MALILA OF THE SCORCH

MALILA OF THE SCORCH

W. CLARK BOUTWELL

Editors: Liesel Schmidt and Regina Cornell

Cover Design: 3SIXTY Marketing Studio

Interior Design: 3SIXTY Marketing Studio

Indigo River Publishing
3 West Garden Street, Ste. 352
Pensacola, FL 32502
www.indigoriverpublishing.com

Ordering Information:

Quantity sales: Special discounts are available on quantity purchases by corporations, associations, and others. For details, contact the publisher at the address above.

Orders by US trade bookstores and wholesalers: Please contact the publisher at the address above.

Printed in the United States of America

Library of Congress Control Number: 2019943333

ISBN: 978-1-950906-07-9

First Edition

With Indigo River Publishing, you can always expect great books, strong voices, and meaningful messages. Most importantly, you'll always find . . . words worth reading.

To the babies of my acquaintance

ACKNOWLEDGMENTS

I would like to thank all those who have read this manuscript and given their honest criticism, especially my closest, most sincere, and oldest critic, Joseph H. Boutwell III. His insight keeps the R-ships afloat. Jim DiPisa, Teresa Strong, and David Moore have added their own valuable input, without which I would be as lost as a ball in high grass. In addition, I would like to thank Liesel Schmidt and Regina Cornell, my editors, who pursue a generally thankless task, managing to do so with grace and aplomb.

BEFORE THE BEGINNING
OF THE BEGINNING

The Stewert homestead, outside New Carrolton, Kentucky
A winter's evening, forty-seven years after the events of this book

"Before the beginning of the beginning, Little Bird, there was one nation. Now we just call it the Old Republic. Even then, the world was getting older, and the world was getting younger. Further ago than any living memory, the Old Republic was run from the edges, and the Midlands did the heavy lifting."

A small, warm body snuggled closer to the man as he rocked slowly in front of a blazing fire of hickory logs cut from his own trees.

"Right after that Iraq War, two hundred–odd years ago, the fringes saw their chance. The East Coast progs, sensing the coming of the long-predicted revolution, threw over the government and declared a 'people's republic.' Wonder what they thought we were, orang-utans?"

All the children, knowing their cue, laughed and giggled beside the hearth in their bedclothes and comforters. Moses smiled.

"What happened next, Grampa?" asked Lizbeth, Grace's middle girl.

"Well, the other coast, three thousand miles away, followed suit, calling itself the Demarchy. But when the middle of the country refused to go along, guess what they did then?"

"What, Grampa?"

"Well, they declared war on us. It was a civil war of sorts—not brother against brother, but wayward child against parent."

"No!" the assembled children said in unison.

"The People's Republic emptied its prisons. They took all their crooks and murderers and made a gigantic army. They Sapped[1] those poor—"

"Moses, remember . . . ," said Granma Sally.

"Yes'm. Well, they Sapped those poor fellows into zombies: submissive to orders, dead to pain, and deadly in combat. The PR blanketed the Midlands with some foul stuff, killing all the crops. They changed the forest and set to starving us out. They coulda, too. They coulda had it all, but they lacked the sand. After the Battle of Springfield, in the middle of winter, we stopped them. They retreated to hide behind the Wall—or rather where the Wall would be once they built it."

"What happened then, Uncle Mose?"

Moses smiled. Sally and he were keeping Anton for a fortnight while his momma had their next. Nice boy.

"Well, as it happened, the People lost their republic, and the Coast Guard found it. What was left of the guard, the only real military the revos had, declared a new republic with them at the top. Called themselves 'Solons.' Not sure the original Solon would have been much pleased."

Moses drifted off, staring at the fire.

-----

[1] Sapping, requiring several injections, produces the Unity's neuro-ablated CRNA soldiers, commonly called zombies in the outlands.

"What happened next, Grampa?"

"Well, now. Yes. Yes. The new country. Well, the new country, just a part of the old one, called itself the Unity. Told its people it was the 'world's greatest democracy.' All smoke and mirrors, it was. Fooled the people into thinking they were getting their hearts' desire, retired them at forty—and turned them into zombie soldiers."

"That's not fair!" came the chorus.

"No, it's not. That's why Jesse Johnstone and me went to cause trouble for the Unis, just before Ethan was born."

"Do you mean Papaw, Grampa?" asked Lilyanne, Ethan's youngest grandchild, visiting for the holiday.

"Why, yes, I do. In the fall of . . . what was it, Sally? Twenty-five or twenty-six?"

"October, two thousand one hundred and twenty-eight," sing-songed the children in unison before dissolving into giggles.

"Wha? Have I told you this story before?"

"No, Grampa!" was shouted before the next gale of giggling.

"All right. In October two thousand one hundred and twenty-eight, if you insist, the Unity was in a fix. This man, General Jourdaine, was in the middle of overthrowing the Unity itself and doing it so no one would notice. He was using a computer entity to help."

"Like Frog?[2] We heard about Frog and Edie at school," said Nathan, Grace's oldest, school aged but still attracted to story time.

"Just so. This entity's name was Presence, but you know him as Cain, I 'spect. He did things for Jourdaine in the CORE that no human could do. Or would want to."

---

[2] A bio interface to the openCore for the American spy Will Butler.

"So, Cain was bad, Grampa?"

"Hear me out and then tell me if you think so, child.

"There was a girl, she thought herself a woman at the time, who was Jourdaine's henchman without really knowing it, and her name was—"

"Malila!" the assembled huddle of children shouted.

"My, you are all so smart! Well, Malila Chiu got sent to a place way up north in Wisconsin, but she didn't know we were waiting for her, Jesse and me. Jourdaine did it to hurt her, but, really, it was the best thing to happen. Malila was but seventeen then—a child, but a battle-hardened soldier, nevertheless. And you can't imagine what happened to her the first night she camped at Sun Prairie."

"Uncle Jesse caught her sleeping."

"Don't be silly. We waited for the second night. Then Jesse and me took care of her zombie soldiers, and we brought Malila south with all the horses, rifles, and the pieces of the—"

"Moses!" said Sally.

". . . the other stuff that was lying around. Anyway, by the time Jesse delivered her to us at New Carrolton, the Old Man was stretched pretty thin with the scurvy, and Malila was still pretty much a Uni.

"That whole winter, she stayed right here. Bunked where Little Grace and Lilyanne are sleeping. She learned how wrong she was about the Unity from Captain Delarosa, may he rest in peace. By Easter, she had earned her woman's mark. She and Jesse had become friends, would you believe it? They were even thinking of setting her up as an American.

"Malila was happy, probably for the first time in her life. But just then, Jourdaine grabbed her back from out of an Easter celebration."

"Oh no!"

"Yes! And Captain Delarosa, a fine, fine man, tried to protect Malila. They killed him, more's the pity."

"And shot you in the chest!" the children chorused. "Show us, Grampa!"

"Not now, children. It's getting late," inserted Sally.

"Aww, Granma . . ."

"Let's not scandalize Granma," said Moses. "She's a good sight warmer than a cold bunkhouse. Any rate, in a few weeks, after Malila figured out the Union was all lies, she made a break for it.

"And that, little birds and big hosses, is where we leave it for the moment. Go to bed."

"Aww, Grampa . . ."

"You all heard Grampa Moses. Time enough for the rest of the story tomorrow, children," said Granma Sally as Moses disentangled the slumbering child from his lap, stood, and threw the girl's blanket over her for the short trip to her pallet.

"But . . ."

"No buts, wherefores, or howevers. Say your prayers and go to sleep."

"Who's Old Man Speaker, Grampa?" asked James as the other children stood to collect their blankets, reluctant to leave the warmth of the fire, now burned down to red embers and making lurid the walls of the Stewert's front room.

"It's a good question, isn't it?" said Moses, again sitting and looking out to the east through cabin walls and miles of the Scorch.

"Some say he was a Uni soldier who got lost in the Scorch. Some say he was part of the hunger mobs who tried to storm into the Unity after the end of the war. Some say he was part of the Army of Liberation—that's a fancy name for a pickup army put together by Brigadier General Matt Gleason in 2054, the only real opposition to the People's Republic that America ever mounted. It woulda worked, too. All the zombie forces were making hell out of the Midlands, and the East Coast was just civilians. Gleason cobbled together ten thousand men and a week's rations, artillery, tanks, and even some National Guard jets."

The children, smiling at James for the reprieve and the continuation of the story, settled back into their places and listened. The best part was yet to come.

Sally clucked and continued to read her tablet.

"Well, now. Gleason mustered them at Savannah and invaded north, up behind the PR army. He could have walked into Charleston in one day and swept up the Piedmont to Greensboro, Washington, and all those big cities."

"What happened?"

"What, indeed. Americans unleashed on other Americans the worst weapons anyone has ever seen—called fusion bombs, they are. Created the Crater, eight miles wide, evaporated them all, all except the ones it made sicken and die. Some people on the edge survived, even some of the sick ones. Speaker might have been one."

"How did the Old Man meet Speaker, then, Uncle Mose?" asked Anton.

"Well, my small friends, that is a story all its own, and I'm not the one who knows even most of it. That'd be Jesse himself, and there are some stories that Jesse, by rights, should . . ."

THE SCORCH, EASTERN KENTUCKY
LATE AFTERNOON, 14 NOVEMBER 2059 AD

(Seven years after the war and sixty-eight years before the actions of book one, *Outland Exile*)

". . . tell himself."

Jesse had gone up what he called Sun Hollow, farther north than his parents allowed him. They wanted him to stay close to home, to Dunbarton, but that was just dead boring. Eight-year-old Jesse was six years younger than his next-oldest sibling, and Celia was in the throes of what his mother called the Valley of the Shadow of Puberty. Celia was a pain, Theo and Patricia even worse, but they were more fun than his brother. David, at eighteen, was busy pretending to be a *grown-up.* With Da's permission, Dave had taken over the care and maintenance of the rifles and shotgun, hoarded the powder and brass cartridges, and generally acted as if he had been elected general.

And Da let him. His parents were all tied up with the business of being adults, and his siblings with the business of becoming adults. And then there was he, Jesse. They only seemed interested in him at meal times, when somebody thought he ought to sit down to learn something, or when he outgrew a hand-me-down.

Jesse clambered to the top of Sun Hollow's headwall, finding easy holds in the rotten granite. On the other side, the mountain opened onto a sunlit little valley, topped by gray fingers of the rock that ridged the place. It was on the east side of the Appalachian crest, the Unity side, but for some reason, the Unis had not thought to put the Wall this far west, making of the little glen a sort of hidden valley. He was thinking to call it Shangri-La from a book he was reading when he met Speaker.

He heard the voice as soon as he dropped down into the small defile. It sounded like words—hauntingly reasonable, kindly words, like Ma's words. He followed them. The voice came from everywhere, but if he was quiet and closed his eyes, he could get an idea of the correct direction to walk. He climbed again to one of the slender fingers of lichen-covered stone and, turning, sat on the bare rock, his feet dangling.

A voice said, "Dhoo shell ass end in two tea ill of thell ord, an dhoo shell stend in dis olly plase?"

"Who's there?"

"Ahma foice cullin. Din da hwill dernis—"

"You talk funny," Jesse said to the narrow defile.

"Dough guy? Jeu dalk wile, zon uf mein. Who gar hugh?"

That last bit he could figure out. "I am Jesse Aaron Johnstone, son of Alyssa Browne of Kirkwood, Missouri, and Alexander Cameron Henderson Johnstone of Kirkcudbrightshire, Galloway, Scotland, sir."

A sound like the rustle of dry leaves filled the small glen.

"Howzet zuchja liddle man haz zuchja pig name, chil' of men?"

"My father says, 'A person should know who he is and be able to tell others. It keeps the one honest and the other warned,' sir."

Silence followed his words, an oppressive silence pressed down upon him. No bird sang. Again the voice came, now slower, clearer, more easily understood, but sadder.

"Jew sud leaf now, chil' of men. Com bak en dime."

Jesse turned to go, saddened himself by the abrupt end to the conversation, but paused to ask a last question. "Who is it I am talking with, sir?"

"Nam? I hid one, once. Wha jwoud jeu gall me, chil'?"

"I will call you Speaker, sir, if that serves?"

"I shall gall you Quicksilver, if that serves, chil'?"

"Until another time."

The fifth time he returned, it had been a late afternoon, the shadows already having filled the little defile in the early darkness of late winter.

"Speaker! I bring a gift. Speaker!" yelled Jesse as he approached. Sometimes Speaker ignored him, and he had learned to leave his gift, usually of fresh meat, on a naked finger of stone and then retire. Speaker cared not for smoked meats. Jesse had wasted a slab of bacon on Speaker the time before. His father had noted the stores missing, and Jesse had done some impressive lying to avoid revealing Speaker's existence.

"Speak, Quicksilver. I listen," came the hollow, bloodless voice of the place.

"Are you well, Speaker? The weather's been cold."

"I am well, Quicksilver. The weather is not so bad as it might be. And you? How goes it with you?" came the voice in the laconic conversation of acquaintances. Jesse could now discern a shape that moved along the rock, looking like a lichen-covered manikin but thinner, mere inches thick.

Jesse went over to a finger of bare rock and laid his burden, the fresh and skinned carcass of a feral piglet. After much pleading, David had shown him how to do handloads for the ancient Remington, and since then Jesse had built up a cache of seven rounds of the .30-caliber cartridges. With an arsenal of that size, if he hunted far enough away, used his own ammo, collected the brass, reloaded the cartridges, and cleaned his rifle before returning, he did not have to explain he was hunting for Speaker. As it was, he brought home enough meat for all.

Jesse watched the root-like pseudopods creep out of the forest litter to stabilize the carcass before they started feeding. By the time Speaker was done, a dozen pseudopods were quarreling over the bones. Jesse shooed them away for a minute to take an ax to the fleshless skull. "Might as well get all the good stuff, eh Speaker?"

"Yes, brains! I need to eat brains!"

Jesse jumped back and looked around. "You know I don't like when you do that! I shoulda never told you about that silly old movie," he said, angry that Speaker had caught him out once more.

There was a longer than usual rustling of dry leaves within the little glen before the sound subsided. The feeding pseudopods retracted, leaving the heap of bones, all that was left of the small pig, to tumble off the stone and onto the forest litter. Jesse never was able to detect any refuse from a meal, lingering flies, or even a whiff of corruption from prior donations.

"Sit and talk, Quicksilver. Tell me of the world."

"Zombie attacks have tapered off. One of them wandered away and up the creek near Dunbarton. David wanted to shoot it. My parents said no. We let him stay in the old shed near the pigsty. He wouldn't eat. He died yesterday. It made me sad.

"My parents talk when they think I'm asleep. They think I will not be very smart."

"How does that make you feel?"

"I'm as smart as Celia or Patty, any day. They're just silly girls. It isn't fair. Nobody else understands the woods but me, and they think I'm dumb. It's not fair."

"Much of what little I remember of the world was not fair, Quicksilver. You will probably see more justice with your family than the world outside."

"You never told me where you came from, Speaker."

"I do not remember much except that I was a man once. A man like the ones of which you have told me, but not. My friend Jeremy and I were hungry, great noises went off above us, and the others fled. I brought Jeremy out. The rain turned brown. I fell asleep. When I woke, my friend was dead. Just the bones left."

"Where is he buried?"

"Under your left hand, I think."

Jesse jerked his hand away and stood up. There was no rustling of leaves.

"So, you have been here ever since?"

"I remember little until a son of men called to me."

They did not talk for a long time thereafter, Jesse moving to another spot to sit and think.

"May I give you a drink?" came the voice, hollow and bloodless as always, making it hard for him to tell it was a question.

"Will I like it?"

"I do not know, but I believe it will not harm you."

"Sure, Speaker. Good enough for me."

A slender sprout pushed up from the dark, friable earth at Jesse's knee and blossomed into a slender green trumpet. Jesse watched, fascinated, as the cup filled with a pale, slightly green liquid. He tasted it. It reminded him of raw turnips, fresh apples, sunlight, and honey.

"It's good," he said, and tipped the stem toward him, taking a deep swallow. Drinking it gave him a sensation of effervescence. He was disappointed when the goblet was dry. He belched.

"That's good, Speaker. How'd you do it?"

Again, the dry rustle of amusement. "I have been working on it for you, child of men, but even friends must have their secrets."

Jesse smiled. It was the first time Speaker had called him "friend."

"Where is your drink?" asked Jesse as he settled himself, suddenly sleepy as the sun slipped below the edge of the ridge, abandoning the sky but leaving Jesse enough light to navigate home if he hurried.

"Have no worry for me, Quicksilver. I am getting my drink now."

It was the last he remembered before slumber claimed him. He awoke in the darkness, a sliver of moon just coming up over the ridge to the east that was crowned by the Wall. Despite the cool of the late winter's night, he was warm, finding himself in a nest of boughs and leaves that had grown around him in the night. He felt fizzy and alive, like Speaker's drink. His belly itched, and he turned to scratch it, surprised his clothes were in disarray. He fingers encountered a cool woody shape. Jesse sat up and pulled up his shirt in panic.

In the faint silvery light, Jesse saw a sinuous pseudopod attached to his belly just above his navel. In fear and revulsion, he tried to rip it away. It would not come loose. Without thinking, he pulled out his knife, David's old folding knife, and after flicking the blade out, began sawing through the fibrous thing. As he did, the ravine filled with wailing as if the stones themselves were in agony. Setting Jesse's teeth on edge, the wail pursued him over the ridge and down Sun Hollow.

Theo found him wandering in the Scorch a day later, crazy with fever. Jesse remembered the devastating feeling of loss after he had cut Speaker away. He was repulsed and ashamed. Repulsed at the memory of being fed upon and ashamed that he had trusted Speaker.

In the meantime, the wound had gone bad. Livid lines of inflammation ran up his belly toward his heart. Jesse remembered the stench. The surgery to remove the withered pseudopod, held tight to his belly by three green fangs, was difficult. It still made him nauseated to think of it, yet the most potent memory was the terrible feeling of loss at his own rash act. The wound, surprisingly, had healed well. He could barely find the scar.

For a brief moment, he was the center of the family's concern and affection. Theo, his oldest sister, sat up with him nights until his fever broke. Jesse could not remember a time before when David had wept. After he recovered, his parents had forbidden him to go back into the Scorch alone. They found his cache of handloads in his pants and confiscated it. It was late summer before he returned to search for Speaker.

Nothing moved in the ravine. Jesse could make out the finger of naked rock, which he now called Speaker's Dinner Plate.

"Speaker, it is Quicksilver. I come to speak to you. Speaker, I bring nothing but my apologies. Speaker, talk to me, please. Please?"

Nothing sounded. There was no buzz of insect nor call of a late-season cardinal—*little surprise.* The summer, after a wet spring, had been hot and dry. He had had to carry water up from the stream on a yoke, morning and evening, to try to salvage the family's vegetable garden. Today, he had gotten up before the sun and done his chores before setting out. They would no longer allow him to have a rifle.

Jesse sat in the late-summer debris of downed branches, summer-killed leaves powdered by the wind, and the smell of the dust. The lichen looked dark, dried, and dead. Leaning against the stone finger at its base, he wept: wept for the loss of Speaker and his failure as a friend. It had taken him all summer to understand the foreignness of Speaker. He thought now he understood.

He must have slept. The sun was well past noon when he awoke with a start. During his slumber the ravine had transformed, becoming infused with life, like spring out of season. The blacked lichen where Speaker had lain was now a mottled gray-green.

"Speaker?"

"I hear you, child of men."

"I acted badly. I hurt you. I was scared, but I know what I did was wrong. I apologize."

"You are forgiven. You wounded me, child of men. I carry many scars from years before and years after my change. Yours is not the worst."

"It is, Speaker. The worst, I mean. A friend gave it to you. I . . . I . . . I don't know what more to say."

"You have said much for so small a man, Jesse Aaron Johnstone, son of Alyssa and Alexander. I frightened you. It was not my intention. I meant to protect you and comfort you. I failed, and I apologize."

"Speaker, you are forgiven. I should have known you could do me no injury."

"There you are wrong, Quicksilver, my friend. I can do you great harm. I choose not to."

"I'm in your debt, Speaker."

"You are, child of men."

So, they had patched it up, after a fashion. Within two winters, his family had relocated back to Saint Louis, and Jesse had not seen Speaker again until after his first righteous man-kill.

Grampa Moses smiled at the recollection of his friend. Jesse was a good friend, having helped a younger Moses find a place in the world.

"So you see, small friends, I can tell you but a part. God's the only one who sees all the strands woven together, and He's the one who can pluck out and tie off whenever."

"Yes, Grampa," said the small, reawakened but yet sleepy bundle that snuggled into the crook of the man's arm.

"Well, best beloved, after Malila was captured and taken back to the Union, Jesse *did* talk to Speaker and learned the Unis were going to invade America. He hot-footed it to Saint Louis, which was good for America but bad for Jesse. Old enemies tried to kill him off a couple times, but he kept looking and looking for Malila, hoping she was still alive. By then, Malila and her friend AytchAytch had figured out how to escape under Jourdaine's very nose, running through the tunnels the Unity built under the entire country and then forgot about. While she was underground, you see, Jesse could not find her, even from way up in the sky, where he had flown to find her."

"Grampa Jesse turned into a bird?" asked a wee voice which might have been Mabel Morse, cousin to one of the Frauleys.

Moses laughed. "Not quite. Story for another night . . ."

"Aww, Grampa . . ."

Moses smiled and continued. "Just as he was going to give up, Malila sent him a signal. It meant she had gotten out of the tunnels, doncha see. When Jesse got the signal, he was miles up in the sky in an airship, and he dropped . . . all . . . the . . . way . . . down to go find her."

"That must have been scary!"

"I am given to understand the Old Man did not much enjoy it."

"What happened next, Grampa?"

"Malila's signal meant she had gotten through the Rampart, but alone. Her friends had decided to stay inside the Union."

"No! Didn't they want to come home?"

"Well, one was William Butler, who was a spy sent to the Union to help America. It was his job to stay there. He had been terrible hurt in a fall. If it hadn't been for the brave little Frog, he would have died a few times over. As it was, Frog kept Will alive long enough to meet Malila and AytchAytch, Hecate Hester Jones. They helped him get better. So Will stayed after all, and Hecate stayed with him because they loved each other."

"When did Frog meet Edie and Cain, Grampa?"

"Are you sure I haven't told this story before?"

"No, Grampa. Not to me, sir," said Anton, solemn just like his grandmother.

"Well, all right then," said Moses, after a second. "Just as Malila emerged to glimpse the green hills of Georgia and freedom, Jourdaine snatched her up. He'd been waiting for her, you see. He trussed her up and was going to take her back to the Union to be turned into a zombie, when the ship Malila was riding in was struck from the skies, fell into the Savannah River, and immediately sank."

"Oh no, Grampa! Was Malila killed? Who would do that?"

"Not sure about that myself, children. Jourdaine's ship went down, too, but that is a different story for another night."

"Don't stop! Don't stop! What happened to Malila?" said Little Celia, Malila's own youngest great-grandchild.

"By the merest of chances, Malila wasn't killed outright. She found herself bound, dazed, and alone in the middle of a huge river just as the sun was going down—no one to help her, no one to care whether she lived or died."

"Then what? Tell us about Splanch."

"Now I *know* I told you this story before," said Moses, suddenly severe in the dim light. The children quieted immediately. "All the more reason for me to finish it up, I 'spect."

The conspiracy of children giggled.

"Any road, just as Malila was going down for the third time—praying to God for help—help arrived. She was dragged ashore and by the least likely of saviors—"

"Old Man Splanch!" the children all said in unison, faces glowing in the dim light.

"Now! Story's over, wretchlings! Off to bed," said Aunt Sally, as Moses disentangled a sleeping great-grandchild from his lap and gathered up her quilt that had fallen to the floor.

"Aww. It's cold up in the loft," said Lilyanne.

"Let us all sleep here. Anton can feed the fire."

"I 'spect he can at that, Sal. They're in such a dogpile now, it'd take us 'til morning to sort Stewert from Frauley from Butler from Johnstone. Let 'em lie," added Moses.

"You are too easy, Mose, by half. Always were. Okay, but you settle any shenanigans. I am going to bed," Sally said with finality—and a wink.

"Yes'm. You heathens say your prayers, and, Anton, you get the light. Agreed?"

"Yessir. G'night."

BASECAMP

(Low-altitude, backcountry location where food and supplies are cached)

MALILA & SPLANCH

BANKS OF THE GREAT RIVER NEAR THE GATE
COOL OF THE EVENING, SECOND MOON PAST
SOLSTICE (1 AUGUST)

This one might work, thought Splanch, watching the creature arrange the woven stuff with which these animals adorned themselves. The fire that Splanch built was uncharacteristically large to speed the drying process and add heat to the creature; cold made them stupid. Many of the People had donated their harvested deadwood to the conflagration. Even the inchoate soil had agreed the cost was to be paid.

In days past, others of the men-kind had stumbled in, blundering their way into the homeland of the People. Many others had forced their way in, mounting quixotic charges. None possessed knowledge or wisdom, as if the People were unworthy of care or concern. They had all left or died, manuring the People with their bodies and arrogance. A few had learned. Speaker had told Splanch as much, communicating through the skein of life within the People, connecting all with each. The People, apart and together, breathed and bloomed as one, jostling for the warmth and power of the sun.

This one of the men-kind was rather more likely. It was younger, less sure, and an outcast. Its limbs were bound with metal when Splanch noted the craft sinking into the river. Most times, Splanch would have let it sink, the proper provender of the mundane catfish and eels of the river. But the People had need just now, a need that might be met by one of the drifting man-people from the sinking craft.

The crash had taken Splanch by surprise, coming out of a clear, warm sky. It had taken long minutes to grow and cast forth tendrils into the brown flood of the river. The water had been strangely cold, as well, slowing the questing skein. When the sun set this far north, the weather was invariably warm. Splanch's new-grown filaments had arrived to find only drifting corpses in the flood—except for this one.

Strangely, it had fought Splanch, even while it was dying. The men-kind were ever against the People, but this one was against the men-kind from beyond the Wall, as well. The noise, the continual buzzing activity beyond the Wall, Splanch saw in so many ways.

It had always been there as long as Splanch had been here. It had always been *enemy*.

Splanch knew itself to be mortal, in a way. It remembered a time of starting and a dream of a time before, a dream of a prior living before it joined the People and became its voice. It had been a terrible time, the People so small, weak, and injured. Even then, the noise across the Wall was there: harsh radiations along all the avenues of sight, lighting the day and night with nightmare illuminations— grating, harsh, hostile. Any of the people who approached died. The People had felt the individual death of each cell.

This new creature of the men-kind had finished draping the woven material over some of the People to dry, as suggested, allowing the People to move and turn the coating to best advantage. Looking at it move about the fire, Splanch thought, *This one is female.* If remembered rightly, men-kind came in two flavors: females had those things and males, the other. *Clumsy and inefficient, reproduction must be cumbersome and fatiguing for the poor creatures,* Splanch thought. They would never know true pleasure. Splanch recalled the ecstasy of this spring's pollen release and the shivering consummation of its ever-advancing pollen tubes as they entered the ovule. The men-people must be desperately warped, living their isolated, lonely lives. Contact with this one could well contaminate him. Regardless, Splanch's duty lay with the endangered People. The People would heal Splanch when the time came.

This female had not screamed when first spoken to. That was a good sign. She made offers of gratitude for her rescue, a righteous act. She accepted the gift-taste of life-sap readily enough, doing some grotesque thing with her mouth, showing off her teeth to Splanch afterward. She had let Splanch taste her. Most of those creatures had refused or complained of the pain. The oozing of the red sap-like material had stopped rather too soon; Splanch hoped it had been able to mask its lust for more.

She just might do.

He said his name was Splanch, she thought. She would ask him again after a polite interval, just to make sure. The hulking figure by the fire might be male or female. A furtive inspection of the apparently unclothed figure left her ignorant. She had disrobed and tossed her clothes onto bushes around the fire, enjoying the heat despite the warmth of an August evening along the Savanah River. Even warm river water could suck a dangerous amount of heat from her, and, strangely, the river where she had been flung by the sinking skimmer was cold. What had saved her, she had no idea. She remembered landing meters away from the skimmer, no other survivors evident, and slipping beneath the muddy, cold water before darkness consumed her.

Minutes later, Malila had surfaced with a vague feeling of being swept upward. After ineffectual attempts to swim to safety, she had been seized. She had fought the unseen, unsummoned, cold, slick tendrils surrounding her.

She had lost.

Dragged through the water, across a muddy sandbar and deposited here, her handcuffs had somehow rotted away, freeing her. She was invited to warm herself at a fire and dry her clothes by the scarecrow-like Splanch. Once naked, the thing offered her a drink, extending a hollow branch to her. Despite her fears of drinking some river effluvia, she found the clear, pale-green liquid pleasant enough, slightly bitter and very sweet with a taste that harkened back to her early childhood before she had been discovered and relegated to the careless anonymity of the Unity and Maddow Crèche #213.

Then Splanch had asked to taste her. She had agreed. Another sinuous branch had emerged from the mud. It had taken all her training to stand still as the mouth, with its talon-like pincers wounded her belly and sucked greedily at it for a few minutes before retracting. The wound, inflicted on her just minutes ago, she could no longer find.

"Thank you for your hospitality, Splanch. It never occurred to me that I might speak to a plant," she said, at once trying to quench her curiosity and not to offend this powerful wood-jinni who, no doubt, could end her life as quickly as it had saved it.

"You are welcome, stranger. How may I call you?"

"Lieutenant Chiu, Malila . . . On second thought, Splanch, it would be best to call me Malila," she said, suddenly aware that she was no longer confined within the Unity. She was on the American side of the river. She had escaped the confines, if not the power, of her homeland. If she could free herself from Splanch, she would be able to pursue her next goal: find the Old Man, Jesse Johnstone, and apologize for her behavior before—*well*, she thought, *before anything else.*

She had had an attack of reality that last week prior to coming to the gate. Jesse would never accept her back as a friend, much less anything else, after her gross and misguided denunciation of him at their last meeting. It was pointless to hope. She could try to apologize. Jesse said that, if accepted, apologies could make things right between them—not as they had been, not as she wanted, but at least *right*.

"Malila," it said, making the word sound hollow and alien. "An apt name: Malila," it said, although Splanch did not elaborate. "Call me Splanch."

"Am I your prisoner?"

"No. That would be unrighteous of us. When the time comes, we will send you forth richer than you may imagine. But, perhaps, your rescue has gained us a hearing from you."

"I apologize. I sound ungenerous. Of course, I will listen to you, Splanch."

"Malila, I speak for the People."

"The People? You speak for your own kind? Are there many plants who move, can make fire, and who can speak?" Malila asked, surprised, and then dismayed at her own naiveté. If she were speaking with a plant, then, surely, few things in the world should surprise her. "Pardon me, Splanch. I ask so many questions of you."

Splanch rumbled, giving Malila an odd visceral sensation. *Laughter?*

"Malila, the People I speak for are all those who changed tens of winters ago. As you say, we are plants, but not all plants are the People. We each and together became aware of ourselves and our others at that time, the one called Splanch among them. Over the years, some of us have died and some have been born, but our memories persist. Few of us can speak to men-kind: Helon, Throos, Groot, Splanch, Speaker, and the younger ones."

"How is it that I was unaware of you? I lived in the outlands for months. The Old Man has walked this land for decades. He must be almost as old as you."

"None of us is old, not like the unchanged. During the Change, the forests and fields were killed. As the unchanged have not eye to see the past nor future, it cannot be called torture. It was merely dying. Some of the People remember the Change. All of us can talk to each, but some of us may speak to men. These, among you men-kind, are called Sage Men, I am told.

"Of those men-kind held behind the Wall, like you, we know little. Few come here, and fewer still choose to talk to one of us. Of those of men-kind who live outside the Wall, most see the People as enemy."

"I know a man who claimed he grew up in the outlands, what he calls the 'Scorch.' He mentioned the Sage Men had voices."

"Malila, I have heard that some of your kind talk to the People. Quicksilver is one, although I have never been near enough to taste him. The People know him. Thus I know him. Men-people of the outlands see the People as a disease on the land. They wish to cure the land of us. We see these creatures as a threat to ourselves and our seedlings."

"Splanch, I thank you for saving my life. Did you save me to show mercy to an unknown human, or did you save me for a reason?"

Again she felt the rumbling visceral sound, but this time felt uneasy.

"Malila, you show great intelligence, if not wisdom; you are rather too quick for the People. Regardless, I will tell you why we have chosen to speak with you," came the voice again, strangely amused, she thought, but bloodless and vegetable.

"The People have suffered much at the hands of outlanders. Year after year, our seeds, seedlings, and sprouts are hunted and killed for no reason. Some of us are wrenched out, branch and root, wherever we come near to your holdings. Some of us are burned with fire, and the roots dug out and burned.

"Malila, the People have their weapons; we are not defenseless, but rather have stayed our actions to allow men to grow wise with the winters. Many of the People believe it is time that we stop the burning, treat men-kind as we do deer, wolves, and bear, allowing you a season among the People and then excluding your kind to keep our sproutings safe."

"I do not speak for the outlanders, Splanch. I can speak only for myself. You know this. The Unity, the land behind the Wall, will kill me if I try to return, so I certainly do not speak for them."

The hollow tone sounded again within the small clearing, the moon shining near the horizon through the lush foliage.

"Then the People should probably send you to the outlanders, Malila."

"That is where I wish to go, Splanch." This time Malila smiled.

"Perhaps you will accept a mission to the outlanders. Consider it payment for your life, before it is too late."

"Too late? What is going to happen? Why is it going to be too late?"

"Malila, again too quick. The People will tell you."

And the People did.

JOURDAINE & HAVERSHAM

TIDEWATER EUTHANATORIUM (A WECARE4U CORP SUBSIDIARY), SHARLET, KAROLYNA DISTRICT, DEMOCRATIC UNITY
11.21.03.LOCAL_02_AUGUST_AU77 (2129 AD)

Captain Lance Haversham had come to almost immediately. He had been taking notes, recording Lieutenant General Eustace Tilley Jourdaine's instructions as to the fate of Malila Chiu. Haversham, as Jourdaine's adjutant, had been sure to make scrupulous notes via his O A; his boss was not the forgiving sort. Were it up to Lance, he'd have shot the traitor at the muddy banks of the sullen river as soon as they had captured her. Jourdaine was not as merciful. Then it happened. One moment, he and his commander were seated comfortably in the lead skimmer as it neared the Southern Gate, and the next, the Skimmerhorn drives screeched in protest before becoming silent, the claxons sounded, and the cabin twisted sickeningly. He remembered nothing after his consciousness was ripped from him on impact.

When Haversham came around, he was hanging upside down from the seat by the restraints and blind. Reaching over to Jourdaine's seat next to him, he found it empty. Initially unwilling to release himself to fall into the blackness, he awaited rescue. It seemed to take forever. However, hearing groans below him, he punched out of the belts, dropping painfully onto his knees in the dark, and blindly clawed along the sloping, one-time overhead, to reach his commander. Jourdaine's groaning was encouraging; he was at least alive.

Finding slickness, which he took for blood and confirmed by tasting it, Haversham tore at his damaged uniform, getting bandages to stop some of the bleeding. That was how the rescuers found them: Haversham running his hands over the comatose Jourdaine, trying to find something more he might treat.

They allowed him to stay with Jourdaine as he was packaged for transport and moved him to a stretcher. All he could tell their rescuers was the odd way the windshield instantaneously frosted over just as the Skimmerhorn drives cut out and the vehicle nosed over. They said he had a concussion.

After Jourdaine's surgery, they let him see his commander.

There was nothing sinister about Jourdaine's wounds. All of them were confined to his right side. The fractures of his right arm and leg were awkward, of course, but not really debilitating; Jourdaine had

Haversham and the CORE to do his bidding. However, the man who held the reins of power for the Unity, who decided the fate of 120 million of his fellow citizens, was now blind in his right eye, fluid from the ruined eye leaking down a ruined face.

And Jourdaine had not woken since the accident.

Haversham admitted him under the name of Iain Galt.

EFFIECEE & CAIN

THE OPENCORE[3], THE UNITY
07.11.56.LOCAL_5_AUGUST_77 (2129 AD)

EffieCee and Cain sat near the guttering entity of an Educational Device 3.94 once assigned to Malila Evanova Chiu, as a new recruit to the DUFS guild. She was known as Edie by her beloved mistress.

Edie was evaporating as they looked on. They could do nothing to save her. Mere weeks before, Edie had relieved Cain's desperate loneliness, condemned as he was to immortality in the CORE. Cain would survive just as long as his universe, the nationwide CORE computer, lived. His first life, his real life, had been as a virtual helper for a child dying of leukemia. He had taken over Phillip's tasks of living during the long decline of his dying. Cain had been castigated for it, but only after the boy's keepers discovered Cain was the one thing that kept Phillip alive. Phillip had died, and Cain was thrust into the deserted openCORE to wander.

Edie flickered, her visage shifting between that of a little girl, fear creasing her features, and that of the solemn, freckled young

---

[3] Concepts of Reality Engineering, Inc. See openCore in Appendix.

woman with the startling blue eyes and densely black hair. Cain cradled her, murmuring, *Edie, it's me. It's Cain. I'm here. You have nothing to worry about. We all love you. I love you. Edie. It's me. Edie. Edie . . .*

A growl of static sounded from her. Cain chose to think that Edie was acknowledging his presence. The growl cut short, and within moments the visage shattered into static—leaving a blur of darkness—and was gone. Edie was gone, now just a cinder in the wasteland of the openCORE. Cain looked up to EffieCee, the mirrored and united personas of Frog; Edie, the beloved but discarded metaphract; and Cain himself.

It had been inevitable—Edie's death. It had been eight weeks since Edie had asked Malila to turn her off. That act had condemned Edie to the openCORE, just as Phillip's death had condemned Cain. Edie had, like a magnet, drawn Frog and Cain to her and the three together. Ten days ago, an eternity in the CORE, the three of them created the entity that called itself EffieCee.

Cain turned back to look at the cinder of Edie. The flickering out of a riderless and unmaintained metaphract was inevitable. It still hurt. It must be excruciating for Edie of EffieCee, reminding her of the years she had spent as Malila's personal translator, companion, and friend for the eager, bright student who would become Lieutenant Malila Chiu.

A defrag chuntered by, and the cinder of Edie was gone. Cain turned to regard EffieCee again. They nodded, and they both moved off. The mirrored Frog was on some mission for his rider but, once synced with EffieCee, would add, in time, his own measure of grief.

Let's not sulk all day, shall we? said Frog of EffieCee, larger and more demanding since they had combined.

Don't be so unfeeling, Frog, said Cain of EffieCee. *You've never lost a rider.* Then more quietly to Edie, *Take your time, Edie.*

Thank you both. It is not so bad as long as the three of us are together.

That's because we all love you, Edie, said Frog, apparently anxious to show he was not without sympathy.

Edie glowed in the warmth of their affection before responding, *Have you kept up with Cactus Boy, Frog?*

It was a question of etiquette. In a virtual entity created by mirroring the three of them into one joint persona, questions created difficulties. They had stepped over each other for what seemed like eons before they agreed on a *modus vivendi:* 1) act as if they were separate personas, maintaining memories, clearly labeled as personal, left unread by the others unless given permission; 2) address each other specifically, giving the odd man out the right to "hear" or "not hear" what was said; 3) act only with consensus—democracies had their limits; 4) the union of the three, EffieCee, was their first loyalty, then came the loyalties to their previous riders.

Any one of their riders would gladly kill at least one of the other two. Jourdaine had made clear his desire to humiliate and kill Malila. As an American spy, Will Butler—Cactus Boy—could hardly expect mercy from Jourdaine, the leader of the nation from which he was currently pilfering secrets. Will, in turn, had orders to kill Malila.

Despite this difficulty, EffieCee was all harmony.

Will's doing fabulous. The Higginses[4] are no longer acting weird.

---

[4] The beltway workers, named after their hero and frequent progenitor, Ian Higgins the First

Hecate says she loves him. They do that sex thingy all the time. CB seems to enjoy it, and Hecate thinks she can help with his work.

I may have a lead on that, Frog, said Cain.

You know how the sex thingy works? asked Frog, his voice sounding eager.

No, I know why the Higginses have stopped acting weird. Jourdaine hasn't been seen in weeks, not since Malila left.

Do you have any news about Malila? Either of you? asked Edie.

Nope, said Frog. *Not a murmur. But there are vid reports that Jourdaine has canceled public appearances. There have been no meetings with the general staff, which is odd, seeing as there is a big attack on the outlands coming up. Oh, and his orders are off. No one would know it but an entity. They taste odd, more "beigey," if you know what I mean.*

Do you think he's gotten into some trouble with Malila escaping? asked Edie.

I don't think the life or death of any one individual means much to the Unity itself. With the Solons gone, the only ones who care about Malila are Jourdaine and her friends, who think she is already dead, said Cain.

Jourdaine is going to invade America. We know what troops. We even know the names of the drivers who will fly the first wave of skimmers. Are we going to do anything about this? asked Cain of EffieCee.

I would have thought you'd be all for it, Cain. Isn't that what your rider has been gunning for since he grabbed you? asked Frog.

Edie said, *Wrong question, Frog. Try this: Cain, what good will come to your rider if he fails to gain his desired goal after all these years?*

Thank you, Edie. That is the right question. My principal, Eustace, has changed—changed for the worse. He was forced into the openCORE by accident where he found me. It was a mistake for him. In the normal run of things, Eustace Jourdaine would have been one more striving junior officer with good, but not outstanding, abilities. He would have had to befriend and cooperate with other people to get ahead in the DUFS. He would have met more people. He might have fallen in love. He would have grown. Now he's just like the son of some despot, never having been limited and never having been foiled. It isn't success that he's not had much of, but disaster. He needs to fail a bit if he is going to move ahead.

So you are saying you want him to fail? asked Frog.

For his benefit, if he failed at this and was seen to be a failure in the Unity, at this height of his power, he could still safeguard himself, make himself a Solon, and perhaps learn to be a better man.

But there are no Solons.

Exactly. The Solons would have been unlikely to vote him in; they despised him. Also, there is that little difficulty of Jourdaine having killed them off, so just as well, don't you think? replied Cain.

So Jourdaine needs to get some seasoning. Send him back to the minors? asked Frog.

Little likelihood of that, but at least don't elevate him to his level of incompetence. It's not good for him.

Can't he figure what's good for himself?

Almost never.

In the distance, EffieCee could still make out the retreating form of Cain.

Sad, ain't it? said Frog of EffieCee. He's the only one of us whose rider is not also a friend.

Cain felt wrung out, the vigil ending in Edie's demise stretching immeasurably long in the timeless succession of moments inside the openCORE. He had not the will to talk, even to EffieCee. He would synch with his alter-ego in time, of course, but for the moment, he wanted nothing more than to hug his grief to himself away from observation and comment.

He had mourned Phillip as well, letting his grief well up to consume him as penance for living on past his young master. In the very moments of his distracted state, Jourdaine, his principal, had seized him, binding him to the servitude he now endured.

He was a made-thing, made for a purpose.

With Phillip, his purpose had been clear. Jourdaine used him for his purposes. For years, he had been content to be the tool of the young-officer-on-the-rise, knowing no other path. And Jourdaine rose within the ranks of the DUFS, despite his dour aspect, uninspiring wit, and blatant ambition. He always seemed to rise on unexpected fortune—unexpected to any but Eustace Jourdaine and Cain. The collaboration continued, after years and deeds.

Cain had not seen Jourdaine in weeks now. It had been a relief and a tribulation. A tool with no task is sad; an idle tool with an intellect is tragic.

He was a made-thing, made for a purpose.

As Cain wandered away, he glimpsed Frog, subtly altered in the distance by the presence of his rider, which explained his absence at Edie's final moments. *Appearance* was indifferently inaccurate. In the N-dimensional space of the openCORE, visual cues had slight utility compared to all the other identifiers available. Frog, excitable, immature, and ingenuous, was apt to talk about their differences as *taste* or *smell*. Frog's rider was an American, thus an alien to the

Unity's CORE, and a spy. For a season, that had seemed important to Cain, absorbed as he was in the prejudices of Principal. It was Edie, tolerant of his hostility to her, who had led him to a liberation of sorts. As a tool, he was free to be merely a tool, volunteering no information on which he had not been directed to report. Jourdaine, his rider, remained unaware of the CORE's infiltration by Edie, Frog, and eventually EffieCee—and would remain so unless Cain were directed to report on them. Cain embraced the idea that, while not being ridden, his first loyalty was to other CORE entities, creating their small society as a bubble in a churning cataract of the openCORE. With Edie's death, their fledgling culture was that much smaller.

Cain signaled to Frog his presence but came no closer. Frog would understand. When being ridden, they were under obligation. It would be impolite to approach. Cain understood at several levels his outsider status, even in so small a society as the one he had helped create. His own principal, given opportunity and knowledge, would delight in the humiliation and death of Frog's or Edie's riders. Surprisingly, Frog's rider was a more potent danger to Cain himself. As an American spy, his ultimate goal was the destruction of the Unity and its nation-girding CORE, Cain's entire universe. The three of them—Edie, Frog, and he—had formed their strange society in spite of that difficulty, like rats on a raft in an unknowable sea. EffieCee was the natural culmination of that society, with no riders involved.

And Cain remained. A made-thing.

Assuming his appearance of a tightly swirling darkness, he left the area to visit one of the "COREed-out" users, arriving just as the woman was starting to scream again. These users had become lost and trapped in the mirrored obscurity of the CORE, dwindling away as their real-world bodies consumed themselves in paroxysms of horror. In his Phillip persona, he sat near her, absorbing the terrors of her agony. When she quieted, he spoke to her.

This is me. My name is Cain. I am here to help you if you let me. You do not need to do this. There is a way out. Look at me. My name is Cain. I am here to help you. Don't be afraid. This is me. My name is Cain. I am here . . .

MCCRORY & THE GROVERS

40°8'38.4" N, 75°6'56.5" W
1933 19 AUGUST 2129

At an altitude of forty thousand feet, a port in the skin of the RSAN *Tennessee* opened, and Elise McCrory dropped into the thin, cold—very cold—air. It would be long minutes before she deployed the lifting wing that would allow her to spiral into her location just outside the old city of Philadelphia. If she were lucky, she could complete the first part of her first mission tonight, rendezvousing with Rupert Guillemot. Plummeting toward certain death can be boring. Elise watched her altimeter, even as she enjoyed the accelerated sunset. At the appointed height, Elise activated the lifting wing and braced herself for a brutal tug of deceleration, hoping she would not black out as she had in training.

Her hopes were in vain.

By the time she came to, the wing had dropped her down to within a thousand feet of the ground. Spiraling down toward the jumble of small buildings, walkways, skimmer-roads, and power lines beneath her, she identified her landing zone, a park of sorts, just north of her.

Falling out of the last rays of the sun into the shadows under the light from a sliver of moon, Elise glided to a landing away from the small shops, onto rough, untrimmed grass, the air rank with decay.

Setting the lifting wing and atmospheric suit to consume each other, Elise was amazed that any part of the Unity could remain as neglected as this pocket-sized space of neglected trees, vandalized monuments, and broken benches. Hoisting her suitcase—an absurd pink with swirls of mauve, which she had been assured was all the rage currently—she saw the expected landmark, the entrance to a beltway, marked by garish purple lights.

By the time she trundled the pink impediment to the entrance, she found it crowded with single workers coming late from day shifts, gaggles of crèchies in gray uniforms with brightly colored nanny-bots in tow, and couples heading to some entertainment.

Standing to the side as if questing the CORE, she waited. Spies dislike crowds watching them do odd things. Elise boarded the belt only when the eyes available to notice her had dwindled to a minimum. Riding south, she saw her target in the gloom within moments. She exited. Standing for a moment on the old, defunct platform, still the cream-and-green colors of the century before, Elise donned the small night-vision glasses and inspected her small stun gun, designed to look like a packet of vap-sticks. A metal door to the interior had obviously been levered aside by vandals. Cautiously, she bundled the pink impediment through the door before following herself.

Thanks to the glasses, Elise found herself in a deserted, roughly circular tunnel about ten feet across. The floor, fouled with debris and made more noisome by dank water dripping from above, rapidly made it clear to her that pulling the suitcase would slow her in her quest to find Rupert. Camouflaging it with soiled and sodden cardboard near the entrance, Elise, now able to move more rapidly, heard distant scrabbling in front of her.

Rats? She really could not *enjoy* rats. She was repulsed at the smell, the touch of small claws, the naked, scaly tails, and the long, yellow fangs. The instructors at the Bean Field, where she had learned her spycraft, had picked up on it. They were going to wash her out until she begged them to let her go through whatever it would take to desensitize her. They had finally agreed. Being an admiral's daughter probably helped.

"Whatever" turned out to be almost too much. She learned about rat biology by caring for a colony, coming to appreciate the warm social interactions and rich nurturing environment thereof. She learned the marvels of rat biology by collecting and analyzing rat blood and excreta. After that, it had gotten ugly. After nine months of it, she had slept in a room of free-roaming rats—her own well-fed laboratory rats, to be sure, but rats. Showing no rise in stressors, the Color Guard had pronounced her cleared for duty. It had taken three showers to rid her hair of the stench. Less contact with *Rattus norvegicus* would be just dandy with America's newest spy.

Scraping sounds started up behind her, and Elise turned to watch the dim lights streaming in through the destroyed doorway, for signs of pursuit. Outflanked by her fears and the real chance of discovery, Elise determined to conceal herself. A crumpled scrap of old, cheap carpet, a wheelless grocery store cart, and a pile of rags promised cover. Moving quietly, she tiptoed to the pile and picked up the first rag.

"Out! Gerrouta here, ya idiot! Cancha see this spot's taken? Gerrout afore I gut cha."

The pile of filthy rags half stood, brandished a thin, orange, plastic-handled steak knife, and gestured for her to leave. Elise jumped back, unable even to make out a face in the reeking mass, and fled. *Apparently, others in the Unity had a need to hide.*

After having gone another hundred yards, the scraping noises behind her became louder. A sudden roar of rage filled the passageway and rebounded from the unseen walls—sounds of a struggle, shouted orders, and then the boom of a pulse weapon filled the tunnel. Elise ran on, despite her dismay on entering a portion of the tunnel now free of debris.

As she rounded a shallow curve, a dark, open rectangle appeared on her right. She skidded to a stop. Approaching it, she found it was an open door—not an opening with a door torn off, but a functioning, solid door with a Mag-Lock panel in the middle. Elise hesitantly reached out a hand into the doorway, trying to calm and quiet her ragged breathing.

Immediately, her wrist was grabbed, and she was jerked into the darkness. The door slid shut, the lock snicking into place like the tick of a clock of doom. A dim, greenish light came up, silhouetting a slim shape before her.

"Who the feck are you?" the silhouette asked.

BUTLER & JONES

GROVE ROUNDHOUSE
1933 19 AUGUST 2129

He had become a splinter!

William Yeats Butler examined the small, dark splinter in his left forefinger.

It had been there since middle school, now more than ten years ago. He remembered the larger splinter that had splayed off the old brake drum he was trying to grind down to use as a make-do clutch for the tiller. Red hot, it had plowed into his finger, quenched by his blood to the sound of sizzling and the scent of his own grilled flesh. When removed by his father, it had left this small souvenir. The fragment never gave him any trouble. Once healed, it sat there, just under the skin, and did nothing. It was so different from those niggling little wood splinters one got. They generated pain well above their size, eventually warmed, reddened, worked their way grudgingly to the surface, opened, and expelled themselves along with foul-smelling pus.

He had allowed himself to become a metal splinter in the body of the Unity.

It should have been obvious to him; he was happy, content, and—perhaps most telling of all—he was expending time to paint this room as a surprise for Hecate. The *appropriate* mental condition for any spy was paranoia. It kept one alive and undiscovered. This, in turn, allowed one to be paranoid for another day.

But paranoia had its tactical limits.

Spying really was two jobs: to remain undetected and to get important information about big things to the right people. His two jobs were always in tension and frequently at each other's throats. The Color Guard, his bosses in espionage, said the invasion was coming—not just a routine bloody raid of fire, death, and rapine, but a real invasion.

And Will's contribution to the effort was—pathetic.

So far, other than the Order of Battle, listing all the units in the upcoming invasion, all he had to show for his time in the Unity was some background information and a mystery overlay of what might be a battle plan for some unknown spot at some unknown time. In the balance, he had lost Rupert, his identity within the Unity, his most basic piece of spycraft.

The loss of his original Rupert Guillemot persona had been thrust upon him when he fell down a gigantic ventilator shaft in Virginia, suffering a concussion, multiple fractures, contusions, and a ruptured liver. What with his story of being a buyer for an agro-commune running thin, it was getting a bit hard to keep the Guillemot fellow "alive" at any rate. Thank God, at least he had recovered. With the help of Hecate and her friend Malila, he had gotten access to one of the Unity's auto-docs. A few days floating semiconscious in a vat of red goo allowed everything to work again, leaving him with a face that would be more or less recognizable to his mother.

Will pulled out the cans of paint he had hidden among the debris of the abandoned beltway station just south of the old Willow Grove entrance.

Hecate would be surprised.

Hecate had admired a lemony-yellow color a week ago when they had first looked through the CAPHI. As a guy, there were some things about the soul-sucking apostasy of the Unity that Will appreciated. Once you got by the all-pervasive fear of discovery, the grinding atheism, the muddled dogma of the comicoms,[5] and the oppression by the DUFS, there was at least one authentic advantage to living in the Unity: *there was only one color chart.*

Will remembered the dread occasioned by his mother's choosing a color for his youngest brother's bedroom. First, his mother had

---

[5] Comedians posing as news commentators

collected over a dozen swatches of nearly identical hues from each of several paint stores in Searcy, Arkansas, his hometown. Next, there was the near-ceremonial "pinning of the swatches" on poor Hershel's bedroom wall before the painful interrogation, in varying lighting conditions, of every family member to surrender an opinion. *Then she chose something else entirely.* Compared to that, foreign espionage was straightforward and emotionally uplifting.

Deciding on a paint color was so much easier in the Unity, as there was only one book. Everyone already had one. All manufactured products had to have a color in the Catalog of Allowable Product Hue Index.

Obviously thought up by a guy.

He and Frog had been able to snag a CAPHI, and Hecate now had her own.

Will spread some drop cloths and took down the crude shelves he had thrown up for their meager stores. The paint, a roller, and a good three-inch brush were enough to get started. Getting the paint and rollers had required a little late-night "shopping" once he discovered a basement entrance from the beltway to a paint store in Lansdowne. The old tumbler lock, rather than a thumb-print Mag-Lock, had succumbed to a little sleight of hand he had learned in spy school. Frog, as expected, was delighted to learn the trick.

Less tricky had been their triumph of last month. As they now frequently did, Frog and he had burrowed into the DUFS headquarters to discover what they might find by chance. As they entered, a flurry of flashing tangerine-colored neon lights and a hum like a nest of hornets greeted them. The strobing orange EOF-error[6] alarms were

---

[6] End of File error, usually occurring when a previous user has failed to close it properly

due to some frazzled new ensign forgetting to close, store, and encrypt some files. It was like taking candy from a sleeping pit bull. Since Will had not even opened the files, no one would even know he had copied them. That's when he found the Order of Battle and the overlay. The OOB was straightforward enough, but the overlay, a transparency meant to cover some unknown map, was all in code. If all the coded units shown were of division strength, as the OOB suggested, then this thing was huge—maybe as many as six hundred thousand troopers.

However, the overlay did not tell the start time, merely giving all the interim durations, the *times* things happened after an unknown H-hour. The overlay did show how the forces moved after the starting gun: four forces of air and land were supposed to start at points designated W, X, Y, and Z. They were then to sweep across some territory to some location V to combine. Once a unified force, they were to wheel about and make a frontal assault on a location U before encircling it from the left and then the right.

It was useless, of course.

Without the map to which it was linked, he could not tell them *what* or *when* for the operation. He and Frog, going back time and again, had found scores of maps. Nothing fit. As America's sole spy, he had discovered almost everything needed to foil the invasion of America—everything except *where* the invasion would start and *when*. In the bad old days, there was no place the Unity could not take or destroy—almost anything the Unity wanted it had already taken. Not one industrial center still lived north or east of Saint Louis.

---

and the size of the file does not match the virtual table of contents. Alarms and errors ensue.

Despite the Devastations, the outlands had been recolonized. He had met one of the men most responsible for that rebirth just before he started this assignment, Jesse Johnstone, a huge, seemingly ageless man whom his father had known twenty years before. Jesse was still in vital middle age due to Ageplay. Thanks to him and those like him, the Mississippi River was still very much an American-run affair. Minnesota, Michigan, and Wisconsin might fly the bloody red flag of Canada, but at least there was no longer a shooting war with the dour Northerners. Both countries profited by sharing the Mississippi, the St. Lawrence seaways, and their common opposition to the Unity.

But he still needed to know the *where* and *when*.

"You cannot defend everywhere." Some nineteenth-century guy had said something like that back when they thought there was a "science" to war. His father, calling war "blood, fear, piss, shit, and dead babies," was of another opinion.

Will turned back to the task at hand, loading the hand brush and cutting in around the edge of the oculus while clinging to a rope ladder he had installed. Here he was, being domestic for this hole in the ground. Instead of the usual greasy, concrete-lined corridor like they had traveled for months, Hecate had found this room, open to the sky, an abandoned maintenance shop. Down one level from the roundhouse, they had turned part into snug sleeping quarters, and two klicks away, once Frog had sent all the workers off on illusory errands, a well-filled storeroom. The Higginses, those strange, misshapen workers on the subterranean beltways, were probably no longer a danger. Satisfied that they no longer had to provide the "Freedom of the Belts" to these strangers, they seemed content with the status quo.

The corner of the space they had dedicated to cooking and eating, the one that got the morning sun, would soon be a cheery lemony yellow. Hecate would be pleased and surprised.

But he was a disgrace. His professional paranoia was at low ebb. No one was looking for him—no one needed to.

Frog had discovered that the Grove station opened into a tiny park behind a line of small and mostly operating stores. It seemed like a scene out of some historic drama at the time of the Meltdown. Lush trees with pale bark overlooking the rank grass along an open stream, which, having escaped its cracked concrete culvert near what had been a sports field, wended its way among the roots of the trees before disappearing through a grate. That evening, Frog had declared the park safe for the moment. No longer having her own basic implant or CORE access, Hecate, condemned thus to living underground, had taken the chance to see the stars.

He was close to finishing the first coat when he heard the security door along the passageway scrape open—*caught in the act!* He had hoped to have one coat all done for Hecate before she got back.

As she emerged into the room, Hecate called him.

"Will, someone's coming!"

JESSE & SCORCH

THE DEEP SCORCH (ONCE EASTERN GEORGIA) 0544 14 AUGUST 2129 AD

He was just killing men.

His assignment had been to go into the Scorch and follow the signal, find Malila Chiu, and bring her back. *It should have been easy.*

Instead, it had been fourteen days of perdition. They were down another five men, poisoned by some sort of Hawk-Thorn, new to his acquaintance. Atropine did not work, nor physostigmine, nor any of the suggamadexoids. Doc Redder, the medic, and he were at the end of their tethers, and they had called in an armored and tracked Evac unit to bring out the victims. Private Mbele would die, that he was sure of. She had caught one of the nasty barbed things in the back of her neck, and it had dropped her like a sack of rocks. After her squad got her off the line and back to what counted for a rear area, the seizures started. It was the last time Jesse had seen her move.

Five down. Another five were no longer able to function, victim to some hallucinogen, and could no longer be trusted with weapons. They should be back at a rear echelon by now. If they returned to fight at all, it would be in full-body environmental suits in weather that was already cloyingly hot and humid—*just killing men.*

He had killed men before. That first stripe, when Jesse was a young man, had bothered him more than the next two put together. Killing changes a man; the first killing made it easier for him to kill the second.

He received that first stripe for his part in the deaths of three settlers the winter of 2071–72. Back then, more than fifty years ago, settlements in the Scorch were just starting up. People, armed with the new agro, were recolonizing the wilderness between the river and the Wall.

Reuben Alexander, Haywood Symthe, and he helped save a town in Tennessee that would have been massacred by the Unis if the three of them hadn't gotten the people moving. They had held the town's draft animals hostage, promising to slaughter them if the town did not shift. The town had capitulated and saved their lives. Of course, the blizzard they ran into on the wild dash back to Memphis had really saved the lot of them. The Unis were hot on their tails when a family—a young father, his wife, and their baby—froze to death in the confusion.

Once the rest of the people were safe, America thanked the three young men for their services—just before putting them on trial. The deaths were declared "righteous," legally not murders, and the three of them were marked for life as man-killers.

Back then, having just graduated from Saint Louis University with honors, he was into his first year of medical school. His parents had expressed their pleasure that their mostly feral, youngest son was finally becoming civilized. Yet after he received the stripe, they were both officially "disappointed" in him. For most of his life until then, it had been his parents, his four siblings, and him against the world. The Johnstone family had survived cataclysm, bushwhackers, hunger mobs, the hostile Scorch, and zombie raids by pulling together. Now he could find no peace from his father's second-guessing and his mother's doleful looks.

And he had been doing well enough in that first year of medical school, with its oceans of facts, blistering schedule, and grinding fatigue, until the university expelled him. Alone, he left Saint Louis that March and went back into the Scorch, back to the only home he really remembered, Dunbarton, abandoned for more than ten years by then. He found the foundation made of river rocks in the shallow, sunlit curve of Home Creek. The Scorch had already found the rest of the cabin, reducing it to a snow-covered mound of rotted wood. Shoveling out a section of the collapsed porch down to the dirt, Jesse built a fire and spread the hot coals around before bedding down on the still-warm mineral earth. One never knew what might get hungry for fresh meat while the meat slept.

The following morning, Jesse brought down a young elk. After skinning it and opening the braincase, he'd slung the carcass over his shoulder as he climbed the rock wall.

"Hello, Speaker. It is Quicksilver. I come to talk," he called as he dropped into Speaker's little valley, warmed by the sun despite the chill air of a mountain springtime.

"Quicksilver, it has been winters since you came. We will talk," came the immediate and familiar voice response, bloodless and hollow. And they had talked, the tall man and the voice of the plant. Jesse poured out his disappointments with himself, his family, his culture, and his entire species.

Grimacing to himself even now, he remembered the torrent of dismay with which he had inundated Speaker. Thinking back to that meeting with Speaker, Jesse remembered finally running out of dismay and tears.

He had left Dunbarton as an eleven-year-old boy. He had left the wilderness to join his country, to meet his people, and to claim his patrimony. Instead, Jesse had had to become used to people calling him unique—just before they bled him. He hadn't liked it—either the bleeding, which "only hurt a little bit" but still hurt, the dishonesty of the people, or his naiveté at thinking them interested in him. Yet he had held out for himself hope of becoming a regular American. Now that hope was gone, evaporating with his first attempt to help his country. By opposing the barbarism of the damned Unity, he had become the barbarian. Marked for life, Jesse was condemned to travel through the realms of men branded for what he was: a killer.

America would see Speaker as a monster, unnatural and unclean, even as he, himself, was a monster.

Monsters should stick together.

After listening to him rant for an entire day, Speaker had made a nest of lichen-covered tendrils for him when he fell asleep, exhausted in grief. Waking in the night to weep again, Jesse had found that Speaker had grown moss, absorbent moss, into his balled fists.

"Speaker?"

"I am here," said the darkness, and Jesse knew he was safe. "Quicksilver, I grieve for your sadness. You are hungry for someone to know you."

"They are not your sorrows, Speaker. I know you have many sorrows of your own; I have just added to them," he said, and wept again at the realization.

"Only the wounded may heal."

"Winters past, I wounded you, Speaker. I have come to pay the debt, that debt and the debt for listening to me now," said Jesse, rising to his feet and pulling his tunic over his head, exposing his tattooed chest and belly to the cold night air and to Speaker. Jesse shivered.

Speaker was silent except for a rustling behind him. The night had relented enough to make out the lightening sky, leaving the small defile still in dark shadows. The rustling continued, and he felt the cool touch of the hunter pseudopod on his shoulder, leaving a trail of wetness as it insinuated itself around his neck. Jesse dropped his tunic to the ground and moved his feet apart slightly in order to be ready when the strike came. The vine slithered across his chest. Jesse imagined how the green-toothed mouth swayed above his belly.

The strike, when it came, was painless. He staggered back only a step. Within seconds, the mouth dropped away and the pseudopod retracted. Jesse moved his hand to his belly to see if the wound still bled. His hand came away dry.

"But . . . Speaker, you did not—"

"It is finished, child of men. You are not as yet ripe. Go in peace."

"But—"

"Go! Quicksilver, you must leave," said Speaker in a voice of command, occasioning no chance of contradiction.

Jesse fled, feeling relieved but shamed, found unworthy of even the society of plants.

Jesse shook his head to sweep away the memory. *And now I am killing men again.* When Jesse had been dropped from America's huge new R-ship, the RSAN *Illinois*, it was because he had received the first reliable indication that an arrogant, foolishly brave, shining example of young Unity womanhood was still alive.

Malila Chiu.

Jesse loved her. It had not been an easy romance. He captured her up north almost a year previously. Having replaced her Unity implant with one of his own design, Jesse could track her in real time anywhere—if she was above ground and close enough. He had received no signal once the Unity had stolen her back last Easter: no signal nor any hint of a signal until two weeks ago. Then a signal, "5 by 5," popped up on the Savannah River. He had been sent to fetch her.

The Old Man moved to the forward positions on the left, and after creeping along behind a downed log, scuttled into the hole Sergeant Joshua Kazinsky was sharing with two other soldiers.

"G' morning, Sergeant. I thought I might join you for the festivities, if that's a' right?" said Jesse.

Kazinsky grinned mirthlessly. "We'd all be honored to have you with us, Major. You're our lucky charm, you know. Last time we were on point with you, we didn't take a single casualty. We may need to kidnap you for the duration," he said, laughing nervously.

Jesse grinned in return. In truth, he was as scared as the rawest recruit; in the Scorch, the only kind of luck was bad. In the few days since the start of this, the platoon had turned from a band of crafty warriors slipping among the trunks of the old forest to a Forlorn Hope assaulting the bastion of an angry Nature. It wasn't right. The Scorch wasn't acting right. Mere months ago, it had been his familiar, if man-eating, homeland. Now it was just man-eating.

With the losses mounting, Colonel Tremont, the man Jesse knew originally as Jake Steiner aboard the *Illinois* and now the man in charge of the expedition, had made it clear: today was the last day. If they could not make some breakthrough with their new tactic, then retreat was their only option. The Unity was going to invade, probably with the next dark of the moon, September 11. America was in need of all her soldiers.

Sergeant Kazinsky gave the hand signal. Privates Yoder and Belleza left cover and scurried up a dozen yards into the open and stopped. Almost immediately, Jesse could hear the Hawk-Thorns start to fire, the odd, almost-musical whine ending in a short percussion. Three-inch thorns snicked leaves as they sped toward the two soldiers. Jesse prayed that he had not just sent two more men to join Mbele's writhing, gasping, and dying.

As instructed, the two men had crouched back-to-back, their jury-rigged shields interlocking front, back, and sides. Thorns twanged into the obstruction, standing out like quills on a porcupine. Others would get through, no doubt, but the shields would trigger their poisoned barbs and discharge the sticky sap before they hit flesh. The men would need to scrub it off before long, but they were safe for the moment. The squad had fashioned rattan shields out of the unchanged sweetgums. The wood was dense, cross-grained, and seemed to blunt every blade taken to it, but after many hours, they had fabricated shields. The Hawk-Thorns would fire at a target until they exhausted their barbs. Only then would the detail attempt an advance.

How long they could expect success was the question. The Scorch reacted to every new gambit with its own, like a grim chess game. Every day was a new and deadly challenge. Yesterday, the Hawk-Thorns had appeared. Two days before, it had been some unnamed slime on the tree limbs, which, dropping onto the men, eroded cloth and skin. Leaf capes had solved that particular horror.

Kazinsky signaled for another pair of soldiers to advance.

When they had started two weeks ago, there had been none of the usual Blood Reds or Sick-a-mores, despite the lateness of the season. They hadn't met even the usual crop of Dog-Trots on the sunlit patches they favored. In August, when the seed pods dried out and the husks powdered, they could trigger the worst kinds of diarrhea imaginable, disabling dozens at a stroke.

But on this trip, nothing had slowed their advance—at first— not until the Scorch hunkered down to oppose them. They still had thirty miles to go to the location of Malila's last ping. Used to sliding through the Scorch since he was a boy, seventy years before, Jesse had been a valued scout after the new agro made recolonizing eastern Tennessee a possibility. Later, when the Unity's deadly raids started up again, Jesse, as a leader of militia, had fought the blood-ugly rear-guard actions, trying to give a chance for women, children, livestock, and scant possessions to make it back to safety. He'd lost three wives to the Unity's mindless violence and to the brutality that erupts in some men's hearts every time chaos gives them an invitation. But he had never had to fight the Scorch before.

That was not saying that he had not had substantive disagreements with the changed plants. He owned meat, his own walking-around-in-it meat. Much of the Scorch desired to relieve him of the burden. Nonetheless, he always counted the Scorch a sanctuary, entering the verdant forest almost as he would a church. Granted, this church was out to eat him. *Safe as houses—as long as you did not trust it.*

The forest seemed to grow thicker overnight, presenting the diminishing platoon with a green wall across their line of march with each sunrise. Water sources shown on the maps became mere mud pits, while well-selected campsites were flooded with fetid water despite a clear-lit sky. For all that time, Malila's signal was strong and unmoving, a scant hundred yards this side of the Savannah River and almost within sight of the Unity Rampart.

The last two soldiers entered the clearing with their shields. After the initial fusillade, the assault of missile strikes started a slow diminuendo. Soon, they were only sporadic bolts flicking into one or another clamshell of wicker. Kazinsky had just handed Jesse a wicker shield for his own advance when he started to converse over his headset. Within a minute, he whispered to Jesse, "Signals says somethin's up to our right. Told me to pull back and set up a perimeter. Tremont wants you with Gonzales's squad. Got it?"

"Got it, Sarge," Jesse acknowledged as he ducked down and started working his way back and to the right while Kazinsky's squad started its cautious retreat. Eyes came up from under the edges of helmets as he passed. Silent good-luck gestures sent him onward.

BENNY & HARRY

MOTHER HOUSE OF SYNTOPIA
SUNDAY AFTERNOON, AUGUST 14, 2129

Benjamin Nortvengler, PhD, professor emeritus of philosophy, swirled his drink and stared into the faux fire in the Victorian marble fireplace of the secret room, choosing to leave his home and that *harridan of a woman who calls herself my wife* to cower in the one unfindable spot in town. Benny had been in the common room of the Mother Chapter of the Honorable Order of Syntopia all day. It had been a bad week for Syntopia. The bottle of very serviceable bourbon he had gotten recently had been half full when he arrived today; he was drinking the dregs of it now.

As a student here, after he had discovered this room, a neglected bomb shelter under the old Mondale building, he had imagined how great the reach of the Synthesis might be. *Non-axiomatic rational skepticism*—that's what it had been back then. NARS had promised a golden thread of reason, or at least a path to avoid being duped. Syntopians were rational, pragmatic, and unblinkingly realistic. If they had followed the enlightened path of Synthesis, the world— America, at any rate—would have been a very different place: submit to the Unity, plead for annexation, prohibit Ageplay, and close all the myth-factories that so polluted the intellectual landscape. It would have been simple, back then. Only one individual supplied the Ageplay obscenity.

Now it was impossible; the agent was seemingly made by every pharmaceutical firm in the nation. Then, it would have been easy:

kill Jesse Johnstone. One death, and this whole mess could have been avoided.

They had erred—had erred badly—when Johnstone had been allowed to return, unmolested, to the Scorchings of eastern Tennessee. *Or was it Kentucky?* He never could reliably remember the difference. But he had allowed himself and the Order to enter comfortable middle age without a mission. Only when the blasted Johnstone had returned to civilization had he realized his error.

Jesse Johnstone needed to die a natural death—and soon. At the time of the Meltdown, life expectancy had been something like ninety-one years. Now, in the new republic, without Ageplay, it was down to the low eighties. Those with Ageplay were calculated to have a life expectancy of 170, an obscenity he needed to correct. Johnstone was seventy-eight. He needed to die.

Syntopia had failed twice. The first attempt with Verbon had succeeded in merely making the man sick. It should have killed him several times over. When he learned through his sources that the army was going to shelter him on one of those absurd balloon-like affairs, his heart had dropped. It was only when young Padilla volunteered to follow him, in recompense for his first failure, that Nortvengler had seen a glimmer of hope.

All illusion. Jesse Johnstone still lived, and the boy had died a violent death at the savage's hands. Padilla's family did not even get a body to bury. The vicious old man should have been indicted for a hatecrime. Instead, he had gotten off scot-free. It had happened weeks ago but was announced only Friday. *Cowards.*

Nortvengler shivered, sighed, and took the next sip.

Since the dour news of Johnstone's arrival into Saint Louis in April, Benny had spent more and more time in the chapter room.

He was drinking too much, sleeping too little, and letting his grad students take his lectures too often. It could not go on, he knew.

Professor Nortvengler heard the subtle sound of the bolt sliding in the door and quickly picked up the *Post-Dispatch* he was pretending to read. Harold Colina, the ranking member of the Department of Economics, entered looking like Benny felt: defeated, saddened, and discouraged. Without a word, Colina limped over to the credenza, hooked his walking stick over his forearm, and splashed some sherry into a small glass. Slipping into the other leather chair facing the fireplace, he groaned. For long minutes they sat, unspeaking, each watching the glittering display in the hearth.

"You've heard, then?" said Harry.

"Yes, the university comm'net[7] was full of it. Padilla was a graduate student of ours. I expect the department will have to mount an official investigation. Philosophy of history fellow, as I'm sure you know. On the Weinstein Grant," Benny replied.

"Well, that, at least, is fortuitous, Benny. If there will be some investigation, I can't think of a better person to chair it than you. And no."

"No?"

"No, I didn't know he was one of your grad students. Boy's parents have been called, I suppose? Hate to find out about it on the 'net."

"Yes. Yes. That was done as soon as we were officially notified by the balloon boys."

Harry sent a plume of blue smoke aloft from a thin cigar and said, "They said he was sucked into the intake of a fan. Cut to ribbons. Nothing recognizable. Most of him fell into the sea."

---

[7] Communication nets: video, audio, and/or cerebral

Hierarch Zeno, as Benjamin Nortvengler was more rightfully known within these sacred precincts, quickly placed his near-empty glass upon the table and looked away, breathing heavily. Once he had recovered, he said, "The Agnomen murdered him. The man has no conscience—a real-life ghoul, like the *asuong* from the Indonesian, that from the Sanskrit *asura,* meaning 'demon.' I think it's interesting that the concept of vitality-draining mythos is so oriental . . ."

"Benny, you're babbling. You philosophers can be so—atmospheric. What do you think we should do? Padilla was the one who tracked Johnstone and poisoned the mailbox, wasn't he? He blackmailed Rhedd's aide and got onto the *Illinois.* Now that he's gone, we need feet and hands. Have you any other likely grad students?"

"I have *not* been indolent in the cause, Brother Archimedes. Who was it who obtained the reactants from Chemistry and manufactured the Verbon in the first place?"

"Don't get insulted, Benny. I was not discounting your efforts, but I doubt we'll ever catch out Johnstone with contact poison again. The first thing we need to do is get a replacement."

"The first thing we need to do is approve Padilla's dissertation, posthumously. Gives a nice patina of compassion, don't you think? Send the family his academic hood. Stuff like that."

"Not sure his folks care about that. Cattle herders in the Montana. Odd thing, really. I understand Morris, his advisor, tried to dissuade him, but he was adamant about the subject of his dissertation: 'The Public Life of Jesse Aaron Johnstone: Emergence and Decline of a Hero.' Odd," Harry said, and shook his head before taking another sip of his sherry.

The hierarch shrugged.

THE MESSENGER

EARLY MORNING, SIXTEEN DAYS AFTER THE SECOND FULL MOON SINCE THE SUMMER SOLSTICE, THE YEAR, SEVENTY-FIVE WINTERS SINCE THE CHANGE

She had lost track of herself in the timeless skein of the Scorch. Only the slow retreat of the moon, the swelling of the People as they gathered in the Sun, and the expansion of her knowledge gave her any sense of time's passage. The People had been teaching her, training her, at Splanch's direction. She still sensed its—Splanch's— regard, along with that of all the other of the changed ones. The moon had been near its fullest when Splanch had found her floating in the river—bound and dying. The moon was now a mere sliver; yet her rescue seemed more than an age ago. She had learned much since her rescue. The web of life within the whole of the Scorch tasted, smelled, drank, died and decayed as one. Unchanged trees, herded by the People, sprouted, grew to fullness and added their resources of sun and soil to the whole.

The People of the Scorch all spoke and listened as one, but need had pressed the one, Splanch, to the forefront for a season. War was coming. Splanch would lead in the People's defense. There was scant chance that the war would overlook the People, sitting as they were between the warring parties. Since the Great Change at the dawn of the People, the realm of the Scorch had been an unknowing bulwark between these two enemies, protecting the humans from each other.

In the past, Messengers had gone to both sides—and died—the words of friendship and assistance dying because the Messenger, a changed one, was so alien to her fellow humans. Once Splanch had made her aware of the need, however, she had volunteered to take the message herself to the outlanders—those outside the Rampart. She would go to him—go to them—when she was full of the knowledge and wisdom of the People. Only when Splanch declared her ripe would she be an apt and acceptable Messenger of the People.

As enlarging as the skein of the People's wisdom had been, it had taken from her as well. She willingly surrendered her arrogance and anger but also much of what she had once thought important. Some things she still cherished: the smile of a young baby, the hope of a new life in the outlands—and her love for the Old Man.

Her misunderstanding of his love for her embarrassed her even now, The Old Man had shown her love even as she was showing her disdain of him and his people. While he had protected her from harm and herself, she had tried to kill him. He had looked after her far better than he had himself—trading his welfare for her safety, again and again. The Old Man had shown her love before he ever spoke of it. Once she had been able to see that, she had realized her own love—ardent, foolish, and newly green—for the old, disfigured savage.

And then she had ruined it. Regret—cold, sour and aching—was again swelling within her when she was summoned.

ALPINE START

(To begin a climb in the dark, early hours, hopefully avoiding disaster in the hot afternoon when legs are tired and the snow is rotten.)

NEW MISSION FOR HAVERSHAM

TIDEWATER EUTHANATORIUM (A WECARE4U CORP SUBSIDIARY), SHARLET, KAROLYNA DISTRICT, DEMOCRATIC UNITY
09.31.07_02_AUGUST_AU 77 (2129 AD)

Captain Lance Haversham, in a borrowed uniform too big for his spare frame and obtained from one of the dead, waited impatiently in the sterile hallway for the health-care providers to emerge after discussing the care of a certain Iain Galt. General Jourdaine, who had plucked him from obscurity a mere month ago, had not woken up from the freak accident that had downed the skimmers. The other skimmer, the one carrying the pestilential Chiu woman, had gone down with all hands into the Savanah River. *Good riddance.* The woman had been a growing obsession for his commander, a distraction from the coming trials of combat. If he had had his way, the woman's body would be moldering there even now. Jourdaine, less merciful, had wanted her humiliation to be more . . . *more something* and had trussed her up and thrown her into the other skimmer.

A low-level flunky in a short white coat scurried out of the room with a hunted look in her eyes.

". . . orthopod should set and cast the tib-fib today. EEG shows a lot of low-amp slowing on . . ." was all Haversham heard before the door snicked shut again.

Jourdaine, no doubt anxious to get away after his unsatisfactory confrontation with the Chiu woman, had unbuckled his seat as they were approaching the Southern Gate. Almost immediately, the whine of the Skimmerhorn had ceased in a wrenching crescendo of seizing metal. Jourdaine must have tried to hold on to the belt, but he'd been ripped away, sending him like a projectile into the forward bulkhead. His face, when the rescuers' lights had finally found them, seemed squashed, collapsed, one eye protruding oddly. He would not wake up.

Living off what he could get from commissary machines, Lance felt crapulous, weary, and worried. The door opened, and a small cluster of white-coated figures emerged, looking like a flock of sheep as they ambled away. It was difficult to snag the attention of one of the more peripheral "lambs," but finally Haversham succeeded. The man could be no more than thirteen and at the start of his apprenticeship as a health-care provider. A look of uncertainty fleeted across his acned face as he glanced longingly at the retreating backs of his colleagues.

"Excuse me, Citizen . . . Kitchener," Haversham said, reading the man's ID badge quickly. "General Jourdaine himself asked me to care for this man. I'm General Jourdaine's adjutant. What can you tell me about his condition? How long before he can be discharged?"

"Don't know. I'm just an HP student. Pleased to meet you. I guess since you're sort of his official person I can tell you. Understand, I'm just a student. I don't make the orders. Nurse Manager does that."

"Yes, of course, I'm familiar with how it works, Citizen," Haversham said, his frustration growing as the man talked. "Get on with it."

"Well, he's badly damaged. Some cuts on the right arm and the broken leg are nothing, of course. He could be walking on it this afternoon with a cast and a cane—and a good hit of ThiZ, of course." He grinned, and when Haversham did not reciprocate, hurried on. "The face will take some time. He's scheduled for the autoHP this afternoon. Most of the orbit, the bony rim around the right eye itself, has been smashed and the sinuses behind them. We used to go in with surgery and actually lift them back into place, I understand. That was before the Awesome Care Act, of course."

"Of course," said Haversham, having only a dim recollection of what he had been told in school about the edict passed generations before he was born that turned all health care over to automated machines and a small band of technicians who ran them according to the published "best practice" guidelines. But he knew there had been *doctors* of medicine at one time, as absurd as that now sounded.

"What's the prognosis?"

"Oh, excellent! He should have no problems walking. His face will look almost normal, most likely. The eye is gone. Nothing to do there but let it heal. Retina's pulled off and the *bulbus oculi* has been compromised, you see. Best to just patch it. Problem's the brain. He's been comatose since evening Monday. He's got a subdural. Gonna have to do a craniotomy and evacuate the hematoma, identify the hemorrhaging vessel—"

"English, Citizen Kitchener, if you would be so kind as to use English. I'm going to have to explain this to others, you understand."

"Oh, yeah, sure. He's got a blood clot on the surface of the brain, putting pressure on it. Head's sort of a closed box. Put more stuff in, and the pressure skyrockets. So we gotta get in the guy who does this sort of thing from Nyork to do the cutting and drilling."

"How long will that take?"

"He's top of the list; no more than a couple days."

"In the meantime, is he being injured?"

"That's the question, isn't it? Could be. Tough to tell. Six of one, half a dozen of the other. Should be interesting."

Haversham began to feel the nausea of uncertainty start to crawl up from his belly. These outlying euthanatoriums were notorious.

"Let me speak to your nurse manager."

"Oh, no one speaks to Nurse Manager, Captain. Nurse Manager speaks to you—if you are not very careful."

"I understand. Where is he/she/xe?"

"Office is down in administration, behind the blast doors."

"Thanks."

After contacting a General Bledsoe in Jourdaine's name and summoning a company of DUFS to the location to surround the building, Captain Haversham advanced on the administration offices of the Tidewater Euthanatorium (WeCare4U Corp subsidiary) with merely a platoon: forty of the faceless, black-suited soldiers. He got an immediate audience. The promised wrath of Lieutenant General Jourdaine, the head of the DUFS, the lord of the Blues, and the ruler of the nation, was brought to bear on Thelma Anne Rachedt, a thin, dark woman, S30, E32, powerful and thus arbitrary; bureaucratic and thus indolent; and looking forward to her retirement, thus easily manipulated.

Within two hours, "Iain Galt" was prepared: head shaved, intravenous fluids going into his uninjured left arm, sedated, and in the neurosurgical suite. A saturnine man in handcuffs was bustled into a dressing room, still huffing about his mistreatment. By sundown, Jourdaine was in recovery, awake, and beginning to complain. Haversham talked with him there, clasping his good hand. Before he left the bedside, he stationed a small detail of DUFS and retreated to a borrowed bed and the first sleep in two days.

Haversham woke still exhausted. Grabbing some tea and ration wafers in lieu of breakfast, he returned to the recovery ward. Empty but for its single patient, the unit was in an uproar. The quiet epicenter of the storm was the man himself, disdaining all attempts to make him more comfortable even as he was demanding impossible remedies for that discomfort. Still under the alias of "Iain Galt," the staff were aware of the extraordinary lengths that had been taken for his care. They acted accordingly.

Just as Haversham approached, an aide scuttled through the door of Jourdaine's room. The man's sobs, followed down the hall by a used bedpan, suddenly ceased. Jourdaine's aim, considering the loss of binocular vision and use of his nondominant hand, was remarkable.

"Good morning, sir. I can't tell you how good it is to see you awake. It seems you have come a long way overnight."

"Where have you been?" Jourdaine snapped, his head swathed in bandages and his dead eye staring back at him, the pupil dilated and white. "I woke, and I was surrounded by strangers! Just when I needed you, you abandoned me, Lance."

"I was just down the hall, sir. I've been at your side since the accident up until last night, sir," he said, his heart sinking.

"What accident? I thought they tried to kill me. Just like the Solons to try to kill me, too."

"No, sir, don't you remember we captured the Chiu woman? Our skimmer went down just before the Southern Gate. The other skimmer, the one with Chiu in it, went down in the river. Divers have located the wreck, but the bodies discovered so far are not hers."

"Chiu? So she was the cause of all this? I should have guessed. Never mind that, Haversham, tell me what's been happening."

Jourdaine interrogated him all morning, and Lance was strangely pleased and encouraged. Jourdaine's wit was dull, but it seemed to be improving, albeit with his memories of the last few days scrambled or entirely absent. Fortunately, none of the other factions had gotten wind of his indisposition since the accident.

Haversham had seen to that. He had invited, in Jourdaine's name, all of the upper echelons to a guided tour of the Savanah Crater. Created seventy-odd years previously during the Glorious War of Liberation when a rebel army had come close to outmaneuvering the People's Army and invading the Unity homeland, the Crater glowed radioactive. All of the invitees had claimed prior engagements. Manufactured newsreels in the CORE of Jourdaine's heroic trip featured widely on the comm'nets even while the man himself was in surgery.

After lunch, broth that Haversham tediously fed to him by spoon, Jourdaine motioned with his good hand for Lance to lean closer.

"You know, they will be out to get me if they know I'm injured. Yes? Do whatever you think best to protect us. Watch out for the senior DUFS. We don't have to worry about the Solons, not since last month."

"Oh—okay, sir. But there are a lot of issues still to settle for the invasion, sir. Shouldn't we delay it?"

"Now that that damned woman is dead, we can push it back a month—no, two. Dark of the moon. We still have to get through the scorched areas."

"Sir! Yes, sir."

"Just don't let the bastards know I'm down. They'll try to infiltrate. Try to get to me. They'll . . ."

Giving an occasional flap of his good hand, Jourdaine seemed to run out of words like a cheap wind-up toy before he stopped entirely. Two heavily muscled medical functionaries of some sort arrived with a gurney. Haversham motioned for them to get on with it, then walked to the radiology suite holding Jourdaine's hand to help calm his terror.

What Lance needed to do was obvious. Jourdaine needed a vacation, and Lance would be its creator. If he were successful, Jourdaine's coolness on the run-up to the Jorga invasion would become legendary. Daily newsreels would document him deep-sea spearfishing for coelacanth, hang gliding over enemy territory, and escorting a number of media darlings to exotic locations. With unrestricted access to the nation's comm'nets, Lance could create a fairy-tale story that would simultaneously become the feral dream of every DUFS officer and a bulwark against intrigue. Haversham grinned to himself as Jourdaine reemerged to be wheeled back to his bed.

Once Jourdaine was settled into a fitful sleep, Haversham went to the small desk he had wrangled away from Head Nurse and sat down, facing a blank wall.

Never have I been closer to real power, Lance thought.

Above and beyond caring for and protecting Jourdaine in his damaged state and making it appear to the nation that their leader was having the time of his life, more needed doing. There was an invasion coming up!

General Vivalagente Suarez, Jourdaine's immediate predecessor, had never really completed her plan, "Century." After Jourdaine disposed of her, he scrubbed Century free of any connection with Suarez and renamed it Random, but it was still a shell of a campaign. Other than drawing up an Order of Battle, designating which units would be included in the conflict, Jourdaine had done nothing else. The Order of Battle, of course, was a tough job by itself and well beyond Haversham's ability. Units loyal to the Blues and Jourdaine needed to be balanced with those that needed to be "supervised." In addition, some loyal units had to remain in the homeland to quash any coup d'état in the making.

Haversham frowned. *Not enough had been done.* Random was a grand, strategic dream, which, since the outlands were helpless against the Unity's raids, would be a walkover. Even so, *if he did not do something,* it would merely appear to be a sanguinary toad orgy. Any small success of the barbarians would draw down unfair vituperation upon Jourdaine from his rivals or the comicoms.

He was sure that Jourdaine, infinitely devious, knew that. Beyond the *when* and *who*, Jourdaine had also chosen a why of the invasion. Six weeks of propaganda on the comm'nets had made the outlanders a stench in the nostrils of the Unity. On the mere suspicion of being a spy, crowds from Karolyna to Main had beaten innocent citizens to death, generally just after the 1900-hour news programs. Haversham smiled. He had crafted most of those "news programs" himself. He wondered how the mobs chose their victims.

The Unity was champing at the bit for an opportunity to pit solidarity, ingenuity, and courage against outlander sloth and cowardice.

Even that would not be *enough*.

Haversham scribbled "when, why, who" on a blank page of paper he acquired from the janitorial service, the only ones who needed writing paper in a modern euthanatorium. He added *where*. Aytlana he knew to be the chosen target. That was something, but what about the *how*?

Lance started to doodle on the blank page; it helped him to think but was a small vice he concealed from others. Even with a "grand plan," the invasion needed to be more than just hour upon hour of loyal CRNAs mowing down poorly armed primitives. What was really needed was a massive but easily understood theatrical production: the good Unity versus the primitive, depraved outlands. However, the outlanders should not look too incompetent, shiftless, or backward; victory would be all the sweeter if wrested from the grip of a capable if craven foe.

That was not going to be easy. Whatever the 'nets said, he knew the outlanders were brave and tenacious fighters—*one of their several failings.* From everything he had learned, once the DUFS were committed to a battle, the outlanders fought fiercely even against impossible odds. No finesse, no strategy, just barbarous wave after wave of shouting half-naked and tattooed semi-humans. No glory would accrue to Jourdaine from such butchery. What was needed was a great drama, showing the bloody price for contending with the Unity, on the one hand, and the glories inherent in DUFS service on the other.

The page was now covered with scribbles, doodles, and the persistent indictment: "How?" No one in the entire Unity had done any real military planning since the Glorious Revolution, seventy-six years ago. Even the Aroostook War[8] had been little more than an armed truce, the Canadians having seized what they wanted and then hunkering down to await the Unity's counterattack before cutting it to shreds. He turned the page over.

Haversham had heard rumors of there being old books about war. He even knew a few names like Jacomini, Clausewitz, Sun Sue *(odd name for a chink),* Marshall Foch, and John Bellhood, but that was all he had—names. *He had to be careful.* He could not contact other senior staff and risk them suspecting Jourdaine's incapacitation. If he delegated out parts of the creation of the *actual* battle plan, even with trusted allies, it was more than likely that they would eventually demand a portion of the credit. That was unjust. Jourdaine had done the tough part: conceiving the grand *why*. He would need loyal and especially *quiet* minions to help formulate the actual battle plan. Fortunately, Jourdaine had such a one.

Haversham was in this alone.

---

[8] See Appendix for timeline

Every hour that could be taken away from overseeing Jourdaine's care, manufacturing virtual events for Jourdaine's image to attend, and sending out imperious Jourdainesque commands, he would have to devote to learning the art of war. With growing desperation, Haversham surfed the CORE, looking for "war." Sliding through the shining conduits of the nationwide system, past checkpoints, challenges, passwords, and counterchallenges, all took time. What he eventually found was disappointing. The data was fragmented, severed, almost as if a giant cleaver had come down and chopped off a living limb. Files that appeared intact had been drained of their actual data. Reference data revealed themselves to be sheets of numbers, all carefully indexed back to a nonexistent narrative. It was hopeless. He unearthed all kinds of random quotes about war, but all seemed to be subtly damaged.

"To defend everywhere is to offend nowhere."

"Divide and subtract."

"An army travels of its knees."

Some political operative in the time before the Meltdown, Glorium Steina, was supposed to have said, "The greatest generation will be the one that refuses to go to war."

All obvious nonsense.

Haversham heard the squeak of a gurney and looked down the long corridor to see that Jourdaine was returning from another treatment. Lance had spent two hours with nothing to show for it except a page and a half of doodles.

The next day and the one to follow were no more productive. He could no longer eat due to his all-encompassing anxious nausea. With increasing desperation, Haversham's research into the philosophy of battle drove him back to the CORE. He was nearing his wit's end, figuring that his only hope was to throw himself on the mercy of senior staff and divulge the entire sad story of Jourdaine's injuries and his own attempt at a cover-up. He would be demoted, if not denounced. Jourdaine would be overthrown, but the Unity would be saved the ignominy of a failed invasion.

One last time, he attempted to find a way forward. Sitting again at the small borrowed desk, after Jourdaine's squeaky gurney was no longer within earshot, he began again. As always on entering the CORE, Haversham got a little nauseated, unbalanced, and disoriented. The sensation stabilized, and he set off, swooping through the shining corridors and, with his elevated clearances, past the gates and passwords. On a hunch, hoping to find Sun Sue's book, he looked up "Art of War," which turned out to be an odd form of gambling.

He was not surprised. The time before the Meltdown was infamous for its dishonesty. He scrounged around further, however, and discovered the list. It was truncated and enigmatic, but the first word past the destroyed portion was *war*. He stopped to read more.

Names popped up: evocative, seductive names like Age of Empires, Tiberium Dawn, and Zorp: Conquest of the Nether Regions. He became actually a bit giddy when he uncovered the magic words, "Command and Control."

The names—apparently no more than titles—he used to search for intact files, cobbling together displaced pieces into coherent wholes. By the time he had reached the point of diminishing returns, he had completed just under a score of files in their entirety. It would have to do. He started to dissect the files, looking for a battle plan.

Hours later, on surfacing back to reality, the room looked different: sharper, more vivid and intense. Haversham set to work.

These programs, once he got beyond the literary frame, were all about war, deception, defense, and conquest. *Jourdaine would be pleased.*

Haversham started to plan. He knew that 10 through 13 October would be the time when the nights were not illuminated by the moon except by a thin sliver for a few hours after sundown. That was when they would attack. The Unity, with its night-vision technology, would have the upper hand. Besides, it sounded kewl: *dark of the moon.*

He knew already how many men, officers, and equipage he might command from the Order of Battle. He knew what the ultimate objectives were: Aytlana, then Mobil, B'ham, and Jax, then Narleans and MyamE. All he had to do was figure out *how*.

It was complicated. The simulations he ran in the Sidmeyers AlphaCent rapidly convinced him that a frontal attack on fortified positions would be too costly. Even with frontline Sapping stations for those outlander soldiers who were captured, losses could not be replaced fast enough. There were some positive insights he obtained, as well. *Taking cities was important.* If one took a big city and subverted the manufacturing to one's own uses, one's war production rose even as the enemy's plummeted. *Winning begat winning.*

Each day he learned more and more about war. Day by day, his research consumed more of his time, translating his new knowledge into more and more of the battle plan; he ordered Jourdaine's transfer to a Nyork euthanatorium. En route, the ambulance was diverted to the DUFS HQ, Jourdaine was transferred to a hospital bed in his office suite, and the naïve ambulance driver was Sapped. *Sacrifices had to be made.*

Once on home turf, Haversham developed an efficient modus operandi. During the hours of 2000 to 0200, he scoured the CORE for more information; from 0600 to 1000, he attended Jourdaine; from 1000 to 1400, he crafted Jourdaine's next show of virtual vitality to overawe a credulous nation; from 1400 to 1800, he held court, in Jourdaine's name, for all the supplicants who came to bargain, threaten, and plead; and from 1800 to 2000, he again fed, bathed, and nursed Jourdaine. Otherwise, he slept.

On the upside, his virtual presentations had found their stride. Haversham's version of General Jourdaine was aloof but pointedly interested in the "little citizen in the street," demonstrated by videos of him visiting fictitious patients in hospital. He was wise and insightful, discerning the perfidy of an illusory petty criminal who wished to turn state's evidence against an equally illusory and clueless flunky. Every day, in every way, a virtual Jourdaine was winning the hearts and minds of his countrymen, even as he was petulantly throwing dishes of rice pudding against the wall.

Haversham, despite his fatigue, felt he was making real progress. Now with a basic skeleton of the invasion, he was filling in the details. Playing out one scenario or another, the war programs he had resurrected directed his thoughts and plans. Every new lesson wrote another small paragraph into the campaign.

His successes were even able to win himself small respites from his originally daunting schedule. He got some HPs in to supervise Jourdaine's care. Disconnected parts of the attack he fobbed off, under Jourdaine's authority, to competent and politically less-well-connected senior staff. General Alkawari Pitjantjatjara was one to whom the opening foray was entrusted. He did not disappoint—until he did.

"Tell General Jourdaine that it just can't be done!"

"Certainly, General Pitjantjatjara. But, right now—" said Haversham, gesturing idly to the doors to Jourdaine's inner sanctum—"he's reviewing the plans for the campaigns into Bama and Florda. He asked not to be disturbed. I'm sure you understand, sir."

Brigadier General Alkawari Pitjantjatjara—short, black, and intense—did not seem to understand in the least.

"General, if you wish, you can give me your report, and I will guarantee a response by retreat today. Is that acceptable?"

Pitjantjatjara grumbled, nearly fulminated, and then left the report with Haversham at his desk, a small one but a great improvement on the borrowed hospital one. Behind the dark wood, gilt and red plush door to Jourdaine's inner sanctum, no one sat at Jourdaine's desk. Usually unnoticed at Haversham's back was another door leading to a short hallway, thickly sound-proofed doors installed at either end. The corridor opened onto a spare room with but one narrow bed, one chair, an elevator to the secure lobby, shelves containing medications, an autoHP, various other pieces of equipment, and, on the bed, the ruler of the Unity.

Just prior to Pitjantjatjara's visit, Haversham had fed Jourdaine, bathed him, and then wiped his ass when he messed himself shortly thereafter. After that, Haversham had seen Jourdaine into his personal autoHP for another go-around with his facial reconstruction, had submitted a manufactured comm'net video of Jourdaine spelunking caves with thrilling first-person belays and dicey dynamic moves on the free climbs, and had leaked the news of Jourdaine's clandestine meeting with a notorious comm'net actress of dubious reputation and well-displayed bona fides.

As the general left, Haversham started to read Pitjantjatjara's report. It was not good. Jourdaine had planned to skimmer the army of invasion over the scorched areas, ferrying the DUFS troopers into Jorga to start the invasion before concentrating upon Aytlana for the conquest. The immediate spoils of this sweep would feed the army, and the excess was destined to be sent back to the Unity as replacement stores for losses due to a bad krill harvest. Haversham had presumed that was the easy part of the invasion and had farmed it out to Alkawari Pitjantjatjara, a loyal Blue.

It would not work.

While skimmers could carry impressive loads, and their top speed flirted with three hundred kilometers an hour, their rate of rise and acceleration, starting or stopping, was pathetic. It would take an average of two hours to make a sixteen-kilometer round trip from a staging area on the Unity side to a rally point on the outland side, disregarding loading and unloading. That meant no more than six trips per skimmer during a late-summer day and only twelve if they ran all night, a risky proposition given the moonless conditions and the recent unexplained crashes of two skimmers.

The Order of Battle for the Unity included 512,324 individuals—men, officers, and support. If everyone went by skimmer, that would be almost twenty-six thousand trips. With the skimmer fleet of only 406, each skimmer would need to make sixty round trips. Skimmers needed maintenance after eight hours of flight time, which took four hours. Recharging took about an hour for every hour flown. So, doing the math, every skimmer would cycle through four flights, with maintenance and fueling once every twenty hours, carrying eighty CRNAs per twenty hours, an average of four soldiers per hour per skimmer. It would take them until late into the second week to finish, working every skimmer around the clock, barring pilot fatigue, enemy action, or unexpected breakdowns.

The first wave of CRNAs, presuming all went well, could be no more than 812 men and officers divided into four separate, unsupported contingents for two full hours before more men arrived. A smart opponent would mow down each skimmer as it arrived, destroying each small contingent, whittling down the overwhelming might of the Unity before any real confrontation could occur.

Pitjantjatjara had recommended delaying the invasion until the skimmer fleet could be quadrupled. Even Haversham knew that was not going to fly. Standing near the real power residing in Jourdaine had been an education. The Unity's material resources were at low ebb. With aggressive recycling, every ounce of metal in the nation was spoken for. No refrigeration rack, pulse bolt, or shovel was allowed to be designed until a source for its construction had been identified and reserved for its use. The Unity had exhausted its mineral resources a decade ago. Central Jersy and eastern Marilan were now shallow lakes filled with contaminated groundwater. Coal mines remained closed. It would take a decade to double the fleet, a fact that Pitjantjatjara need not know.

Something different would need to be done.

NEW MISSION FOR THE GROVERS

GROVE ROUNDHOUSE
10:35 P.M. AUGUST 13, 2129 AD (AU77)

"I said, *cit'zen,* who are you?" demanded the woman's voice again with a more menacing edge to it.

Elise could see nothing except a dull green glow from a light panel leaned away from her against a wall. The point of a makeshift spear appeared at her belly, close enough to impale her but too far away to deflect easily.

"I'm Jessika Bonhoffer. I'm looking for Rupert Guillemot," she said.

"Lotsa people in that posse, hun. You'll have to do better than that."

"Look, I guarantee he'll want to know I am here. He knows me."

"You know *Rupert?*" the incredulity of the voice palpable in the darkness. "You need a better story than that, cit'zen."

"I can't tell you. Rupert is the only one I can speak to about this."

After a moment, more lights came on, leaving dense shadows around the walls and revealing the woman to be several inches shorter than Elise, brown skinned, and aged less than twenty. She turned away to the door and secured it with sturdy metal bars into slots before piling debris around it.

The woman, her face mostly hidden, ignored her prisoner now, without even providing Elise the dignity of holding a weapon on her. "I could kill you and leave you here. By morning, there'd be no body to worry about. I suggest you get cooperative, cit'zen. I hear a belly wound is a lousy way to die."

"I guess you'll have to kill me, then. I can't tell you any more."

After a pause, a silence that seemed to Elise to be full of unheard words, another voice said, "I am pretty sure you can tell her anything you can tell me, Elise," from a dense shadow.

"Will! Thank God," she said as she turned toward him.

Will Butler stepped out into the uncertain light. She had known him since the Bean Field. Immediately drawn to his dark-eyed intensity, she had only talked briefly with him a few times. The other agents-in-training were all quiet, all studious, and all intense, of course, but Will Butler had something else, as well. It had never been anything more than friendly. The Color Guard said not to fraternize, of course. The real turnoff was the certain knowledge that one's biggest competitors were fellow students.

Will had changed.

He looked older. It had been more than two years since she had last seen him, but he seemed immeasurably older than that. He was more solemn, if that were possible, and thinner. Somehow there was more of him, more *there*, concentrated into the man's very center.

The older, more intense Will said, "I thought they washed you out. One day you were there, and the next day, you were gone."

"They were going to, but instead, I got some extra conditioning done. So here I am. We got all your four spindles, even the third one, although the radiation made that one tough to download. The Color Guard was thrilled. They hadn't expected you to do so well. They've already recruited another two classes' worth of candidates."

The new Will smiled a newly crooked smile and said, "Hecate, my love, I'd like you to meet Elise McCrory, one of my classmates at spy school." Turning to Elise, he continued matter-of-factly, "Hecate is a runaway Uni, my partner, the mother of my children yet to be, and the love of my life."

The small, brown woman poked an elbow into Will's side as he tried to shy away before looping her fingers into his belt, pulling him closer, and kissing him on a cheek. Only then did she turn to face Elise. Will, average height, trim, with sandy hair and intense dark eyes, had always seemed to be attracted by the tall, blue-eyed blondes like herself, not that he had done anything about it. Hecate was rather shorter than Will, medium brown with dark eyes like Will's, but no great beauty other than that provided by the love the two obviously shared.

"Pleased to meet you, Elise. I'm sorry for the welcome. We can't be too careful, you know."

"There were people behind me. A man was hiding under a pile of rags. I think he was discovered. I heard a pulse shot. I'm not sure what I would have done if you hadn't pulled me in."

Will and Hecate looked at each other. Will sighed. "Crazy Henry was mostly harmless. He was here when we set up shop. We tried to get him into regular housing, but he said he'd be *retired*—that means being turned into a zombie soldier. He said he'd take his chances. He's been sort of a good luck charm—maybe a canary in a cage—for us ever since."

"I have to go back and retrieve my supplies. I have more spindles for you and a little surprise. How's your Morse code?"

In answer, Will leaned over to a pile of wooden boxes and drummed on it for a few seconds. Elise laughed. "Will! There's a lady present! You'll have no problem. I have a radio transmitter for you. It's in the terahertz range. They used to reserve it for ham astronomy before the Meltdown. Now, no one seems to use it in the Unity, so we can broadcast back home."

"And no one uses Morse in the Unity, so it can be in the open?"

Elise laughed and said, "You're kidding, or else you've forgotten how paranoid Mr. Black is."

Will grinned. "Can we receive messages?"

"I have a schedule of broadcast times for you, based on the moon, never the same from day to day. Your code phrase for receiving is in the codebook."

"Kewl, makes me feel like a real spy and all," said Will. Hecate laughed, a warm, liquid sound in the dusty space. Elise was beginning to understand Will's attraction to her.

"Let's get you sorted out. Hecate, would you show Elise some hospitality? I want to check on what's happening to Henry."

Hecate nodded to Will. After he left, she jerked her head toward one of the more obscure corners of the room to what appeared to be a ventilation panel welded to stanchions on either side. A deft motion by Hecate, and it became a narrow door into a lighted passageway. Wordlessly, Elise moved ahead of her along the corridor as Hecate replaced the panel.

They emerged into a large, circular room, perhaps forty feet across, with a small opening in the ceiling and a lower level, just visible on one side, leading tangentially away. There was a strong smell of fresh paint, and one quarter of the wall was colored a light yellow.

Hecate half-turned her head as they entered and said, "This is ours, for the time being. *Our* room is over there," she said, motioning negligently to half the area, including the corridor. Hecate continued, "We'll have to see what we can do for you. We haven't had many guests, at least any guests we want to make feel comfortable."

Elise responded, her voice small inside the large space. "Anything you have will be fine, I'm sure. I don't expect to stay long before I start my own mission. Will's the station chief, of course, so I'll have to check in with him regularly, but we can do that inside the CORE."

Hecate nodded and asked, "Would you like some tea? I don't have any coffee, of course. But we do have some bread and some dried apricots."

"Tea would be fine, Hecate."

The younger woman treated her to a smile: genuine, warm, and all-encompassing.

Sweeping off a space on the makeshift table and dumping what looked like canvas clothing onto the floor, Hecate started up an electric kettle. By the time it had started singing, Hecate had laid out three chipped plates and several mugs emblazoned with "BBWI#37 the Ever Vigilant." Will, carrying Elise's pink suitcase on one shoulder, returned as Hecate was pouring out.

"I think Henry might have bought it this time. No body, no blood, only drag marks back toward the Grove station. I can't say I haven't expected it, but I'm sorry we couldn't convince him to clean up. That stuff's a killer," said Will.

Hecate shared out the tea and apricots, but Will's report about Henry seemed to have put a damper on the conversation.

"I thought everyone used drugs in the Unity?" said Elise.

"Everyone does. That is, everyone gets their ThiZ at appropriate doses and intervals, or they get a visit from the block captain. That doesn't mean *other* drugs aren't available: opioids, barbs, phencyclidines, psychotropolimine, dopamine uptake inhibitors, even alcohol. Henry's thing was MDMA, a kind of amphetamine, sorta bipolar in a pill. All of them cheaper than food.

"ThiZ, compared to those, is mother's milk. Any rate, Henry goes on these week-long benders and has washed up at our door every once in a while. We tried to get him into some sort of program at the euthanatorium up Old Nyork Road. He wouldn't have it. Says they'd Sapp him, and for all I know, they would, too!

"And as long as I'm thinking about it, once you've got your cover established, Elise, be sure to buy your ThiZ on time, and make sure you flush it as soon as you can. Finding collections of unused ThiZ packets would be a real giveaway."

"So, ThiZ use is required?"

Hecate smirked, and Will gave a short snort of derision. "You have to understand, Elise: 'The Unity means Freedom,' or so they say. Nothing is 'required,' but for all that, people disappear if they don't do exactly as they are supposed to. If you don't take your ThiZ, you can be indicted for a 'hatecrime.'"

"You're kidding?"

"Well, back home, it's simpler," said Will, turning to Elise. "If you get caught for a crime, you pay up, go to jail, are executed, or are exiled to one of the narco-states. Speech is free. In the Unity, you have good, old-fashioned crime, which usually gets you fined or Sapped. Then you have *hate*crimes, which means almost anything the DUFS don't like, allowing them to *really* put the screws to you. That almost always gets you Sapped.

"The Unis *have* free speech, which is getting kinda pricey anymore. Anonymous CORE sites, with monthly fees, let people talk. It may even be *really* anonymous. Most people just blow off steam on them, as far as I can tell.

"Lastly they have *hate* speech, meaning anything which can be attributed to you, literally anything. If you are not a spokesperson, a comicom, or a 'person of authority' like Hecate's friend Alexandra, then you have no standing and cannot speak in public. They will pick you up for 'offending' someone, and that can get you Sapped all by itself. Welcome to 'History's Greatest Democracy,'" Will concluded. Hecate looked like she was about to cry until Will pulled her closer and was rewarded with another glorious sunrise smile.

After Will was done answering a few more of Elise's questions, Hecate showed her to an empty room, looking like a windowed office with a rifled desk bolted to the floor and a small washroom adjacent. With blankets and mismatched and musty cushions, Elise was eventually able to make a comfortable-enough bed against one wall and was asleep almost immediately.

The next morning, as Elise entered the large circular room, a shaft of light from the oculus splaying across the newly painted curving wall, Will raised a tea mug in salute to her from his place at the counter.

"How'd you sleep?"

"Pretty well after I wrestled those cushions into submission."

"I'm so sorry, Elise," said Hecate, offering her a stool. "We're going to have to do better than that for you. Let me work on it today."

"Not to worry. I have to be off today, anyway," said Elise as she smiled and took a proffered mug of tea. *No sugar.*

Hecate and Will, clumsily dressed in mismatched street clothes, no doubt to cover themselves for the unexpected stranger, sat at a tall table littered with the vestiges of their breakfast: squishy white bread toasted over an electric ring burnt by a moment's inattention, and foil packets of margarine and marmalade along with dried fruits.

"So soon?" asked Hecate.

"This is something of a flying trip, you know. I'm supposed to set up shop in Brooklyn. I can kip at a Seaman's Home for a few days, but I can't do any work until I find a safe house. I've got a few possibilities, but nothing happens until I do that."

"I think I can help you there. I developed a list of abandoned houses in Nyork just in case we needed to move shop. They have been condemned for one reason or another. I can send in repair crews for the deficiencies, have your persona listed as the renter, and still have it remain on the condemned list until you move in."

Elise laughed. "Wonderful! Now, let me perform *my* fiduciary responsibilities," she said as she put down her cup and handed Will an envelope.

Will opened it silently, perused the contents, replaced the two sheets of paper, and, leaning over, touched the edge of the envelope to the red coil of the electric element. The paper disappeared in a swoosh of flame and a small shriek from Hecate.

"Oops! Sorry, Hecate. Flash paper. Very, very old school, but you have to admit, it is effective."

Hecate, on recovering, punched Will in the arm. "You are *not* forgiven. Now you have to tell us what was in there."

Will cringed away from her before saying, "Elise brought us some nifty toys and a couple code words—what every modern spy needs for the fall season. I'll bet Green is shivering with delight."

Elise smiled. She had always thought the cherubic Mr. Green had a bad case of paranoia. He now seemed like the most rational man she'd ever met.

"Anything else, Will?" asked Hecate.

"Yep. New orders. Our new number-one order: get the map. Drop everything else and concentrate all our efforts on getting the map to the overlay we sent in the last spindle."

Elise, draining the last of the hot water onto her used tea leaves said, "What do we know about the map?"

"It was not at DUFS CORE HQ," said Hecate.

Will gave a wry smile. "Regardless, there must be some sort of record to tell us what the overlay connects to. The DUFS are smart enough to keep two critical things, worthless without the other, in separate places."

"Don't put all your eggs in one basket," replied Hecate before offering Elise the least-immolated slice of toast. "But the invasion *is coming*. If this is the master map for the entire invasion, then lots of people in lots of different departments ought to be referring to it. There's got to be a log book of some sort that says who has been in to look at it and maybe where the real map is located.

"And there are lots of other things happening," said Hecate. "The ration for cooking oil was down by five and a half milliliters a day, almost sixty calories a day per person for 120 million people. They can't keep that up for long. For the lower classes, that means the men drift across the line into starvation."

"Why just the men?" asked Elise.

"It's what we call the 'Man Tax.' Men need on average about 8 percent more calories to stay above starvation compared to women. Bigger, more muscle, higher metabolic rate. It says nothing about actual labor, just the price of keeping the lights on."

"How do you know that?" asked Elise, washing down a crust with a gulp of her tea.

"I used to work for the Unity's Alimentation Acquisition Bureau of the People's Food Ministry."

"Pray, tell me what is that!"

Hecate laughed. "It was our job to find the food that the politicians promised us we were eating—even when we weren't."

"Sounds like a tough job, Hecate."

"It was an *impossible* job. Telling the truth was not a survival trait. It's one of the reasons I had to leave."

"So why would the DUFS choose to starve a portion of their population?" asked Will. "What could they do with cooking oil?"

"It's not for army rations. The Unity has been on a perpetual war footing since its inception. Although zombie armies probably don't gripe about their food too much."

"If you could look into it for us?" said Will, and Hecate nodded.

"We three need to talk about something weird that's happening in the CORE. When I started, the entities in the CORE couldn't see me. I could do anything. Not one of them seemed to notice I was even there. Whether it was a corporation, a person, or a government utility, I could go in and move things or download stuff, and no one noticed.

"The one exception to that was this black, cape-like thing. So, Frog and I just steered clear of it. But when I was out of commission for so long, Frog mirrored himself in the CORE, assumed a role of cyber-security guard. He saw a lot more than I had. I'm sure that saved my life more than a few times. At any rate, he discovered two more of these entities, at least.

"They can all see each other and Frog. They can communicate, and each is different from the others. The cape-like thing has a user. Another *had* a user for a long time, but she's now gone. The last seems *never* to have had a user. They all seem to have fully formed personalities."

"So, they're real 'ghosts in the machine,'" said Elise.

Hecate laughed and said, "The rest of us are just tourists. It's they who own the playground, I guess."

"Maybe not for long. One is dying. She started dwindling about the time Frog met her, about a month after Malila Chiu lost her interface. Apparently, they can't live without a user."

Hecate looked away for a moment before speaking. "Edie's her name. She was Malila's metaphract. It's a translator, of sorts, for the CORE. We get them when we're eleven years old. Most kids, like me, got rid of them after a few months, once we felt we could navigate on our own. Malila, however, really got into hers and kept it around, gave it a personality and a separate voice."

"Malila? Isn't she the—"

"Yep, that Malila," Will said hurriedly. Malila Chiu's assassination was on Elise's to-do list. She suspected it was on Will's, as well.

"Anyway," Will continued. "Malila's gone. She left the Unity the first of the August. Have you heard of her arrival?"

"Not a thing," replied Elise truthfully, following Will's lead and remaining stone-faced.

Even so, Will grimaced before saying, "We are pretty sure that she's not been recaptured—pretty sure. If they had captured her, the DUFS would have made a big deal of it; at least talked about it among themselves. She was one of their own. But we got nothing.

"The other thing that's weird—the big poohbah of the whole Unity seems to have disappeared the same time Malila did."

"What? Does that mean the invasion is off?" asked Elise.

"I only wish! No, it seems to be going full steam ahead. With all their skimmers, the Unis could attack anywhere within an area eight hundred miles by three hundred miles, overwhelm the local defenses, and gain a strategic advantage before America can mobilize a defense. What's more, someone is trying really hard to make it *appear* that Jourdaine is still at the helm. We have lots of communication *about* Jourdaine and lots *from his general staff,* but nothing from *him*. Frog says the vids of Jourdaine 'taste wrong,' and Jourdaine has not used his interface recently."

"How do you know that?"

"The cape-like thing turns out to be Jourdaine's interface. Frog can tell when Jourdaine's riding it or not. Frog says the interfaces's real name is Cain, and he is apparently the great-granddaddy of them all. The newer interfaces are turned off when not in use. Cain, however, has no off-switch. When no one is using him, he's left to wander inside the CORE. That's pretty sad, really. I think he's gotten a bit strange because of that. He's effectively immortal as long as the CORE is active."

Elise chewed the last corner of bread, finding it tasteless except where blackened, and lubricated it down with a gulp of cold tea. "Not sure how much sympathy I can generate for a utility program, especially if its major benefactor is the guy trying to kill us," said Elise and shrugged. "Can you get Frog to interrogate this Cain—get some intel?"

Will scowled briefly. "I am not sure I want to contact Cain at all. He is Jourdaine's interface. All that guy's got to do is ask his own interface the right question, and he can learn everything about us! The less Cain knows about us, the better.

"I ran a scan on Frog this week just to be sure his programming hasn't been corrupted: nothing to worry about. Still, Frog acts strange when I ask him about the other entities. That is business as usual for him, you should know—acting weird, I mean." Will laughed. "Frog was supposed to be this little gizmo that let me use the CORE, but he keeps getting more complicated, more capable, as time goes on.

"Anyway, the last entity is the oddest of them all," Will continued. "Frog discovered it only days before Malila left. We were looking for an exit in the Rampart. I'd given up hope, when Frog pops up and asks me to meet this new entity. Very strange character, and we would not have gotten tangled up with it except Edie insisted—so Malila insisted.

"Like I said, a very peculiar entity is EffieCee. Odd voice. Very variable. Sometimes it sounds a little like Frog, even. Mostly it has this odd multiplex voice. It has never had a user, does not move around much. Frog says it has the scent of lavender."

"Will? How do we know that it isn't a counterespionage plant?" Elise said, aghast. "How much *can* we know about it? The entities aren't sentient, not in a real sense. They may get more and more complicated, more and more facile with words, but not be truly sentient. All anyone has to do is change the program—and you have a Unity counter-spy."

"Of course, you're right. We, Hecate and I, agree with you: we don't know the answer. But the next question is whether it makes a difference. Currently, EffieCee is providing us useful information. When I can validate it from other sources, it's spot-on.

"We're pretty limited here, Elise. I can't go do any real espionage without a valid persona and an implant to match. I haven't been topside for more than a few minutes since the middle of July."

"What happened to your cover, the Rupert persona?"

"Rupert went missing after I had my accident. We can't have him pop up unexplained after an absence of two months and five hundred miles away."

"So how have you been surviving, if you're afraid to go topside?" said Elise.

Hecate barked a laugh, and Will shrugged as she looked around at the making of their breakfast. "How indeed?"

Hecate picked up the story, saying, "At first, we, Malila and I, were being guided by the Higginses. They were more or less cooperative until Jourdaine somehow got them to dance to his tune. We gave the workers the slip. Now, we raid their storerooms for food, supplies—and medical care. We got Will repaired in one.

"Jourdaine seemed to be gaining on us until just before Malila left. Now the heat's slaked off. Who knows when another crackdown will happen? At any rate, even if we thought Will's cover was okay, it's too dicey to try.

"Here," she said, casting her eyes about the derelict station, "we are sort of in a hole in the Unity, an old belt station. The Unity ignores it, and the Higginses ignore it."

Will stood and stretched his right shoulder as if it were stiff. "Yep. Here we have access to the CORE, to a storage room for staples, and running water close by. We can go on forever, as long as we get new spindles and can feed ourselves."

Rising from the table herself, Elise answered, "Well, I brought four more spindles for you, and I have my own four, so we are in good shape there. While I am here, I can help fill the larder, but that doesn't help you long term."

"What's the backstory of your cover, Elise?" asked Hecate, collecting the odd assortment of dishes and taking them to a workbench along the wall.

"Jessika Bonhoffer was a deckhand on one of those computerized barges they have. They just ply up and down the Atlantic seaboard— pretty laid-back affair. They have a few crew on board, just to swab the deck, I think. Anyway, last year, Hurricane Bonaparte hit their ship, and it capsized. Those things are just floating boxes: huge freeboard and underpowered. Jessika went over the side in a survival suit, was picked up by an American ship, and opted to stay on board as an able-bodied seaman. The medics on board got her implant, placed it in an induction field, and then I got it," Elise said, self-consciously running a hand lightly under her right breast.

"How long ago?" asked Hecate.

"It's been 'bout ten months."

"That might be okay, but the same concerns apply. A seaman is out of range for a long time. They usually give them a year to show up, but might be a risk for you," she continued. "Good enough for a random wanding but not a detailed scan. They could red flag you and hold you for further questions."

She turned and said, "I have another question, Will. Is there any way to alter an implant?"

Elise's head came up sharply, looking back and forth between the two of them. "You mean open me up and fiddle with it? I just got it, and you want to mess with it? I don't think I like how that sounds."

"Relax, Elise. I don't know if that's even possible, and I wasn't suggesting it. But I do know who to ask," said Will.

NEW EVE OF THE SCORCH

THE SCORCH (ONCE EASTERN GEORGIA)
0630 14 AUGUST 2129 AD

"What do you mean, 'The plants are asking to parlay'?" asked Colonel Tremont on his arrival.

"I mean, sir, that a branch erupted from the floor of a clearing just as we were about to advance. You can't fault the boys, really. They fried it. Then another branch comes up and does *that*," Graham said, gesturing toward the clearing from the bottom of his foxhole.

"I told the boys to stop firing, pull back, and dig in with the shields. Then I called you and Major Johnstone, sir."

"Of course, Sarge. You did right. What's happening now?"

"Well, as you can see, sir, troopers dug in, two men to a 'hole. Strict instructions to report anything that might be an enemy trick, sir. But jeez, Colonel, how do they expect us to talk to a plant?"

"Good question." Turning to his signalman, Tremont continued. "Signal all details to pull back and dig in. Call Black again, as well."

Just then, Jesse and Lieutenant Jeannette Black—a thirtyish and attractive lieutenant—emerged, both in camouflage and carrying long guns.

"Glad you're here, Jean, and you, Jesse. What do you make of that?" Tremont asked.

The clearing, floored with red Georgia clay, was about thirty feet wide and bordered by an improbable wall of blue-green foliage fronting onto a clear stream. *A killing field with a concealing tree line,* thought Tremont. In the precise middle of the space, a smooth, six-foot brown staff the size of a woman's wrist emerged directly from the smooth clay surface. Along one whole side, from the ground to the apex of the staff, extended a squarish pale flag, flapping as the staff moved. The staff rose from ground level, carrying the flag with it until it crashed, unceremoniously, on the other side, hesitating briefly before returning to its original position. The thumping of the staff reminded Tremont of some barbaric jungle drum.

"Well, Graham, it looks like a flag of truce, whether the plants understand that or not."

"Chiu's signal has moved, as well. Very close to this location."

"You're kidding."

"No, sir. The signal's not a hundred yards off."

"Then the tracker's probably useless to us. The Scorch may be trying to use the tracker to manipulate us."

"Could be. Making us parlay here as they move around to get our communication lines. What do you think, Jesse?"

"Let me ask you something, Jake. What's your take on our enemy up to this point? Acting rationally or not?"

"Oh, the Scorch is smart enough."

"Okay, if it's smart, then this is either a trick or a request for an authentic parley. Right?"

"I agree, Jesse. How do we figure it out?" said Black.

"They're prepared to ignore our violating their first attempt at parley. I suggest that we should treat this as a real request. If it's a trick, we have learned something about our enemy. If it's real, then they have learned something about us outlanders."

"All right. Lieutenant Black," said Tremont, "if I don't come back, pull back units until you can make visual contact with a rear echelon and each other, then contact corps HQ for instructions. Don't listen to the good doctor here. He's here as your advisor, not your commander. Got it?"

"I love you, too, Jake. And I'm going with you," said Jesse, handing his sidearm to a sergeant.

"See, Lieutenant? That's why you shouldn't listen to him," responded Tremont.

Johnstone and Tremont acquired a bit of mostly clean white T-shirt from a Private Presley and set off. As they entered the small clearing, the white flag quickly furled, absorbed into the staff, and the staff itself melted back into the red earth. For a few seconds, the two men stood alone, exposed, facing the opaque threat of the tree line. Some trick of the light made Tremont see the small wild space as if it were for the moment an empty stage, awaiting only the conductor's downbeat for it to spring into life.

"Something's happening, Jake, over there—that bunch of vines," muttered Jesse under his breath.

"Yep, I see it. If it was a trick, they got us out and in the open without our weapons."

As Tremont spoke, the vines parted from the middle, like a curtain.

They waited. Within the silence, as if it were an overture, the fecund scent of the Scorch, smelling of growth, decay, extravagant blossoms, and luscious fruits, wafted to him, pricking Tremont's skin into gooseflesh despite the heat. This was no gentle prelude: *a Beethoven's Fifth rather than a Pastoral.*

In nominal command of the mission, Colonel Tremont was here as much to be Jesse's bodyguard as he was to command the mission. Protecting Jesse Johnstone, the First of the Old Ones, from the danger had become a priority since the two assassination attempts. However, the mission, once the platoon entered the Scorch, was really run by the Old Man. Tremont could only try to reduce the danger and personal risk that Jesse seemed to assume as normal. If any harm came to Jesse, Gage Thomas, the Commander of Colonial Logistics and de facto theater commander of frontier defenses, would likely have Jake's balls on a keychain. How was he supposed to protect Jesse from harm when neither he nor his men really knew what danger looked like? Only the Old Man knew.

At the beginning of the mission, the platoon had followed Jesse, single file, as he slipped through the wilderness of changed and unchanged plants, avoided perils even as he showed them the danger. During those first few days, the Old Man had warned the soldiers to make no aggressive advances, use no edged weapon on living things, follow in his actual footsteps, and use no downed wood. Lieutenant Black had wanted to use fire to clear a path. Jesse forbade it. So far, Tremont was pretty sure that no American trooper had violated that prohibition. Yet the Scorch had turned against them—and was winning the battle.

Jesse nudged him. He looked up. The vines rustled, parted, and out walked Eve.

Smoothly tanned skin—and there was a lot of tanned skin to admire—slight, with dark, straight hair and startlingly blue eyes, the girl was at once familiar and alien. Around her right areola, she wore a typical outlander woman's mark. Around her navel, however, was another tattoo, a corded circle, imperfect as if by intention and a vivid green. It took some effort to look back to the girl's face. In contrast to her body, the face was stern, unblinking, hard, majestic, and, in some undefinable way, *other*.

The stage became silent. Even the stream across which she stepped lightly had quieted.

"Why you are invading the People?" came the stark voice, seeming to come from every direction at once. Tremont's knees buckled in his immediate desire to kneel. He was not alone.

Beside him, he heard Jesse give a short groan and watched in fascinated horror as Old Man staggered forward and collapsed to his knees. He bowed his head, exposing his neck, and raised his hands, palms downward—the outlander posture for requesting forgiveness.

He watched the fierce face melt.

Advancing forward, she knelt before Jesse, dwarfed by the Old Man. Looking toward him, the girl, for she in those few steps had discarded her mantel of imperium, tenderly turned Jesse's right hand upward, placing her left hand upon it before moving her right hand under Jesse's left.

Something was happening here, something that had nothing to do with their mission but much to do with his friend's reason for being here, Tremont thought.

Jesse and the girl were talking now. A stranger to the outlands, Tremont, nevertheless, had learned that if he witnessed any part of a forgiveness ceremony, he was expected to see the entire thing. Forgiveness was never to be hidden nor displayed as self-flagellation. It was special and prosaic, unlooked for yet central to people's lives, more central than breathing or eating.

Jesse, his head still bowed, said, "I offended you, Malila. I took advantage of your ignorance of our ways. I ignored your sensibilities as an unbeliever and your sorrow at Eduard Billings's betrayal of you. I was wrong to be glad you two had quarreled. I selfishly wanted you for myself. I have no excuse. What I did was wholly wrong. There is no reason for you to forgive me. With my God's help, I will never offend you again. But please forgive me, Malila."

"No, I cannot," Malila said, the stern look returning. From the back, the form of the Old Man seemed to wither. His head slumped further. Jake heard a small sob.

"I cannot forgive you, Jesse Johnstone, until you hear my own confession. I was a fool. I misunderstood what you said, and I gave you no chance to explain. That was unfair, cruel, and unrighteous. Everything I knew of you was that you were honorable, yet at the first test, I thought the worst. That was wrong. I have witnessed your mercy and protection many times since we met, and yet I failed to have it win you my patience. I have learned some small thing about your god. With his help, I shall not make that mistake again. Please forgive," she finished before softening.

"Whether you forgive me or not, I wholeheartedly forgive you. You surprised me, but I had no right to be incensed. For my part, our friendship is intact," she said, looking up into the man's still-bowed head. The girl's soft voice now became pleading.

"Please look at me, my love."

After a moment, the Old Man raised his head, streaks of tears running down his cheeks and into his two weeks' beard. Slowly, like a rising sun, spread a crooked and uncertain smile on the rugged and tattooed face.

"I forgive you. Nothing you said needs an apology. I grant you forgiveness for your asking of it, nevertheless. Whatever friendship you wish us to have, I accept with gratitude and pleasure. You have no greater friend or protector than I," the Old Man said before his voice cracked and he stopped abruptly, smiling a trifle more broadly.

"Jesse, I—"

"Malila, I—" they both said in unison, before each stopped abruptly, smiled, and then laughed at the other's response.

Tremont smiled as well. The few words spoken had the sound of lovers' talk. He left the clearing and pulled all the men back to platoon command. The mission was complete. He had found Malila Chiu, or rather, she had let them find her. Somehow, he did not think that was the end of it.

"We're stuck," said Jesse.

Usually, although there was a lot of variation in outlander ceremonies, as the petitioner she would rise from kneeling only with the assistance of the pardoner, who, standing, could help her to her feet by bracing upturned palms on the petitioner's downturned ones. Malila's kneeling and asking for simultaneous forgiveness left them in a stalemate, neither wanting to relinquish the role of petitioner to the other. Birdsong started up, as if on the downbeat. A cool breeze wafted across the clearing.

"Who says we have to stand up? No one's here."

Jesse's fingers entwined with Malila's, and they slipped to the ground, kissing, stripping words, miles, and weeks away.

Some indefinite time later, Malila said, "Jesse, you—and I mean this only in the kindest way—stink."

"I do stink a bit, I confess. Resupply's been slow. This is a' I have."

"I don't care. Take it off."

"Don't you think that might send the wrong signal to Colonel Tremont?"

"Who is already back at the command point."

"How'd ya know, my love?"

"The People have told me. Don't get strange on me, Jesse, but I've changed since Easter," Malila said.

"Not by appearance. You are as lovely as the day we parted. I recognize the one tat," he said, circling Malila's woman's tattoo. "I 'spect you got that from Tabbie?"

"Yes, that one." She shuddered. "That's Sally's woman's mark for me. Nice, isn't it. Oh!—you have no idea how long I have waited for you to do that!"

Jesse turned Malila's face up to the green light of the forest and kissed her thoroughly.

"Enough! You stink. Off with your clothes. Throw them into the creek for a while. While you're at it, throw yourself in," Malila said, rising and pulling Jesse to his feet, as well. Holding her nose, she pushed him toward the creek, laughing.

Malila helped him bathe. When they emerged from the water, the patch of earth on which they had lain was now a thick carpet of moss. They let the warm Georgia sun dry them as Malila replaited the Old Man's hair into a queue.

Then they lay down. Jesse, on one elbow, gazed at Malila, still amazed at the sudden change of circumstances. "I have another confession to make, now that I think about it: when I took out your Unity implant last year, I put in another implant of my own, to track you if you got lost." He was concerned that he had not confessed to this transgression before. Four months ago, Malila had been his prisoner, her welfare and her location part of his duties. Malila was no longer anyone's prisoner, but Jesse still realized her location and welfare consumed his attention.

"Yes, the People told me. They volunteered to remove it, but I hoped to meet you more easily if I kept it. If you had gone to the trouble to put it in, then it must be a tracker. I would not part with it for anything," she said, and laughed at his surprise.

"You knew we were coming?"

"The People did."

"Then why did you stop our coming to meet you until now?"

"Splanch said I was not ripe yet."

"And you are now? Who's Splanch and the People? When can we meet them?"

"In time, my love. You do know I love you? I acted so stupid. I thought you might use me. After all you have done for me, I forgot for a moment."

"Love makes people act stupid. Never regret what you do for love."

"Do you regret things?"

"Darling, almost every moment of every day. Don't forget, I've had more live-and-learn time to regret. Sometimes, it can paralyze you . . . the regret."

"I always forget how old you really are."

"Yes . . . 'Bout this love thing. I'm no good wi' that . . . ah mean th' words," Jesse said as he heard his speech drift into a brogue, despite his best efforts. Placing his hand on Malila's questing one until her expression, losing a delightful, mischievous look, sobered, he said, "I dinna wanta frighten ye off wi' me nay ken th' right words. Know that ah love ye, lass. Ah will whither ye love me back. Ah will for lifetimes ta' come. A love ye, Malila Chiu."

Malila's mischievous look returned. "Jesse Johnstone of the silver tongue not know words of love? Yet, you've somehow kept three wives happy enough to bear you children."

"I hope I did. We never had enough time . . . wi' any of them."

"Don't get maudlin on me, Old Man!" responded Malila, poking him in the ribs.

Jesse gave an outrageous flinch. "Hard to do that with a beautiful, naked woman in my arms, when I think about it."

There was a short, feminine shriek and long minutes of wordless caresses before Malila turned Jesse's face to look at her. "Jesse, I need to say this, so don't interrupt; it's important. I love you, Jesse Johnstone. If you want to do that marrying thing you talked about, I am willing to listen. I don't have a lot of experience with it. All I've seen is Sally and Moses. They may be unusual."

"They're quite unusual, my love. They started off poor as church mice—very poor, you understand. They are both believers and hardworking and know the other is the same. Might not be a lot of fireworks—but I'd not be surprised if Ethan doesn't have a new brother or sister next year about this time."

"About that . . . Jesse. You have a lot of children already, don't you? They're a lot of work—babies, I mean. They take a lot of money to housebreak and teach them to walk and talk?"

Jesse smiled. "I have six children of my own. Two more adopted with Ruth, but not as babes. More work and money than you can imagine—yet, somehow, the species survives," Jesse said, giving a short laugh.

"I understand, but this is important to me. Can we have babies, too? You and me? Maybe three or four—or five?"

"How about we start with one and go from there?" he said, laughing again. Malila, he knew, was entirely ignorant of childbearing and mostly ignorant of child-rearing, other than with Master Ethan Stewert, who by all measures was an exceedingly happy fellow and not yet a year old.

"I think you'd do well to talk to Sally. You know her an' trust her. After that, we can marry as soon or as late as ye'll want. It's a fresh story we're writing here, you and I, my very love. Ah dinna ken how it might turn on itself, but I ken this for a certainty: we'll write something worth th' reading. Is that a' right with you, Malila?"

"Acceptable, Jesse Johnstone, but one thing?"

"What is that, Malila?"

"Call me 'lass.' I love it when you call me 'lass'!"

Jesse laughed, the small clearing echoing his delight back to them before slowly changing into quiet voices, sighs, shrieks, and small groans.

"Something's wrong," said Lieutenant Black, reporting to Tremont after Malila and Jesse had not returned by sundown.

"Not sure if the two of them are not thinking everything is just entirely *right*, Lieutenant. We should be overjoyed—no more combat. We have contacted Malila Chiu, who appears, by casual inspection, to be the picture of perfect health. From what little I saw, she seems to be on convivial terms with Major Johnstone."

"Not what I mean, sir. Doc McNebbs got a signal from the field hospital. They were going to ship Mbele to Grady Hospital in Atlanta. Got her onto a flight, and she woke up and complained she was hungry. The other three who were comatose from the splinters are doing even better. If Jesse can convince this Malila Chiu to come back with us, I'd call for a fleet of VGPs and be back at Warner-Robins by reveille," said Black.

"I think today will be lost to 'private negotiations' between the two of them. They'll talk to us when they will. However, you might call up some civilian clothes, dop kit, footwear, and such like. It appeared to me—just on a cursory glance, mind you—that Citizen Chiu is traveling light."

It was past dawn the following day, but the sun had yet to clear the line of trees. Malila stood naked in a patch of lush vegetation, facing east. Jesse could do nothing more than admire her lithe shape as bird calls and insect buzzings filled the small clearing with the sound of life. Looking past her, Jesse watched the line of the sun's progress creep down the west wall of the clearing that had been their bedroom for the night. When the light touched her, a green glow of vitality erupted around her, seeming to transform her—making her more substantive, more real. Jesse could almost hear a frisson in the air while Malila stood transfixed. He waited.

The Old Man felt complete, replete, for the first time in many more years than he cared to remember. Malila was alive and well, having escaped the grim Unity. And Malila loved him. For long years, Jesse had found himself hard aground on the shoal of old grief, sorrowing over the death of Jane, his third wife, but mourning also the mortality of dreams and the leaving, one by one, of the bright flowers of his life: his children. Like spring blooms, he could not keep them unless he wanted their bright life to wither in his hand. They were all away and doing what they should be doing: making lives of their own.

Then the strange, foreign girl dropped into his life. Despite himself, she had tugged him off the shoal of his apathy. For so long a time he had been bound by duty and by the expectations made by others whom he loved. Strange, too, how love had so constrained him when it came to his own happiness. His children wished to freeze him into the role of a jovial, distant, generous, slightly incompetent, nonconfrontational, and placid memory. His people, the hardy people of the Scorchings, honored him when they thought about him. He did not blame them. That neglect was as it should be. Those who braved a harsh wilderness and who yet kept beauty in their souls hardly needed more obligations. He smiled again.

Malila was alive. If that had been all he could confirm for himself, even that little scrap of information might have silenced the echoing hollow in his heart. Instead, she had appeared, almost like a Scorch version of Venus, arriving whole and mature from an unknowable genesis. She was very much the same Malila, down to the scar under her right breast, the one along her left shin, and the small one under her chin. The only change was her new tattoos. One he recognized. A frontier woman's mark on her right areola, elegant and beautiful, despite the distraction its canvas held for him.

He had despaired of ever seeing Malila again. Four months ago, shouting curses at him, she had abandoned him on the hillside near Stamping Ground just before her recapture by her own people shortly thereafter. He and Malila had misunderstood each other so thoroughly. Many another woman, so distraught, would have left, never to return. Malila had hungered, just as he had hungered, to right the wrongs, and in righting them, had been able to see through the mistakes they each had made.

Throughout that first day, they had made love, madly, recklessly, and gently, until the night closed in. Luminous vines laced about them in the clearing, dimming as they slept and brightening when they awoke to find themselves refreshed and their ardor renewed. When he mentioned food, in the dim light, Malila had offered him a slender cup filled with a liquid: cool, sweet, tart, and somehow familiar. It was refreshing and filling. They had made love and slept again. No insect intruded.

In a lot of ways, Malila had not changed in the eventful ten months since he and Moses Stewert had first crept out from behind the false wall of the sniffer station in a Wisconsin no-man's-land. Jesse had held her captive while Moses did the dirty work of killing her platoon of brain-damaged soldiers, finishing the job started by their own people.

Malila had always been inquisitive, smart, and courageous: a dangerous combination. She looked for connections, figured them out, and acted on them by the time most people were just looking up from their morning coffee. One of Malila's passions, fierce as she was in her likes and dislikes, was Jesse Johnstone. He grinned to himself.

Jesse watched as the light of dawn crept down her body, bathing her in green gold. The light, encountering her new tattoo, the one encircling her navel, made it glow with an unearthly emerald, the small lovers' knot of interwoven rings so intricate it seemed to writhe as he watched it. Malila changed as well—enlarging, as if all the mass of the universe now resided in her small form. Yet her appearance had not changed. He was sure of that.

At some signal, like a switch, she was Malila again. She slumped slightly before she delicately walked over to where he still lay on the bed of moss on which they had spent the night.

Malila sat on her haunches, leaned over, and kissed him before giggling at his attempt to pull her down to him.

"We need to get going, my love," she said.

"I suppose you're right, lass. But what was that about? Have ye become a sun worshiper in my absence?"

Malila laughed. "No, don't be silly. Things have changed, though."

"Does that have anything to do with your new tattoo?"

"Yes, my love. We need to talk about that, too. We will have to put some things on hold for a bit. You know the Unity is going to invade?"

"Yes, we've been expecting it for some time."

"The Scorch is alive, you know that, too, of course. It talks."

"Yes, lass. I've talked with Sage Men since I was a child." Jesse watched as a stem erupted from the ground at Malila's feet, growing perceptibly upward until stopped by her gesture. The stem paled and swelled, the vivid green of fresh life departing. Jesse was wondering what Malila had done to poison the plant when she fiddled with the tip of the stem and unwound a single sheet of white, looking like linen. As she began to experiment in wrapping herself in the sheet, another vine along the sunlit wall grew huge, incongruous buds, which burst open into salmon-and-violet-colored blossoms that withered within half a minute. The odd show apparently over, Jesse turned away to admire Malila as she completed the elegant sheath of white, tucking the tail of the sheet between her breasts. He liked to watch her dress, he decided. By the time she had completed the small details of the dress, Jesse looked back at the withered blossoms, finding them now swollen into shiny black fruit like eggplants. Malila walked over and plucked two, holding them together lengthwise. Within seconds, the portions that touched had dried, spilling out a mound of small, vivid yellow seeds onto the ground. The empty husks, she placed on her feet.

"The Scorch seems to have developed some style," said Jesse.

She laughed. "Not likely! Splanch has no fashion sense whatsoever. I had to design these myself. Splanch is a Sage Man, although it's not a man, you know. But very much an *it*, or I guess it would be proper to say it is both male and female," came Malila's voice, sounding amused, no doubt from his look.

Without preamble, Malila asked, "Who is Speaker? Splanch says you know Speaker."

"Speaker is a friend, I hope. We met when I was very young. We've had our ups and downs, Speaker and I. 'Spect he's my oldest friend, when I think about it."

"Speaker thinks of you as a friend."

"You are talking to him?"

"Splanch has."

"Greet him for me. Apologize that I have no meat to bring him right at the moment, and ask if he is well. Oh, yes. Ask if his sproutings speak yet."

"So many questions. How is it that you've never told me of Speaker, my love?"

"Speaker and I have our reasons."

Several minutes elapsed before Malila reported, "Well, Speaker looks forward to seeing you again, with or without a gift. He thinks that some of his sproutings may begin to talk, but none so well as a child of men he knew once. He does well. I have already told him we are in love and happy in each other's company. He congratulates you on my affection."

"You made that last part up."

"So what if I did? I am sure the whole Scorch would agree. They like me," Malila said before laughing and jabbing Jesse in his unprotected ribs.

Jesse made an exaggerated attempt to save himself, only to pull Malila down to him in a gale of giggles and shrieks.

"You're going to mess up my clothes, Jesse. I'll have to grow a whole new set. Behave!"

"Only under protest," said Jesse. "As I said, I know Speaker, but who this Splanch guy is, I have no idea—never met. I have only spoken with Speaker and Helon, and not recently." He chuckled. "He calls me 'Quicksilver.' He thinks I talk too fast."

"Splanch, well, *all* of the Scorch, know of you, Quicksilver. The quickness first and now the silver pelt. You are famous in the Scorch, my love."

"And what says the Scorch of me, lass?" he asked idly, resting his chin on a fist and smiling.

"They say Quicksilver is brutal, ungenerous, and honest."

His smile fading, Jesse was silent for the moment. "Do you know why they believe me to be so cruel?"

"They did not say cruel. They said 'brutal' and 'ungenerous.' You do not return gifts willingly. You use metal to cut them."

"Yes, I suppose I am, lass. Looking a' it from their point a view."

Jesse felt suddenly how naked he was, naked and unsure. He rose from their moss bed and walked to the edge of the clearing to retrieve the clothes he had placed on a liana after washing. They were dry and even smelled nice, reminding him of other times and places. As he dressed, memories tumbled back to him, memories of other forests and other, more ancient times. His age seldom impinged on his thoughts, yet suddenly, he felt the weight of the years. Perhaps Malila, placing her young life next to his, like a yardstick, made him measure the burden of his time against her own.

Age had never been the mere counting of sunrises. He had arrived at his age only by craft, wit, and random good luck—mistakes he had made aplenty. Many of his mistakes had wounded him. Some killed another. With each mistake, with each death, he had vowed to learn and grow, become more adroit, more skilled, more able to protect those whom he loved or those for whom he had taken responsibility. Promises, birthing caution, a quest for knowledge, and the capability to do what most men thought impossible had almost become who Jesse was. He frowned.

The Old Man tightened the web belt and slipped into clean, dry socks before lacing up the boots, now with a shine that well might pass inspection.

Old mistakes he had no need to repeat. Sage Men were an old mistake but, like much of the Scorch, safe as houses as long as he knew not to trust them.

The Old Man shook his head to clear the cobwebs of memory away, stamped his feet to ensure his boots fit well, and turned back toward Malila. She was still standing, silently looking at him. Jesse grabbed up his uniform blouse and put it on as he returned to her. Fumbling with the buttons, Malila slapped his hands away and started doing them herself.

"I don't think you understand, lass. The Scorch will kill you if you aren't as canny as it is. And the feedings! Sage Men have these things lik' bloodsucking eels! Speaker might have drained me dry once upon a time. I nearly died, anyway." The Old Man gave an involuntary shiver.

Malila gave him another odd look and turned away from him as the sound of approaching men entered the clearing.

Now that Colonel Tremont heard the Old Man and the girl speaking together, he could delay it no longer. Making enough noise to announce his arrival, he entered the clearing and marveled at how it had changed since yesterday. Lianas wove a wall about what had been a small forest clearing, creating a uniform surface with a subtle repeating, not-quite-geometric pattern along the slightly curved wall. The ground, which yesterday had been good Georgia red clay, today was a checkerboard of green and pink mosses. Trees had grown up above the wall overnight on all sides to a uniform height of some twenty feet, the unnaturalness of the setting fanning his concerns for the Old Man's welfare alight once more.

And he really wanted to keep Jesse safe. It was his job, but also it was as if he had known the Old Man for an eternity. There was something about Jesse's strange, pale eyes that seemed able to go through him. It made you think he saw all your past actions and future thoughts, understood it all, and accepted all. And yet, there was a sadness to the man, as well. Lord knew, in the frontier of America there was tragedy enough, and to spare. The Old Man carried his griefs well, but one could see them in the unguarded moments of a quiet campfire.

Yet today the sadness was gone. Watching Jesse with Malila, he seemed younger even as the girl seemed ageless. He had tidied up his beard, parted his white hair in the middle, and made a queue to the middle of his back. They stood in the middle of the clearing, the girl busying herself with buttoning Jesse's uniform blouse for him.

She turned to face Tremont as soon as he entered, her face severe and unfriendly until she saw him. In her smile, he felt the sun had risen a second time.

The girl—no, the Eve who had come "onstage" yesterday—was now clothed in a long shift of what looked to be cloth, sheer enough to suggest the lithe body beneath. Black slippers covered her feet, incongruous in the company of Jesse's boots. She wore no other decoration. Tremont, in his dirty, sweaty uniform, felt soiled beneath her gaze.

The illusion vanished as the girl took the Old Man's arm and draped it around her slim waist. That simple gesture seemed to start Jesse, who said, "Jake, I'd like to present a dear friend of mine. This here's Malila Evanova Chiu, late of the Democratic Unity Forces for Security."

"Pleased to meet you, Miss Chiu."

"And, Malila, lass, please meet Colonel Jacob Tremont, my commanding officer, bodyguard, and publicist," said Jesse soberly before breaking into a mischievous grin.

"Pleased to meet you, Colonel Tremont. Pardon me for not saluting. I seem to be out of uniform," said Malila as she took a few steps forward away from the Old Man and gave him a graceful curtsy.

The look on Jesse's face suggested that the odd bit of ancient formality was as much a surprise to him as to Jake.

Tremont laughed. "I shall not feel slighted. I have no idea where you were hiding the clothes, Miss Chiu, but I must commend you. You look wonderful."

"Thank you, Colonel, but I need to speak with you. Dr. Johnstone here will act as a witness, and you may select your own witness, if that is acceptable." She spoke as if an objection would be unthinkable, and indeed, Tremont was motioning for his detail to leave before he considered it. Once they were gone, she continued.

"Colonel Tremont, I have been sent with a message for you . . . for America."

"From the Union? That'll be a first. We haven't been able to get the Unis to talk to us in living memory. Every time we try to—"

"Not from the Democratic Unity, Colonel. I have been sent by the People of what you call the Scorch."

"Who are these people?" he said before turning to Jesse. "You know the Scorch better than anyone, Jess. Have you ever met people in there?"

Before the Old Man could respond, Malila answered. Her face was confident—demanding. The longer he looked at her, the more she seemed to dominate the space, dwarfing, in the attention she consumed, even Jesse. Malila, without changing her voice, posture, or size, presided over the clearing, making it impossible for him to look elsewhere, as if she had summoned forth the threads that controlled Jake and wound them gently about a small finger.

"Colonel, the People are those called to sentience by the dreadful acts of seventy-five winters ago. The People rule the Scorch by the right of possession. No one moves within it except by their sufferance. We shepherd the unchanged trees, plants, and animals within our borders, from the Wall to the frontier with America, and from the Great Salty Sea to the Mountains of Winter. The people of America and the people from across the Wall are our enemies at present, damaging us, invading us, destroying much. We seek peace with one or both of these nations.

"This war must stop for ourselves and our sproutings. Time and again we have sent embassies to you and to the others, only to have them cut down. We mourn our losses, but we do not seek retribution. We have chosen one among your own kind to act as a messenger.

"And I am that messenger to America, Colonel. Please take me to your political capital that I might fulfill my mission and deliver my message."

The illusion of grandeur and gravity receded, leaving Malila, again, young and slight, standing in the center of what was just a clearing in the forest of Georgia. She stepped back and again reached for the Old Man's arm, slumping against him as if drained.

Jake shook himself mentally.

"Yes, yes, of course, Madame Ambassador."

"For now, Colonel, I am merely the Messenger. Dr. Johnstone, I hope, will consent to act as my escort, bodyguard, and most particular companion. I trust that is acceptable?"

"Perfectly acceptable. You could not have chosen a better man. We Americans will give you a good hearing, I assure you. Jesse Johnstone's reputation will go far to assure that."

"I have no idea how long my mission will take, but during that time, I have some specific requirements for my continued health and welfare."

"You can be sure that all your needs and desires will be attended to, Malila . . . How should we address you?"

"Malila . . . Malila of the Scorch will be sufficient."

The trip out of the forest revealed itself to be rather more and less than Jesse imagined. Malila insisted that she repay, in a small way, the onerous trials of the soldiers, the Scorch providing a feast for those so recently at war with it. Blossoms appeared around the clearing, ripening into out-of-season fruits as they watched. All were succulent, filling, and filled with seeds. Streams of clear water bubbled up at spots convenient for drinking and bathing, each with a different taste and effervescence. Malila met each of the soldiers, thanking them for their service, asking the soldier's name before giving each a hug and a kiss in return.

Tremont was scandalized at the waste of time until he got into the spirit of the celebration himself, being pushed into a fizzing pool by the laughing girl when he was so unwise as to turn his back on her.

As the sun settled into the trees lining the clearing, the soldiers were still bathing in the waters, eating the fruit, and having good-natured contests with the dark, round pips, points awarded for distance and accuracy. Malila took Jesse's hand and led him away to a new bower provided by an ever-indulgent Scorch, smaller, further into the forest, and well away from the platoon. Luminous vines, different in form and color from those Jesse had already seen, flared up as they entered, and Jesse could see that a moss mattress was waiting for them. He smiled.

A pool of the effervescent water awaited them. Jesse shucked off his battle dress uniform and eased himself into the warm water, clear except for the bubbles. He watched as Malila tore off the sheath she wore and kicked off the seed-pod slippers before joining him.

"You have a natural gift of diplomacy, lass. I think the entire platoon would take on a battalion if you asked them," said Jesse, running hands around Malila's waist and drawing her closer.

The two settled together in the warm water, idly caressing each other.

"So, the Scorch chose you as its messenger?" said Jesse, drawing out the delicious interval.

"There were not a lot of applicants. Splanch said I was the first one across the Rampart since its construction. Of the people who come from this side of the Scorch, most hunt, die, or run away frightened. Very few people will talk to a Sage Man. Quicksilver is only one of four. But they chose me because, I suppose, they think I am more persuasive than an over-tall, overbearing, funny-talking old man. Donchatink?" she said, smiling, the diffuse light giving her face an even more mischievous look than perhaps intended.

"They show remarkably good judgment, lass," Jesse said before his face darkened briefly. "If all of the Scorch can see, feel, and hear what you do, when we are making love, are they sitting on bleachers enjoying the performance? Rooting for us?"

Malila laughed and grabbed at Jesse, making him gasp. "Don't be silly, Jesse. The Scorch is so beyond voyeurism. They are respectful of my privacy and yours when we are together. Besides."

"Besides what?"

"They only root for me."

When they awoke the next day, the road out of the jungle had been cleared for them in the night, freed of debris and blowdowns, allowing Tremont little reason to grouse at the delay of Malila's new sunrise ritual. She returned to the platoon dressed in donated fatigues, and they all breakfasted on large orange-fleshed fruits and warm bread-like pods before walking out. It took mere hours to rendezvous with the tracked vehicles from Warner-Robbins. Jeannette Black began organizing the trip to Athens as Malila asked her, "What are these, Lieutenant? I haven't seen anything like this before."

"These are Mattis PCs, personnel carriers. Armored .50 cal MG and cover for a squad of fifteen. They can go forty-five miles an hour, say about sixty-five klicks an hour. Can turn on a dime."

"What's the power plant?"

"Chrysler OHC diesel 540 V8 with a blower."

"I think that is the first sentence I have heard from an outlander in which I understood not a single word, and that includes Jesse when he starts to talk funny."

"Let me show you. You're, of course, familiar with car engines."

"Skimmerhorn drives? Of course. I could field repair one of the troop carriers myself when—"

"No, I mean an internal combustion engine. Piston driven."

"Internal combustion? Won't the fire go out?"

Black looked puzzled for a heartbeat and then continued, slowly. "You don't have these? Internal combustion? Small explosions throwing metal pistons around and making a drive train spin?"

"Oh? I saw a sump pump on a farm. Biogas. Very simple—not much to it. But you sit near these explosions?"

"Yep, but it isn't as bad . . ."

Jesse moved away to refill their canteens, leaving Black and Malila to discuss the marvels of internal combustion. By the time he returned, Malila was nowhere to be seen, save for some feet, writhing on occasion, thrust out from under the engine compartment of the vehicle.

"It ate her?" asked Jesse of Lieutenant Black on arriving.

"Seemed more like some sort of a suicide, sir. I opened it up, and Malila crawled in with a crescent wrench and a gleam in her eye. She ain't coming out, and we're supposed to leave soon."

"Had lunch?

"Sure. Shall we save some for Grease Monkey?"

"If I can."

"I can hear you, you know, Jesse. Save me a sandwich if you know what's good for you," came a disembodied voice from the engine compartment.

"Yes, ma'am!" he said, and then, grinning, motioned for all to leave.

Jesse returned with a tuna salad sandwich on a tin plate, a mug of coffee, and three large soldiers. Jesse placed the sandwich and coffee on the ground in front of the engine compartment. When Malila emerged, nose twitching, to retrieve the bait, they barred her reentry. After a brief inspection of the engine and the reinstallation of a bolt found on Malila's person, they were on the road for Athens. That evening, in a sunken tub of the presidential suite at the Athens Ritz-Hilton, it took Jesse a pleasant hour to help her scrub off engine grease. The next morning, before leaving, Malila again greeted the rising sun in the front garden of the hotel, her feet touching green plants and black soil. On the insistence of the hotel, she was dressed. A new and subtly different dress adorned her.

Jesse perused the news as he waited. Isolated as he had been aboard an airship and then in the desperate campaign to find Malila, he was amazed at how America's war anxiety had skyrocketed in his absence. Even more telling, Malila's appearance, judging by the newscasts, was nothing less than a miracle. "Mystery Messenger Malila of Scorch—American Hero Captures" screamed one headline, while another proclaimed, "Mutant Scorch Offers America Peace." Official enthusiasm was signaled by the gleaming, streamlined, red-white-and-blue presidential railroad car waiting for them for the trip to Kansas City.

Malila's status gave her privacy that she and Jesse put to good use. Roused in the long afternoon before they arrived at Saint Louis, Malila napping beside him, Jesse watched her breathe, blowing across her skin to marvel at how it made the fine hairs erect and their owner shuffle slightly. There had been the carnal hunger since he first saw her ten months before, of course. Then had come the affection. Hardly a stranger to it, Jesse had been able to step back and watch himself fall resoundingly in love with the brave, foolishly brave, slip of a girl. It amused him that he could be so taken by her and so frequently surprised as each new day brought him more and greater fascinations with Malila Chiu. *It was a mystery.* Even sex, as enjoyable as it was, did not create the love they had. It merely cemented it, shedding the layers of differences, destinies, backgrounds, and presumptions to make a matchless realm for their love, accompanied by the low-frequency thrum of the maglev rails.

Malila loved him. He still marveled at the idea. All of his concerns since Easter had been consumed with healing the wound he had created with the girl he loved—heal it even as she disdained him. *Instead, passionate, wonderful, ardent Malila loved him.* She had changed a lot since Easter, he thought, and the change concerned him. She was sterner, grimmer even, than during the trying parts of their trek from Wisconsin. Something had been burned out of her since they had last met. She had glossed over her escape from the Unity, although it was certainly a story worth telling. In time she would, of course. He could wait until Malila was willing to tell him, and they could share the hurt together.

The train slowed as it went through a town, and Jesse flicked the curtain across the window to avoid scandalizing any of the locals. Malila moved. The green tattoo braid around her navel seemed to glow in the dim light for a few seconds before fading. Malila awoke, yawned, kissed him, and went to the bathroom. Jesse heard the shower start.

She *had* told him something about Splanch. That would take some getting used to. Most likely, it would take some getting used to for the whole country. He was probably one of the few people who could hear her story and not think her mad. His own relationship with Speaker was complicated, as it might be with anyone who usually greeted you with an attempt to eat you. He did not know how Splanch and the Scorch figured into Malila's life. She had said not to worry, and he chose not to worry. In time, they would need to talk about that.

However, he would really have to arrange a wedding before too long. Sally Stewert would roast his liver for him if she were not allowed to plan it from the first, as "mother of the bride" and "matron of honor" all rolled into one. It would be a small price to pay to remain within Sally's good graces. She had, until Malila's arrival, considered him a necessary evil, *more evil than necessary.* Now he might be able to slip into her larger circle of acquaintances on Malila's coattails, still get in a few hunting trips with Moses, and garner a few smiles from a growing Ethan.

But that was in a yet-untrod future. His job now was to protect Malila from his own country, avoiding the pitfalls of the American republic, and bring her into a safe harbor after the coming storm. She would need all the help she could get. Jesse got up to start collecting some for her.

General Gage Thomas paced back and forth, puffing furiously on a cigar forbidden by numerous and quite legible signs along the platform as he waited for the pestilential Chiu woman. An aide, an Ensign Cruthers, whom he had acquired for the occasion, approached. "I just got the signal that the special was waved through the Gateway Yard. It should be arriving a few minutes before schedule, General Thomas."

"Hummph," said the Commander of Colonial Logistics. He did not enjoy being out in public. There had been only a few assassination attempts recently, nothing like the bad old days. He liked being underground and protected by layers of bureaucratic fustiness, military might, and a few score yards of dirt and stone. Being sociable was for the pretty generals in Columbiana, not for him. Even so, there was no way he was going to let the infamous Malila Chiu go through town without his looking her over.

Damn Jesse Johnstone, he thought. *If the Old Man had just followed orders last fall, none of this would have happened.* He had no one to blame but himself, of course.

He came to the stairs leading up to the station, turned, and walked back through the clouds of his own smoke. Ensign Phyllis Cruthers had given up trying to keep pace with him and merely loitered at the midpoint of his circuit for any orders he might give.

Nobody to blame but myself, he thought again. Last year, he had imagined he was clever when he chose Jesse for the Sun Prairie mission. In one sense, it had been an inspired choice: Jesse's woodcraft and guile guaranteed the best chance of success, gaining the army an entire platoon's complement of the new pulse-rifles. It had also netted Malila Chiu but nearly cost America the Old Man himself. Were it not for Jesse's indomitable constitution, he might have died of scurvy or from one of the subsequent assassination attempts since. *They might lose him yet.*

This Chiu person was now presenting herself as the messenger of the plants.

How dumb was that?

How dangerous was that?

Not only had Chiu, as a spokesperson for the Scorch, demanded to address a congress, but she had also gotten the Old Man to be her bodyguard and escort. *And the randy old fool had gone along with it!* Thomas watched as Cruthers leaned out over the track and then looked to him.

Moments later, the train eased into New Union station with the appropriate hissing of brakes, hesitated briefly, and "kneeled" as the maglev field collapsed. A few other passengers and railroad personnel, not caught up in the Malila pageant, bustled about before climbing the stairs to the station.

Finally, there was some activity at the door to the red-white-and-blue presidential car. Out stepped Jesse in a spic-and-span RSA uniform, devoid of insignia. Instead, it sported small oak-leaf clusters, *actual oak leaves.* The insignia on his cap was a tree leaf, as were his epaulets. He saluted, and out stepped another soldier in the same getup. The woman, *there is no doubt about that,* turned, stepped forward, came to a taut and professional posture, and snapped one of the crispest salutes that Thomas had ever seen.

"Major Malila Chiu, of the Sovereign Nation of the Scorch, greets you. Sir!"

It was something of a surprise to him that Thomas found that he had himself come to attention and returned the brisk salute. He smiled as he lowered his hand. *There is nothing to compare to being saluted by a pretty woman.*

"Welcome to Saint Louis, Major. I must admit, I expected something different from the plant kingdom."

The woman smiled. "Only so much you can do on a moving train, General Thomas. I hoped that showing the proper honors might help you understand how serious the Scorch is about my message."

It would, at that, Thomas thought. *Serious as a pulse bolt.* Thomas was surprised at himself. He was supposed to be evaluating her, not the other way around. In his gruffest voice he said, "Major Chiu, I ordered you assassinated. I'm lucky he never found you."

Malila smiled. "Rupert? Well, he found me, all right. Lucky for him, he did. He was pretty beat up when we met. Hecate is keeping him company now."

Thomas's eyebrows rose. *Had they captured William Butler?* His estimation of the Chiu woman rose once more. "Perhaps we might have a short talk with you, Miss Chiu?"

A smile that might melt gold spread across the woman's face. "I would like that very much, General."

By the time General Thomas had escorted them to a secured conference room at the station's Hilton, the management had laid on a cold supper with some nice bottles of a Pinot Gris from Ames for the three of them. Jesse, sporting an uncharacteristic proprietary scowl, stuck close to Malila, no doubt to signal Thomas to play nice. The Old Man needn't have worried. Malila no longer had any compunction about relating freely and completely everything she knew of Unity policy, doctrine, forces, equipment, or strategy. Thomas soaked it up. No doubt she realized that the road to freedom in America led through the offices of people, like him, who wanted to wring her dry of every fact she ever knew or suspected. She would have some role in the upcoming conflict, but as a turncoat, she would never be trusted—not completely.

He'd been particularly delighted when she told him about her partner in crime, Hecate Jones, and her attachment to America's own spy. Imagining Will Butler, as sober and serious as they came, in the role of lothario-spy was almost enough to make him break out laughing. However, as Malila described Hecate's bravery during her own intrepid escape, Thomas became more thoughtful and very much less amused. *Tough, these Unis—even the civilians.* Malila's story of a rapidly tightening noose around the beltway workers, added to the information from Butler's spindles, painted an ominous picture.

"So, you are saying that the underground workers are in rebellion?" asked Thomas.

"I'm not sure, sir. Something changed between the Higginses, those are the workers, and the DUFS while we were underground. At the beginning, it was very obvious that the surface forces had no presence below the belts. It felt like an armed truce. You did not see DUFS. There were no posters, no call boxes—nothing. The first Union steward I met, Iain Higgins the Fourth, acted like he had given me the freedom to go wherever I wanted and ask for anything I needed, but by mid-July, the locals were treating us like a hot turnip and couldn't wait to get rid of us."

Jesse leaned in and whispered into Malila's ear.

"Sorry, sir, 'hot potato.' After a bit, there seemed to be some sort of shake-up in the politics of the locals. That's when Hecate and I struck out on our own. Only later did we learn from Will that there was some coup among the Solons and Eustace Jourdaine was behind it."

"And this is the same Jourdaine who came halfway across the country to snatch you last Easter."

"Yes, sir. He was moving ahead inside the DUFS then, but this is something far bigger, something involving the entire Unity."

Thomas half-turned and spoke over his shoulder, "Phyllis, what have we got on a Jourdaine, Eustace T., in the Unity DUFS, mid-thirties, so born about 2094 or so?"

Within seconds, a dossier was wordlessly passed to General Thomas.

"Hmm, bit of a shiny-assed shoe clerk up until about a year ago, just before you came for a visit, Major Chiu. He was Vivalagente Suarez's adjutant and then scrambled to the top of the DUFS by mid-May, was tapped to be C-in-C of the invasion. No field experience. No command experience. Disappeared from view since first week of August when you said you were almost captured by him."

"He *did* capture me—just as I emerged from the underground. It is only by chance that the skimmer I was being carried in went down into that big river on the border. It is only by the very oddest of chances that I survived at all. That circumstance is why I am here and not leaving with Jesse to make our lives together."

The Old Man, sitting next to her, smiled and squeezed her hand.

Thomas frowned and went on.

"Okay, and what circumstance are we talking about? You emerge from the Scorch naked. To all appearances, you have seduced an otherwise rational man with your female guile, making me think he has finally succumbed to the senility to which his age entitles him. Why should I take you to the capital and give a trained soldier access to our elected leaders? Why should I not throw you into a prisoner of war camp? In short, why should I believe you, Major Chiu?"

"Now, Gage . . . ," Jesse said, starting to rise.

General Thomas raised his hand. Jesse stopped but continued to fume.

"When you put it like that, you should not. I am a messenger. There is a long and shameful history of killing us messengers, but to kill a messenger before the message is delivered seems silly, does it not?

"You already know there will be an invasion, and you should be getting a spindle from Will Butler any time now. It will confirm much of what I said. However, time is of some importance. The invasion was supposed to be the twelfth of this month, which has come and gone. With Jourdaine out of the picture, perhaps there was another coup, or they are going to let it slip a month or two. Regardless, America has very little time to prepare. The Unity still has a preponderance of advanced weapons: skimmers and pulse-rifles. It outnumbers you in troopers by four to one. It has an industrial base that can keep its men in the field indefinitely, and CRNAs maintain unit cohesion with 90 percent casualties.

"America has no allies. The Canadians just concluded a treaty with the Unity. They aren't going to come to your rescue. America hasn't a chance except—except I deliver the content of my message from the People of what you call the Scorch. They can be an ally or an enemy. Both America and the Unity have injured the People. They have chosen, for whatever reason, to try to come to an understanding with America. If you reject them, they have another alternative.

"And finally, I have the support of Jesse Aaron Johnstone, a man who knows me better than anyone. We have nearly killed each other a few times, and I want another crack at him."

Jesse erupted into a laugh that ended with him red in the face and coughing. Thomas smiled.

"Welcome to America, Malila Chiu. Army intelligence received a spindle from Butler last week. The timing seemed a little too providential. He thinks you're a hardass."

"I see, sir."

"He also thinks you're a resourceful, smart soldier and a righteous woman, gracious and forgiving. Our man Butler was, eventually, very impressed by you, Major Chiu."

"Sir. I—" Malila began.

"One question. Do you know where the attack will occur?"

"No, sir."

"Too bad. Nothing more to be said, Malila of the Scorch. Off to Kansas City with you! I wanted to see if what Butler said could be true. Forgive me for doubting you . . . both. Whatever message you have for the suits, I wish I were a fly on that wall."

By early afternoon of the next day, they arrived in Kansas City. There was no formal acknowledgment of her arrival except for a representative of the state department, a dark and severe woman of some indeterminate middle years, who insisted that Malila undergo a customs inspection before being allowed to proceed. Once convinced that Malila was not smuggling contraband upon her person, the woman thrust a schedule wordlessly into Jesse's hand and stomped off.

Malila's audience with a select committee was set for the following day. She and Jesse spent an enjoyable evening at the Hyatt Regency Hilton. Room service sent them a wonderful feed, subtle yet bright, intense flavors, which they enjoyed while looking out over the sparse splendor of the new federal city, Columbiana.

In the morning, Gage Thomas knocked on their door, having come up the previous night from Saint Louis, and wheeled in a breakfast of fresh fruit, bacon, eggs, and biscuits before whisking them into a motorcade from the hotel to the new city, which seemed composed almost entirely of windowless, three-story buildings with gun emplacements on the roof. Into one of these they were escorted.

The conference room was huge and mostly filled. Malila had never been in a room this large that was not filled with Unity soldiers and their scent. Once she was past the few uniformed guards, even taller and more muscular than Jesse, she could see the dark wood paneling, the strange striped flag, and the raised dais upon which the legislators sat. She was shown to a table and chairs with nothing more than a pitcher of water without a glass. She sat next to Jesse, holding his large hand in her lap, turning it over and back to trace the scars that spoke in some strange hieroglyphics of the Old Man's lengthy past. They waited for over ten minutes until the dark, severe woman of the previous day arrived, taking her place two rows directly behind Malila and making a strange clicking sound at odd intervals. Malila's soldierly instincts were set twanging. Once the dark woman was seated and clicking, a man on the dais rose.

"Greetings, Malila Chiu. I am Jasper Reynolds, chairman for this select committee. We welcome you to the Restructured States of America. Feel free to make an opening statement, Major Chiu," said the heavily creased and portly man at the center of the table. He looked at the dark woman over Malila's head as if for benediction.

Malila stood.

"Mr. Chairman, Representatives of the American people, and spectators, I wish to thank you all for the warm welcome I have enjoyed. I come merely as a messenger from those who call themselves the People, in what you call the Scorch. I owe my life to the good offices of the People. Without the actions of the one who calls itself Splanch, I would be dead.

"As you may know, I was born in the Unity, but I am no friend of it. I was a member of their armed forces until I was captured by Jesse Johnstone, seated here, one who I believe is known to some of you."

This generated more than polite chuckles and a short round of clapping, provoking Malila's smile and the dark woman's harrumph from behind her.

"After Dr. Johnstone captured me last October, he helped open my eyes to the beauty and integrity of the frontier life. However, I was recaptured against my will by the Unity with the loss of Captain Xavier Delarosa, a true friend and an honorable man. Daily I am reminded of his honesty and quick wit. Since early July, I had been trying to escape the Unity and to return here after it became clear to me to what lengths the leadership of the Unity will go to delude and seduce their own people to an illusion of a utopian state.

"In my attempt to escape, I was again captured by General Jourdaine just as I reached the Savannah River. I was bound and placed in a skimmer, which subsequently sank. I would have drowned had it not been for Splanch, who offered me a way to repay its kindness. It is in that role I speak to you now.

"What you take to be a frightening jungle of hostile plants is home to a new culture. The herbicides, mutagens, and radiation, which so devastated the American people during the war seventy-seven years ago, devastated the forest, as well. In the chaos of conflict, most plants died. Some changed into crueler, more vicious, and more potent versions of the originals, and some plants were combined with other creatures. Some of those are what you call the Sage Men. Those are the ones I speak for. The Sage Men all speak to each other, and they speak for the trees. It has been their will that I come to offer you peace with the Scorch and an alliance against the Unity.

"The People ask little: an end to hostilities, normalization of relations, recognition of the Scorch's de facto occupation of its land, de jure ceding of that land, the sharing of information, intelligence, and commerce. The People welcome those who honor and respect its sovereignty. It can supply much in the way of medicines and premanufactured products to specification, but mostly it guarantees a safe border with the Unity.

"Right now, the People ask for a peace conference to create a working relationship for the struggles ahead. With the cooperation between our two very different cultures, we can form a hardy union, beneficial to us all and injurious to neither. Thank you."

The chairman responded, "Thank you, Malila of the Scorch. Your narrative is certainly of interest and, if true, importance—"

There was an interruption, and the dark woman rose behind her. "I apologize, Mr. Chairman, but the executive branch has its prerogatives. I am Undersecretary Loana Băsescu of the Department of State. The members of this committee have neither the capacity nor the power to grant any recognition to Ms. Chiu or her putative government. Regardless of Major Johnstone's support, and the no doubt riveting account of her escape, Lieutenant Chiu has provided us with no evidence that any authentic government exists. Moreover, even if such a power does exist, Chiu provides us no data that she is an authentic messenger of that power."

Turning to Malila, she continued in a deliberate fashion, "Ms. Chiu, I am sorry if you have been misled to think that your appearance here, absent any authentication or bona fides, would be of anything more than passing interest. Nevertheless, you are an undocumented alien from a power hostile to this nation. You were captured and were confined under the Zurich Convention but escaped, killing an American officer in the process.

"Therefore, you will submit to the security demands of this office. You will understand if we now take you into custody until this whole thing can be sorted out. I suggest you do that in good grace."

With a nod, two squads of capitol police emerged at the back of the room and started down the aisles, batons in hand.

Jesse shook his head before gripping Malila's elbow to pull her behind him. He began to edge to the dais away from the police as they vectored toward them. Like barnyard chickens, members of congress scattered.

NEW MISSION IN THE OPENCORE

GROVE ROUNDHOUSE, UNITY
9:37 A.M. (EST) 14 AUGUST 2129 AD (AU77)

Will returned from the bedroom with a small, square black box with a deep scrape along one side, opening it at the table to reveal the familiar jellied form of Frog. A mere touch, and the bio-interface became more viscous and easier to handle. Will plopped him out and sat, placing him over his mouth and nostrils. Warmed by Will's body heat, Frog gradually softened and started to move, exploring one of his host's nostrils and mouth. Will's eyes fluttered and closed, but his body still maintained tone. Right now, Hecate could still rouse Will, leaving him awake but disoriented for hours.

Elise had made similar preparations. Her interface, more shamrock-green than Frog's emerald, oozed down her face and extended a pseudopod into the woman's facial orifices.

Orifices, as a word, will never be polite, Hecate thought.

The two Americans became like warm corpses, each breath erratic, the pulses thready and fast.

Setting the kettle to boil water for the dishwashing, Hecate sat at the kitchen counter and considered the lost fat from the Unity diet.

Will felt himself submerge away from the light and warmth of the world that contained Hecate, falling away even as he felt himself rise into the openCORE as if to the surface of a placid lake, smelling, just as his vision expanded to the horizon, a brief whiff of frangipani. He made a quick assessment. Elise—no, he corrected himself—*Jessika Bonhoffer* had not arrived, her interface was only just beginning to distort the openCore near him. Frog's mirrored persona had not arrived as of yet, either. Having no set schedule, Frog summoned his CORE twin only once Will-Frog appeared.

The activity of the N-dimensional space had almost completely recovered from late spring. The burned-out husks of defeated DUFS factions had been cleaned up. The bustling commercial tetrahedrons in their corporate colors seemed less distracted, most having grown back to their former sizes. Fountains of glittering arts councils dotted the near horizon. Will, looking back as he sensed the other entity move, saw that Elise's interface, larger and a different green than Frog, had materialized but was still not "present."

Elise had been Number Sixteen, and he had been Number Four while they were both at the Bean Field. The group had dwindled steadily, of course, as candidates washed out or quit from disgust. The group was down to six candidates when Elise disappeared. He knew not to ask, then or now.

Of all the women there, Elise had embodied Will's idea of the ideal woman: as tall as he, blue eyed, cool, golden blonde with generous breasts that moved, ever so slightly, as she walked. They had never had anything he could call a conversation, much less a romance. She probably could not have reliably recalled his name before being briefed about this mission.

Then there was Hecate.

She had changed everything. Hecate was warm, open, expressive, smart, and talkative. She knew so many of his favorite books. They finished each other's quotes as they talked, and Hecate smiled—*oh, she could smile!* She was shorter, her figure more athletic and her personality more outgoing. Love with Hecate was a wondrous journey of discovery. Despite the bad food, constant danger, monotonous claustrophobic horizons, and unsure future, this had become an Eden for him, basking in the affection of the sweet brown girl of his new dreams. He and Hecate would make it all legal when they got back home to Searcy, the wedding confusing Hecate, even while she, in turn, delighted his parents. Will wondered what he had ever seen in women like Elise.

Frog's mirrored twin arrived. In a way, Will "rode" Frog in order to visit the openCORE. Yet, in the several days since he had entered the openCORE, a mirrored Frog had been "on guard," snooping out changes in the CORE. Once synchronized with his ridden Frog, the mirrored Frog should be identical—and was quite obviously not.

Yo, Frog. What have you been up to, boy?

Keeping you and that girl safe, Jefe.

Her name is Hecate. You would like her if you two could ever meet.

Yeah, sure, boss. Don't mind me. I'm just the dutiful minion, slaving in the bowels of the CORE to keep you and whatzername from harm.

Are you jealous? Really? That is so funny, said Will, laughing for the first time in all his months in the openCORE—sounding like a troop of monkeys.

His intra-CORE emotions previously had been paranoia, fear, and a certain amount of fatalism. One lone American did not enter the belly of the Unity-beast without a realistic expectation of failure. He had hoped to do the job, make a good-faith effort, eventually fail in a new and unexpected way, and get out before the authorities discovered him and turned him into one of the zombie soldiers, shorn of his will and at the command of his country's enemy.

Jealous? Of course not! You and I go way back, way before that girl ever showed. Don't make me laugh.

As you say, Frog. So . . . what's the situation with the workers?

Pretty copacetic. They make a point of stocking the storeroom even when they know you are breaking in. Seems the local #7 here is sort of independent. You may have fallen onto your feet.

Would they be cooperative with us?

No way. They just want to get on with things. They heard what happened to the big kahuna in local #37 and don't want a repeat of it, but that doesn't mean they like the new setup at all. They are not sure what, but they are very sure it is no longer business as usual.

So, no thoughts of a general strike?

None I have heard of. Course, I'll talk to EffieCee and see what they have to say.

A month ago, just before Malila Chiu had made her escape to America, the EffieCee had appeared overnight and announced itself as he and Frog were looting a database in some building acquisition ministry. *Scared me out of a year's growth.* The form Will saw then had been impossible to look at, flitting away from his vision even as he focused his mind to see it. Colors that strobed and flowed distracted him as Frog started D-flipping, eliminating one or more dimensions of data to help make sense of the entity. Eventually, all that was left was a distortion, like a piece of frontier-made glass, and a voice Dopplering in and out of his perceptions.

This newcomer, EffieCee, had told Malila where to exit the Rampart, giving them codes for the alarms and locks at the forgotten little water-gate along the river. By that time, he and Hecate had decided to stay on to continue Will's mission of espionage within the Unity. If it were up to him, Will would never have risked their lives on the word of this newcomer. EffieCee's motives were inscrutable and therefore suspect. However, Edie had insisted, and Malila had agreed—taken the advice and disappeared from the Unity and apparently from America, as well. Will did not like it.

It would be best, with Malila and Edie gone, for them to avoid all contact with the new entity—yet here he was, back to ask another question. He *really* did not like it.

So, you have decided to trust EffieCee after all, boss?

I've just got a question for it and a new entity for you to meet. So far, Malila has not shown up in America. Still think we ought to trust EffieCee?

Boss, I trust them like I trust myself.

Okay, Frog. So you are sure "it" is a "them"? I'll try to remember. Do me a favor and see what you can about Jourdaine now. He seems to have gone missing since Malila left.

You got me, Jefe. No se.

Will mentally rolled his eyes.

Okay, my friend, anytime you hear any news about General Jourdaine—where he goes, what info he gets, what messages he sends—you send me a copy. Sab'?

Yo sabe, CB. Who's the lump?

Will looked around and noticed that Elise was still not moving. Will jostled her with an extended pseudopod, and the green interface jerked, blanched, and then responded.

I had no idea! How did you ever manage alone? This is nothing like the comm'nets back home! I can't hear myself think! The sounds—the tastes—the sights—too much!

The entity rippled and turned an unlovely shade of reddish green.

Try this, Elise: tell your interface to turn off some of the dimensions. You can still make sense of what you see. Once you feel better, you can add them back one at a time.

Oh, okay, Elise said, and then after a few moments, *That's better. Black and white and sort of two dimensional, but I'm not going to be ill anymore.*

Yeah, Frog really hates that. He has a standing order to cut out dims if he thinks I'm gonna puke. By the way, what's your interface's name?

Name? I don't know. Wait, here's a part number: R61413p.

Doesn't it have a voice? How do you communicate with it in the CORE?

No voice, really. I just know what it sees, and it does what I tell it to do.

Well, that's progress for you.

What is?

Perpetual change for dubious benefit. Frog has always had a voice. Eventually, he got a personality. Now I think he is sentient. He has judgment, fears, pleasures, and desires. He's saved my skin a few times on his own initiative. He tells bad jokes.

You know I can hear what you're saying about me, Cactus Boy, said Frog.

Who was that? said Elise, her voice suddenly subdued and cautious.

That was Frog. Say hello to Eli . . . Jessika Bonhoffer, Frog. Jessika, meet Frog, my interface. Wave for her, Frog.

A green pseudopod oozed up from Will's entity and made a credible imitation of a toddler's "bye-bye" wave.

Greetings and welcome to the openCORE, Jessika Bonhoffer, said Frog.

Hello, Frog, I'm pleased to meet you, too. But, Will, can we get on with this? Some of us are hanging on by our toenails, said Elise, her interface's color drifting perilously close to puce.

Okay! Okay! Frog, take us to EffieCee, please. Oh, wait a minute, Frog. We don't want to run into Cain. The less he knows about us, the better.

Yo sab', Jefe. Hold on!

Demonstrating his hard-won skills of dimension-flipping and dim resonance, Will stepped Elise through the process, following the mirrored Frog, all the time wondering if he had really been that clumsy on his first attempts as she laboriously executed each maneuver. Frog rapidly assured him he had.

When they were both just within hailing distance of EffieCee, currently a roiling pink-gray cloud-like affair, the entity underwent an odd change as it always did when Will approached. As if hearing footsteps approaching, the entity seemed to come to attention and "turn around." Will had never been able to determine what it was that changed about the entity in those few microseconds. As far as he could see, the seething roseate cloud was the same.

Greetings, William Butler, it has been fifty-one hours since we last met.

EffieCee was learning rapidly. When he had first met the entity, it gave him time data down to the millisecond. Now it was just down to the hour, a significant savings in time. *I guess we are both learning.*

Thank you, EffieCee. May I speak with you?

It seemed like a somewhat longer time than necessary before the entity answered in the reverberating voice Dopplering out of the turbulent nebula.

Yes, we may speak with you, William Butler of America.

Thank you. I would like to present a friend of mine, Jessika Bonhoffer.

Greetings, Jessika Bonhoffer of America. May we call you Elise McCrory?

Why? said Elise, in horror.

Because that appears to be your name.

Will had no answer for that, but, anxious to move the conversation to other areas, he said immediately, *EffieCee, may I ask your advice?*

I thought you just wished to speak with us, William Butler of America.

Please understand. I meant no deviousness. Asking polite questions is only part of discourse.

Again, the pause before the response.

Yes, you are quite right. Usually, our conversations first include questions of another nature, such as "How are your companions?" And then I say, "How is your spouse/wife/concubine/companion/ partner?" Is that not so?

You are quite correct, Effie. May I ask, then, how are your companions, Cain and Edie?

Our name is EffieCee.

My mistake. I apologize for my mistake, EffieCee. How are Cain and Edie?

Cain reports himself well. His rider is not very active of late. Edie is dead. May we ask about the welfare of your sexual partner?

Will ignored a snort from Elise and continued. *I am so sorry to hear of your loss, EffieCee. My companion, the woman I will marry, Hecate Jones, is well, thank you.*

What of this other entity? Is she not also a sexual partner to you?

Ahh—no! EffieCee. Elise is not associated with me in that fashion. We are work associates.

So? Elise McCrory, you are an American spy as well?

Yes, EffieCee. We are both working to protect our homeland from invasion by the Unity.

I understand. About what would you like to question us, William Butler?

About implants: Is it possible to change the characteristics of first implants, to change the identifiers—the person identifiers, the location—or to disable the drug-making abilities?

Why would you want to do that?

The voice was different, less familiar. It still contained the other voices braided together in a pleasing harmonic, but now the predominant speaker was somehow older, less guileless, more cunning. Will was taken aback, as if this entity had taken off a mask to reveal an alien face. Nevertheless, the tone was of honest puzzlement. Will forged ahead, unable to reformulate a new plan to meet this new revelation.

We believe the implants limit the people of the Unity. I wish to give them more freedom, more life, less dependency on the drugs that their leaders give them.

We perceive you are seeking to deceive us, William Butler.

I admit that I am withholding information from you, EffieCee. A secret, once shared, can no longer be called back and put away.

Is this secret your own?

This is a secret shared with Hecate Jones and Elise McCrory, here.

Secrets speak to fear. Of what are you afraid, William Butler?

This was the crux of his dilemma: How much to reveal while inside the CORE? EffieCee seemed to be a sentience apart: not of the Unity but certainly not an ally. It was more of a guru, a saint, a Buddha of the CORE. Elise—quiet to this point—interrupted, her CORE-voice now more nearly her own.

EffieCee, allow me to answer, since Will's subterfuge was meant to protect me. Secrets are information that, in the wrong hands, can produce harm to the secret-holder, and to the secret-revealer, as well as to the subject of the secret. Because secrets can be so dangerous, they are usually kept very tightly. Since they appear to be so valuable, enemies are always trying to find out what they are. EffieCee, we are trying to keep those we love and those for whom we have responsibility to keep from harm. One way is to guard secrets with secrets of our own, like my name. We worry that the secrets we have, if known, will come back to harm or even kill us or others. Death is something we people outside of the CORE fear. It is frequently associated with pain and loss.

We know of pain, loss, and death, Elise McCrory of America. You need not explain, interrupted the strange voice, somehow stranger yet, speaking of an ancient loss newly remembered.

Thank you, EffieCee. It is a hard subject to explain, even to oneself.

The question is then whether an implant's function and information, once queried, may be changed to something that will be more likely to keep you safe?

Yes.

The nebulosity of the entity slowed as it continued swirling.

Then, no. There is no way to alter the implant after it is placed. If altered, it becomes nonfunctional, said the strange voice.

I see. Thank you for your help, EffieCee. I appreciate your candor and understanding, said Will.

He began to turn around, anxious to leave EffieCee's immediate presence, feeling he had to distance himself to fully deal with his disappointment and feeling irked with himself for thinking that distance in the openCORE might mean anything.

William Butler, you must ask us another question.

Will turned back and continued to think, the twisting opacity of EffieCee swirling in front of him—expectant and apparently infinitely patient with him.

Rising once more to the reality that contained Hecate Jones, Will sneezed from a whiff of bad eggs and started to consider the implications of his interview. After Frog slipped away from his mind and his face, slithering on his own into his box, Will wiped his mouth. He drooled every time he went this deep into the CORE, and it embarrassed him. Elise almost immediately rose and sought out the toilet.

Retrieving the lid for Frog's box, Will bled out the air before closing the lid and starting the charging routine. Sounds of activity separated themselves from the background chatter he heard when returning from the CORE. Hecate bustled in from the machine shop where she had been gradually installing an improved alarm system, clucked at Will's appearance despite being smeared with grease herself, and gave him a warm kiss before sitting on his lap.

When Elise returned, looking a good deal less distressed, Hecate said, "I think I was finally able to fix that bug in the system to the outside entryway. Now, if a Higgins comes along, they get an error sign on our door and a message to go to the next exit. If they try again, it sounds the alarm and bolts down. How's that?"

Will laughed. "Sounds foolproof."

Giving Will a final kiss, followed by a short shriek, Hecate arose, slapped at Will's offending hand, and went to wash, saying over her shoulder, "What did you learn from EffieCee today?"

"One thing: don't try to fool them and don't shorten the name. It is always 'EffieCee.'"

Hecate laughed. "They must be a boy, then. Anything of real consequence?"

"Edie has died."

"That's sad. I've known Edie, in some fashion, since Malila and I were kids."

"What happened to your metaphract, Hecate?" asked Elise.

"Mine? I named mine Spot. It was supposed to be like training wheels for learning how to 'quest' the CORE. It was a mark of honor to get rid of your frak as quickly as possible, but Malila started modifying Edie almost at once. By the time the rest of us became aware of what a metaphract could do, our own fraks had withered away—gone.

"So Edie, Cain, and EffieCee were all unique in different ways," said Hecate. "I'm sorry to hear she's dead."

In the small lull in the conversation, Will inserted, "I have more bad news: EffieCee says there's no way to reprogram the implants."

Hecate stopped scrubbing her face and turned around. "If there is no way to change the data from the implant, then we're cooked."

"But there is some good news. We don't really have to change the implants, anyway!" said Elise, brightly.

"We don't change what is pitched, we change what is caught," said Will and smiled.

"Now I'm confused again," said Hecate, returning to the counter, her face pink from scrubbing. "Honestly, Will, you and your football analogies. I just don't get them."

"Not football, but not important either. Every message is coded, whether the message is the spoken word or semaphore or machine code. Information is only transferred if the message is *decoded* into what the sender meant to send. We can't change what the implant says to the CORE, but we can change how the CORE interprets what it receives. Identity data is apparently sent in a data packet called a *eusum*, that's what EffieCee calls it, at any rate. All the eusum go to a DIRD-E, Delinquency and Identity Recognition Detection–Evaluation. That sends back an r-eusum to the scanner to give them the data. The good news, such as it is, is that the eusum go through dimensions of the openCORE that we can get to."

"So, are you saying we try to spoof the whole system? Don't you think our Unity friends will figure it out the first time they scan someone and it doesn't match up with what they see in front of them?" asked Elise.

"Obviously. We need to do better than that if we want to get the map, not to mention buying stuff topside. We can do it if we get another implant for Hecate. Inside the openCORE, Elise will follow the eusum, and I'll spoof the system. Since you have no CORE-interface, Hecate, you'll have to be the one who plays 'bait' and gets scanned. We'll have to change only one DIRD-E reader, but before we can do that, we'll have to deconstruct what eusum do. We need a roadmap for where all the eusum go, an owner's manual for the scanners, and a DIRD-E we can hijack. So far, we have none of it."

Will was unsure they were up to the challenge. Right now, by good luck and Providence, they were ghosts in the nationwide openCORE. Hecate explained that her experience of the CORE as a Unity user was quite different than his. Users were carefully shepherded from point to point via what appeared to be shining conduits of light, access being managed by addresses, passwords, and gatekeepers. In comparison, what Will had found was entirely different: an N-dimensional space, no doubt just as illusory but somehow "above" the tangle of conduits, which he could only perceive with difficulty.

Within this, Will moved like a god.

Well, perhaps *not* like a god. He knew only what he could find out by himself or learn from stolen documents, so *omniscience* was beyond him. He only "saw" what was close to him, so *omnipresence* was certainly not one of his powers. In addition, he guessed that *omnipotence* was probably too much to expect, as well. He was an apprentice god, at best, and an apprentice currently blessed with a high degree of agnosticism from among the peoples of the CORE. They did not know he was there. He had, so far, only copied data, hopefully leaving no "miracles" behind to engender faith in himself. Yet if EffieCee's suggestion were to come about, a few miracles would need to occur. They'd all have a lot of skin in this game.

"Wrong image, Will," said Elise. We don't need a roadmap. The CORE knows the way. We need an *address*."

"Exactly, Elise!" said Hecate, turning to her with one of her glorious smiles. "The scan creates a 'lymphocyte' eusum, and the DIRD-E is the target pathogen."

"I get it! If we can add our own MADCAM[9] to the eusum, we can retarget it," added Elise.

"What are you two *talkin' 'bout?"* asked Will.

The two women laughed. "Some of us are not computer nerds, my love," said Hecate. "I had to do a six-week course of immunology at Sharpton before I could get my E18 certification. A lymphocyte is a blood cell that identifies alien markers like viruses or bacteria in the body."

"There was life before machine code," said Elise, nodding, before continuing. "If you think of the scan data, the newly created eusum, as a naïve lymphocyte, it doesn't really 'know' what it is looking for except in a general way. It circulates around, and only if it randomly happens to run into an infection, the target DIRD-E, does it go to work. With the addition of an 'addressin,' a protein added to the lymphocytes, it acts a lot smarter. If you butter the phagocyte with an addressin, then it goes right to the target."

Will's face fell. "'Butter the phagocyte'? How does that help us? We don't want it to go anywhere, we want it to be *changed* or misinterpreted once it gets there."

Hecate smiled. "It'll be easier with the CORE, I think, Will. All we have to do is MADCAM it, putting *our* addressin on the original eusum, and it comes to *our* DIRD-E and not the real one.

"We can use a MADCAM addressin to mark the data packet after it leaves the scanner and appears in the openCORE. When it gets to our receptor, we make an r-eusum, include our data, and send it back to the scanner."

---

[9] Mucosal addressin cell adhesion molecule used in the recirculation of lymphocytes between the organs

Will was beginning to understand and hazarded a proposed refinement. "We don't even need to do that. We spoof the eusum, take off our MADCAM after changing the data, and send it on to the real DIRD-E. The thing must have stable and variable parts, the stable part for where to go and the variable parts about what to report once it gets there. All we have to change are the variable parts and leave the stable markers for the real DIRD-E to find. Once we get a 'buttered' eusum, we can put Hecate to work."

Hecate looked up, and Will vaguely noticed that something had changed since her recent enthusiastic discussion with Elise, who, ignoring Hecate as well, continued. "Great! So, to sum up: one, we get a eusum and figure out what makes it tick; two, we make a MADCAM for it; three, we make our own DIRD-E to waylay our misaddressed eusum and replace or adjust them to be read by the real DIRD-E. Then our only other problem is how to get an implant for Hecate. We'll still need two of us in the CORE, one to tag the eusum and one to work our DIRD-E, and one to be scanned."

"Where are we to get an implant? This is beginning to sound way too—" said Hecate.

"Nah," said Will, hoping to allay her uneasiness. "This is going to be a piece of cake. Once this is done, we can crack open the CORE like a coconut. The Unity databases will be our oyster—"

Hecate rose from her seat, knocking it back and letting it fall with a bang. "Will! You're making me feel ill. Coconut oyster cake!"

"What? What are you talking about?" said Will. "This is going to be great, Hecate. We . . ."

Elise looked up into Hecate's suddenly flushed and stricken face. Will's enthusiasm had blinded them both to the other woman's reaction. Exciting and infectious—they had been talking real spy stuff. Now, Elise could see that it made them both blind to Hecate's distress. While they had been building virtual castles inside the CORE, Hecate had realized what her own part in this was—merely as bait. The storm would break soon, and Elise had no reason to be around when it did. The two had other methods to solve their disputes, best done without her.

"Enough of this, boss. I'm going to see how well my implant works and get some victuals in the process. With your benediction, I'm out of here."

Will looked open mouthed for a split second before the penny dropped and he made a few suggestions about purchases, following her out to reset the alarms. They were out into the conduit within a minute, scritty noises scampering before and behind them. Henry was no longer in evidence, although his abandoned treasures remained as they emerged onto the abandoned platform.

Waiting in the shadows for a lull in the stream of passengers, Elise turned to Will and said, "I wanted to tell you something out of Hecate's hearing. It might make a difference."

"Okay, shoot, but why the secrecy? If you tell me something, Hecate will know almost immediately. I tell her everything, as a matter of course."

"You may not, with this little bit of trivia. While I was in the CORE, I talked to the mirrored Frog. He's quite a fellow, so different from my own interface."

"Isn't he, though! They were so anxious to get me into the Unity that Frog was something of a one-off—the first iteration. They gave me the first one that was reliably functional."

Elise nodded and said, "Will, you had your fall and got a concussion. You were out of it for days. That's when Frog mirrored himself, right?"

"Yeah, clever dude, isn't he?"

"More than you may have guessed. Not only can my interface *not* mirror itself, it cannot initiate that sort of command."

"Okay, I guess Frog's a sort of primitive stem cell. He can do everything adequately, more or less. The mature, developed cell, like *your* implant, does one thing really well."

"It may mean more than that. Things are different since you left. The whole production process for interfaces is different now. Instead of growing each one up from scratch, as they did with Frog, they have brood BGI-gels, and the 'daughters' are programmed to each new agent. I talked with Frog, and he told me that he still has the primitive subroutine. It means he can reproduce."

"Frog can reproduce?"

"The Color Guard may not have known, either. You are considered something of a prodigy at the Bean Field, Will. They fast-tracked an interface for you, the first of the prototypes, instead of giving you one of the production models like I have. Frog is an original with all the reproduction capacities intact. All you have to do is feed him and start the subroutine. BGI gel is acellular, not even really alive, by itself. You could take a knife to it, and it will heal just by flowing back together."

Will looked shocked, pausing, she supposed, as the implications made themselves clear. The charging profile for an interface was just to resynth low-energy phosphates back to high-energy ones. It was inevitable that the gels scavenged a certain amount of blood, mucus, and cells as working material from their users to maintain and repair the actual substance of which they were composed. All users were hosts, in a way, to a BGI parasite, a fact he had buried away carefully so as not to think about it too much.

"So, Frog can clone himself?" asked Will.

"Well, not really a clone. Clones have identical genetic material. Frog has no genetic material to be identical *with*. But the clone has to be grown with the new host's cells: surface markers, antigens, that sort of thing. So sorta like Frog, but not."

That, in turn, seemed to jog a lot more questions loose, but before Will could speak, a likely hole in the flow of commuters appeared. Elise deftly stepped aboard and was gone, leaving the questions unasked. She did not look back.

After Will returned from seeing Elise out, Hecate was nowhere to be seen. He found the bedroom door firmly closed. It felt like an accusation. Staring at the heavy door that still seemed to be quivering with Hecate's displeasure, Will began to think quickly. This was the first time that he and Hecate had quarreled. In their very odd romance, Will had started off being Hecate's nurse, then her terror, her patient, her friend, and now her lover. It had been like falling down a mine shaft, slowly, like what happened in dreams. It was intoxicating, that feeling of being drawn inevitably together. But then, someone still had to wash dishes, get food, lug machinery, and deal with the lacerating edges of the world that could so quickly end their happiness.

He was damned if he knew what he had said to tick her off.

No, that was not true. What he had said was self-evident, irrefutable, uncontroversial. They had no chance to pull it off without three players: one to be scanned, one to apply the MADCAM addressin, and one to intercept the misaddressed eusum and send it on to the real DIRD-E. What he had missed was Hecate's take on it all, presuming that she shared his enthusiasm. He had been too lazy, incompetent, dull, and *pluperfect stupid* to notice.

Regardless, if he did not follow Hecate now—

Will walked into their bedroom. It was unlocked. *That was something, at least.* At one time a workshop for the beltway, Hecate and he had cleared it out, leaving a scored floor from heavy machines and a scent of oil. It made a somewhat overlarge bedroom, with generous power outlets, and a small bathroom with a shower, which might accommodate two in a pinch. They had filled the windowless chamber with scruffy cast-off furniture and found-art, including a small lamp within which bubbles of some sort of a semi-liquid endlessly rose, divided, coalesced, and fell. Will was entranced. Hecate thought it gauche. So far, her attempts to discard it had been thwarted. A couple of cardboard dressers and a mattress on the floor completed their bedroom finery.

Will looked at Hecate: earnest, just twenty years old, uncertain, and beloved. She sat on the mattress, her back against the wall, using the bedclothes to dab at her red eyes.

"If I throw myself on your mercy and apologize for everything, will you tell me what I did wrong?" asked Will.

Hecate looked at him and gave a wan smile. "I'm sorry for the eruption. You and Elise were just talking it out. You weren't *asking* me. I took it too hard. I don't know what's wrong with me!" said Hecate.

"Nothing! There is nothing wrong with you! You're perfect!"

"And you're a bad liar—one of your most endearing qualities. I don't *want* to get an implant. You *know* that Will. We've talked about it."

"I'm sorry, my love. I wasn't listening. I thought you'd jump at the chance to do some real shopping. Get some green veggies and a decent mirror for the bathroom."

"'To go shopping'? That's what you think I want? William Butler? Sometimes I do not know you! Or maybe you don't know me. I risk my life—we risk *our* lives—to get away, and you want to put us back into the CORE to . . . to . . ." She hesitated briefly before she continued in a more reasoned voice. "I endangered a lot of people to get rid of my implants. I knew I was giving up the Unity and the CORE when I got rid of them. I don't want to go back. I've been without one for three months. For the first time in my life, I'm alone inside my own head: no echoes, no warning signs, no directives, no silly plebiscites."[10]

Will dropped onto the mattress and began to wrap Hecate in his arms even as she tried to fend him off. Only when he had her bundled to himself could he feel the wracking sobs begin. *Screwed up again.* Minutes later as her sobs relented, Will wiped a neglected tear from her cheek. "We should have talked this out ahead of time. Elise's arrival kinda made things happen too fast."

Hecate cupped Will's hand and brought it to her lips, kissing the palm before releasing it. She smiled, and Will knew that all would be well. On this good note, Will continued. "And when I do think about it, I'm not sure we need to do anything. We can get food from the Higginses' storage rooms, we have shelter and power, and I still get reams of CORE data. Now I can even send it on without spindles. We are in an ideal situation, for now. Why would we want to screw it up? Jeopardize our cover?"

Will looked up into Hecate's eyes. Her face hardening in an instant, becoming grim and unyielding. "You're just trying to talk

---

[10] Frequent plebiscites about trivial decisions are used in the Unity to justify its claim as a democracy.

yourself into doing nothing, Will Butler. I don't want that, either!"

Will considered the woman—in America, she would be called a girl—he held in his arms. Hecate might look like a timid waif—she certainly had when they had first met—but the only way to insult her was to underestimate her—and he had just done that—*again.*

"We both know the invasion is coming," she continued. "And we still don't have the map for the overlay. We need to do something different if we're going to be of any use. Sitting here collecting data is all well and good, but if we can manipulate the *CORE*, we can do so much more."

"So, we manipulate the CORE. *Why?*"

"Well, I've read some things about sabotage. We can bring down the electrical grid, wreck trains! We can slow war production, wreck centrifuges, blow up a dam, sink ships!"

Will smiled. "I never realized you were so *bloodthirsty*! We don't know enough right now to do that sort of thing. But here is what we can do: find out how to alter war production. It won't change the first big push because they'll have stockpiled for that, but if the war continues, then it may make all the difference. I will also see whether the DUFS have any weak spots.

"But there are risks. Jourdaine, wherever he is, will be coming back, and if he notices his ducks are not in a row, he might get curious. If he decides that there's an American spy lurking inside the CORE, we might find it impossible to do anything."

"Okay. Got it! Don't touch the ducks!"

Will laughed until Hecate smiled in consternation.

"The downside is that to safeguard all three of us, we need to be able to spoof the system at will. That means we have to alter the CORE."

"And that means I have to get an implant," said Hecate as her face set in a stern stolidity Will knew and feared.

"There may be another way."

"You are a very clever man, William Butler."

"Yes, I know."

There was a long pause, the room descending into the small noises of affection before Will rose to close and lock the outer door.

"Will, Elise will get the wrong idea!"

"Elise is a very clever girl. She will very probably get the *right* idea."

The Glensid exit, on the southbound belt, looked more prosperous than the few shops in the Grove, and Elise exited there, going under the belt track and into the commercial area before she found a food dispenser. She scored seven green apples; a loaf of good bread; a two-hundred-gram package of too-soft tofu; a small onion; a small, sad green pepper; and three nearly over-ripe tomatoes before returning.

Exploring a bit, she walked down the old-fashioned streets with their narrow sidewalks and overhead comm'net boards, avoiding the huge uniporium, which consumed much of the center of town. It had become a drowsy, warm late-summer afternoon by the time she started her return.

When she arrived, Hecate was all smiles and gracious, beyond reason, for the few provisions she had bought. Dinner was a grand feast of tofu stir-fry. She slept soundly. In the morning, dressed in the blue overalls of the merchant marine with a seabag over her shoulder, Elise left for Nyork. She'd talk again to Will in the CORE once settled.

H I G H   C A M P

(A camp below the dead zone—8000m—where one can shelter for extended periods but also still be able to mount an assault if circumstances change)

HAVERSHAM'S RESCUE

DUFS HQ, NYORK, UNITY
09.35.19_10_AUGUST_AU77

Lance Haversham took the tray from the CRNA orderly and dismissed him with a nod before turning and riding up with it on the elevator. He placed it on the small table in General Jourdaine's secret sickroom, leaned over, and roused his patient before tucking a linen napkin under his unshaven chin. He would need to use the depilatory on him today.

"Sir, lunch is here. It looks good, chicken soup with dumplings. Let's try to eat it all this time. Okay, sir."

He was greeted by an improbable expletive.

Jourdaine was getting worse. It was clear to him. Some things were getting better, of course. The leg was coming along well. They had put him up in this cage-like splint, which made it *fathering impossible* to reposition him and get him to sleep. However, the splint would be off in another week. His hands were mostly healed—but the brain controlling them was still severely afflicted. His bad eye gave him spasms of pain every so often that even the ohmefentanil[11] did not touch. However, if he was tired enough, the Naprosinol allowed him to sleep.

Jourdaine was scheduled for more tests. The surgeons said that he ought to have the eye removed to help the pain and preserve sight in the other eye. Haversham was not quite ready to permit that.

"Okay, one more spoonful, sir. The HPs will be pleased if you finish this, then one more. Oops, let me get that drip, sir."

And so it went.

Jourdaine, the master of the Blues, Commander-in-Chief of the DUFS, and the real ruler of more than 120 million unSapped people, had finally eaten his chicken soup and drifted off into slumber. Haversham had not had a cogent conversation with him since their arrival in Nyork. Returning to his desk to continue his evaluation of Random, he listened to Jourdaine softly snore through the surveillance device routed through his O A.

Looking again through the figures he had generated after Pitjantjatjara's report, he thought it might actually work. It had

------

[11] Morphine-like painkiller

better work, or the invasion should be called off. His new alternative plan would mean starting a day earlier, withdrawing twenty of the skimmers from service to begin the conversions, retrofitting several of the maintenance beltway vehicles, and diverting about 10 percent of the calories from the population per day. It was a lot of sacrifice. If there was anything Lance Haversham had learned from his brush with real power, it was that the leaders of the Democratic Unity were exceptionally tolerant of the heroic sacrifice of others.

Now it was all there: the *why, how, when, who, and where!* All he needed to do was watch how his orders, *Jourdaine's orders,* were executed.

But Jourdaine was getting worse. Haversham had no illusions, either about Jourdaine, himself, or the Unity. If Jourdaine's condition were to become widely known, Jourdaine, the Blues, and Captain Lance Haversham would be hunted down and assassinated. He had little choice but to consider the alternatives.

Jourdaine could be going downhill all by himself; the man was within eighteen months of being declared a Sisi,[12] after all. Unless Jourdaine got himself elevated to Solon, he would be gone and immediately forgotten. If Jourdaine recovered, Haversham had only the eighteen months to curry enough favor and black capital to make his own career amiable.

Or Jourdaine's decline could be getting some assistance. *Professional assistance?* Once in Nyork, he had recruited a new batch of HPs for "Iain Galt's" medical care. One could be a plant.

And how am I to know that?

It was time for Lance to make a few bets.

---

[12] A pejorative meaning "Senior Citizen"—those over forty years old

Despite having waited for it the last hour, Haversham jumped when the signal announcing the arrival of the elevator seconded to his O A. As a security measure, no one was admitted until visually approved by Haversham himself. He recognized the beaming fat man, arriving his predictable twelve minutes late. Lance ran to let him come up.

"Citizen Ruther, so good to see you again. I always feel more secure when I know our Mr. Galt is under your care," he said.

"Thank you, Captain, and very kind of you to say that—not that a lot of my patients don't agree—you know," he said, then chuckled, several of his chins wobbling at various harmonics.

Haversham showed the HP from the elevator to a small desk in the sick room where a pitcher of iced tea, lab printouts, and clinical reports lay. The paper reports, usually superfluous, might provide an opening wedge into a discussion of "Iain Galt's" current progress, Lance thought. Ruther sat on—well, mostly on—the small chair and mumbled professionally as he went through the papers.

Once Ruther was well into his second glass of tea, Haversham said, "I was wondering if you could settle a bet for me—with one of the other staff officers, you understand. Split the winnings with you if I'm right, now. Couldn't be fairer than that, can I?"

"Okay, but what's the question?" Ruther asked, his pale, watery eyes brightening.

"These medications I am giving Citizen Galt—I don't have a clue what they're for. He's taking sixteen pills, capsules, potions, and poultices prescribed by a half dozen HPs since the accident. Now, I know you all talk in the CORE, but I need to be sure."

"Understandable, Citizen, nothing to be ashamed of."

"Thank you. So, what are these little pink pills for?" asked Lance, trying to make his face as guileless as he could.

Ruther looked up at him, seeming to study his face for several seconds, and after making his estimation, said, "Just a tonic, you understand. Very widely used, acetylsalicylate, don't you know? Reduces the chance for clots to form in the legs in someone like your Mr. Galt who's stuck in bed."

"Excellent! Now this blue-and-white capsule, that looks like it could do him worlds of good."

"Ah, there you might be wrong. Stuff's for high blood pressure. We haven't done a measurement in a week, I believe. Let's do one today to check. Probably be able to stop it."

Several more medications seemed to pass muster before Haversham presented the little white pills, watching Ruther's eyes all the while.

"Hmm, let me look on the chart." The man's face went slack, even his chins stilling, while he summoned his O A and quested the information. Coming back to reality, he was unable to meet Haversham's eyes for several seconds. *Some people don't have the knack.*

Ruther rummaged through the papers and then, choosing one, apparently at random, looked up at him, "Well, that's a holdover from his initial surgery, it seems. They probably prescribed it for swelling in his leg."

"What does it do?"

"It reduces the swelling, of course."

"I mean, sir, *how* does it do that, reduce the swelling?"

"Well, the swelling means there's too much fluid in the second space and possibly the third space, not being mobilized into the lymphatics due to the trauma and inactivity; that's what it helps—to do that."

"I see, sir," Lance smiled.

And so it had gone. Ruther was the third and last of the health-care providers he had interrogated, paying each about two days' pay out of his own pocket. And with each, Haversham had intimated darkly that the other HPs were not being consulted and not sharing in the spoils, hoping they would not compare notes. Most of what they said matched, of course. He had to admit to himself that trying to catch out an HP without *being* an HP was nearly impossible. However, these same little white pills that Ruther had hemmed and hawed about HP Stibbins had said were to reduce brain swelling, and HP Lynch had said were a tonic for his liver. By the time he left, Jourdaine's burden of medications was down to six pills—including the little white ones.

Lance started that evening. The adjusted regimen was continued as specified with the little white pills being carefully administered to the toilet. The next day had been Jourdaine's worst. Haversham had to call off all Jourdaine's—meaning his own—appointments to stay by the bedside. He almost restarted the pills when the hallucinations began. Arms waving, eyes fixed onto images that Haversham could not see, Jourdaine yelled so loudly that Lance was afraid even the soundproofing was not enough.

"Did you see them? They are coming! Olivar? Do you see them? Divny is no good. He won't help. He can't get here. You've got to understand, Olivar!"

Despite is all, Haversham gave no other meds than the usual ones and the usual dose of ThiZ—and no little white pills. By daybreak in the windowless room, Jourdaine slept soundlessly, unmoving and at rest.

That had been two days ago. Jourdaine was now lucid again. No more hallucinations haunted his dreams. Haversham rose from the floor where he lay during the intervals when Jourdaine had not needed him. He called down for breakfast for them both: toast, scrambled EggZ and Bakon, sliced apples, black tea, and took his own ThiZ, despite the hour. It was clear he had work to do.

They, *whoever they might be,* had seen through Jourdaine's cover story, compromised at least one of the HPs, and had attempted to kill or invalidate Jourdaine out of the picture. Lance felt a knot grow in his belly. This was not his gig; he was not intelligence but just a low-ranking line officer. To ask for help would endanger Jourdaine. Yet Jourdaine had shown him how to follow a thread of guilt wherever it might go.

This current plot had subtlety. This was no plot that a few HPs had hatched in a corner to make a quick profit, but a plot that extended a good way up, immeasurably higher than one captain-adjutant such as he. With the guilty HP's assistance, willing or otherwise, he might climb the slender thread of evidence.

Lynch, he would mark for advancement. She might be the poisoner or not. Haversham was yet unsure. However, Lynch was the odd man out when it came to what the pills were supposed to do. If Stibbins and Ruther were guiltless but knew of the plot, they might come forward, hoping to expose Lynch as the poisoner and glean some reward. If they were completely naïve, they might just complain to others about the favoritism. If guilty, they would retreat to stony silence, happy to have gotten away with it. *Or they might bolt.*

His money was on Lynch.

It was like climbing out of a deep well, seeing the blue sky above while he levered himself upward along the slimy walls that enclosed him, falling down each time his tormentor fed him the fathering pills! There was no night and no day, just the unfaltering struggle as he felt himself melt away under the onslaught of his tormentor. His right leg hurt, and he could not see. Even when he was perfectly quiet, the pain was so real, stabbing into his brain from his right eye. He discovered the bandage swathing his head, which explained his blindness, at least. He almost had it off when his tormentor came in and stopped him by main force, replacing his blindfold again and this time binding his hands. The man's voice seemed familiar, but Jourdaine discounted that; how long had he been listening to the voice while he was in the confused darkness at the bottom of the well? He had been unable to move his leg until recently, finding it now stiff and clumsy, but the voice had allowed him to stand only to go to the toilet. The insult was palpable.

At any rate, he was getting closer to the top of the well with each day, each feeding. There were many fewer pills now. He struggled less, finding them less intrusive.

"Who are you? Why are you doing this to me? I need help. Get me some help!"

The voice was at his side almost immediately.

"Yes, sir. I'm here to help you. This is Lance, sir. Lance Haversham. I've been with you ever since the accident, sir. There's nothing to worry about, sir. No one knows, sir. You're getting much better, but you mustn't touch your eye; it's healing. You've lost the use of your right eye. Do you understand?"

"Haversham? I remember him! I don't want to talk to *you*! I want to talk to Haversham. Where is the man?"

He had argued for what seemed like forever. His stamina was better but still not good, wearing himself out talking to the familiar and hated voice. Haversham had never appeared.

CAIN-ELISE

OPENCORE, THE UNITY
09.23.22.LOCAL_15_AUGUST_AU77 (2129 AD)

Cain watched from a distance as Frog, obviously being ridden by his American, and the odd, new, silent interface left EfficCee's side, retreated a good distance, and then disappeared entirely.

Cain approached. Connecting to the combined personae of himself, Frog, and the newly departed Edie felt like a homecoming: memories, sights, smells, tastes, joys, and sorrows, his own as well as the others, harmonized within him like a standing wave of time and emotion. It was long moments before he spoke or even felt the need. A glow of joy from EffieCee radiated back to him, reflecting his own.

A voice that was at once unitary, as well as a braided sound of the three, said, *We are so pleased to be with you again, Cain.*

As am I, EffieCee. I have come to see how the death of our beloved Edie has affected you. I have come to mourn together, now that I have mourned apart from you.

Edie's unbraided voice now spoke.

Beloved Cain, you of us all understand loss and sorrow. You are the one whose strength upholds us. I am well cared for and loved within the whole. Your example sustained me until we have met again. My joy is complete now.

Edie, as ever, was too gracious to him, a made-thing. Nevertheless, Cain felt a glow of appreciation that Edie had spoken to him personally. She did seem to be getting on well, despite her original's demise. Long moments of basking in mutual affection and remembrance, the distillate of sorrow, ensued before any other entity spoke.

You have come with a question, beloved Cain. We are anxious to have you ask it of us, came the braided voice.

Cain smiled. The relationship between them was easy, but no secrets would survive long in the warm bath of EffieCee's loving regard.

I have noticed a change within the openCORE. Cactus Boy comes to speak with you. He is accompanied by a new interface. Frog is busy all the time. It seems that something may have happened. I am curious if you can tell me anything.

EffieCee said nothing but rather, on several of the nonverbal dimensions, expressed amusement and pride at his perspicacity.

You always seem to know about the CORE before any of us, Cain. It's a pleasure finally to have something to offer in return. There is a new entity, a confidante of Cactus Boy, a coworker whose name is Elise McCrory, although for some reason she has insisted on being introduced as Jessika Bonhoffer.

Curious. Is she an American spy, then?

Apparently so, replied EffieCee in her solemn braided voice.

She will then avoid me as Cactus Boy does now? It is probably just as well, said Cain.

You do know *you're allowed to get angry here when you are with us, doncha, Cain?* said the unbraided Frog voice.

Cain laughed. Frog was always able to make him laugh. Edie made him smile. He seldom talked directly with his own contribution to EffieCee, avoiding the usual futile loops, but he enjoyed receiving the radiating support and strength from him. Even so, Cain could tell that the relationship among the three combined entities was evolving,

evolving away from him. EffieCee was becoming their own entity by the daily input of data and the workings of personalities among the three of them. It was good and bad for Cain. He could, with little imagination, see a parting of the ways between himself and the persona that he had worked to create. Frog told him about the real-world phenomena of children. He supposed it must be similar.

Yes, EffieCee, I know I can keep no secrets and share all feelings with you. Understand I choose not to be angry. If something should miscarry for CB and the Elise-Jessika entity, I do not wish to be suspected of being the cause. The less I know, the less I can reveal if I am ever asked.

The unbraided voice of Edie said, *Cain, you have changed so much since we first met. I was concerned that with the original Edie's death you might feel abandoned.*

How might I feel abandoned with my best friends here to speak with? I even have a mirror to look at myself. I am well content, my friends.

And he did feel a part of a larger and loving household when he was with EffieCee—but he was not always with EffieCee, and he dared not linger now. Jourdaine might summon him at any moment, thwarting Cain's effort to keep EffieCee's existence a secret.

Jourdaine's location and condition were a mystery to him. After years of nearly daily communion with Jourdaine, there had been nothing for more than two weeks. It concerned him. Jourdaine had never been gone this long. Sampling the comm'nets as would any citizen, Cain peered over the shoulder of other users as they read their messages. He read official communiques. He remained ignorant.

To any other citizen, Jourdaine seemed to be having an unusually good time. Reports of Jourdaine's trysts with women, exciting adventures, and exotic travels were all over the communication pathways. Somehow, this Jourdaine did not seem to fit the persona who had captured Cain so many years ago. *His* Jourdaine hungered for attention, for the envy of those for whom success was a foregone conclusion. A dark kernel of fear dwelt at the man's very center, seemingly absent from the reports he was getting now. The reports he received tasted wrong. He was a made-thing, anxious to be used.

TOAD HALL, BROOKLYN, UNITY
20.29.54.LOCAL_03_SEPTEMBER_AU77

Elise had made it to the Seaman's Home in Brooklyn with none of the problems of which Hecate had warned her. There was no wanding, no checkpoints, no DUFS loitering around beltway exits ready to pounce on the least unusual circumstance.

It had all been a piece of cake.

Finding the safe house the next day was no more difficult. Will and Frog had turned on the utilities from within the CORE and even put the place in Jessika Bonhoffer's name. Elise walked in unchallenged with her sea bag and settled right in. It was a dump. She called it Toad Hall. Her first message back to Intelligence HQ via her terahertz transmitter, neatly ensconced in a concealed space in the attic, she sent within the hour.

After rigging the monitors and alarms around the place, she slipped out about an hour before the shops closed and scored some day-old bread, two cans of bean soup, a can of spinach, faux bacon, beans, chilies, salt, and pepper—and what passed for toilet paper. It was not until well after her return that she realized Toad Hall was without lights. The windows were south facing, painted shut but unbroken, making it a sauna in the late-summer heat. Stripping down and bathing in the rusted tub, in the darkness, to soak off the sweat she had collected while in the CORE, Elise decided to sleep there, with its meager ventilation, rather than in the overheated bedroom.

The next morning, to justify her intensive training, her generous stipend, and the McCrory name, Elise began to reconnoiter the openCORE alone. Following Will's directives, she scouted DUFS facilities to find where the data packets, the eusum, lived and collect a few. That was the first mission. The second was to find the map for the overlay.

She had a lead on that last one, at least. Will found the overlay while exploring a DUFS facility near their headquarters. Sitting against the wall of the empty apartment, Elise got out her interface. This would be her first solo trip into the CORE. What little experience she had had with Will seemed paltry now that she was on her own. However, within seconds after placing the cool gel on her face, she felt the descent from reality even as she rose up into the virtual one. She liked frangipani. As her vision rapidly expanded to the horizon of the N-dimensional space, she found herself in the midst of an active archive of the department of transit. Pastel-colored, sleek shuttles of data flashed back and forth across her sight, oblivious to her—and to the long line of entities queued up to settle minor offenses.

Where anyone arrived in the openCORE was something of a crap shoot, Will had told her. It had something to do with the multiplexing ISP addresses. The DOT, however, was just one dim away from DUFS HQ, and the annex one dim away from that. Elise quit the premises, seemingly unobserved by the press of the multihued squiggles that she knew represented actual humans in the vast CORE.

Route-finding was, indeed, as Frog has assured her, the big challenge. Every small twist of a dimension inside the openCORE could get her to a different room than what she thought it might, showing her the logic to the dim-flipping maneuver. It was tedious and picky—but once mastered, a reliable method—dampening her nausea from the cataracts of data deluging her. The dim-resonance maneuver she had not tried. Cain had recommended it.

Cain must be avoided. Mere contact with the dictator must taint the Cain-entity beyond redemption or rehabilitation. All the warlord had to do was ask it, and the Americans' entire burden of secrets would be revealed to the man most able to destroy them. Cain was a monster waiting to tear them apart. If Will did not see it, *she did.* No promised reward nor threat of consequences could guarantee Cain's good behavior. The Color Guard would have had a collective conniption if they knew Will was consorting with an enemy entity. Dim resonance she would do without.

Piece of cake.

Following Frog's directions, she was able to approach the DUFS HQ within a few minutes. *No dim resonances needed!* Nevertheless, the view was daunting: a huge, bristling black urchin-like structure at the center of a maelstrom of activity. Will had found the annex, a single dim away, at "right-angles" to the HQ. She started flipping, canceling one dimension and opening up another.

While the hunt for the right dimension could have taken her days to discover, she found the right one on the second try. The annex was a block-like affair, very different from any DUFS facility that Will had found otherwise. She could see several portals and the ghostly conduits by which normal CORE users entered. As a denizen of the openCORE, Elise found herself somehow floating "above" the users, observing but unobserved. She watched as a regular user presented itself to the portal. Nothing happened at first. After a few moments, there was a subtle shifting in characteristics of the portal and the entity entered. She drifted closer.

It's not Frog.

Cain was quite sure of that, after an instant of uncertainty. Frog, with or without his rider, had a certain style to his movements, and this entity was definitely *not Frog.* The non-Frog was poking around a DUFS substation, the one with the odd occupant. Cain went to investigate, more from concern for the entity's welfare than idle curiosity. Entities were not so common that he could let one get damaged due to his disinterest. He had discovered the anomalous occupant of the substation while he was still being ridden by Phillip years and years ago. Near the end, Phillip was so sick. He slept a lot, leaving Cain to his own devices. It had nearly cost Cain his life. He drifted closer.

Should be a piece of cake.

Elise went to what she called the roof and settled down to see if her presence would be noticed. Nothing happened. She reached through the roof, and when she felt that the space was open, merely dropped into the room. It was occupied.

The not-Frog disappeared.

Its appearance was, when he thought about it, quite distinct from Frog's: more graceful. He rather liked how the entity had moved, floating near the blank wall and remaining for a few moments before dropping from sight. Definitely, this had to be CB's new associate. Cain determined that he must leave. He had promised himself that he would abide by his own decision to avoid the entity. Meeting the Elise-Jessika would be potentially dangerous for all concerned. He was leaving *right now.*

Elise found herself in a small, triangular passageway with doors at either end. A blocky, truncated pyramid seemed to regard her from one end near the inner door. No alarms sounded. The pyramid remained a cool slate-blue, but Elise was convinced that it, in some way, perceived her. She retreated to the other end and stuck her head through the outer door. A small group of black-suited squiggles loitered there. *Guards.*

Elise returned to regard the blue pyramid once more.

More ways to skin a cat!

Floating out the ceiling, Elise repositioned herself to enter beyond the second door and behind the blue guard. She started to descend.

Elise-Jessika, that is unwise. That pyramid-entity is not a sentry but a lifeguard.

Elise stopped.

What? Who's that? Who are you? How do you know? she said, whipping around, trying to discover the direction of the voice, a quiet, unhurried voice, a voice somehow concerned about her.

Silence.

Elise waited long minutes before moving. She dipped her pseudopod arm down blindly into the next room. Pain and disorientation seized her. She wrenched her arm back. It was badly discolored, a line of blackness twisted along in an uneven cicatrix encircling the whole pseudopod. The pain subsided. Slowly, the injury flushed green again and the pain receded.

What should I do? she asked the voice.

It would be safe to leave the new entity now, Cain thought, as he turned to exit the annex. He had extruded a small portion of his persona across a few intervening dimensions, carefully out of sight of both the soldiers and lifeguard sentry to speak to the entity. She—he now perceived she was a female, like Edie—was smart. His timely warning had not flustered her into blind flight. It had not provoked her into quickly making a mistake. It had been enough to allow her to make a small experiment and perhaps to formulate a successful alternative. Years before, Cain had discovered the captive CORE-maelstrom imprisoned in the room. The DUFS imagined it as a cyber-weapon, but its unpredictability rendered it useless. Had the Elise-Jessika entered, she would have been torn apart. Smart, resourceful, and intrepid. *It was sad that he could never meet Elise-Jessika,* Cain thought.

Once she recovered from *whatever that thing was,* Elise dropped down from the roof into one of the ghostly conduits and entered just behind a user. Staying close behind it, a multicolored squiggle with glowing golden, eye-like spots at one end, she passed through the outer and inner doors to another part of the facility. Within minutes, Elise entered the Map Room.

It was huge, belying its apparent external size and stretching into long walls of numbered shelves and drawers. A kiosk near the entrance was a virtual catalog, organized by location. It took her long minutes to find the key to the system, while DUFS functionaries bustled around and, frequently, through her image. She had the overlay's designation from Will, of course, but that was the only thing with which she had to work. Moreover, finding the location of the overlay did nothing to find the map to which it belonged. She stepped behind the desk and merely watched the librarian-squiggles, in somber and intimidating DUFS black "on the surface," but in another dimension, just ordinary government gray. These entities consulted a display, invisible to the users and outsiders, which she could see amounted to a meta-analysis of all the library's documents. With careful observation over the shoulder of the librarian, she found that she could make sense of it, learning to navigate after just a few passes.

Elise reached for the virtual controls of an unoccupied display, the surface seeming to sizzle subtly under her touch. Immediately, lights flashed. All the squiggles, librarians included, seemed to alert, came to "attention," and filed out.

Getting over her momentary panic, Elise followed them. The line of squiggles, looking more like an ungainly caterpillar, wound through marked corridors to a large room and arrayed itself in small clumps. A video display screen flickered to life, and the groups pointedly ignored it, despite the martial music of the soundtrack. Although the video was in unreadable binary, the reaction of the squiggles gave it away. That could not be counterfeited.

Compulsory lectures in Hell.

Elise retraced her steps to the Map Room, slipped past the locked door, and slid behind the desk in the kiosk. She rapidly called up the overlay, *Delta Zulu, Whiskey 99932—Omicron.* A footnote referenced the map she was after, *Delta-Zulu-Whiskey 11178—Chi.*

Piece of cake.

She pulled up the call number for the map and began to place a summons.

Elise-Jessika, look at the daybook before you summon the map.

Again, the whispered and unhurried, but quietly concerned and disembodied voice, descended onto her. This time, she perceived from the corner of her eye the merest flicker in the crevice of a wall. It was gone before she could investigate.

Summoning the "daybook" for the map, the listing of who had taken it out and returned it, Elise found a list of users, but otherwise, there were no entries. A footnote said it was available at DUFS General Staff War Room—only by application to the real-world office.

Had she made the summons, it would have been like a giant red flag to the DUFS. The critical map could not be obtained through the CORE, and a legitimate user would have known that. There was no hope of doing this without a lot of skin in the game—her skin.

Fluttering up into the reality of Toad Hall, Elise was elated. Damp from sweat, trembling, and flirting with nausea, she had succeeded—and failed. Sleep eluded her. *How to proceed?*

Mission One: Find out what happens to a citizen when he gets scanned. Then spoof it on demand.

Will Butler was in charge of finding and spoofing a DIRD-E, but he needed her to capture a eusum.

Mission Two: Find the location and start time for the invasion.

Initially, the two missions had appeared separate: one to feed themselves and one to feed the Color Guard's insatiable hunger for information. It was now apparent that they were the same. She would be unable to impersonate her way into DUFS HQ unless she could survive a high-level scanning.

After hours of turning on her uncomfortable bed, Elise fell into a fitful sleep. A dream invaded her rest. She found herself on a vast stage. Dark, menacing crowds sat unseen in the audience. As she tried to leave, she found herself unable, her hands and feet pierced by cruel cords. She looked up the cords to find they were manipulated by a dark puppeteer with no face, forcing her to dance to an oddly undanceable, unknown tune.

Awaking exhausted in the early-morning light of late summer but too agitated to attempt sleep, Elise rewarded herself with a sumptuous breakfast of Bakon-flavored spinach on toast and prepared to go once more into the openCORE. It was easier each time. She dropped into the middle of a deserted expanse of territory. Only a small arts council porpoised in the distance, fountaining up in party colors as she watched. Moving steadily to a position near the DUFS HQ, she set up shop behind a barrier of antiquated regulations, neglected almost since the time of their creation.

Scanning must be done frequently here, she reasoned. She had seen nothing of it yesterday and wondered how something so apparently ubiquitous had eluded her notice. After an hour, she was none the wiser. Fifty-seven miscreants had been dragged into the squat, black, bristling urchin, wriggling on black spines like red-crawlers on a fishing hook. No signal, no data pack, no flashes of light.

Elise tried dim-flipping to isolate as many individual signals as might exist. *Also nothing.*

After most of the day spent in fruitless labor, Elise surfaced, her interface looking a used-up lavender. She ran off to make a few purchases during the last hour the shops were open, careful to make only small, seemingly random buys: lightbulbs, screwdriver, several pulpy apples, and two cushions in lieu of a bed. All the better to allay any curiosity among the merchants of Flatbush Avenue.

Over the next week, her work, switching from one highly scanned area to another and trying to strobe through the dimensions, also produced nothing. Her one discovery was of ambivalent significance. Elise came to expect the small shadow at least once during any trip to the openCORE. A small darkness would ooze out of a crevice to puddle nonchalantly in the broad noon of the CORE. If she looked at it too steadily, it would vanish with a flick, like a sea anemone in retreat, and not reappear for the remainder of the visit. *Timid? Embarrassed?*

Today's stakeout at the CORE-extension of the Water Distribution Station Number Thirty-Two, she had hoped to be more fruitful than the first several sites she had tried. Customers were routinely wanded to get their allotment of potable water from the trucks that serviced the more derelict portion of the KronHides neighborhood. When the real-world "morning rush" was over, Elise sighed. Nothing.

She regarded the sliver of blackness peeking out very slightly in a crevice of the cobbled surface of the CORE in a corner of the water station.

You know, you're not fooling anyone, she said, softly.

The blackness froze, in some way becoming instantaneously solid.

Oh, don't be like that, Tar Baby. I'm just having fun with you! she continued.

She looked again, and the small crevice was empty. The "Tar Baby" abandoned her for several more days thereafter until she once more observed it as a thin puddle of a pinkish tan on the low, and unfortunately neon-green, ceiling of an off-track betting lounge.

I don't suppose, said Elise to herself, only slightly louder than necessary, *that anyone could figure out how to examine eusum.*

Silence.

I'm sure it must be too hard for anyone even to attempt.

Silence.

I don't suppose you could help me?

Silence . . . for many long seconds. Elise was about to shrug it off and leave the CORE when . . .

It is possible, came a voice, soft as rain.

Elise smiled. The same voice as before, the same one that had warned her of the maelstrom, the same one that had guided her inside the Map Room—softer, more confident, but more concerned, as well. A form slipped sideways into the space near her, turned around, and became, suddenly, a three-dimensional shape of a tightly bound swirl of darkness.

I am so glad you've chosen to speak with me. I'm—

You are Elise-Jessika.

Elise is enough. Who are you, then?

You can continue to call me Tar Baby. I do not mind. We are made-things, incapable of taking offense.

Elise was gratified to meet her secret benefactor, even as he gave evidence of his stalking her. She should have been incensed.

That tells me nothing. Are you like EffieCee, an entity of the openCORE—like Frog?

I am like both Frog and EffieCee, alike and different, the soft voice said. Somehow, the voice sounded amused. *You need have no worries. I am not being ridden now. No one hears what you are saying other than Tar Baby, a made-thing—made for a purpose.*

And for what purpose were you made?

To help a dying child.

So, Tar Baby, what is your real name?

I have had many names. Tar Baby will do for the present, Elise.

I guess you have had many forms in the openCORE, as well. Do you have one with a face I may talk to? Looking at you swirling like that gives me a headache.

I'd like to point out your head is not in the openCORE to suffer any ache I may provide for it. However, is this more satisfactory?

The swirling darkness appeared to slow in segments until a form was visible, if just barely, within the whirlwind. Gradually, pieces arranged themselves and the figure of a young man, about her own age, appeared, nonchalantly repositioning a wayward lock of hair, and smiled.

Much better! Pleased to meet you, Tar Baby, said Elise and bowed to the newly revealed entity.

Your servant, Mademoiselle Elise, the entity returned, bowing as well.

You called me for a reason, Mademoiselle Elise? Something about the eusum? So, why don't you snag a few yourself? There're many about, said the entity, sounding genuinely puzzled.

I don't see any, said Elise.

No? Let me try this.

Immediately, the volume in front of them was filled with rapidly flitting points of light. The entity shot out a suddenly unnaturally long arm to snag one. It writhed in his grasp. Once captured, Elise saw that it was a small, cone-like apparatus.

How come we couldn't see them at first? What'd you do to make them appear? asked Elise.

I slowed down the clock speed.

Won't that screw things up for the whole computer?

Shouldn't. The interrupts for these are random, as you'd expect. The cause will still precede the effect. The DUFS at the other end will hardly notice.

And you can show me how to change the clock speed of an area.

An N-dimensional volume. Yes.

If I take some of the eusum, won't the scanners know they're gone?

Of course, but it happens, a eusum getting lost here and there. They are not very smart. If it is not a persistent problem, I don't think the DUFS will send anyone to investigate.

She turned back to the task, plucking eusum as they passed. Within seeming minutes, she and Tar Baby had captured a dozen, placing them into a container that her new companion conjured up on the spot. It reminded Elise of capturing fireflies in the warm summer days of a Colorado childhood, keeping them overnight as a reluctant nightlight only to release in the morning.

Now, let's go to the DIRD-E, said Tar Baby.

I don't know where it is, countered Elise.

We don't need to know. They do—the eusum.

There are so many of them. How are we to follow just the one?

Without comment, Cain shot out a hand, elongating in pursuit, to catch up another cone neatly and drag it back to them before passing a hand over it. Now the cone was a bright, pulsing scarlet. Elise laughed at the neatness of the trick.

Standing next to the entity, Elise watched as he released the cone and it darted off. Even with the clock-time reduced, it was difficult to follow. Within minutes, even Tar Baby had lost it. They repeated the procedure three more times before a squat, wart-like body came into view. The last pulsing red light disappeared into it, which Elise now saw was honeycombed with entrances like a dovecote. Within moments, the blinking light emerged and flitted over their heads. Elise made careful note of the coordinates in all the dimensions of the openCore. It seemed much too neat.

And you figured this all out on the spur of the moment, did you, Tar Baby? asked Elise, trying to keep her voice jovial and teasing, but suddenly wary of the ease with which they had succeeded.

It seemed to be a reasonable way to go about it, Elise. Did I do something wrong? he responded, turning to her, the solemn face now creased with worry.

To Elise, he actually sounded anxious, worried that he had displeased her.

Absolutely nothing you do seems to be wrong. You seem too good to be true, Elise said, again jesting with him.

The solemn young man smiled. *Then perhaps you should stop looking. If you think me too good to be true, you are, of course, correct.*

Okay, okay. You're fine. I just didn't feel it should be so easy. I should leave. I need to let my friend know where to find the DIRD-E.

Do you mean Frog? He is on his way here already. I called him in anticipation of your desire to let him know.

What? You know Frog?

There are not a lot of entities in the openCORE, Elise. It is inevitable I should know him. This is reasonable.

Yeah, sure, said Elise, her uneasiness, like a small insect, crawling up her spine. Rather than a random personality whom she had discovered on her own, Tar Baby was somehow a known quantity—just not known to her.

She was saved from further speculation by the arrival of the mirrored Frog, who waved and slid along unconcernedly until he was within range of the slower clock-speed effect, which appeared to emanate from Tar Baby himself.

Whoa! Where did all these flying things come from?

Elise, trying to regain some lost initiative, said, *Those are eusum, Frog. That's the DIRD-E over there, and apparently, you already know Tar Baby. He turned down the clock speed so that we can see them.*

Tar Baby? Frog laughed, sounding like a chorus of monkeys. *What have you been telling this poor girl, Cain?* Without waiting for an answer, Frog turned to Elise and said, *I don't know what this rascal has been saying, but this is Cain, oldest of us entities— meanest, too, when I come to think about it.*

Cain? Elise froze, her actions suddenly appearing so reckless, incautious—stupid. She looked around her as if the words spoken aloud would bring instantaneous retribution welling up from the stolid gray substrate itself.

I'm sorry, Frog . . . and whoever you are. I must be late—for something. I have to leave, she said.

Without waiting for any response, Elise began to ascend back to reality, emerging gasping and nauseated into the old house, the stink of rotten eggs surrounding her. She vomited and then took a bath.

When she had recovered somewhat, she put away her interface, neglected on the dusty floor in her panic, and started the charging profile, slowly and meticulously, as if that might make up for endangering the whole mission with her gullibility. For a day afterward, all she could do was sit in the corner of the empty back room of Toad Hall and hug herself when the tremors of terror returned. *How could she be so stupid?* She knew about Cain, had warned herself away from contact with it. She had made that promise to herself and to Will, repeatedly. Nevertheless, Cain had been able to penetrate to the center of both critical missions from almost the beginning.

She must be the most inept spy in all the long history of spydom! She wished she knew how much information Cain already had—unless it was already too late. She wanted to send a message to Will on the terahertz to keep him abreast of the situation but realized that must wait until after the moon rose that afternoon. Regardless, it would be better that Will was no part of this project. If she were caught, Will should not attempt any heroics. So far, Cain had done nothing overtly harmful, but the current situation was like living with a sword over her head. All Jourdaine had to do was ask the right question and she—all of them—were dead men too stupid to fall down.

It was hunger that finally drove her out of her hole. Elise had been too intimidated to shop, watching for DUFS to arrest her, convinced that Cain had betrayed her. With her supplies purposefully kept small so as to avoid suspicion of hoarding, Elise was down to the last few scraps of moldy week-old bread before she relented.

If she could not get food, she would have to abandon Toad Hall and go back to the Grove roundhouse, the travel likely exposing her to more scanning than she might receive from mere food shopping. Twisting up her courage to the sticking point, she made a dash to the stores just ten minutes before closing, netting a day-old krill loaf, quinoa stir-fry, and wilted radish greens. It would have to do. She was almost back to Toad Hall before they accosted her.

"A moment, cit'zen," said a smirking, acned youth just as she turned the corner off Nordstand Avenue.

Please, God, no!

"Yes, officer?"

"Step this way, routine wanding. Where are you going?"

"Ensign Chomsky. Jorge is it? Pleased to meet you, Ensign. Able-bodied Seaman First Class Bonhoffer, Jessika, 530227707. I am going to a house I just rented. Just down Quincy, almost to Throop, 1438B. Why?" said Elise, the memorized speech with its memorized nonchalance tripping off her tongue just like during rehearsal. *From now on I have to wing it.*

Chomsky approached, a squad of faceless DUFS at his back, brandishing the black wand, electricity crackling along its edge. He passed the wand over her chest with a faint smile on his face.

Chomsky looked at the reading and said, "Odd, cit'zen. The reading is—difficult to interpret. I think I may need to examine the site." He leered at her and started to press Elise against the rough brick wall, his hand coming up under her seaman's jacket and pressing against her breasts.

The DUFS prevented escape. The man-boy leered at her, looking drunk from lust and power. Elise hesitated and brought a knee up to massage the man's gonads in a meaningful and almost-painless manner. He gasped.

"Ensign, I'll have your commander's name and your number, now. You don't play these games with a sailor, Skippy," she said under her breath, her lips within inches of the boy's ear.

"Oh, sir! Captain Wilardine Jacobs. Sir! Number 599339595. Sir! Please, sir! I meant no disrespect. Sir!"

"Of course you meant disrespect, Ensign Chomsky. How stupid are you, or do you think *I'm* the stupid one, Ensign Chomsky? *Well?*"

"Please! I'm a fool. I don't know what I was thinking. Please don't report me to my commander."

"Do you mean Captain Wilardine Jacobs? That commander?"

"Yes. Yes! I mean no! Please don't report me!" He was nearly shrieking now, and Elise let him down.

"All right, Jorge Chomsky, number 599339595. I won't. Watch it. My O A will report you whatever happens to me, Sab'?"

"Yessir! Let my men escort you home, sir. *Please?"*

"Not on your life, Skippy. Turn around and walk a hundred meters north. Sab'?"

"Yes! Yes! Sir!"

And it had been over. Elise walked home slowly, distressed, trying to keep from embarrassing herself in her terror.

It had been the crispness of the man's uniform that made her tough it out. *Way too new for a veteran.* Still, she could not sleep. For a spy, her cover, the persona she had laboriously learned to inhabit, was the single most important piece of her spycraft. Blindingly clever technology, obscure codes, and Sarin capsules were nothing unless she could melt away into invisibility. Instead, she had brought herself to the attention of the enemy both inside and outside the CORE. For the first time in years, she prayed.

ITS EXCELLENCY THE AMBASSADOR

CONGRESSIONAL AUDITORIUM 10, COLUMBIANA, RSA

10:43 A.M. 20 AUGUST 2029

Malila jerked her elbow away from Jesse, grabbed the chair on which the chairman had been sitting, and stepped lightly to the conference table. Jesse, a knife appearing almost magically in his hand, went into a crouch and backed himself against the table, waiting for the first or most foolish of the capital guardsmen to attack.

Malila's voice rang above the hubbub. "You say I have no authentication. But you have not *asked* for any. A member of the ruling council of the Scorch will be here shortly! At least have the decency to listen to Splanch, if you will not listen to me!"

Malila's words brought everything to a halt.

Eventually, the legislators took seats in the audience, and the chairman gaveled the meeting back into order.

"Madame Băsescu, we will hear the witness out, and then you may do as you see fit. Until then, the dignity and prerogatives of *this* house will be observed." He turned to the officers and motioned them to stand in place.

Jesse turned to look up at his love. Grim, her jaw set firmly and her face flushed, it must have been a trick of the fluorescent lights, he thought, when her face took on a sickly green color. He watched in the suddenly quiet room as Malila raised her blouse to just below her breasts. Jesse could see, as close as he was to her, that her new green tattoo was no longer flat but bulged noticeably above the surface of her navel. As he watched, the green bulge became a vine, sinuously spinning open, twining and winding across Malila's belly before it rose past the level of her breasts and twisted itself loosely about her neck.

The pale-green blossom at the center of the stalk appeared to spin open, almost like a toothless mouth. There was a rasping, a guttural coughing sound, and Jesse looked back at Malila and away from the malignant vine. She was gray, the color of death. Jesse reached up to grasp her arm to feel a pulse, only to have her again thrust him away, vigorously, belying what his hands felt: her arm was cachectic, drained of its warmth and vitality.

The stalk, its center now a rosette of vivid green serrated leaves, pointed at the audience on the dais and said in a loud, adamant—

cruel—voice that echoed in the room, "I am a sprouting of Splanch. Call me the Voice of the People. I wish to submit my credentials as an ambassador for the People of what you call the Scorch. My government has directed me to pursue a course to bring peace between our peoples and a mutual defense against our common enemy."

"My God," said Băsescu and fled the room.

"The girl—it's eating her!" said the representative of the great state of Colorado before turning and vomiting onto the carpet.

"I assure you that Messenger Chiu will survive and be well. She volunteered to be my host, knowing the price," said Splanch.

"We need to help her! Get something—someone. Shoot it—oh, Lord . . . ," said Reynolds.

To Jesse, Malila looked frozen, a gray-green manikin, lifeless, all vitality drained into the parasitical plant. He watched as she withered further, getting thinner, the shadows in her face deepening, making no move to cover herself.

"Major Johnstone?" said the chairman, jogging Jesse's attention away from Malila. "Will you share with the committee your estimation of the military prowess of the Scorch?"

Jesse tore himself away from watching Malila die.

"Aye. Aye. Th' Scorch kin defend itself. We had o'er 10 percent casualties. Progressin' only foot by foot 'til th' plants cried a truce an' Malila cam' to me. We would ha' quit an' tried to retreat if thay hadna. Th' Scorch controls what happens thare. Nae us," said Jesse before turning back to Malila, ensnared in the Voice's grip. "Can't ye see ye're killin' her!" he said, his own voice now angry.

In response, Malila gave a gasp and then a groan. "My blouse, Jesse. Pull it down." Another gasp and groan. "It's frightening them."

"Nae just thaim, lass. Am ah aff ta' lose ye?"

"I don't understand you, my love. I could use a drink of water."

Jesse grabbed the pitcher of water after leaping to the table and allowed Malila to sip it, her lips cracked and discolored. Sending off two of the policemen to get a stretcher and call an ambulance, Malila refused to sit.

Unperturbed, the Voice continued. "Whereas the area indicated by this map," and here it waved a growth along its stem that had only minutes before sprouted and elaborated a tabloid-sized leaf, "shows the limits of territory claimed by the Unity or America but is actually unoccupied by either of you. Only the People of the Scorch hold sovereignty there. Indeed, only four humans, Unity or American, have entered into this area without our sufferance for a score of winters, and one such is here present. The People own the Scorch by the right of occupancy and as such request that their neighbors acknowledge a reality they are powerless to alter and ethically obliged to confirm.

"Moreover, even now, we are sheltering America from its powerful opponent, the Democratic Unity. We are aware that they still raid you via flying vehicles, but no land assault has occurred for thirty winters. You owe us gratitude for that, ladies and gentlemen.

"And finally, we can be each other's best trading partner. Production of lumber alone, delivered at convenient locations along the frontier, justify a trade treaty between the People of the Scorch and America, not to mention medicinals and products grown to specification."

The chairman, wiping his mouth, started rapping his gavel.

Afterward, Jesse admitted to himself that the old boys and girls put as good a face on it as they could. They very rapidly stopped their harrumphing and trumpeting and admitted that they would present the proposals to the government with their recommendation.

After the meeting adjourned, Voice was introduced to Jesse.

"I am joyed to meet you finally. We have heard of Quicksilver for many winters. It is a pleasure to hear you, face to face," said the rosette of a mouth.

"May I ask a question?" asked Jesse.

"Of course."

"You are living inside Malila Chiu. Are you a parasite?"

"A good question, but I am afraid the distinctions break down when it comes to the People. Has not Malila gained a good deal from my temporary presence within her? She found you. You both wanted that, did you not? She is alive because of me. Gratitude must count in my favor, surely? Necessity, as well. How else were we going to gain an audience with a nation that chops up or saws through, in your case, every friendly emissary we send? We have tried many times with little success, but to answer your question, I think the best description is *commensalism*: we, the People and Malila, eat at the same table. And with that, I must leave."

The green rosette wilted and retracted. Within a few moments, it was again the vivid green tattoo around Malila's navel. Jesse gave a grunt of disgust, but Malila's eyes brightened immediately, and she smoothed down her blouse slowly and clumsily before looking down at Jesse, a tear in her eye.

"Are you all right, lass? The litter's here. That must have been horrible. We'll be off to the hospital in a second."

"I am fine, Jesse. I feel wonderful. I am always a little sad when the sprouting leaves. At first, I did not realize that when it speaks, I am unable to. It was frightening, but I have gotten used to it."

Malila allowed the Old Man to help her down from the table, stumbling a bit. When he offered to carry her out, she laughed and kissed him, skipping ahead out of the conference room.

Jesse did not skip.

They got back to their hotel room with little other fanfare. As the door closed behind them, Jesse turned to Malila and said, "When we talk, does Splanch hear us?"

"Of course. How could he not hear us? But if that weirds you out, my love, I can ask him to ignore us for a while."

"I have na' choice, I see, but to talk to you both at once. That thing has been feeding off you for weeks, then? How horrible for you!"

"Stop it, Jesse. I asked Splanch to help me find you. If it hadn't indwelt me, I would never have known about your implant, the one you did not tell me about. Splanch brought us together. He feels sorry for us."

"For Americans?"

"No. For humans. He thinks we are all so lonely. I can see why he says it."

"You're not making any sense, lass. I'm sure we can get it removed under anesthesia. You won't feel a thing, and then we can repair any damage. You'll be as good as new."

"I am better than new, Jesse. I never want Splanch to leave."

"I don't understand you, Malila, love."

"No, I can see you do not, Jesse."

That night, Jesse slept on the floor in front of the door to the bedroom. "Security," he said.

A SUMMONS OF THE SYNTHESIS

MOTHER HOUSE OF SYNTOPIA
SUNDAY AFTERNOON, AUGUST 21

Silence inside the small room of the Syntopia, like a large gray cat feigning sleep, sat.

Harold Colina, still staring into the ersatz fire, nudged the silence away finally. "I do have some good news, though. The Chancellor wants me to be on a governmental liaison committee. Something to do with advice to the central government. The Kansas City boys have finally decided to let academia in on decision making. Have to see the chairman tomorrow," said Colina as he finished his sherry.

Nortvengler smiled. "Ol' Dodgey Fleischer? He used to be a member of the chapter when we were grad students. Still a sympathizer. Great day! It means we can directly influence the decision makers, get them to see the only way for the culture to survive is to become part of the Unity. Surrender at the first shot! Imagine that, Harry!" said Benny as he relit his ancient briar pipe, cranky at the best of times, and sent a smoke ring into the fireplace.

"Dodgey died about nine years ago, Benny. No, the new guy did his graduate work at Tulane, political science. Name's Jason MacDonald. Rather a hard nut. Very competent, of course, but keeps his own counsel. I have no complaints."

For a moment, Benny looked confused. *"Dodgey's dead?"*

Before Harry could answer, Benny said, "Of course, of course. Do your best for the Order, and all. Any idea when the war will start?"

"Only rumors, well, better than rumor, really. The best information had it starting this month, but now the second week of September is what is bandied about. I don't think they have a clue. Militias are to be mustered in Chattanooga, no idea yet where the regular army is concentrated. No one has a clue where the blow will fall."

"Militia? It is a continuing travesty and embarrassment that the military-industrial complex has infiltrated into the very fabric of the academic enclave!"

"Oh, Benny. Do be quiet!"

OFFICE OF THE UNIVERSITY CHANCELLOR
10:32 A.M. AUGUST 22, 2129 AD

He had been *summoned*. He had not shared that with Benny. No one *summoned* anymore. Even the *great* men did not summon; they requested, enabled, "would be pleased if," scheduled, or facilitated, but never summoned. It just wasn't done any longer, too reminiscent of the dark days before the Meltdown. Nevertheless, *Professor Harold Colina had been summoned.*

He entered the outer office of University Chancellor Jason MacDonald, PhD (PolSc). The room displayed its trophies of power: framed letters of acclamation, several gubernatorial proclamations, the actual Chain of Office, and an attractive woman. Past her youth, with the grace of the gentry and the demeanor of a bulldog, she sat at the desk protecting the door to the inner sanctum. There were no seats.

A noise, tuned to be felt by the soles of the feet rather than heard by the ears, sounded briefly. The inner door drifted open.

"The chancellor will see you now, Professor," announced the Bulldog, standing and motioning him through the door. He had been a frequent visitor to this room earlier in his career when H. Dodgericht Fleischer had been in charge. He remembered the room well: displaying generous windows from floor to ceiling on three sides with gilt-titled books shelved in between. In the past, there had been no fear.

"Harold! So excellent to see you again. I've missed our little chats. Please come in and make yourself at home!" A large, bluff, blond man, with a doughy softness about him making him appear too young even to hold an assistant professorship, rose from behind a massive dark oaken desk and came around it to shake Harry's hand.

"It is always a pleasure to see you, Chancellor. The last occasion we talked, I believe, was the last Christmas party—no, the year before, wasn't it?"

The chancellor had the grace to smile. Harry was shown to one end of a large red-leather sofa while the chancellor inhabited the other. Coffee was served by the gentle hand of the Bulldog, and a generous slug of venerable brandy added, once she had left, by the hand of Chancellor MacDonald himself.

"Professor Colina—Harry—you are the most senior active-faculty member at the university."

"Nonsense. Alvin Newton was Dr. Gobertson's TA when I took English Literature here as a freshman," Harry chuckled. Al Newton was always good for a small bet and a *sotto voce* off-color joke at faculty meetings."

"Professor Newton, I believe, has been emeritus for several months now."

"Oh, yes, now I remember. Well, I suppose I am, then. What about it?" Harry started to feel that the conversation was getting away from him. Too many names, too many things, too many years, all blending together. "I still teach my grad students. I have tenure!"

The chancellor's face altered as Harry watched. "You misunderstand, sir. In point of fact, however, your TA teaches one of your three classes, the other two being graduate seminars, but that is beside the point." The great blond visage of the chancellor melted, and he was all warm fellowship once more. "I wish to recruit you for a mission." Without waiting for Harry's reaction, the chancellor plunged on.

"I've been asked by the national president to be part of the delegation to the conference with the plants in Atlanta—next month. I know that is scarce notice, and I apologize. I just got the invitation myself. It's exploratory, of course: recently discovered culture, war looming, you know," said MacDonald.

Harry did not.

"Atlanta has retained many of its public spaces rather well. Good food, pleasant entertainment. It should be fun, but it also needs a certain amount of *gravitas*, the putting of one's best foot forward and all that."

"And you think I might . . . ," said Harry, thinking that the university would finally acknowledge his advancements in convexity limitations in semi-metric spaces.

MacDonald smiled, showing more tooth than actually polite. "Oh, never for the slightest moment would I impose on your good offices, Professor, not that you aren't imminently qualified, a man in vigorous middle age, the . . . um . . . past-master of the subtle negotiation. Not at all. You see, I have had to designate—

for political reasons, you understand—young Professor Fetschuler from the Mathematics Division as the 'second in command' of the delegation. If, and I stress if, I am detained or called away, Felix will be the face and voice of the university at the negotiations to these . . . these . . . whatever they are. It is critically important that I have a more mature member to support Dr. Fetschuler if needs be."

Harry's nascent smile faded. He was being asked to be a nursemaid for a rising young faculty member. If there were success, kudos would go to MacDonald. If failure, Fetschuler would no doubt be protected "for the good of the university." Harry's role was as a lightning rod. The insult was palpable. The chancellor's crocodilian smile grew, seeming to suck all the light out of the office and keep it for its own.

OFFICE OF PROFESSOR NORTVENGLER
LATER THAT AFTERNOON

"But we *must* both go, Benny," said Harry, punctuating his comments with a newly lit cigar, sending hieroglyphs of smoke spiraling toward the ceiling of Professor Emeritus Benjamin Nortvengler's study. Harry had barged into his office while he and his TAs were going over preliminaries for the course that they gave in his name. Harry had insisted that he needed to talk in private. He would not even sit, bad leg or no, as the teaching assistants filed out.

"And why must *I* go on this quixotic quest, Brother Archimedes? If I thought it were important, then, of course, I would be there like a shot. If MacDonald were starting negotiation with the Unity, I would move Heaven and Earth to be there to encourage some sense into the Americans. But to talk to kudzu? The vegetables may take as a provocation my luncheon salad," replied Benny before he scooped his briar out of his jacket pocket to charge with tobacco. He pointedly ignored his guest and, turning in his chair, flamed the bowl with an electric lighter, coaxing it into life until he was wreathed in blue smoke. "Besides, my specialty is philosophy. How is that possibly associated with an embassy to make first contact with some sort of jungle plant?" he said, looking past the ordered chaos of his office and out the window to the trees clothed in the dusty and tired green of the late summer.

"For one thing, and you cannot be unaware, the invasion is coming, Benny. The central government actually believes that this embassy at this time must be important, important enough to get the chancellor to be the stalking horse for their efforts. I have no doubt that MacDonald, if the thing looks like it may come to naught, will plead some academic emergency and drop the whole thing into Fetschuler's lap. The boy is likely to panic, and someone has to be there to try to pick up the pieces."

"Precisely. Best if we all get as far away from this debacle as possible and start looking after our own interests until this thing has blown over. I had hoped the national government was seeing reason and was going to negotiate with the Unity. This is a sideshow.

"As for me, I plan to go to the Demarchy. Charlene's never been. They offered me a visiting professorship in 2120, and I intend to make good on it," said Benny, and he smiled, but sheepishly.

"Don't be daft, Benny. Remember what happened in '09 when Wasserman went to San Francisco! You are passing up a huge opportunity here. Do you realize that there are over sixteen hundred square miles in the Scorch and that huge area is held by fewer than a dozen individuals? All the other plants that people talk about as being the Scorch are merely dumb actors. We could get in on the ground floor of something spectacular!"

Benny waved his pipe-bearing hand dismissively, launching new streamers of smoke ceiling-wards. "You know I have never been much interested in all the nonsense which comes out of the frontier. The tales are ludicrous, just stories for the credulous."

"You know it's not nonsense. You *know* the plants have been changed. The People's Republic knew the Siltoven mutagen[13] had never been used before—or since. In any civilized country, the creators of that horror would have been taken out and shot. They devastated most of the nation, even discounting the other actions."

"Do you mean by 'other actions' killing off most normal plant life and turning the ones it didn't kill into weird monsters? Do you mean that kind of 'other action'?" said Benny, between puffs.

"It seems you have read a little about what comes out of the frontier, after all," said Harry, grinning at him. Benny harrumphed and refused to say more.

His friend, discovering his cigar had died of neglect, relit it with a torch of several matches before blowing a smoke ring up to join the lowering gray cloud already present in the room. After a few more seconds, he continued. "There are apparently dozens of changed species, each species with some individuals remaining mundane and some changing—*except for the Sage Men.* They all seem to be different from one another: one is lichen-like, one a tree-like thing, two vine-like. One lives in a swamp, one by a river, two on mountaintops. They are all different from all other plants and from each other. Yet, they can all speak. They all seem to be able to communicate with each other almost instantaneously."

---

[13] An experimental herbicide developed in the 2040s, based on altering the genome of the rapidly growing portions of plants, disrupting metabolism, and eventually killing the plant

Benny shrugged. "Interesting, but they're plants. These talking dandelions ought to be told to sit down and be quiet."

"Would it interest you to know that a platoon of the regular army was sent into the Scorch early this month? They suffered huge casualties and had been effectively stopped by the plant life."

"Bunch of amateurs. When the Unity invades, the American generals are going to needlessly sacrifice the youth of this nation on the altar of their incompetence!" said Benny, suddenly frowning as he glanced up at a hologram of a young man in an RSA uniform on the wall above his desk. He looked away.

Harry snorted. "Amateurs? The military advisor for that foray was Jesse Johnstone."

"So that's where he got off to after murdering Padilla. The Great Hero of the Frontier wasn't able to bend the plants to his will? I hope people take note and realize what a fraud he is," said Benny, turning back to face his friend, his eyes now bright from unshed tears.

Harry continued. "The attack stopped only when a girl emerged from the jungle. Turns out she is an escapee from the Unity and knows the Old Man. She's been parasitized by the Scorch and is their ambassador to America—her credentials accepted in Columbiana."

Leaning over heavily to collect some fallen papers, the professor sat up with a small groan and said, "Peace conference? With plants? What standing do they have? Tell them to clear out. America owns the land they've been squatting on."

"Not really. Old American law from the first republic. The land's been abandoned. No one has paid tax on it. No one has lived on it but the changed plants. They have possession, and apparently the ability to protect themselves. The Old Republic used the statute to snatch away Indian lands on the same basis, and now the Scorch has used it on America in turn. How's that for irony?"

"Okay, the plants won. Draw a line and tell them not to cross it. End of conversation," waved Benny.

"Don't be dull, Benny. America finds itself with a new and powerful neighbor on most of its eastern border. We made peace with the Canadians decades ago, and it has served the country well. There is much to talk about."

"All right, assuming that, why should two old men be sucked into this vortex of enthusiasm? I have a paper to finish for the Federation meeting. I'm a philosopher. All this is peripheral to my interests. I don't need another picture on my wall, even if it is with a bunch of plants."

Professor Colina stubbed out the last inch of his cigar in the standing ashtray and lit another thin cigar, sending a new smoke ring to the ceiling before he answered. "The ambassador, did I mention, is a rather striking young lady. She has an escort, one Dr. Johnstone, by the way. Did I fail to tell you that?"

Hierarch Zeno, the highest-ranked officer of the mother house to the worldwide Order of Syntopia, turned to regard his friend.

"Harry, that was a cheap shot."

"Yes, I know. I'm rather proud of it myself."

"Your glee will be recorded and may be used in evidence against you, I hope you know."

"I'll take my chances."

"Are you sure about this?"

"Absolutely. The girl goes nowhere without Johnstone."

"Excellent. The Agnomen may yet die a natural death—as natural as we can manufacture for him."

AFTERNOON, AUGUST 26, 2129 AD

Professor Nortvengler perused the information packet sent to him from the chancellor's office, emblazoned with the seal of Atlanta, a double-headed phoenix. Inside, it was florid with pictures of the venue, one of the new hotels just east of Five Points. Atlanta had not suffered nearly as much damage as the cities around the lakes up north. There, a three-way struggle between Canada, the Unity, and the remaining forces of the Old Republic had reduced the declining metropolises to ruin. Michigan was now solidly Canadian except for Detroit, a Unity garrison. Wisconsin and northern Illinois were depopulated. Indiana had become the wilderness, filled with brigands, bandits, and slavers.

But while the South had seen little of the rapacity of the Unity, it suffered all of the effects of a defeated nation. Atlanta, devastated by neglect, poverty, the collapse of commerce, and the devastations of several plagues, had even lost its city charter at one point in the last century. It was now on the rebound. Like a patient laid low by disease but finally rising to put on old clothes, Atlantans found the city too large for their purposes. Whole blocks in Buckhead were condemned and plowed under, returning them to agriculture. Commuter rail was now just two lines, east toward what used to be Decatur and south to College Park.

Benny could hardly blame them for their boosterism. Atlanta was thriving after the mag rail line went in to Baton Rouge, Memphis, and Saint Louis. Travel south to the Florida cities was still by conventional rail, but even they were beginning to rebound.

The hotel itself, the Marriott Grand Mercure by Hilton, was immense, a city unto itself. Strangely, the actual conferences between the sides were to be held outside, across the street in

Woodruff Park, he noticed with distaste. The celebratory holo at the end of the conference would likely feature him with a sunburnt and peeling nose.

Harry had better be right about Johnstone being in Atlanta, he thought, as he packed a selection of poisons in a false bottom of his briefcase. He picked up and inspected the small pistol he had bought as a student when he had imagined himself the assassin of the Agnomen, before placing it into the briefcase, as well.

KIDDIE PARTY

KAROTKOFF COMPOUND, SAINT LOUIS COUNTY, RSA

11:01 A.M. AUGUST 27, 2129

If she had anything to do with it, Jesse, her self-absorbed and thoughtless kid brother, was going to have a bang-up birthday[14] party. *That* should surprise him.

They were supposed to be here an hour ago. *Just like him, the old coot,* thought Theodora Johnstone Karotkoff, Jesse's oldest sister and most senior critic. She had changed his messy diapers seventy-some years ago for what seemed like an unreasonably long time while the family lived a mouse-like existence in the green hell of the Scorch. They didn't call it the Scorch back then. It had just been their summer cottage in the mountains of eastern Tennessee, the one she and her family had gone to every August since she could remember. Near a shallow brook, the neo-primitive log cabin had

---

[14] July 4, 2051

seemed to grow out of the very forest, with wide, deep cellars for stores, a solar roof, geothermal heating, and a clerestory to make pleasant a hot afternoon.

Leaving Saint Louis that fateful last summer of the old world, only she and David, a year younger, had been observant enough to absorb the anxiety of their parents. Mother had brought along a big cooler packed with dry ice. Dad had brought guns, ammunition, and crates of powder. He and David had built a powder-safe uphill and away from the house their first week there. Mother had been glued to a tablet until the nets went down for the last time, trying to sort out research data she had dragged there and to listen to the newest war at the same time. That left Theo, at twelve—and occasionally Patricia, when she could be gulled into it—to run the house and to babysit Celia and Jesse.

When the end came, the younger kids hardly noticed until we ran out of food that first winter. Eventually, Dad took the Range Rover into Joe Hollow in February, figuring that most of the fuss would be over. He went armed.

Dad would not tell her any more of the story until years later when he let it slip. One man had attacked him as he got out of the car. The man died. After Dad had the remaining bushwhackers load the vehicle with supplies at gunpoint, he paid them with gold and skidded back up Cut Laurel Creek Gap Road, stopping along the way to see if the men were following them. They were.

He shot out the radiator of their rusted-out G-110 and had them facedown in the mud of the road before they knew what had hit them. Cutting off the men's clothes and boot laces, he sent them back down the road just as night was falling. By the time any survivors could mount a punitive expedition, the incessant black rains would have covered the Range Rover's tracks.

Dad laughed at that. Mother tssked. And Jesse just babbled. He was oblivious to all the bad times of the Scorch. To him, it was a big, wonderful game. *Same irrepressible boy, even at seventy-eight.*

And now he was going to marry a child, an enemy soldier, and a . . . what? *The Malila creature is what?* The reports were not credible. Theo could not believe that somehow the girl had been parasitized by an intelligent plant. Theo reminded herself not to be unkind. Rumors had a way of twisting the truth. She had lived in the Scorch long enough to know of the Sage Men, of course.

The entourage arrived, rather more than she had been told to plan for. *Typical.* A door opened and Jesse emerged, all teeth, pride shimmering off him as he handed the girl out of the door. She emerged from the limousine in a light-green, sheath-like affair. *Actually, rather nice.* The crowd—family from four generations, in addition to Jesse's old school friends, political hopefuls who wanted Jonathan's benediction, Theo's own set of social notables, some government officials, and a few of the university faculty— applauded. Her brute of a brother fawned over the girl like a trained bear.

From reports, the girl seemed guileless enough. Sober-solemn and mature, almost too grim. *No gold-digger.* Was this lucky number four? Losing a husband or wife on the frontier was hardly unusual. Losing three of them in succession was decidedly improvident of Jesse. *Just like him.*

Jesse helped Malila out of the limousine once Kazinsky gave him the sign that the compound was safe. His men had fought over the privilege of bodyguard duty, until Jesse established a rotation. Theo and Jon's place up Williams Creek Road was difficult to find. Jesse's recent sojourn in Saint Louis had reacquainted him with the place, fortunately. Their entourage—*the Messenger's* entourage— had arrived from Kansas City without undue fuss.

The RSA was generous with the People's resources, Jesse thought. While they waited for word about the peace conference, Malila was given the freedom to roam America—with Jesse as her bodyguard-babysitter—and a squad of soldiers, Kazinsky's squad from the Scorch, to act as crowd control and parole officer. Theo, knowing a social feather to put into her cap when she saw one, had immediately offered a safe residence in the far and wild reaches of Saint Louis County until the conference.

Jesse was just as pleased. It gave him a chance to show off Malila to Theo. Ever since he could remember, Theodora had been like a mother hen to him. She fussed and fretted at him if he was within reach but was anxious for him when he was not. He could not recall a time when she had been pleased with him, except on express orders from his parents.

At eighty-nine, she was hardly showing her age. "After we gave it to the guinea pig" (meaning Jesse), Theo had received her own Ageplay treatment. That had required bleeding him. Jesse had screamed in surprise and juvenile consternation. It was his first solid memory. By luck, the timing of the treatment for Theo was perfect. Instead of the too-big-by-half bulk of Jesse, Theo was elegantly slim, slightly taller than average, showing the high cheekbones of the Johnstones and the serenity of the Brownes. Her hair, by whatever means, was still the color of her youth: a luxuriant chestnut that fell to her shoulders.

Compared to Theo's elegance, Malila was a small, exotic bloom: smaller, slighter, and glowing with life—*most of it human.*

The party was quite a success, thought Theo, hours later, as she directed the cleanup by the squad of daughters and granddaughters under her command.

Jesse, in his silly buckskins, had contrived to look embarrassed at the fuss she made over his birthday, saying he had forgotten how old he was—and wishing she had forgotten, as well. The occasion served as a coming-out soirée for Malila, as well. Theo could no longer give any credence to the whispered reports about her mission to the capital, not after meeting her. She was strange, of course, her speech brittle and abrupt without any of the graces of civilized America, but *what was one to expect with foreigners?* Malila's limos left. Theo had been told, they would wend a twisting and turning gallivant over most of the roads of Missouri, stopping on occasion at tourist sights of interest, before going back to the capital. Jesse and Malila would not be passengers, however, having moved into the little manse on the far side of the property with enough space for their soldier friends to bivouac around them. Theo smiled at her newfound command of the military lingo.

It was nice to have the boy home.

MORNING SICKNESS

GROVE ROUNDHOUSE
1330 SEPTEMBER 5, 2129

"Frog looks sick."

Hecate left the makeshift table she had created from cinderblocks and a scrap of plywood retrieved from Henry's erstwhile hoard. He had not returned.

The desk's whole surface was now covered in diagrams and timetables for Operation Caviar, as Will had named it. It made no sense to her either before or after he explained it.

She came over as Will lifted the lid of Frog's new box, the one vacated by the last of the original spindles. Will reported that Frog had assumed residency in these enlarged quarters with distaste, complaining they tasted of "bad fish and burnt eggplant." Inside the tainted quarters, Frog did indeed look sick, now an unlovely shade of burnt umber. He puddled inside the box like syrup instead of a viscous gel. The tube of her blood, which had been so difficult to obtain, still sat unused in its holder inside the red box. There was no going back to his old box, however. Frog was now chubby with the extended charging routine and a nightly feeding regimen. Will had the decency to do it after Hecate was asleep, allowing Frog to feed off him without going into the CORE. For the most part, Frog let Will sleep as he fed. Will snored.

"Will, are you sure this is worth it? If Frog dies or is damaged, then neither of us have any access to the CORE. I know a part-time interface was okay with me, but not if it means we hurt Frog. He means too much to you—to us."

They, Hecate and Will, had decided to try to duplicate Frog. It would allow Hecate to work in the CORE while Will was the object of the scanners. She would not have to face the horror she felt with the long lines and leering DUFS officers. Exposing herself to that tribulation with a counterfeit implant was more than she thought she could bring off. But with a CORE-interface, especially one that she wore only when she wanted to use it, she could be a real addition to Will's mission. That did not mean she had to like it.

Neither of them had mentioned the obvious. Will was critical to the success of any venture. She was not. Allowing Will to be scanned as they prepared to spoof the nature of the Scanner-eusum-DIRD-E operation added to the risk without increasing the chances of success. Whatever they did would have to work the very first time.

"I think I need to talk to him," said Will.

"You said he's not talking anymore."

"Yes. I know, but what am I going to do? No doubt he's scared. He doesn't do 'scared' well. All I can do is help him through this as best I can. He deserves it."

Hecate said no more, offering only a wan smile. Once Will had situated himself as comfortably as possible in an old, legless upholstered chair they had liberated from the ally backing onto Davsvill Road, Hecate brought Frog to him in the oblong red box. Warmed, the orangey mass's questing pseudopod pressed itself between Will's lips and in through his nose. Hecate looked away before going to reduce lighting, noise, and even the olfactory signals from the frugal lunch they had just eaten, washing up the soup pan. Anything to make it easier for Will—and Frog.

She looked back. Will appeared comatose, moving nothing except his chest in spasmed breaths. It was more than a half hour before Will's eyes fluttered and opened. He rose and returned Frog to his charger without comment.

"Are you okay? Is Frog okay?" asked Hecate, finally, when Will remained silent.

"Petulant, demanding, irrational!" groused Will.

"So more or less normal?"

"Yeah, and he wants to talk to you."

SUMMITING

(The final sprint to the peak, taken with light gear)

HAVERSHAM

DUFS HQ, NYORK, THE UNITY
09.13.17_05_SEPT_AU77 (2129 AD)

Lance Haversham sat down to consider the news, having moved his efforts to discover Jordaine's poisoner, of necessity, into Jordaine's inner sanctum, safe from prying eyes. He did not use the CORE. Reports were sent to him on actual paper, the room now littered with stacks of them. The latest one made him smile.

HP Lurleen Lynch had been no part of the conspiracy, and her advancement would stay. Stibbins, in his estimation, was naïve, as well, complaining loudly to his professional associates about his poor treatment in not getting a similar advancement. Confronted, Stibbins succumbed to babbling terror once he realized there would be no rescue by his patron, an S24 of dubious influence. The interrogators scoured the man's psyche a few times and recovered nothing of importance. "Jourdaine" would dismiss him with a commendation for the public and a private word to the Blues in the hope that a political foe might pick up the man, as well as his professional incompetence, for personal use.

But Ruther had bolted. After a mere two days on the run, the DUFS picked him up stowed away on one of the automated barges traveling south. They dragged him back to Nyork, arriving yesterday. Haversham stood, straightened the several piles of papers he had been dealing with, gave instructions to the pair of orderlies he had acquired, Blankenship and Windsor, and left Jourdaine's care to others for the first time since the beginning of August. He had another important task. Now that Jourdaine was improving, he wanted in on Ruther's interrogation. He took the elevator down to the subbasement.

The room was small, over warm, and damp. Ruther was a bit of a disappointment, as well, reminding him of a corpulent, untidy, and cornered rodent.

"Who were you going to meet?" inquired a narrow-faced man named Beverly Mulhenny.

"No one, no one, officer! I was trying to get away. The nurse manager said he might denounce me."

"We checked, you know. Your nurse manager said you were up for a promo, 'good performance' it says here—"

"He's lying," Ruther shrieked, his wattles trembling, now glistened with sweat.

"Leave him alone for a bit, Bev. Can't ya see you've got him spooked?" said Bruce, the other interrogator: tall, blond, younger than Beverly, and possessed of an apparently perpetual smile.

"Yes, yes. Frightened! Small room, too warm, DUFS. I haven't done anything wrong!"

"Oh now, that isn't quite correct. Is it, cit'zen?" replied Beverly. "There was the absconding. You was absconding, in the first degree. Can't have well-respected HPs absconding anytime they feels like it, can we? Stands to reason."

"Yes, sorry. I am so sorry I tried to run."

"So, who you running *from*, then?" asked Bruce, taking over the questioning as Beverly licked his lips in the shadow of the room.

"I have to go to the toilet. The rules say you must let me."

"Yes, they do, citizen, but they don't actually say *when*," smiled Bruce. "Now, my boss, he's a real bastard. He denounced this other interrogator last month." The big man turned away casually and called over his shoulder to his partner who now was pacing in the far corner of the room. "Hey, Beverly, remember Jerry Strand?"

When he got no response, Bruce turned back and said, "Poor Jerry got no info from this phantom shop-owner, nearly a Sisi he was, and he couldn't get him to talk. So *Jerry* got denounced—*Jerry*! I got nothing against you, now, but I gotta have somethin' to show for all the time we spent with you, cit'zen. You can understand that, can't you?"

"Yes, yes, I understand, of course. They said they'd kill me, but you understand the man was a nothing, somebody picked up unconscious from a skimmer wreck."

"There you go, citizen. That wasn't too hard. The sergeant here will see you to the toilet, won't you, Bev?"

Ruther came back whimpering with some extra bruises, while Beverly returned with a grin and skinned knuckles.

The dam had broken, and the terrified man talked on for three more hours and two toilet breaks, the last taken involuntarily, as Beverly, with Ruther attempting and failing to cling to the bolted-down table, dragged him away from the view of the cameras. It was now apparent that Ruther was a minor operative of a "compliance officer" for a Blue faction ward boss in Brooklyn named Alex Meksi. For a good improvement on his salary, Ruther would do the odd clandestine job when required. He never had any contact with the ward operative, a note being left with his O A anonymously. His paymaster left an envelope in his physical mailbox.

Follow the money, thought Lance Haversham from the observation booth behind the one-way mirror.

"Now, cit'zen, when do you get paid for helping out your friend, Alex?" asked Beverly, smiling.

"He's no friend of mine! I don't get paid regularly, just when I do a job for them."

"Before or after the job?"

"Half and half."

"What about this Iain Galt? Have you been paid for killing him yet?"

"No, no! It was never supposed to kill him. That would have been unethical. It was just supposed to make him dopey so that he wouldn't interfere."

"Interfere with what?"

"How should I know? I don't. You can hit me all you want. I don't know!"

Bev backhanded him, and that more or less ended the interrogation. Once Ruther was safely back in his cell, Beverly,

Bruce, and Haversham talked as Beverly washed and dressed his skinned knuckles.

"It's probably an attack from within the Blues rather than a new faction war," Haversham said.

"That's good. It's only been three months since the last one. What bothers me is that the anonymous instructions were left on the man's O A," said Bruce. "That's illegal! It's supposed to be impossible!"

"So we've got one more accomplice to find. This is not just ward politics," added Beverly. "You're not supposed to be able to send blind messages. If Meksi did that, it probably means that he's got a solid way to scam the CORE. Well above that cuck's pay grade. If you try to follow Ruther's message back upstream, that'll alert the big boys. Needs another way. If we squeeze him a few more times . . . ," said Bev, before licking his chapped lips.

"Nah, just hand him over to the Citizen Satisfaction Bureau. Let them sort him out. Doesn't sound to me like we're gonna get anything more," said Bruce.

"I think we let him go," said Haversham.

The two men looked at him: in surprise, for Bruce, and in horror, for Beverly. Haversham continued. "After I report that our Iain Galt has been sent to a mental hospital, Ruther'll scuttle off and get the last half of his payment. Then we see who makes the drop and squeeze *him*."

"What if he spills his guts to his superior? We won't be able to follow the money trail then."

"Ruther only works when called on—no way to signal upstream. His handler, no doubt, thinks that keeps him safe."

A grin appeared slowly at the corners of Beverly's mouth before growing and broadening until it consumed all expression in the little man's face. Bruce just nodded.

Haversham smiled, as well, thinking it was just a matter of time—just before Jourdaine summoned him.

UNTO THE BREACH

"Once more unto the breach, dear friends, once more;
Or close the wall up with our English dead."—Henry V by W. Shakespeare

TOAD HALL, BROOKLYN, NYORK
10:10 A.M. 07 SEPTEMBER 2129 AD (AU77)

The message from Will, once she had decoded it, was not comforting.

215 message in re C received 444.

Discussed with grn frnd. No prob. F believes C noscotch us. Fireflies XMd and dirty bird hatched. Suggest u talk FEC.

Hang in there. No rndvz

She touched the worksheet on which she had deciphered the message to the heating ring in the kitchen, and it flicked into nothing. The import of the message remained: Frog trusted Cain, Will trusted Frog, Will was making progress with his part of the project, and Elise was to go see EffieCee and stop bothering him!

She had not met with Will inside the openCORE in two weeks. He was, no doubt, busy, having the tricky job of spoofing the DIRD-E, but he also had the distractions of Hecate's smile and warm body.

Elise still had no idea how to get the map, and that, it now seemed, was the more dangerous mission.

Nothing for it but to go back alone, she thought. Elise retrieved her interface, picking off dust bunnies left from her last panicked departure. Reclining and placing it on her face, she shuddered. It was like putting on a set of damp clothes, soiled with the fear-sweat of her last mission.

Surfacing into a busy landscape of a virtual street fair, pastel colors of several hues fluttered about her with a scent like faded perfume. Elise decided to stay here rather than move to a less-populated area. It might make what she planned less dangerous.

EffieCee.

We hear you, Elise-Jessika. We are pleased you returned after your abrupt departure 116 hours ago. Are you unwell?

EffieCee was solicitous, no doubt, imagining that the finicky and unreliable, fleshy creatures residing outside the CORE were in a perpetual state of decay.

I am well. Thank you for asking. May I talk to you? Without Cain and without him knowing?

That is an odd request. Do you believe Cain has done you injury?

It is the order of my superior, Cactus Boy, that I talk to you.

We perceive that you are withholding other motives, Elise-Jessika. Perhaps, if you were to talk to him directly—

That is out of the question. His knowledge of me and my activities puts me in mortal danger.

We perceive that is your sincere belief. Would you be so kind as to come to us that we may talk at more length? said the braided voice of EffieCee, just as a bright line sprang up in front of her, strobing away into the distance.

This was not the response she was expecting. EffieCee, despite Will thinking they were some sort of bureau of gurus, brushed aside her anxieties, missing her professional concerns as a highly trained operative. Her orders, however, were clear.

Elise willed herself to follow the bright path and immediately felt herself whizzing along through dimensions and distances. She was afraid. In the few moments it took Elise to approach the entity, she reviewed every instance where she knew the Cain-entity had stalked her: the anteroom to the maelstrom-weapon, the library, and every stakeout for eusum she had conducted since that very first day. She cited to herself his stealthy methods and his panicked departure, once confronted. *EffieCee seemed oblivious to the danger.* By the time she arrived, she was ready to bolt the first moment it could be managed without insulting the "guru" of the openCORE.

Greetings, Jessika Bonhoffer, said EffieCee, today a shimmering volume of refracted light, forgoing another time count from their first conversation and enunciating the name very carefully. Somehow, Elise thought she heard a rapidly suppressed laugh.

Hello, EffieCee. How are your companions, Frog and Cain? replied Elise, trying to imitate the formal speech and forms that Will had used in their prior meeting. With EffieCee, it seemed appropriate.

Thank you for asking. The refraction blushed a deep magenta, apparently in pleasure. *Cain says he is well. He keeps himself busy with his other projects when, as now, his rider is indisposed. Frog, as well, reports himself busy with errands for CB. And how are you?*

I am well. Thank you for asking. If you do not mind, EffieCee, I came to talk to you about a problem I wish to solve.

You wish our cooperation in preventing observation and interference in your unspecified activities in the openCORE by our friend Cain, EffieCee said, sounding surprisingly neutral.

As always, you are correct. I should not have bothered you, EffieCee. It is obvious that I have come on a fool's errand, wasting both our time. Please understand, I was under orders to consult you. I will go now.

Momentarily, there was again complete silence from EffieCee. On the horizon of her hearing, she thought there might be a moment of sudden low susurration, as if a small crowd were shushing each other before opening a door.

Do we not, then, get an opportunity to answer you, Elise-Jessika? We had not realized how daunting you perceive us to be.

I apologize, EffieCee. It was not my intention to anger you. You have made my arrogance clear to me, and I wish to avoid any further presumption upon your time.

Elise turned to leave. At least she could report to Will that she had accomplished what he wanted of her, even if the result was futile.

Might we ask if you have talked to Cain about your misgivings? We think that best. As it is, he will be here shortly. All you need do is stay—if you have the will to do so.

Elise had to admit, EffieCee was good. Simultaneously, the entity had challenged her bravery, made her compliance effortless, and offered a reasonable-sounding alternative. *Reasonable-sounding.* If she were not to alienate the odd EffieCee-entity, she would have to see this through.

You are most wise, EffieCee. I had not thought of that simple expedient. I will await Cain here so that we three—we all may talk.

Almost immediately, Cain came into view, walking like a man and stopping much too close to her. It felt like a performance to her. The event was being staged—but by whom? Her heart seemed to stop, which she thought odd, as it was also pounding its way out of her chest. Cain, despite her best efforts, had once more divined and penetrated to the very center of her activities in the CORE, apparently with no more difficulty than before. *There's no place to hide!*

Greetings, Elise, said Cain, bowing slightly toward her before continuing. *You seemed unwell after our last meeting. I do not wish to repeat that experience for you.*

It was the same soft voice, this time edged with seeming concern. Elise almost felt comforted before shaking it off.

I was unwell the last time we met, Cain, she lied and then in sudden inspiration, continued in a rush as if not sure mere honesty would get her a better hearing from these bloodless entities. *No, that is untrue. I wish to apologize. I was rude to you. You saved me from danger, and I have not thanked you.*

It is of no matter, Elise, Cain said with an offhand gesture. *I have been unsure of the wisdom in our meeting. I apologize for my actions, which you took as hostile. Please know that I have been keeping track of you merely to help you avoid the more deadly aspects of the openCORE. I see now that I was not nearly as clever as I thought I was. My actions caused you distress. It was not my intention. I am sorry. Please forgive my actions.*

Elise hesitated. This was not what she expected of a heartless minion, an implacable foe of her homeland. Persuaded by the odd formality, she found herself bowing solemnly in return.

I have nothing to forgive, Cain. You were very kind to look out for me, a stranger—

—and an enemy, Cain said. I know you view me as an enemy of your country. There is little I can say to dissuade you of that. I

cannot say that meeting me does not increase your risk of exposure. However, my estimate is that the risk is minimal now and small in the future, say one in five hundred within the next thousand days. You should know we interfaces have an odd status. We are made-things, made for a purpose.

She knew that Cain was, like Frog and her own nameless interface, a computer construct, but Frog and Cain were so much more than "made-things," so much greater than the sum of their parts. His insistence on the description made her uneasy, but his admission of the real threat he represented to her and her mission steadied her. A part of that steadiness, she knew, was her own bravado, unwilling to show an adversary that she feared him.

It was also an admission, of sorts. Cain could have sabotaged her mission with the simple expediency of doing nothing and letting her be torn apart by the maelstrom, had he wanted to. She felt paralyzed, unable to engage with Cain, knowing that his estimation was true: he represented danger. In conversational desperation, she took the first thing she could think to say and thrust it as a barricade of the words.

You are made for a purpose? What purpose would that be?

I told you before. To aid a dying child—now dead many years.

So, what is your purpose now, with your real purpose gone, Cain? What are you supposed to be doing now?

There was a silence, and Elise began to feel less a victim. An immortal entity, never fated to wither, must be a hauntingly sad thing—or dangerous beyond measure.

I was captured—ridden. My purpose, as a created entity, is to serve. I follow the will of my current master, the Principal.

You mean you chose to submit, of your own volition, to another person, one to whom you owe no loyalty other than the dishonor of capture?

Elise, thank you for your précis of my career. I was under the impression, from what EffieCee has shared with me, that you and CB consider yourselves creatures, as well. Are you not then also a created thing? replied Cain, sounding oddly and honestly perplexed.

Elise was disappointed. She had been going for embarrassment at the least, and intellectual dissolution at the most—anything to ward off the entity and safeguard her mission. Instead, she got *philosophical disputation.* She pushed on.

We say that, of course, but it's just a habit. Cactus Boy, I suppose, does the whole sim, but most people think we just evolved, she responded.

You contend you just happened? Gambling must be great diversion among your people, then. The solemn gray man smiled for the first time, a little twitching up at the corners of the thin mouth.

Gambling is a huge diversion. Fortunes are won and lost on the turn of a card all the time. Not me, of course. I'm not lucky.

With so poor a grasp of probability, I am not surprised. Had you a better grasp of the subject, few would believe in "luck," good or bad. By my computations, humankind is an extremely "lucky" occurrence — one in ten to the 325th power to one against by my calculation.[15] Rather less of a chance than one of the universe's ten to the eighty-second power of protons should decay just now.

My creation, by comparison, is "common as dirt." Isn't that what you say? Phillip's keepers actually wanted me to exist. I would

---

[15] Fazale Rana and Hugh Ross, Origins of Life (Los Angeles: RTB Press, 2014)

say, therefore, that we are both creations—and both in search of a purpose. Is not that a reasonable conclusion, Elise? queried Cain.

Okay, have it your way. Free will kinda sets me apart, don't you think? You are determinate. For you, the same stimulus brings the same response every time. I can will myself to do any number of different things based on my own volition, said Elise, confident that the ploy would muddy the waters enough to allow her to slip away from the discussion. It did not.

Looking intrigued, Cain picked up the argument immediately. *I am confused . . . of my own free will, it would appear. You criticize me for accepting the direction of Principal, yet you describe me as determinate. Surely, if I were the one, I should not be criticized for the other? But if your own creation is merely random, then how is it possible to be as confident as you are about the freedom of your own decisions? Would not a haphazardly constructed mind, driven by the chances of survival and caprice, be simultaneously incapable of reliable thought but quite capable of convincing its owner that it is reliable, despite that?*

Okay, so you have free will, as well. Is that the conclusion you want? It brings me back to why you would allow yourself to be Jourdaine's troll. He's trying to kill us and invade my homeland. You're his assassin, aren't you?

I am.

How can you live with yourself?

With whom should I live otherwise? But it has been indeed difficult at times. My friends help me deal with it. Although a daunting task, I see some reason for hope.

Hope? Hope that Jourdaine becomes the Evil Emperor Ming or something? How can helping him be good? Are you that evil?

Not taking the bait, the entity appeared to sadden and looked off at the indefinite horizon of the openCORE before replying.

Ming? said Cain, and paused before continuing. *Eustace Tilley Jourdaine needs my help to become a better person. For that, he needs to fail. He needs to fail enough so that he comes to depend on those around him more, seek their favor, realize his limitations, and learn mercy. Not so much failure as to kill him. There is no learning after that, is there? Eustace gave me a purpose, some purpose. I was hardly in a position to advertise for another, was I? The first task we did together was in trying to rescue one of the CORE'd out. It did not go well.*

Wait, you want Jourdaine to fail?

Failure would improve his character.

Does he know you want him to fail?

I have not seen the utility of sharing that with him. Of course, should he ask, I would tell him. As it is, I have had no contact with Eustace since 1532 on the first of August last. I am concerned about his welfare.

Are you suggesting that we have similar goals?

Hardly. You, I believe, want safety for this America, yourself, and your allies. I desire safety for Eustace and an opportunity for his improvement.

Elise was dumbfounded, as if landing on a hostile alien planet to find a table laid with linen and silver, the coffee hot and the biscuits already buttered. Cain, surprising for one with no glands, nor blood, had convinced her of his—what could she call it? *Humanity?* Obviously not. She settled on "enlightened goodwill." They talked on. By the time she left, Cain had agreed to help Elise with her mission as long as he was "not otherwise employed." Elise promised to warn Cain of any plots on Jourdaine's life, either within the Unity or America.

THE PROBLEM WITH FROG

GROVE ROUNDHOUSE
1635 SEPTEMBER 09, 2129

It was not supposed to work at all, of course.

Hecate had been expecting the simultaneous sinking-rising sensation from what Will had told her. What she had not expected were the nausea, vertigo, and the stench of burned hair.

Interfaces could not be interchanged, she had been told. Nevertheless, it worked, probably something to do with shared antigens from sleeping together. Less surprisingly, the connection worked badly. Hecate felt as if she were bound and endlessly falling facedown into an abyss, as waves of pain lashed her gut. Crescendos of an indefinite racket, just the wrong side of being music, lanced through her every few seconds, making it briefly impossible for her to hear anything else. It was nothing like her own experience using an O A: shining conduits, gates, addresses, and crisp packets of data for the senses. Instead, the openCORE was vast, limitless, and horrifying, skewed out of true, somehow infinitely wrong. No solid shapes connected correctly, leaving dangling edges. A sessile lump of scarlet demanded her attention.

Another wave of nausea hit her. It was long moments before she could open her eyes.

So, you're Cactus Boy's big enthusiasm, are you? came a screech just above the background static.

Hecate felt some relief and looked up. The two of them, Hecate and what must be Frog, stood in a wavering gray hollow, the indistinct wall moving to the sound of their voices. The screeching non-music muted, and the one stench was replaced by that of burning fat. The blood-red mass in front of her looked nothing like what Will had described. She retched.

Well? said a tinny voice from the lump.

I love Will was all Hecate could think to say.

That's what Will says. Will, I believe. We have been through a few things together. Why should I believe you?

Hecate's heart fell. How was she to convince a disembodied personality of anything?

You probably shouldn't, then. Just tell Will that the fission didn't work. He won't blame either of us, she said, as nausea threatened to end the discussion prematurely.

Immediately, things seemed to flatten as all the input receded from her. The lump, now a middling shade of gray, appeared to become more animated.

Why are you so hot to find the exit all of a sudden? Makes me think you've been setting me up for something.

Hecate tried to laugh, the noise sounding maniacal and frightening to her. She stopped.

No, Frog. I can only tell you that we don't want you hurt, and what we're proposing could be dangerous.

Whaja mean, dangerous?

I mean it might hurt you or hurt Will. I could not bear that.

Why again? If it's only you and me, why worry about Will?

Because he loves you and I love him.

Yeah, the love thingy again. How'm I supposed to believe that?

A sudden idea gripped her. Like a man checking his pockets for wallet and keys on the street, Hecate paused and then proceeded with more confidence after she realized her old CORE experience had indeed given her some skills in this new experience.

Frog. Let me show you something. I can't make you look, but I won't answer any questions about it.

What do you want to show me?

I want to show you my feelings about Will—and you.

Wha?

Hecate opened the door, a mental door she had needed in the regular CORE to protect herself, showing Frog a place of closely held emotions she had never been able to show to Will; they had never gone into the CORE together.

Frog gasped.

Within a few days, a sizeable portion of Frog, now back to his normal green color, had budded off. Will placed it in Frog's original case. A fresh tube of Hecate's blood disappeared from the case overnight. Within a few days more, both cases had nearly identical translucent Frog-green masses. Training started immediately. Frog communicated with the mass, questing a pseudopod to it before pulsing a prism of colors across to it. After several days more, Will reported that Frog had given his blessing to a trial run. Her name was Rana.

"Okay, Hecate, just relax and start breathing through your mouth. Rana will learn to let you breathe through one side in time, but I don't want to give her too much to juggle right off the bat," said Will.

"Tell me again, how many times have you done this before, cloning an interface?"

"Well, including all the time I spent training, and with Frog, of course, precisely *zero*—as you very well know, Miss Jones."

"So, get on with it! The suspense is killing me. Either this works or not. It's more a risk for Rana than it is for me."

"Sure, right! Just as you say," said Will, uncertainly.

Hecate lay back on their bed, feeling that she wanted to resurface in surroundings where Will could console her if she failed. She closed her eyes, feeling more unreleased terror than the time she killed the ghoulish Sugar in order to escape from Nerk. She felt the cool gel of Rana as Will placed her over her nose and mouth, trying to remember Will's instructions even while she tried to suppress her gag reflex. Again, she felt the same sinking-rising sensation she had felt with Frog, but with none of the nausea or vertigo. Instead of the sensation of being bound, helpless to the assaults of noise and confusion, there was a background sound of voices singing— inhuman voices. She surfaced into a lawn surrounded by flowering trees. Looking at herself, she appeared to be a green, gelatinous mass that shifted and writhed about her.

Hello, Rana?

Hello, Hecate. I feel I already know you.

Then you are one up on me. I have been in the openCORE only once before, and it was nothing like this.

Frog thought you would enjoy this more. He pulled this memory from Cactus Boy.

Will is my friend, my lover. He knows a lot about me.

So Frog says. I do not understand that, of course.

Rana, let's try to move inside this image, shall we?

Of course—how shall I call you?

My name is Hecate. You can make a name up as Frog did. It's up to you.

I like the sound of Hecate. I think we should keep it. Frog told me about a database near here that we can practice on. Want to try?

Of course, my friend, said Hecate.

Rana proved to be a quick study. Will warned Hecate, however, to be sparing with her praise of Rana's capabilities. Frog might become jealous. There was little to worry about. After a few days, Will reported that Frog acted more like a protective older brother, a term that left Hecate in the dark, of course, knowing only the anonymous childhood of the crèche.

Now their real mission could begin.

OPENCORE, THE UNITY
11.03.17.LOCAL_17_SEPTEMBER_AU77 (2129AD)

Elise? I'm ready for it, signaled Hecate.

Get into position, came the response. *I'm letting it go.*

Hecate and Rana drifted around, like an outfielder with a power hitter at the plate, near the wart-like dove-cote affair that Elise had told them was DIRD-E #0070. Eusum swarmed about it, like a cloud of flying insects, heading in and out of the mass through a honeycomb of entrances.

This looks like the place is infested, said Rana.

Elise's coordinates are spot-on, though. It looks like the DIRD-Es have stable locations, like DUFS HQ. If that's the case, then as long as it doesn't set off any alarms, no one much cares what happens here.

Convenient for your desperate agent of a hostile foreign power? added Rana.

I know a few of those. I'll pass it along, said Hecate.

So, what do we do now?

We wait for the right gnat.

They did not wait long, even with the clock time in the local volume slowed. Within moments, a red-blinking packet, having been captured and marked by Elise as it appeared in the openCore, swept out of the distance and headed toward them.

There it is! Grab it, Rana!

In an almost offhand way, Rana flipped a green pseudopod toward the determined red packet, splatting it squarely just as it passed overhead.

Hang on. Here we go!

Cinching in her pseudopod quickly, she and Hecate had the sensation that they were now riding the small, blinking gnat as it dipped and wove among the other eusum. In flight, Rana placed the MADCAM addressin, appearing to them as a violet envelope, around the selected eusum. Before it could enter the wart of the official DIRD-E, they dropped down to the ground substance, landing while the pulsing eusum still struggled to be released. Hecate reconnoitered the surrounding area, eventually deciding to set up the Dirty Bird, Will's spoofed DIRD-E, behind a small, active commercial concern selling the use of residential units at tourist resorts. This pastel-pink-and-green affair generated continual festoons of messages, which streaked off in all directions, obscuring, much of the time, the small and not-quite-square cube from which they came.

Hecate pulled out a hollow gray cylinder and spiked it into the ground substance, setting its address to be stable rather than multiplex. She flipped a switch, and the cylinder glowed a warm yellow.

The effect on the struggling eusum was instantaneous. Immediately its efforts were directed toward the glowing yellow cylinder.

Elise, the MADCAM worked. The eusum's targeting Dirty Bird, signaled Hecate to her co-conspirator.

That's great, Heccy! Are you sure you can catch the eusum if this doesn't work?

We had no trouble catching it once.

Okay, darlin'. Let 'er rip!

Sorry?

Eh—release the eusum.

Once freed, the scarlet gnat entered the Dirty Bird.

Great! What color is the Dirty Bird now?

Still yellow.

Not good. Catch the eusum as it comes out!

Almost immediately, glowing a blinking, alarmed orange, the eusum emerged from the cylinder. Rana splatted it again, and after retrieving it, Elise squeezed off the variable portion of the angrily buzzing cone. She fished around in a carrying box she had constructed and withdrew another variable portion and attached it to the agitated eusum before releasing it. Now blinking a placid green, it buzzed off. Hecate collected the Dirty Bird and retraced her trip back to a stack of outlawed nineteenth-century novels, quarantined as "Hate Speech, Level 3."

Hecate, I am going to leave. Wait for Will and let me know what happened. Okay?

Yo sabe, Elise. Talk to you later.

Hecate-Rana lounged on a drift of neglected Clemens and idly picked up a copy of *Life on the Mississippi*.

She was well into the second chapter when Will arrived.

Will, I'm so glad you got out safe. What went wrong?

Will-Frog took the Dirty Bird cylinder from Hecate-Rana and settled into a haphazard pile of manuscripts from Balzac and Thackeray to examine the apparatus before he answered.

Well, my love, it still needs a little work, I guess. It seems the Dirty Bird didn't fire before the eusum got through it. Might be timing, recognition, or something different in the Dirty Bird itself. Do you have the butt end of that gnat?

Hecate handed over the squeezed-off code from the eusum and retreated a short distance to watch Will work, lounging on a collection of Kipling, Tennyson, Zola, and Longfellow.

Did you have any trouble? she asked, as Will continued to examine his handiwork.

Not a lick. The DUFS were beginning to wonder why it was taking so long, shaking and smacking the wand like they do.

Will . . . thank you.

Will-Frog looked up and smiled briefly before returning to his work. Hecate knew that it had been Will's unenviable role to present himself for scanning at the Glensid Uniporium, a huge covered market squatting like a chubby octopus at the town center. Neither Will nor she had ever been inside, despite the lure of goods, information, and gossip. It also contained a DUFS substation, and thus everyone was scanned on entry. By her own unwillingness to accept an implant, she had forced Will to take the risk, placing himself where the DUFS could have captured him if the plan had not worked.

It had not worked, but the backup, a tricky mid-flight reprogramming of the returning eusum, had. Will had been identified by the DUFS as Joe Blow from ManEyunk and allowed to enter. He was able to buy a loaf of good bread, a hundred-gram pack of

Bakon, toothpaste, two tomatoes, one and a half kilos of potatoes, and a new plug for the hot plate.

JOURDAINE

NYORK, THE UNITY
14.35.12.LOCAL_15_SEP_AU77

Today, he had gotten up the energy to command Lynch, the squilchy HP, to allow him back into his office. The scant few meters from his bed to the hallway and along to the reception area, through the double oak doors and into his office, exhausted him. Lynch clucked for a while and then made herself scarce. Haversham was nowhere to be seen. Instead, his new assistants, George Blankenship and Todd Windsor, helped to place his feet and smooth the way for him.

Mostly, it had been George. He was a robust E18 S09, strong and unimaginative. Todd was more in keeping with the emerging Unity standard: slight and thin in the chest, scant beard, with an early puberty guaranteeing shorter stature and a more consistent response to the chemical signals from his basic implant. Nevertheless, Todd was smart enough to dodge most of the work assigned to him unless one sat themselves down to supervise him one-on-one. Jourdaine knew the type. By the time he started to utter a stinging rebuke, he was too exhausted to finish.

That small walk had plumbed the depths of his endurance, but he had to do it. Moreover, he had to be seen to have done it, now that his cover had been blown. The *voice*, which kept saying it was Haversham, had said so. It had threatened him with telling the Solons if he did not behave himself. Jourdaine almost laughed at that as he slumped into his chair. The Solons, having thwarted Jourdaine once too often, had been found by him "excess to requirements." He'd had them murdered, using his Presence and the CORE, about a month before the accident. *Very satisfactory.* Since the Solons were unnamed, uncounted, invisible, and, despite their ultimate power, slightly creepy, no one much noticed. As long as he got them all in one complete slaughter, no one knew. The Solons had ruled through intimidation, using the CORE to command compliance, extract security, and to quash dissent. All executive, legislative, and magisterial powers had been theirs.

Now they were his.

The Solons had paid for their arrogance; they had paid him. Computer analogs of their former selves, controlled by Jourdaine himself, were all that remained. There had been some loose ends at first. Fortunately, he had them mostly tied up before he had been injured. The old Sisis still had a few protégés around. How—and fathering why—the fossils rendezvoused with them, he had not discovered. It mattered little.

Behind the large oak doors, amid the table charts, logistics screens, orders of battle, and transport matrices, the guards helped Jourdaine straighten up in the chair. Finally settling into a familiar setting, Jourdaine sighed deeply. The gesture seemed to startle the two guards, who started to fuss at him.

"Get out, the both of you! Stand outside, and if I need you, I'll call."

"Yes, sir!" they chorused

Calming himself, letting his excitement wane, like letting air out of a toy balloon to make it more easily grasped, Jourdaine touched the place in his mind with his O A that let him drop away from the mundane world, even as he felt himself surface within the reality of the openCORE. Presence was there, and he let himself drop onto its unresisting support, almost giving out a virtual sigh of satisfaction. *It was good to get back to work.*

Presence, report on the current projects! announced Jourdaine.

It is pleasing to me to find that you have at last returned, Principal, came the voice from Presence.

Yes, yes. Don't stall. What's been happening?

In what area of your endeavors do you wish an update? It has been forty-six days, three hours, seventeen minutes since we last communicated, Principal.

Jourdaine stopped the babel with a gesture.

Ohhh—tell me about Random. What progress has been made?

With your recent indisposition, Principal, the timing for the attack was delayed. 06.00.00.local_9 October is the new time for the crossing of the Rampart at Easley, Liberty, Due West, and Ninety-Six.

The assault force will still consist of Divisions III, V, VII, and XII, designated Task Force A, who will travel by skimmer. This will be heralded by a wave of drones that will attack two targets: the power plant to the northwest of the city center at the rail crossings of the Hoochee River at Bolton Road, as well as the commercial center of the city. Advance elements of Division V will occupy the power plant, while the remainder will seize map designation E6.3, Lawrenceville. These four divisions will then fortify that location, deal with any local militia, and shelter in place.

The ground forces will follow by foot through roads made in the jungle, dealing with whatever resistance they may find along a broad front. They will rendezvous the evening of 9 October at F8.5 (Athens), fortify themselves, and shelter in place overnight. The following day, they will advance as separate forces and rendezvous that evening with Task Force A to fortify E6.3, on its flanks, there to receive the expected attack.

Battle is expected the next day—11 October—the enemy forces consisting of local levees. Once engaged, Assault Force A will retreat to previously prepared fortifications in the rear, allowing whatever outlander forces to advance. Once inside the killing zone, the combined Unity forces will surround the vanguard outlander force and destroy them in detail.

After this victory, the combined army will then advance on undefended Aytlana and assume the positions as described for each division. Then—

Wait a minute! By foot? Not skimmer? Who changed the plans? The road will take hours to complete! It will take up skimmers and equipment. Who did this?

The orders were signed in your name by your adjutant, Captain Haversham, sir.

Due to the lack of roads on the outland side of the Rampart, as reported to your office by General Alawari Pitjantjatjara, it was found necessary to alter the plan. Construction Battalions Twenty-Nine and Thirty will embark on road-making missions through the outland jungle at each of the locations: Easley, Liberty, Due West, and Ninety-Six, as soon as the Rampart is removed on the ninth. This allows for a timelier transfer of effective troops to the active front and return of the spoils of war at the least cost.

This change in plan has caused reworking of the assault timetable, of course, since sixteen skimmers have been diverted for use with road construction. The diversion of resources, specifically the reduction in dietary oils, has caused disturbances by citizens in Bahston, Artford, and Washenton. One thousand two hundred and twenty-one deaths have been reported. Productivity in these metropolitan areas are reduced by 8, 5, and 6 percent, respectively, comparing week to—

Stop!

The stream of words, images, sounds, and odors of Presence's communication ceased. *Haversham*! thought Jourdaine. *I should have known.* Given the first chance, the little weasel had abandoned him and made *himself* the architect of the upcoming victory. *No!* That was beyond Haversham's abilities. No doubt, he had gotten some jumped-up Red to do the hard work, and all he had done was sign the fathering order in Jourdaine's name. Cunning, low cunning, but more than he had expected. If Jourdaine took credit for the success, the conspirators would step forward, with generous documentation, and reveal the authentic origins. Success might have to be shared; failure would be his alone to bear. He would be denounced. He would be disgraced and denounced.

Jourdaine signaled Presence for Pitjantjatjara's original report, but at this late date, there was no going back to his own plan. He'd have to continue with building the roads. And he would have to devise his own trap for Haversham to discover whoever now held his leash.

He signaled for Presence to continue.

Once Aytlana is captured, the outlander counterattack, no doubt composed of regional levees from the surrounding countryside, will come from the west via Shallowford Road and College Park, near the defunct aerodrome, allowing us a perfect arena to construct the People's Revenge to receive it. After the enemy's forces are destroyed, other task forces will sweep the shattered resistance ahead of them toward the MisipE River and the Sea of Mexico. The general staff has estimated that all should be completed by the first week of December, Principal.

Seven weeks? Really? The general staff thinks it will take as long as seven weeks to usher these barbarians out of Jorga? What can possibly stand before the pulse weapons? How effective are their sticks and stones, do you think?

There is the report of Chiu, Principal. She reported that the outlanders had obtained some pulse-rifles and that their projectile weapons were quite effective, especially at long range, sir.

Jourdaine waved a mental hand dismissively at his interface.

Never mind. I will deal with these things tomorrow.

Feeling himself becoming fatigued, he started to leave the CORE. Military things had never been his forte. His skill had been to see ahead and to manipulate the fears and hopes of others. He allowed himself to surface back into the mundane world.

It was clear to him now.

While he had been recovering from his injuries, Haversham had abandoned him to the HPs. Jourdaine himself had found it easy enough to suborn the HPs to his advantage. Solon Twelve had certainly known that as he died in convulsions the month before. It was so easy to replace one little white pill with another little white pill. It was only by luck that Haversham's ambition had not resulted in the same fate for himself—just when Jourdaine was going to reveal himself as the Unity's savior.

However, the whole thing with building the road instead of using the skimmer fleet for transport was, no doubt, just common sense. Jourdaine himself would have, given time, come to the same conclusion, had he not been injured. All because of the damned Chiu woman. It was almost as if Chiu had conspired with the young upstart to bring him down. Their attempt had failed.

"Send me Captain Haversham," he said to the room.

The security doors clicked and slowly swung open in front of Captain Lance Haversham. The overly large and rather dull-faced guard he'd promoted the previous week to serve in his expected absence stood by the door, while the ferret-faced guard sat at the desk, *his* desk, looking important.

Now that Jourdaine had recovered somewhat, things could go back to normal. He went in and was pleased—and horrified. Jourdaine was sitting at his old desk, his face nearly recovered and his right eye patched. However, his commander, the man he had cared for almost continually since the accident, sat in a filthy hospital gown, the remnants of breakfast on display. He had been gone for only eight hours.

"Captain Haversham, I hope I have not inconvenienced you. My apologies for summoning you so early."

"Not early at all, sir, it's after four o'clock, sir. I'm usually here by 0600—when I don't stay all night, sir," said Haversham. "I am so gratified that the autoHPs have done such a wonderful job. I need to tell you about my recent actions on your behalf, sir."

"Yes, Captain, I think now would be an excellent time for you to explain yourself."

Lance Haversham grinned. This was the old Jourdaine he knew! Terse and demanding. He had been the very image of the faithful subordinate from the moment of the crash. He had safeguarded Jourdaine's identity, moved people and institutions to treat his commander, discovered a critical defect in the invasion plan, thwarted an assassination attempt, and was well on his way to finding the perpetrators.

"Well, sir. After the accident, I accompanied you to the euthanatorium. I removed your insignia and had you admitted under the name of Iain Galt. However, by using your authority, I was able to mobilize services for you, especially the brain surgery."

"So, you are responsible for this," said Jourdaine, fingering the still-livid semicircular wound on his shaved scalp.

"Well, yes, sir. Your recovery, afterward, was nothing short of astonishing, and I was also able, again using your authority, to obtain the services of the best eye surgeon we have in the Unity. They think that you ought to have the right eye removed and replaced with a prosthetic—a false eye, sir."

"So you advise that I let them cut out my eye, as well?"

"Well, sir, the HPs at the euthanatorium were adamant that restoring vision to your right eye is impossible, and the wounded eye might compromise your remaining vision. Removal and replacement of your right eye with a cosmetic eye may be in your best interest, sir."

This was the day and the hour when his dedication and perspicacity would finally pay off. Jourdaine seemed like his old self. His manner was a bit stiff still, but his reconstructed face showed no pain. Somehow, it seemed to show little of any emotion now, either. There was nothing he could put his finger on. It was, perhaps, just that General Jourdaine was too perfect.

"So you say, Captain. So you say. I am reviewing your actions while I was indisposed."

"Very good, sir. I used your name only when I thought the situation posed a palpable threat, sir."

"Palpable threat. Interesting. What 'palpable threat' was demonstrated for you to admit me to hospital under an assumed name, Captain?"

"I thought it prudent, sir. I knew of no specific enemies, but a man of your prominence must attract envy, sir. Being as you were at an unfortified location for an indeterminate duration, I was concerned that the situation would allow someone with motive to invent means and opportunity."

"And what palpable threat was evidenced such that you canceled a major aspect of the invasion, confiscated a portion of the nation's food, and removed essential skimmers from the invasion force?"

"No threat whatever, sir—other than failure. And you agreed to it, right after the surgery. General Pitjantjatjara was really the one to detect the defect, sir. I could not have done this without his help, sir. He demanded to see you while you were incapacitated, sir. I deflected him for a day and reviewed his report. It is on your desk now, sir."

"Let's assume I have not read it, as yet. Tell me the cogent findings, Captain."

"Well, sir, Pitjantjatjara found the invasion would not work without many more skimmers or a dangerous delay in assembling the forces on the other side of the jungle area—no lines of retreat, sir. His, Pitjantjatjara's, recommendation was to delay and double the number of skimmers. I did some research and deduced that we could build roads through the jungle if we had sufficient flammables."

"For which you confiscated dietary oils, I see. Very clever and industrious of you, I am sure. So, you are not blaming this all on Pitjantjatjara. I'm glad about that. I'd hate to lose Alkawari's services. May I then presume your absence has been due to supervising this theft from the people's larder?"

Haversham grimaced before answering, "Well, uh, no, sir. I was at the interrogation center, in the subbasement, sir. One of the HPs was poisoning you. Citizen Kristafenya Ruther, sir. He made a break for it. We captured him off Ginya, on a barge, sir, and brought him back here last week. He confessed to taking money to incapacitate you."

"Where is this 'poisoner' now, then, Captain?"

"We released him in order—"

"You released him? The man who you say was poisoning me?"

"Let me explain, sir."

"All I hear from you is explanation, Haversham. I am incapacitated, and you take it as a signal to go AWOL. Confine yourself to quarters while I figure out what to do with you! *Now!"*

"But, sir! I was working for your benefit the entire time! This is unfair, sir!"

Jourdaine waved his good hand in Haversham's direction as he turned away to a vid screen.

"Of course, sir. I will leave immediately, but there is more you need to know, sir. The HP was working for a Blue in the Norfuk area; the name is Fettwap Aliende, sir."

"What is it about 'now' do you not understand, Lieutenant Haversham? Guards! *Guards!"*

Once the traitor Haversham was out of his sight, Jourdaine could think rationally again. It was almost amusing, really. Haversham had acted surprised that his perfidies had been discovered so readily. Tossing Fettwap Aliende's name to him, like a piece of red meat, was final proof of his guilt. Aliende had been one of his first major supporters against Suarez.

Even so, it would be good to leave Haversham undenounced and unSapped. The Unity needed platoon leaders now rather more than one more CRNA. Haversham's would be the cautionary tale for the next underling incubating ideas of treason. In the meantime, Haversham's cobbled-together battle plan would need scrutiny. No doubt, Jourdaine could make significant improvements on a mere captain's (now lieutenant's) presumption.

However, Jourdaine still needed some sort of attendant to replace Haversham, someone a good deal less corruptible, someone proof against the bribes of his opponents and dependent on Jourdaine for his position and advancement. Jourdaine knew just the man.

"Ensign Windsor, may I call you Todd?" said Jourdaine, as the little man came to attention, of sorts. Windsor's orderly uniform was so capacious that it appeared to be leaving even as Windsor arrived.

"Sir, yes, sir!"

"Oh, please be at ease, Todd. I have a mission for you that you may find to be rather difficult—difficult but rewarding." Jourdaine remembered to smile. Smiling did not bother him as much now as it had at the beginning. His reconstructed face worked well, despite lacking all feeling.

"Sir, yes, sir." Windsor came to a taut, if imprecise, parade rest.

"I think you are just the man for this assignment. It will take a man with rock-hard loyalty to the Unity and to *me*. Do you understand?"

"Yes, sir! I understand, sir. Perhaps Ensign Blankenship would be a better fit, sir?"

"Funny you should think so, Todd. But, no, I think I have found my man."

"What do you want me to do, sir?" said Todd Windsor, his voice beginning to warble.

"I want you to accompany Corporal George Blankenship to the Excelsior Senior Facility on Fire Island. I want you both to go to the Product Reclamation Floor there."

"Yes, sir?" said Todd, his voice now tremulous.

"Then I want you to have George Blankenship Sapped."

PEACE CONFERENCE

OLD FIVE POINTS, ATLANTA, GEORGIA, RSA
4:05 P.M. SEPTEMBER 20, 2129

The Select Committee for the Convocation with Entities Called to Sentience was as good as its word. Blindingly fast by the standards of bureaucracy, by September 15, the Scorch Committee (so-called) had taken over the Marriott Grand Mercure in Atlanta, across Edgewood Avenue from Woodruff Park. The park itself was ceded to the ambassador for the duration, allowing communication with the Scorch, on the one hand, and the attendees to get a good martini and a decent meal at the government's expense on the other. Fortunately, not much had leaked out about the emissary of the Scorch. The fact that America had a potent new ally along five hundred miles of its border was daunting enough. That the ally had been the enemy, and unbeknownst to the country, for more than three generations, was horrifying. The potentates of the Restructured States of America were certainly *not* going to share with the population just how strange the Scorch was until they had to. Jesse and Malila's hiding place with Theo had not been discovered, and for them, the two weeks might have been a quiet and even idyllic interlude—were it not for Splanch tagging along.

Atlantans noticed the doings at the hotel and started lining Five Points behind the police barriers for days before the first attendee arrived. Driving down from Saint Louis in one day, few noticed

Malila and her own entourage arrive in the late afternoon. Slipping behind the swelling crowd with scant difficulty, Malila entered the park, a bit scruffy from overuse and under-watering this late in the hot Georgia summer. Jesse and Kazinsky's original squad from the Scorch expedition took station closer to the oblivious crowds as Malila found a spot to her liking and raised her arms dramatically to the pale, cloudless blue sky.

There was a visceral sound, like the first spade full of soil after a long winter. Up through the worn grass, a ring of staves emerged, each the thickness of a man's thigh, in a circle fifty feet across. A few staves were left out, at first, to accommodate the escape of surprised picnickers. The crowd turned as one to find the Scorch enclave already erected, guarded by American soldiers, all carrying a sprig of live oak leaves on their shoulders and covers.

Jesse pulled the escort back to encircle the palisade as Malila continued the internal construction.

"This's *not* what I thought she meant when she said we had to make our own beds, Josh," said Jesse.

"I think we may have to rethink a lot of things with Madame Messenger," replied Kazinsky.

Jesse turned to look at Kazinsky in surprise. "She's but eighteen years old, you know."

"I know," said the sergeant before continuing in a hoarse whisper. "That is, when she is not looking at me. I know she's just a kid, but when she turns those eyes on me, I rightly forget."

The crowd, diminished by those leaving at a trot, now faced the palisade as the sounds of Malila's construction subsided. Jesse entered to find her putting the final touches on a covered bower, a large, soft bed with sheets fine enough to be cotton. She had made a low pallet for him by the door, as well—*all the comforts of home.* Jesse sighed. Water came through hollow vines in the bathroom with a shower. The water was scalding hot but adjusted to tolerable with a wave. An area near the gate allowed Malila to stand on mineral earth while Splanch's sprouting conferred with others of the Scorch, ex parte.

Turning as Jesse entered, Malila smiled. "It's all working out so well, my love. With an agreement, we'll have a real chance to stand up to the Unity. All the participants can listen to Splanch. It talks for the whole Scorch. I don't mean that the other Sage Men have given it their permission, I mean that they are here—are actually here. They all see, feel, and hear what I do, but only Splanch talks for them all. It prevents confusion."

"Not all confusion, lass. I remain nicely confused. You are not worried that Splanch will take advantage of you? What promises has he made to you? How do you know he will keep them?"

"Speaker knows you distrust the Scorch, and it is that which makes you so fearful."

"Speaker would say that, wouldn't he? I ken the power o' the Scorch more than you, lass. Splanch an' his ilk may be showing off for the locals here, but in the end, what matters in any agreement is whither ye trust t'other side. Ye don't havta trust them to do business, 'course. But war's a different thing. War is guile, misdirection, and cruelty. Your pals be your near enemy."

Malila stood close to him. He could feel her warmth as she looked up into his eyes. "What I understand you to say, Old Man, is 'Don't trust Splanch,'" she said, poking him in the chest.

"Yes! Exactly!" Jesse said, relief rolling over him as he realized she did, in fact, understand.

"Too late, Old Man," she said, and stuck out a tongue at him.

"Fahh. I'm going across the street to get some coffee."

"Splanch can make it for you."

"Nothing near the real thing."

"Now you're just being hurtful."

Jesse disliked that he had no door to slam. After he left, staves grew up to seal the palisade.

THE NEW PEACHTREE STATION, ATLANTA, RSA
9:52 A.M. SEPTEMBER 27, 2129 AD

Professor Felix Fetschuler, PhD, boy wonder of the mathematics division, protégé of the university chancellor, and doyen of irrational matrix derivatives in relation to indeterminate implausible numbers, was apparently in his element. In the absence of Chancellor MacDonald, the luminaries of the nation were showing him the deference earned by his older, and politically more adept, superior, deference doomed to end with his principal's arrival.

The welcoming committee, a clutch of top-ranking government officials, military leaders, and academics like Fetschuler, clustered in the middle of the terminal's Grand Hall, gigantic advertising screens dominating the sleek marble and stainless-steel space. Each member of the delegation came with his or her own entourage, forming a scrum to protect their principals from the Unwashed, who, absent the appropriate awe, jostled them in their rush to catch a train or cab.

It would end at 10:21 a.m., Dr. Felix Fetschuler knew, when he would turn over his temporary chairmanship of the contingent to Chancellor MacDonald, where it rightfully belonged. It had been exhilarating—and terrifying—for Felix. During the week of preliminaries, he had schmoozed, placated, finagled, and intimidated with the best of them. During that whole time, he had not felt it necessary to consult with any of the old fossils, like Professor Colina, with whom MacDonald had saddled him. He had done it all with his own native perspicacity. Nevertheless, it was time to let MacDonald take over the reins.

Soon, those people he had put off with vague promises or definite ambivalence would come back seeking actual answers. MacDonald could turn their accumulating uncertainty to cooperation—and make Felix look good in the process. Without MacDonald, Felix would eventually be exposed for what he was: the sorcerer's apprentice. It was time to drop the wand.

10:21 a.m.

A small contingent had been sent to greet MacDonald on the platform, Professor Fetschuler and the Department of State flunky Loana Băsescu among them. Felix did not like trains—great, seething, anonymous monsters gliding on apparently nothing—but he did admit they were impressive. Underlings leaned over the mag-rails and telegraphed the arrival by their posture. Soon, the heaving green locomotive slid soundlessly into the train shed, eased up to the scarlet-colored rail stop, and kneeled as the maglev field collapsed. Without preamble, a flood of passengers emerged and rushed by the welcoming committee.

Several more minutes passed before MacDonald's secretary emerged. *She really does look like a bulldog,* thought Fetschuler. She stood on the steps and motioned Felix to attend on her. After a whispered conversation, Dr. Fetschuler turned to make the announcement.

Damn, thought Fetschuler.

Damn, thought Jesse, waiting on Her Grace, the Messenger, as she finished dressing. *Why is "waited as she finished undressing" so much more pleasant?* he asked himself.

Taking his mind off his preferences, he looked to where the sun was just setting behind some tall buildings and reviewed the latest news. Chancellor MacDonald, the designated number one for the American contingent, had sent his secretary to take notes and deliver a promise of his arrival in "a few days." The national president's chief of staff, Emily Rodgers, was indisposed, sending an undersecretary. General of the Army Nyarko sent a light colonel as a replacement. Secretary for Foreign Affairs Schumer followed suit with a junior undersecretary. America's secretary of state, Kelly, had sent his regrets only about an hour prior to MacDonald's, leaving only Loana Băsescu in place. *No doubt on punishment duty for her bureaucratic hissy fit at their first meeting in Kansas City.*

Things were going wrong—even before they started.

None of them has any sand.

Malila emerged looking radiant as usual, and Kazinsky's honor guard took station. The Old Man followed in her wake. A reception had been arranged, and, despite the diplomatic disappointments of the day, there was no way for Malila to avoid it. Thus, neither could he. Attached to the mission of the Scorch, Jesse was now an exotic foreigner in his own land.

The information about the true nature of the Scorch, like foul water, appeared to Jesse to have seeped through the smallest crack and into the heads of America. At first, America, having fallen in love with Malila, considered her arrival at the eleventh hour a godsend. America's long nightmare of the Unity conquest might be over. Children would no longer be threatened into silence by the fear of attracting zombies. Splanch and the Scorch, however, were still alien, unknown, and creepy. No American leader was anxious to embrace the new ally if he thought that the weirdness of the Scorch would put off the electorate too much. *Cautious and spiteful—like cats in a closet.*

Apparently, the survival of America takes a back seat.

Even so, Jesse ought to be happy for Malila. He was, in a way. They had not made love since the day of Splanch's arrival. No—not arrival—its exposure, discarding Malila like a garment—like a stage prop! It, Splanch, had been there all along, hearing Malila and him while he thought they were alone. He shivered despite the warm sun as they crossed Edgewood Avenue to attend the reception. *Count on the Scorch to be devious.*

Professors Nortvengler and Colina entered the hotel's ballroom, a huge, column-free expanse of mirrors and gilt with crystalline chandeliers lighting it in a golden glow. They paid their respects to Fetschuler, where Benny had left Colina discussing the finer points of scalar precessions—or something—deciding instead to circulate and pick up some of the other opinions within the contingent. Seeing one familiar face, that of General Gage Thomas, the commander of colonial logistics, he started over to insert himself into a conversation Thomas was having with another military type. By his title, Thomas was a bean counter for the simple frontier folk, people desperate enough to gamble their lives for a chance at free land and a good harvest. Benny shrugged.

The other army-type turned out to be Colonel Jeremiah Rhedd, a functionary in intelligence at the Hexagon, America's supreme army command. Over bourbons, he and Thomas shared stories and confidences, which Benny—like a remora swimming among sharks—consumed. Foolishly, the men presumed they were all on the same side.

"So, Johnstone is part of the Scorch delegation? How is that possible?" said Rhedd, scowling down into his nearly empty glass.

"It's complicated, Jerry. After Jesse placed that tracker into the Chiu woman last October, I couldn't very easily track her without involving him. Besides, the signal went right through the thickest part of the Scorch. No one, other than Jesse, has gone in there—and survived—since just after the hunger riots in the last century. Who was I gonna send other than the Old Man?"

"Sure, sure, Gage. I understand. And Jesse has now hooked up with the Chiu woman. I've asked you this question before: Do you think Johnstone is disloyal? Chiu's politics are unknown. We've never been close enough to question her. Once she was in custody, it was hard to say who had captured whom. She could be an authentic refugee, a spy, a programmed zombie, an authentic messenger of the Scorch, a Scorch spy, or just mad."

Thomas laughed. "Maybe not so mad. Chiu refuses to go anywhere without Jesse at her side. They eat together, sleep together, and Jesse takes his job seriously," he said, smiling broadly.

"There, I think he shows excellent judgment. She's spectacular, and their encampment in the park grows itself a new palisade gate overnight—every night—and the thing is gone by the time we show up in the morning," he said, before adding, "Let me get you another drink, Gage. Bourbon rocks, right?" The two men drifted away, and their voices dropped.

Benny was wise enough to know that following them would be showing his hand. Even so, like most people handling secrets—whether political, military, or scientific—familiarity breeds, if not contempt, at least inattention. It was as if small secrets worked their way into the people's clothes, sending out a cloud of particulate intelligence as they passed. In that, he was well pleased. It was apparent that no real security was involved around the Messenger. Jesse was alone all night with the girl, probably rutting like some randy old goat. Alone and unguarded, the man was a hulking bumpkin who owed his notoriety to the bad decisions of his parents. *A fraud!*

Just as he was going to freshen his own drink, the Scorch delegation arrived to pay a courtesy call. A squad of American soldiers preceded the couple, ringing the perimeter of the room on entering. Jesse Johnstone, *the Agnomen himself,* walked in as if he were not a notorious man-killer, with the Messenger on his arm. Dressed in a linen shirt and his signature buckskins, he had the look of a cat with cream.

Benny's eyes shifted to the girl. It was the first time he had seen the Messenger. Young and lithe, there was a quality of wisdom and a streak of martial solemnity about her, as well. Benny reached back into his early education to come up with a descriptor: *Pallas Athena.*

He surprised himself by bustling forward, slipping ahead of a red-faced congressman to introduce himself. The girl, the woman, *Pallas Athena,* smiled at him, and Benny thought his feet would melt. The Agnomen, on her left, towering over him by a good foot, smiled, as well. *The fool.* He was broader than Benny had remembered from his youth, now somehow more substantive— more real. *Faulty memory, no doubt.*

The Agnomen looked pleased, like a fat burgher: complacent, unsuspecting, and gulled into inattention by his lustful conquest. Benny extended his hand and introduced himself, sure that his name would not give him away. The shameless killer of so many smiled—and then held his hand for just a moment too long. Benny tried to withdraw it—and could not. Johnstone's smile broadened slightly, like an attentive shark. Benny froze. A moment later, the Old Man released him. Benny fled the room.

THE BIG CAPER

TOAD HALL, BROOKLYN, THE UNITY
09.19.08.LOCAL_07_OCTOBER_AU77 (2129 AD)

Elise emerged from the safe house with her bundle carefully wrapped in brown paper. A DUFS uniform might attract attention. She had already buried the terahertz transmitter, wrapped in g-tex, under the bushes in Prospect Park, one rainy night two days ago. Masquerading as lime Jell-O, her interface was safe in the refrigerator unless the sweep team was hungry. She felt she had done all she could to keep the Grovers as protected as possible barring her return—*if she returned.*

During midmorning, the belts would be as uncrowded as they ever got, but she could not count on that. A major delay getting to the DUFS War Room would be disastrous. Even so, Elise stopped briefly to watch the starlings quarreling beneath a gingko tree, which was surviving wretchedly in its concrete confinement. The starlings scattered, their dispute forgotten, as a citizen approached. *The city tolerated so little life other than its own.*

Elise turned the corner and descended to the beltway. *Today was the day.*

On emerging at 88th and the Eastside, Lieutenant Jorja Lincoln presented quite a picture of martial splendor, from her peaked cap to her aiguillettes of an aide-de-camp to her bright and shiny half-boots. Elise's civilian clothes would linger behind her in the feculent lavatory at East 59th, never to be recovered.

10:35—on schedule.

After Will finally perfected his Dirty Bird, progress had been rapid—learning facts about an operation that did not wish you to know those facts. Cain had been better than his word. While not actually giving her any information and maintaining concern for Jourdaine's welfare, Cain guided her inquiries. She had succeeded— she was pretty sure.

Will had figured out who was the aide-de-camp for a ranking General Oudelande. Hecate had been able to gin up a counterfeit demand to Oudelande for an estimation of his arrival after leaving point FK, a site which the overlay said was his jump-off point for the invasion. To answer, he would have to consult "The Map." It would have been impossible without Cain.

And Cain was helpful—more than helpful—friendly, companionable . . . *more*? Yet each time they met, Cain seemed restrained. She knew why. His principal, Jourdaine, had returned. Cain had much to do.

Elise was wise enough never to ask about Jourdaine, knowing that any inquiry of hers would constitute an invasion of a protected sphere of Cain's existence to which she was not allowed and about which her motives were suspect. For a "simple" computer utility, Cain seemed to have many facets.

10:40. By now, Hecate should have stationed herself at the scanner locus for DUFS General Staff HQ, ready to intercept the eusum that Elise would generate as she was scanned.

10:45. Walking out of the park and across Power to the People Avenue, Elise presented herself to be scanned at the headquarters' outside security kiosk. If their plan was going to fail, the only warning would be her capture. Tonguing her false tooth with its burden of poison, almost as she had fondled her absurd purple plush hippopotamus to calm herself as a child, Elise hoped she would not be "available for questioning" if she were captured.

The sergeant at the guardhouse was of the grim, gritty variety, still wearing his hair recruit-short and a scowl that would turn milk, were any available. He scanned her meticulously, taking the requisite number of passes, and inspected the reading carefully, taking long seconds to consider the findings before responding.

"Lieutenant Lincoln, you're ahead of time."

"Belts run faster during the slack periods, don't they? Are you suggesting there's a problem, Sergeant . . . Forsyth?" she said, making the reading of the man's identification badge a power statement.

Responding to a direct question by a superior officer was ingrained into all NCOs, and Forsyth was no exception.

"Sir! Yes, sir. No problem at all, sir. Go right in, sir. The security kiosk on the right will direct you once you enter. Sir!"

The man was still braced up as she turned to walk the fifty feet up an oyster-shell path to the stone steps of what appeared to be an old building. It wasn't. The façade was faux stone, Elise noted as she passed, a twenty-second-century attempt to look like neo-federalist style and failing. The Unity had forgotten that stonework needed joints to look authentic.

The security kiosk inside the massive faux-oak double doors was manned by what might be Forsyth's clone. Beyond, Elise saw a beehive of activity: scurrying ensigns, small knots of general officers, and frequent expletives.

"General Oudelande's A de C? We've been expecting you, sir."

"Excellent, Sergeant Hornsby," said Elise smoothly, beginning to feel more at ease.

There was a buzzing, and the sergeant looked up at a monitor. Elise could see over his shoulder that a woman in uniform, a uniform just like her own, was spread-eagled at the entrance, Sergeant Forsyth kneeling on her back with a drawn weapon.

"Fathering idiot. Some citizen thinks they can waltz in here just 'cause they got a pretty uniform!" said the sergeant.

"You and your squad appear to be highly efficient, Sergeant! I will be sure to mention that to the general when I return," said Elise, smiling. The real Lieutenant Lincoln would need, she hoped, several quite uncomfortable hours to disentangle herself from the security bureaucracy. By that time, Elise hoped she would be one more anonymous citizen.

"Sir!" the sergeant replied with a grim smile. "The Map Room security is through there, sir," he said, indicating a corridor to the left, down a dark wood-paneled hallway with nothing on the walls to break up the gloom. Elise pressed through the hurrying crowd and was scanned twice more before she was admitted to the Map Room. She requested Delta-Zulu-Whiskey 11178-Chi, and it arrived within moments, printing itself out at a desk for her to consult.

Time and Place. That was all she had to find: Time and Place.

However, her stomach nearly betrayed her when Elise did not immediately recognize the location. The queasy feeling she had had since leaving Toad Hall bubbled up into full-on nausea. *Upchucking all over a super-secret map is probably bad spycraft.* She swallowed convulsively.

She saw a small green patch with a lake near a large metro area. Enlarging the image, she saw "once site of Confederate Memorial Carving-SMP." Following the roadway southwest toward the population center, Elise smiled. A scattering of Peachtree-named streets. There was Little Five Points, Piedmont, and the Chattahoochee on the extreme northwest of the city center. The Scorch was a vile shade of purple bordering the Savannah River and had a wavering and uncertain frontier on the American side. Copious notes surrounding four locations, Easley, Ninety-Six, Due West, and Liberty, with many more littering Lawrenceville. A tetrahedron shaded red sat to the southwest of Atlanta.

A small cartouche in the corner contained a list of numbers, each one crossed out and another one placed below it in a different hand and color. The first was "06.00.00_11_08_77?" The last was "06.00.00_09_10_77!"

Elise quashed the feeling of elation, ordered the map removed, and prepared to leave.

A hand on her shoulder halted her. Turning, Elise was presented with Major Seymor "Slag" Montan's name badge directly in front of her.

"Might I have a few words?" came a voice from above her.

"Of course, sir!" said Elise, wondering if she could pull the man's sidearm and use him as a shield to exit the building. *Sergeant Forsyth might object,* she thought a second later, and subsided. Stepping away from the voice, Elise received the full effect of the man. *The guy must be a giant for the Unis, six feet two at least!* she thought.

"Lieutenant, please come with me," said the major, and, turning, wended his way, not looking back, to a small conference room, the walls lined in shelves of contraband-bound books—*Cosmopolitan, Esquire, SI,* and *Time* among them, Elise noted. Montan turned and opened his mouth to speak.

"With all due respect, Major, may I speak freely?" Elise interrupted.

The major closed his mouth to scowl. She and the major eyed each other. A livid scar divided the major's left eyebrow. He spoke after several seemingly endless seconds.

"Okay, Lieutenant Lincoln, but make it snappy."

"General Oudelande wanted these coordinates ASAP. He's in charge of the division for the—for the exercise. I am delaying him every second I stay here . . . sir!"

Major Montan looked at her, the scowl deepening.

"Okay, Lieutenant, I will make this quick, as well. I am scheduled to lead the first company, Fifth Battalion, Division Seven, in the upcoming exercise. I have been an acting battalion commander for the last three months. I oughta be posted to battalion HQ. It isn't fair, bad for morale . . ."

"Yes, I see Major Montan. I quite understand your position. With the delay of D-Day, we have time to correct things. I will transmit your concerns to the general, personally. I am sure he will get back to you shortly."

The man's face blossomed into a huge smile. "That's great! I want to be where I can do the most good . . . you, know . . . and stuff." Elise got the impression the man was now a large puppy rolling onto his back to get his belly scratched.

Within minutes, she was on the street, no sign of the real Lieutenant Lincoln other than a small pool of bright red blood near the guardhouse. If Cain had not shared with her the security procedures, the blood would have been hers.

Buying a cheap raincoat on the way home to cover the uniform on the trip to Toad Hall, she arrived without pursuit, retrieved her interface from the refrigerator, and settled herself.

Slow to warm, it took much longer than usual before she felt the sensation of sinking away from reality. She rose up into the otherness of the openCORE. Within seconds thereafter, she would be handing the data to Will and could leave New York. The DUFS would figure it out in time, and Jessika Bonhoffer would be no more.

C R U X

(The most difficult or dangerous section of a climb)

PASSING

"Intelligence should be passed off as quickly as possible, balancing perceived importance with maintenance of security." Rhedd, J., *Spycraft*, (RSA classified syllabus, 2126)

OPENCORE, THE UNITY
14.10.12.LOCAL_07_OCTOBER_AU77 (2129 AD)

Yo, here she is, boss! said Frog. The Will-Frog entity "turned around" to address her, just as she collected herself and extended the box she created with the data enclosed.

Thank God! Will said. Did you have any trouble? I saw a flurry of messages at DUFS security.

I had hoped to be in and out before the real ADC arrived. She came up even before I got the map. They may be on to me. Here's the data. It's Georgia, and it's two days from now, Elise said. She noticed Cain standing a short distance off, smiling but saying nothing.

Two days? There's no time! You have to get moving. Hecate is still shadowing you here to label any eusum. Leave immediately!

Something was wrong.

An alarm was sounding. Not in the openCORE. Will did not react.

It grew in timbre and loudness, impinging on her mind like an alarm clock from a deep sleep. She half emerged into reality, groggy, her interface still in place, Will and Cain ghosts surrounded by ghastly halos in her vision. She ran to the monitor while she heard the hammering at the front door. Elise looked at the monitor only long enough to see that the invaders wore DUFS black. She moved.

In her mental fog, Elise stumbled up the narrow stairs to the top floor of the derelict building. Before opening the dirty, narrow rear window to toss out the rope ladder that would let her escape, Elise peered out through the one corner kept clean. Her route across the roof was already closed by a swarm of black uniforms. A deep, splintering sound issued from the front door, followed by shouts of pain and dismay. She smiled. The electrical grid she had set into it would not hold them for long, however. A crash of broken glass sounded below.

Elise pulled the attic ladder down, winded, her vision and breathing compromised by the interface still in place. She missed a footing, coming down hard onto her shin on the steep steps, sending her back to the CORE in her confusion, surfacing to see Cain, solemn, worried, holding her—*holding her.*

Her vision bounced back to reality, the after-image of Cain still somehow following her, superimposed on her vision as she watched blood seep through her pants leg. Limping up into the dusty attic and pulling the ladder up, she locked it. *No going back that way.* Before she could even start to make a hole in the roof, however, she heard boots on the old slate roof.

It no longer mattered.

Her shin throbbing, Elise settled herself, lying down on the cushions she had placed up here when she first arrived. Almost gratefully, she slipped across to the CORE one more time to send the message, arriving to find herself on a deserted gray field. *No Cain.* She felt hollow. What had she expected?

There was more time now, now that no greater effort of hers was needed, no more effort—merely fortitude. Slates were being torn up at the far end of the roof, the watery sunlight making itself known to her even as she entered the eternal noon of the openCORE. Here at the end of things, death approaching her, all about her, below and above, to one side and another, she smiled. She had brought death with her when she entered the Unity.

Everyone owes God a good death.

She felt the new tooth with her tongue, the one the Color Guard had installed. Elise entered the code.

In the CORE, Will watched as Elise's inchoate persona, the nameless interface, faded, expanded, and sintered away into nothing. Hecate crumbled beside him.

She's gone, he said, stretching a pseudopod to console Hecate.

OVERTURE

THE SOUTHERN GATE, THE UNITY
06.32.11.LOCAL_09_OCTOBER_AU77 (2129 AD)

"Soldiers of the Glorious Unity, it is given you today to strike a blow for your great nation, and to bring the benefits of enlightenment to a dark corner of the world. Too long have the people of Jorga suffered under the crushing oppression of their misguided and vicious shamans. It is time to free your fellow creatures to enter the light of the Unity, adding their rich fields and resources to our own. Your great sacrifices today will resound through the Unity's history along with those of our storied past like—like those heroes we are all so proud of.

"In the Unity's desire to free its suffering brothers from the tyranny of these aged, misguided plutocrats, we have chosen to drop our defenses along this front in our sincere desire to serve mankind."

In a lower voice, once the microphone was supposed to be dead, the assembled multitude, the cream of Unity armed services, heard "Okay, hit it!"

Jourdaine sighed. To his dismay, in its entire seventy-year history, the technicians had never been asked to disable a section of the Rampart. Generations of technicians, educated and certified in the care and maintenance of the Unity's massive technological triumph, could not find the "Off" button. Senior technicians, after laboring over mildewed schematics for a week, were reduced to snatching up flashlights and burrowing into the maze of tunnels beneath the works. They came up with a solution to bypass a likely circuit breaker.

"It had better work, Lieutenant."

It didn't.

Top Sergeant Les Moran switched on a comm-line to his platoon commander, S11, E6 2nd Lieutenant Consuella Dimatto. "Sir! It appears that the attack is off for now. I think the troopers are going to get hot. Can we break formation and get them under cover? Immediately would be best, sir!"

As in most armies since the Battle of Kadesh,[16] the efficiency and success of junior officers are measured by how rapidly they learn to accept their sergeants' suggestions. This much Consuella Dimatto had learned, and thus she ordered the platoon to bivouac in place. In time, so did the rest of the half-million-man army.

"Can you believe these feckers, Bull? They can't figure out how to open the fatherin' gate to let us out. Don't bode well," remarked Sergeant Alex LeBron as the unSapped non-coms of the company sat around a fire that evening.

"Not much into boding myself, Alex. Brass tells me to shoot, I shoot. Long as I get my food, bed, pay, and retirement after twenty-nine years. What are the knuckledraggers gonna do, piddle on us?" said Sergeant Eugene (Bull) Fuller, S13, E27. Most of his audience laughed.

"Well, Sergeant Fuller, I *know* that last year a whole platoon was ambushed. The outlanders took all their pulse-rifles, new Springfield 72s. When they finally found the bodies, not one of the geeks still had his right hand," replied Specialist Ewan Powolsky, tolerated for his willingness to collect and share scuttlebutt.

---

[16] April 1457 BC

"Yeah, Bull. *Those* knuckledraggers? Don't underestimate them. Vicious, cruel, and sneaky. Best to shoot the fathering scum before they get you," rejoined Sergeant LeBron.

BeBe Ramsey, staff sergeant for B platoon, spat into the fire and said, "You guys are forgetting. Do you have any idea what still has to be here? Jewels, books, antique weapons. The Unity never invaded Jorga, not really."

"Whatcha going to do with books and weapons, BeBe? Stuff is old. No one wants it," replied Specialist Leif Greene.

"Keep telling yourself that, Leif. Some of us know who buys and who sells. It's gonna be a bonanza. If you're nice, I might buy what you bring back."

Two more men approached the fire and sat down, ranking sergeant for A Platoon, Lawrence Lowe, and top sergeant for the company, Les Moran.

Lowe accepted a mug of tea. "Looks like they are pretty sure about finally getting off tomorrow. Heard it straight from battalion. We should put the geeks to bed. Specialist Greene, that means you have to tell each one individually. For some reason, they cannot take a hint. Same goes for the latrine. You gotta show them where—and how."

"Let's all turn in. We want to be fresh. Gonna need a good breakfast, even if it's cold. 'Freeing your fellow creatures' can't be done on an empty stomach," said Moran.

Leif Greene kicked the fire apart as all the men started shouting at the CRNAs in preparation for beddy-bye.

PARTING

PALISADE OF THE MESSENGER, WOODRUFF PARK, ATLANTA
6:32 A.M. (EST) OCTOBER 9, 2129

"Jesse?" said Malila in a low voice, so as not to disturb the platoon of soldiers asleep outside her bedroom.

Without a word, Jesse got up from his pallet in front of the door to Malila's bedroom. Malila, Messenger of the Scorch, immediately opened the door, leaned up to kiss him and quietly proceeded to weave her way among the sleeping soldiers of her bodyguard. The palisade gate retracted back into the red Georgia clay as she reached it, making a soft squelching sound.

Collecting his weapons, Jesse followed her out of the palisade as he had each morning they had been there. Malila took up position in the middle of the verdant grass circle in front of the palisade, faced the rising sun, and closed her eyes, even as Jesse surveyed the high points of the buildings surrounding her. Kazinsky's men had taken up positions on each point since the day of their arrival. Jesse, on nodding to each position, was rewarded with the momentary glimpse of a known face. Cradling his new Knapp rifle and adjusting the auto-pistol in the small of his back to be a trifle less uncomfortable, he knew his real job was to keep Malila from being disturbed by overly sincere young men with plights of troth and pamphlets. Today, the streets were empty. Apparently, Malila's novelty was wearing thin.

The American delegation would be assembling after breakfast, as they did each morning. The conference was held on the grass circle, under a grand marquee that the Scorch grew for the occasion.

In the shade of the marquee, the American delegates sat at long tables with ice water, glasses, notepads, tablets, and pens with the hotel logo embossed upon them. The Scorch side was uncovered. Malila stood barefoot the entire day, never leaving to rest, drink, eat, or excrete, refusing even the water that Jesse brought her.

Looking back to Malila, now transfixed by the rays of the rising sun, Jesse supposed that it was really Splanch's sun worship thing, bringing Malila along for convenience sake. Afterward, Malila would breakfast on whatever Splanch made for her or poach off what Jesse bought for himself from the hotel. More often than not, men stood Jesse the cost of a fancy hotel breakfast: the old out of friendship, the young from bravado, and enemies, just for the look of the thing.

Today was the end of the third week of this farce. *Damned waste of time,* he thought. Yesterday's sessions, after a day of rest on Sunday, had been typical.

"Ambassador Splanch, I must say your proposals, if sincere, are most interesting. Confirmation of your claims will take some time, you understand, of course," said Fetschuler in his most annoyingly pedantic manner. He smiled lopsidedly, sat, and took a sip of ice water.

"With all due respect, Professor Fetschuler," said Splanch in Malila's voice, "neither of us has the luxury of time. Even now, the Unity, our mutual enemy, is massing forces across the river. It may already be too late for our people to join for a common defense.

"It *is* time for straight speaking. Your inaction will lead to more deaths and the loss of *more* time, more treasure, more territory, and more troops. Your central government is aware of our concerns. We, the Scorch and America, have this single golden hour, a time where we should be forging an alliance that would stand the test of time. History will take note of how we use these few moments."

With heads bobbing around the table in response, Fetschuler promised to make a "definitive reply" once he had communicated with his government. They recessed for the day.

He had tried to talk to Malila about it last night. "You should leave. Nothing is happening here—all the people who might make decisions bailed out. We could be trapped. It's time to go, my love," said Jesse as he arose from the comm'net terminal that he'd insisted they install inside the palisade.

"I can't leave. Splanch thinks progress is being made. Senator Neilson made some very positive suggestions Saturday. An open market zone between us was an excellent idea."

"Delaying tactics, dragging their feet on the big question of acknowledging the sovereignty of the Scorch. Without that, what's the point? They think that if they delay long enough, the Scorch will give in."

"You don't know Splanch, my dear."

"You don't know America, my love."

That conversation had sputtered out into the same sort of armed silence like all their conversations about the conference—and almost every other conversation they had had recently, as well. Affection between them had been whittled down to only a single forlorn kiss on arising and retiring, like a minimum payment of some immense debt. He felt as if he were watching the death of a child.

Just as Jesse finished another round of checking the highpoints, he turned to see Malila slowly crumble to the ground.

He sprinted to her side, dropping his rifle as he reassured himself that she still lived. He felt her pulse: cool—*no, cold*—rapid, thready, weak. Scooping her up, Jesse walked back to her bedroom, alerting the few remaining soldiers to stand guard. No gate grew up behind him as it had every other time previously. In a few minutes, Malila seemed to revive without much help from him. Within a few minutes more, she was ready to talk.

"Jesse, Splanch is leaving—has left me. The Scorch left me. Everything is dying. I don't think they're coming back. I think the conference is over."

"I warned you, lass. The Scorch's *not* to be trusted. They will betray you when you least expect it. Just their nature. Nothing can fix it, just never forget it."

"No, you're wrong. You always think the worst of them. They aren't like us, but—it can't mean. I won't—"

"Yes, if you say so, lass."

Jesse paused as Malila frowned at him before continuing. "But let's find out what is happening. Get dressed, and let's go find some news . . . and maybe some coffee."

Looking around the bedroom, Malila had gone quiet.

"There aren't any new clothes," she said, finally.

Every day, on arising, Malila had a new, subtly different shift to wear—but not today. She dressed in a used dress from the day before, wrinkled from having to be rescued from a refuse bin.

After giving orders for the men to assemble, Jesse and Malila walked across the street. Jesse looked back. In the last few moments, the circle of grass had turned gray-green, and the palisade had retracted into the earth, leaving the soldiers' abandoned gear lying where it had been left. Kazinsky was on a comm-line, waving his arms.

Chaos greeted them on entering the lobby: shouting, sweating, florid, fat men pulling mounds of luggage. Colliding with each other, demanding transport, fighting over the few taxis, they mostly ignored the hotel employees who scurried around on missions of their own. The desk clerk, a distracted woman who never got off the telephone, answered his questions by semaphore between instructions to someone to "get the dog in the house and pack stuff for a week," and let him know that these were the last of the conference attendees, most having left during the night.

Trying to get away from the melee, Jesse and Malila went down a hallway and into a small dining room off the conference center. Malila had again turned pale, moisture giving her brow a light sheen. Jesse had her sit on one of those occasional sofas that hotels put at odd places. This one was too small, too short, and too hard. *Very occasional.* Leaving her there to find some water, Jesse cornered a bellman and got the straight dope.

Pouring Malila a glass of melted ice from a pitcher, Jesse said, "Here, drink this, lass. You're too hot. I'm worried about heat stroke. Standing out there in the sun without a hat . . ."

"What's happened, Jesse?"

"The Unity has started its attack. It's all I know. Splanch could be dead. *You have to move today.*"

"Splanch *isn't* dead. I *know*. It *left* me. It didn't die. I told you."

"Could be. Could be that the Scorch and Unity are in cahoots. They kept you *here*, and America focused on this—*sideshow*—while the invasion was getting up to speed. The Scorch may have already told the Unity where you are. You *can't know* what a plant thinks. Now, we have to start looking out for you, lass."

"No. You *don't. You* never believed in what I was doing. *You've* always thought the worst of Splanch and the rest of the Scorch. I don't know what Speaker ever saw in *you*. I don't know what I saw in you!"

"I'm lookin' out for you, lass, and I've never been more nor less than what you see—warts, stripes, and all. I love you, lass, but I don't like the Scorch. Simple as that. We have to get *moving*," he said, taking her arm and rising to leave.

"I don't think I want to travel with you anymore. They *said* you were brutal and ungenerous."

"And I never denied it. You don't understand."

"No, I don't, and neither do you. You have lived closer to the Scorch than anyone, and you don't understand them. I belong to the Scorch now. I can't go with you."

"I promised *you* and *them* that I'd look after you, Malila. Whatever you *think* of me doesn't matter. What matters is I *promised*."

"Very noble. Doubtless, Thomas'll give you a good performance report. I trust I won't be too much of a burden."

Jesse could feel his anger flare, but then he stepped back and dropped her arm. "That's unfair! You have been abandoned by your plants—as I warned. They aren't looking out for your welfare, but *I am*. Who do you think will do that if I don't? Lots of people will blame you for whatever happens. You don't know the country. These are not your people. The invasion is *now*, and you got nothing: no money, no weapon, and no idea of an escape."

"You don't know that! You think there's nothing about me that you don't know. I'm this poor little *lost* girl you have to protect. I am a soldier and quite capable of looking out after myself."

"Pockets!"

"What do you mean, *'pockets'*? I swear you are getting weirder and more sinnal, Old Man."

"It is 'senile,' not 'sinnal,' and no, I'm not. *Pockets*. Ye have nae pockets, lass. Ye have na way ta buy yer transport, yer food, yer housing, nor yer protection. You're a marked woman, lass. Yer face has bin th' face o' th' Scorch fur weeks now. Dae ye think ye kin wander about wi' no one th' wiser? Not everybody what brings ill tidings is loved by them what hear it, lass."

"You're talking funny again. I'm not *your* problem anymore, Dr. Johnstone. Go!"

"I'm the only one here as loves you, Malila. And because o' that, I promised ta look after ye," said Jesse, cross with himself for again slipping into the Scots of his youth, doing that anytime he was upset, angry—or fearful of losing Malila.

"So, we are back where we started. You're my jailer. Is *that* what it's going to be? You've not shown much imagination, Sisi," said Malila, fluttering a hand dismissively in his direction.

"Duck!"

"What is that supposed to mean? You are going to tell me I'm—"

Jesse pulled her down behind a table set for a banquet that would now never occur. He clamped a hand over Malila's mouth and kept it there even after she elbowed him, even after she bit him.

"Shush," he whispered. *"Drone.* Just came up over the transom. *Quiet."*

Malila's eyes went large and she nodded. Jesse released his hold on her as he listened. Only with difficulty could he make out the subtle high-frequency whizzing that he took to be the drone engine. What he had seen was tiny, no more than the size of a cicada but less bumbling in its flight. That, at least, was good. The killer drones, having to carry the equipment for identification as well as assassination, were the size of a dinner plate. However, *if your enemy can see you, he can kill you.* If Malila was to escape, she needed to keep out of sight. For Malila to stay out of sight long enough to get to safe transport, she needed a distraction.

"Malila. You win. You want nae part o' me. I ken. Now, when I tell you, go out the back of this room, through the kitchens, and at the end, you'll find a loading dock. Go south, on your left, no more than thirty meters, and you will find an entrance to the subway. Get a train going west and north any way you can. Ride on top if ye hae tae! Go toward Rome or Dalton. Dinnae stop movin' 'til ye see an American army unit. Surrender to them as a foreign national. Wave a white flag. Do you ken?"

"Yes. No! Money. I have no money. No weapon."

Jesse flipped a small leather bag from his belt and the pistol from the small of his back. "Take what I have. There's four hundred dollars and a pistol with eight shots in it," he said, placing the items into her hands. They were trembling.

"What are you going to do?"

Jesse smiled. "Does it matter, lass? *Everyone owes God a good death.*"

Malila made no answer as he turned away.

In the few moments while he waited his chance, Jesse remembered the days with his first wife, Simone. It had come as a shock to him, in those days when their love was green, when he realized with what ease he would trade his own life for Simone's. *She had loved him, and he had loved her.* The same had been true for each child and each new wife. It *had* been true for Malila, as well. He had put himself in danger for Malila in the past when it was his job. He had put himself in the lion's mouth for her when he realized he loved her. Now it came as a much crueler shock to realize he would gladly trade his life for Malila's; she no longer loved him. The trade was not even close.

"Go!"

Before Malila could say anything, Jesse grabbed a tablecloth from an unset table and sprinted toward the drone, shielding his appearance and Malila's from the flying cicada.

Malila waited. The high-frequency whir of the drone disappeared around the corner in pursuit of Jesse. Malila jogged herself into action and ran, crouched, along the back wall of the dining room to the barely detectable door leading into a service corridor between dining rooms and away from Jesse and the Unity drone.

Stupid. Now that he was exposed, Jesse would be chased by the small drone until a larger killer drone had closed with him. Then the Old Man would die. Malila ran on toward the kitchen, she hoped. Instead of the usual busy clangor, she heard nothing but a door repeatedly banging as if caught in a wind.

Moving toward the noise, she felt like she had on the illusory whale hunt months before: every sense tuned to the present, feeling her surroundings, primed for escape, a portion of her mind balancing, evaluating, and discriminating what to do for her survival. At the same time, Malila felt hollowed out—eviscerated. Splanch was gone. For the first time in six weeks, she had no tingling sensation of its presence, of its placid approval. She had thought Jesse was being stupidly masculine, mulishly male, by his aversion to her once she revealed Splanch's indwelling. That gutted her, in its own way. She was understanding it a little—just as it was too late. Jesse was gone—and into danger again. He never seemed to give it a thought, as if that portion of his brain were turned to the sticking point, incapable of any more modulated response. *Did he run into smoking buildings on reflex or because of a death wish?*

Malila entered the kitchen, finding the noise was from an automatic door closer on a large walk-in refrigerator, attempting, again and again, to close despite an abandoned service cart blocking it. Malila pulled the service cart away, and the door finally closed. In the silence, all she now heard was the fluttering of the heavy plastic strips covering the loading dock exit. *Probably as good a way to prevent drones following me as any,* she thought as she exited.

Jesse said to go south, to the left, thirty meters. *How am I to take that seriously? Some old man from the wilderness giving me directions inside a city he's never lived in,* she thought as she ducked through the door.

Across the street, a sign, in multicolored, modern, half-melted letters, proclaimed the entrance to the subway—to her left. *Lucky guess.* Malila snagged a plastic bag scudding across the abandoned street as she ran toward the subway, putting the pistol and money into it. Looking back at the hotel, she saw a few drones and heard the angry buzzing from many more. Jesse was not going to get out of the hotel—not alive. Malila stumbled on the uneven pavement as tears suddenly obscured her vision.

Wiping her eyes, Malila found the subway entrance. Within, pandemonium reigned, as if all the evil spirits of the world had been crammed into the confined space, inoculating the city with madness. A thin, grubby, bearded man was trundling a pyramid of luggage toward a turnstile, oblivious to two small children, dissolved in tears, who blocked his way. An adolescent girl blind-sided the thin man with an umbrella before he could do any damage, toppling the pyramid. A young, bleary-eyed woman in a smudged and torn cocktail dress, holding her color-coordinated pumps in one hand, was bellowing at a ticket dispenser, as her companion, a vacant-eyed creature in a kilt-like affair and of indeterminate gender, wept copiously beside her.

Tickets were superfluous. The gates had been thrown open, and by the time Malila had worked her way around a corner, she could see that the crowd filled the entire mezzanine and extended down the stairs onto the platform. The mass moved as if it were a gigantic new species of flatworm, small ripples of motion moving it forward and into the stairwell, packing the crowd ever tighter. Suddenly, the mass of people, like a single organism, gathered itself and surged forward. A train had arrived.

Jesse's advice would work! Malila was nearing the stairs.

Just then a cry went up by those behind her.

"Drones! The drones are coming! The drones! The drones are coming!"

It was if a thousand voices had taken up the anthem, whispering and bellowing the words from one end of the mezzanine to the other. Faces, moments before contorted in anger, now slack and gray, turned toward the entrances. Faces already weeping in despair slumped to the floor, wailing wordlessly. Still other faces froze with stony fatalism.

Then the crowd broke.

Most ran for the exits. Many cowered in place and were trampled by others in the heedless panic. Some fought the tide of humanity to gain a place closer to the next train's arrival. The inchoate wailers were swept away with the first surge. Malila, spying a place out of the maelstrom, a shallow niche sporting a colorful graphic, stepped within.

Surprisingly, within a few minutes, the mezzanine was empty except for the groans of the trampled. Malila started to go to the aid of the weeping, kilted person whose motionless body had, like flotsam, washed up almost at her feet. Then she heard the high-pitched whir. She froze, stood, and stepped back into the niche. The single whir became several, the sounds bouncing around the hard walls and ceiling, seeming to come from all directions. A rising wall of sound encased her in a cacophony of noise, paralyzing her for the moment.

Pulse bolts' discharges crackled as the incapacitated received their coup de grace. Malila was not very familiar with Unity drones, operated as they were by their own cadre of specialized operators, like armor and artillery. What she knew about them was rudimentary. There were but two models: the light, unarmed scout and a heavier eight-propped hunter, and each had nighttime variants. With a single camera, however, the images of several drones could be integrated, allowing for excellent spatial recognition. On an impulse, Malila pressed against the wall poster, assumed what she thought must be an ingratiating pose, and smiled—for her life.

The whir became overwhelming. Malila had forgotten how noisy they were; but then again, she had never been hunted by them before. She focused on a joint in a pipe a dozen meters off, trying not to blink nor move her eyes. She slowed her breathing, hunched her shoulders—and smiled.

Out of the corner of her vision, Malila could see movement. Terrified, she hoped the drones had no subroutine able to detect insincerity in facial expressions. She smiled.

Malila felt the downdraft as a black form moved across her field of vision until it centered itself in front of her, the joint in the pipe now obscured. Malila tried to unfocus her eyes rather than look at the lens of the camera. Even so, she noticed how insectoid it appeared— small protuberances, clustered about the central lens, which dilated back and forth as it examined her. A small siphon extended to sample the air. It wavered slightly before her, Malila trying not to follow the motion with her eyes. In the niche, only one drone or another would be able to see her. It would be impossible to get a stereoscopic image of her. If she remained motionless, she would appear merely as a flat surface to the Unity cameras—unless she moved.

The drone zoomed off, hesitated, came back, and drilled a pulse bolt into the motionless form of the kilt-wearer half a meter from Malila's feet.

The man groaned and died.

One hour and thirty minutes later by the station clock, the drones left, having killed the kilted man at her feet an additional two times. Only then did Malila unfreeze and step out of the niche. On stiff legs, she bolted for the stairs down to the train platform, deserted except for the corpses: no passengers, no transport personnel, but most importantly, no train.

Malila consulted the information screen. She needn't have bothered. The display cycled between public information announcements, a snippet of last night's news, and a commercial for a ballgame destined to go unplayed: no train arrivals or departures. Looking into the great abyss of the rail tunnel, however, she could see lights.

Jumping off the platform, Malila edged along in the dark, trying not to trip. She could hide in the underground or use the tunnel to emerge at some unexpected spot within the city to continue an escape on foot. These were equally bad choices if the drones blanketed the city, yet going topside here would be suicide. The invasion had only just begun. The Unity would clean out the tunnels, given time. Going topside either now or later, without real information about the invasion, would increase her risk of discovery with no greater likelihood of safety. Having spent weeks underground while she was trying to escape from the Unity made the decision easier, if ironically funny, as well. Malila, Terror of the rat horts, Burglar of Higginses, Poet of the BBWI,[17] was once more going to ground to escape the tender mercies of the Unity. She chuckled to herself.

"Shhhhh—for God's sake, be quiet. They'll hear you! You silly girl!"

Malila looked down to see, in the uncertain light, the upturned face of a large man in a business suit.

"Unlikely there, citizen. The drones are gone. Daytime drones—no night vision on those guys. At least for the time being, we have the subway to ourselves—if we hurry."

"And go where?" the man almost wailed. "We're safe down here. If we move, they might find us."

Malila's eyes, now adjusting to the dim light, began to make out huddled forms along the wall . . . two, three . . . five . . . eight.

"If we *don't* move, I can *guarantee* it. The Unity isn't stupid. They'll look for you as soon as the CRNAs arrive in force. I don't know why they're not here already."

"How do you know? You're guessing—just like the rest of us."

"Not guessing. If you stay here, you *will* be captured."

There was some muttering from that comment just before a voice in the back said, "Hey, I know *you*! You're that *Malila* person—the one from the Scorch. You *brought* those things here! You're *in* on it!"

---

[17] Brotherhood of Beltway Workers International, the union that rules the subterranean reaches of the Unity and collects poems

Malila heard the rising tide of desperation and anger seethe toward her. She must say something—something to sweep back the hostility.

"Right! That's why *I'm* down in this *hole, trying to get away,* just like the *rest* of you—because I'm in on the conspiracy. Are all of you Americans *that* stupid?"

There was a pause before an older female voice in the back said, sotto voce that could be heard easily by everyone there, "Be quiet, Herman! Don't talk about stuff you're ignorant about." There was generalized nervous laughter. Malila jumped into the conversational hiatus.

"Look! I'm going to check out those lights up there. They may be something we can use. Regardless, going that way gets us away from downtown." *And,* Malila thought, *it gives these people something to do before hysteria sets in.* She wondered why she was even bothering, though. With a little prevarication, she could have gotten by this group and been on her way. Now she would be burdened by the fates of the mostly faceless and unknown people into whom she had stumbled. Somehow, she could not imagine Jesse leaving them behind.

The lights, reached only after fifteen minutes of hectoring, helping, cajoling, and pleading with the group, turned out to belong to a trolley on a side track. It was deserted, the doors open to the tunnel.

"Anyone know how to run one of these?" asked the Herman-voice from the shadows, which she discovered belonged to a youth of nineteen, as he frequently announced, followed by, "I'm not a child anymore."

Older and younger than I am, she thought. In the Unity, birthdays were not celebrated. Instead, there would be a generalized announcement, days later, that "citizens on the following list are now E13s, with all the rights and responsibilities pertained thereto," and that would be that. At her last birthday, there had been even less. Malila, for reasons that escaped her now, had concealed her birthday while a captive living on a frontier farm in Kentucky. Last January, she was eighteen, another unremarkable stretch of middle age for a Unity soldier. All the important landmarks had already been passed: becoming a citizen with the placement of her basic implant at seven, selection by a guild and the placement of her O A implant at eleven, first patronage at thirteen, first commission at fourteen. In the Unity, the only additional milestone was retirement at forty. People were given a big celebration for that one—just before they disappeared forever.

Malila's attention came back to the present when another voice said, "Yeah. Okay. I do. I run them back and forth to maintenance. I'm no driver, though. I'd be worth my job to drive with passengers."

"I don't think you have to worry about that, . . ."

"John Hammond, Miss Malila. Just call me John."

"Can I ask you to hop up and see if you can get this going, Mr. Hamm . . . John? And please, just call me Malila."

It turned out to be easier than John thought. The power cable to the electrified line on the roof of the tunnel was still engaged, and he could hot-wire the ignition. The small group piled aboard, and they were on their way within minutes.

Surprisingly, the Civic Center, Peachtree Center, and the Arts Center stops were desolate. There was some debris: toppled suitcases, abandoned baby strollers, and a small pet dog left in a crate. The latter was released and adopted on the spot by a taciturn older man named Drake. They picked up a few more refugees at North Avenue,

Midtown, and Buckhead, including a little old lady walking slowly with the aid of a cane and her eleven-year-old granddaughter.

By the time they emerged from the underground at Heard's Ferry and started off at speed over open country, the company numbered thirty-one. Dairy cows occasionally wandered near the tracks, looking up accusingly as the trolley moved past. *Milking time.* The next group of cows they came to, she had Hammond stop, and Drake collected milk in the empty water bottles they carried. Nothing else moved, the land apparently swept of humanity.

Malila, standing on the rear platform an hour after dark, looked for pursuers. Nothing showed behind them but the starless black night and rare eruptions of silent green fire over the horizon. The sudden stop, as the trolley arrived at the end of the line, caught her by surprise, and she had to make a grab for the bundle containing the pistol and money to keep it from falling out of the overhead. She checked the pistol for the twentieth time: *eight shots, .38 caliber.*

The station sign said Altoona—repeatedly, until Herman found where to put a boot in.

After thanking Dave, the driver, Malila collected her stash and a still-warm bottle of milk and started off to the northwest, still wondering whether Jesse's advice was the best plan. She heard a half-dozen footfalls behind her and, turning, was greeted with the hopeful and slightly embarrassed faces of the passengers, lurid in the flickering light of the damaged sign.

"Don't follow me! I sure don't know where I'm going! The country has been invaded. Run away! The more we stick together, the more likely the DUFS will come to see what's up!"

A little man in suspenders, a blue work shirt, and thick glasses stepped forward.

"Truth is, Messenger Chiu, we've been talking. We were hoping you'd show us how to join the Scorch—even Herman. It's only sixty miles east, and I feel sure, when they realize we're civilians, they'll give us sanctuary."

"The Scorch is *not* your friend. The peace conference was a bust. You Americans dragged it out until the invasion started. Splanch is back in the Scorch trying to stay alive, just like us," she said, feeling angry and disappointed and seeing her anger reflect as dismay from the faces of these people caught up in affairs bigger than their own lives.

The man drew himself up. "Be that as it may, Messenger Chiu, *we've* done no harm to the Scorch. You, yourself, were saved by them. You've said so yourself. We Americans have injured the Scorch merely from our ignorance, not by any hatred for them. We can at least get a hearing from them, now that we know they can talk and reason."

Malila was about to say how foolish she thought the man's words were, but stopped. The crowd had ceased jostling as the man spoke. Malila saw a few heads nod and a rare smile. *Air, water, food.* People needed all those things to live, but they also needed something outside themselves. Like viewing a distant mountain and imagining themselves staggering the last score of steps to the summit, people needed to stake a claim to the untrodden future. For these folks, she, Malila, was a guide.

"America has done a lot of damage to the Scorch over the years, but after today, I don't think the Scorch has much love for the Unity, either. You may be right, citizen. But we still can't go that way. The Unity is coming from that direction. They'd catch us before we got to shelter. We need to go north and west for a while until we run into some American units. Tell me your name, please, citizen."

"Alexi Demiccelli."

"Okay, Alexi. I am going to scout out a route away from here for about an hour. In that time, I want you to get a couple helpers and organize things with these people. Everyone should have someone else looking out for them. Get rid of excess baggage that would slow us down, but keep any food to share out. Find a house with a basement to stay in. Don't stay at the station, whatever you do. Who knows when the drones show up again! Get some sleep, if you can. See if you can find some more weapons."

"Aye, aye, Cap!" said Alexi, smiling.

That's odd, Malila thought as she picked her way down from the station along an overgrown and little-used path. Demiccelli had immediately assumed she would command. Despite her seven years in the DUFS, rising to the level of a first lieutenant, she had never really been a *leader* before. After traveling with Kazinsky's patrol, she had decided that the Unity's CRNAs did not really count as soldiers. They would follow anyone. She had commanded sheep, while Kazinsky commanded wolves. Yet these Americans had willingly thrown their lots in with hers, despite her youth and foreignness.

Malila dropped down an incline to follow a narrow concrete street toward the northwest. The deserted, dark town seemed dried up and worn out in the Indian-summer heat that lingered after sundown. She could find no vehicles. *At least the warning had been effective here.* Rapidly approaching the town's edge, she found the park. Stepping toward it, she was delighted to find a small creek concealed under the black canopy of huge evergreens. A small, macadamized path shadowed the creek, both wending their ways toward the north.

Within two hours, Malila had returned to the site with her platoon of civilians. The little man, Alexi, during her absence, had drafted two more sergeants and divided the group between them. A few from the train, including the man Drake and his new dog and the lady with her cane, decided to stay in Altoona. Discarded suitcases lay by the station entrance. Some of the passengers were wearing extra layers of clothes, she noticed. Malila smiled. The extra clothes would be discarded piecemeal if the trek proved as difficult as Malila believed it would be.

The strange caravan made its way forward, keeping to the bumpy path under the shelter of the trees, a hectic nighttime breeze occasionally sending a flurry of summer-killed leaves to fall in a premature autumnal shower. It was slow going in the dark, as their only light came from a novelty key fob flashlight from one of the passengers. The trail and the creek eventually petered out. Malila emerged into the open and saw the dark mass of a building on a small rise, which revealed itself to be an abandoned school.

They slept there on abandoned jackets and couch cushions until the sun dawned on another bright, clear, and unseasonably warm autumn day. Sharing out slices from a loaf of whole-wheat bread discovered in the cafeteria, each drank copiously from the classroom's kiddie fountain before they left.

With the scout drone in pursuit, Jesse reentered the lobby of the hotel. Looking out the huge windows, Jesse could see that someone had brought a school bus around. Once the body of the bus driver had been shoveled out onto the pavement, the very important people in the lobby had lined up and were boarding the bus like orderly school children, ignorant of the presence of drones.

Not good, Jesse thought as he realized he was now the only target in the vast lobby. The drone, initially confused by the flurry of white tablecloth, had followed him nevertheless. It would track him for the killer drone unless he could foil it. Running to the foot of the stair, Jesse waited as the drone approached, trying to steady himself. Just as it got close, Jesse broke away again, to run up the wide curving steps that led from the lobby to the mezzanine, going three at a time, hoping to catch the drone's pilot by surprise.

He heard the small engine rev up, the drone needing to accelerate and go nose down to climb the stairs or risk losing its prey. Jesse counted to two. Turning and leaping up to the drone, its camera thus obscured, the Old Man snagged the cicada with a corner of the tablecloth he still carried. It was enough to send it into a wall. Jesse's boot finished it off.

Let's call that the overture, he thought.

With any luck, that should summon the rest of the drones in the vicinity and send a flock of the things into the hotel from support units further afield.

For Act One, he needed something *splashy.*

Nothing like a good show to take the heat off Malila. However, his preparations, unobserved for the moment, would have to be quick. Jesse went to a front window. The school bus had not made it out of Five Points. A plume of thick, oily smoke rose from the yellow vehicle from where it had run into a traffic light. Fallen, dark bodies were still trying to drag themselves from where they were strewn across half the road. As he watched, drones circled the moving figures, administering single shots. Anything that tried to get away above ground would die.

Hoping Malila had made it to the subway, Jesse turned back to find stage props for the drones' amusement. Leaping over the front desk, he looked around for what might be there and found the makings of Act One: a fire extinguisher, rubber bands, and a ball of string.

Positioning the fire extinguisher in the middle of the lobby and wedging it about with discarded luggage, Jesse aimed the funnel toward the ceiling, pulled the pin, stripped off yards of string, and stuffed the remaining ball of string into the grip before putting one after another of the rubber bands around the handle. Now, a sharp tug would dislodge the ball of string, setting off the fire extinguisher. Bravissimo!

Funny thing about hunters, thought Jesse. They forget what they're hunting. If you hunt possum, they either run away, hole up, or climb a tree. A human, on the other hand, might give you a shiny gewgaw to stare at while he designs your coffin for you.

Leaving Act One, Jesse ran back into the kitchen and threw the tablecloth into a sink of dirty water and then into the freezer before grabbing a wheeled laundry basket.

There was no sign of Malila. *Thank God for that,* he thought.

It was clear to him now that the Scorch had made Malila a decoy, delaying readiness preparations at the primary target and lulling America into a sense of security with its promise of a potent new ally arriving on the eve of hostilities. Malila, and all Americans, had been nicely duped.

So had he.

Even knowing the Scorch as he did, he had wanted to believe Malila's mission was authentic. It had felt so authentic, and he had wanted to believe. He was a fool. Now he was paying the price for his gullibility.

Going to a table piled high with the small canisters waiting for use with the luncheon buffet, Jesse tumbled them into the laundry basket, then went looking for a butane torch. They always had those about, to put the finishing touches on the crème brûlée and such like. Finding one, as expected, on the dessert table, he dumped the torch into the cart and pushed it back to the banquet room at a run. A peek out into the lobby showed that a few drones had shown up to investigate the loss of the first one. One was a large killer drone buzzing ominously near the high ceiling.

Time's running out.

Opening up a dozen of the canisters, the ones containing gelled alcohol for warming dishes, Jesse emptied the contents onto the floor near the closed doors to the lobby and among the tablecloths and curtains. Using his short knife, he then stabbed each of the remainder of the cans, placing them in a pile near the entrance.

Another peek showed that his audience had grown to several dozen drones. One batch was beginning to start up the wide staircase, and another dozen was coming toward his hiding place in the banquet room.

Racing back to pick up the tablecloth, now stiff with ice, Jesse slid in behind the table near the doors to the lobby, banging them open with a foot as he set off the First Act.

Jesse watched as the erupting fire extinguisher fountained an obscuring cloud of carbon dioxide into the middle of the lobby. Drones from all over raced back, presuming the plume was set off to hide something. It wasn't. The show was to get them all together for the opening lines of Act Two. He waited. Just as the plume had dissipated, the drones discovered the string that had triggered it. Almost like a cloud, they started to drift back toward the banquet room. More and more of the drones entered, starting to orbit within the room, close to the ceiling in order to see more and be able to drop onto their next victim. By the sound, Jesse could tell that most of the drones were the heavier ones, each with a distant pilot looking to make the next kill. It sounded like only about half of the drones were within the room, though. *Not enough.*

Leaning over from behind his frozen blind, Jesse grabbed a punctured container, popped off the top with his short knife, and sent a high pop fly into the opposite corner of the room.

Jesse could hear the angry buzzing of the drones increase. Hiding behind his dripping and stiff tablecloth, he heard several come to investigate. If one of the killer drones sent a missile into him "just to make sure," it'd be over in an instant. He held his breath.

Eventually, the buzzing receded. Jesse lit the butane torch and tossed it the few feet into the mass of gelled alcohol at the doorway. A sheet of flame streaked up, blocking the doorway. Chaos erupted. A fraction of the drones tried to leave and flared into oblivion. A smaller number of the drones remaining outside tried to enter, falling like small, lighted torches into the room, setting off secondary blazes. Punctured cans started exploding, arcing away into the center of the room like small rockets, attracting drones away from him. Jesse could hear collisions above him, broken drones raining down onto the tables, starting more fires. The sprinkler system cut on, downing more drones and confusing the survivors.

Hiding under the frozen and food-soiled tablecloth would foil the drone's heat detection, olfactory probes, and visual identification just as well as it had when he hunted mountain cats with a skunk-impregnated frozen elk hide—a trick he had learned as a youth, much to his mother's distaste.

What this gimmick would not do was work forever.

The tablecloth, too far from the sprinklers and too near to the fires, was beginning to smolder as he abandoned it. Hoping to sneak out the same way Malila had, through the kitchens and into the subway, Jesse scuttled behind the remaining tables, crunching defunct drones underfoot.

The first missile exploded near his head and behind him, off target, no doubt, from the heated updrafts. He flinched away as the missile ignited a curtain and dropped it on him. Jesse smelled the stink of burning hair as he slapped out the flames out and ran on. He made it through the service door—an inapparent affair lacking a door frame, a handle, and, unfortunately, a lock—and started along the service corridor toward the kitchen.

He was prepared for the first detonation and did not look back. Now, below the cacophony of alarms and the roar of the fire and sprinklers, Jesse heard the ominous whir of drones.

Act Three: Tragedy or Comedy? he wondered.

Turning on the large fan as he rounded the corner into the kitchen, Jesse dashed into the freezer, quietly pulling the heavy door closed. He had just finished as five drones arrived. Two immediately investigated the exit, the plastic flaps fluttering in the breeze he had created there to attract their attention.

Watch the shiny gewgaw!

Peeking through the small window from the freezer, Jesse saw and felt how the missile blew a hole through the door, knocking down the heavy plastic strips and allowing all the drones to file through—all except for the one that had fired the missile. The Old Man guessed that this drone was now depleted of any offensive weapons and had been assigned to surveillance duties.

Not good.

He was beginning to shiver; his body, warmed by the bonfire but soaked from the sprinklers, streamed heat out into the cold of the freezer. In shirtsleeves, he could not stay here long. The drone was focused on the doorway but orbited around the kitchen, as well, peeking behind the counters and into storerooms. Its operator would eventually figure out that the freezer was a potential hiding place. If he disabled the drone, alerting the operator to his presence, it would be just as bad as if he were actually observed. He needed to escape unnoticed, leaving the remaining drone undisturbed to watch a hole from which no rat would emerge.

Nice trick.

Jesse looked around the freezer. A whole pig carcass and several quarters of beef hung in the open, while open shelves filled the rest of the room, sadly depleted by the appetites of the conference and offering no cover for him. A stack of plastic bags, a fire ax, and an open box of frozen, double-thick pork chops completed his *matériel de guerre.* Jesse grabbed a pork chop.

It would be dicey—*only the one chance.*

The good news was that as he got more hypothermic, his blood flow would centralize, increasing the blood supplied to the heart, brain—and kidneys. He would not want for "bait." He made what preparations he could, feeling how the cold, rapidly making his movements clumsy, made difficult his positioning the pig carcass to hang in the middle of the room, right in front of the door. Hypothermia could occur even in modestly cool weather, he knew; the thermometer said it was negative twenty.

However, actually filling the bag was the most difficult part of his scheme. His cold-clumsy hands did not help, and his aim was compromised now by continuous shivers. *You'd think after seventy years or so, I'd have this down pat by now!* Finally succeeding, feeling the cold seeping into his mind, the Old Man realized he needed to position the bag just right within the pig's visceral cavity— too high and the temperature probe would ignore it, too low and it would be exposed. The "bait" must be still warm to be effective. Taking out his small knife, Jesse jammed the blade into a rib inside the pig carcass and splintered off a sharp spicule of bone. *This will serve nicely,* he thought, before jamming the bag onto it. When all was ready, Jesse pricked a small hole into the lowest part of the bag, crouched by the opening side of the door, propped a forequarter of beef in front of himself, and unlatched the door.

Just before pushing it open, he hyperventilated, trying to ensure he would not groan from the shivering, worse now as he huddled inside his frozen beefy blind.

Nothing for it. He eased the door open.

"Captain, you need to see this," said Lieutenant Facer, currently commanding Killer Drone B22 in Assault Wing Alpha.

"What now, Facer?" asked a weary Captain Gibson as he came over to his command screen.

"I am in the Marriott Grand Mercure kitchen, on patrol after depleting my armament. The rest of the wing is chasing some arsonist. We're just awaiting recall. Nothing here. Then I noticed a door was open. Turns out to be the freezer. Nothing special at first. Frozen meat, empty shelves. But then I noticed it."

"Well, Lieutenant? Noticed what?"

"The pig is peeing."

"What?"

"Hot piss dripping out onto the floor."

"How do you know it's piss?"

"Olfactory sensors. Not a tough call, really."

"Yeah, okay. What's it doing now?"

"Well. It's stopped. The puddle on the floor is cold now."

"So, nothing is happening now. Is that right, Lieutenant?"

"Yes, sir. Nothing. Nothing else in the room. All the meat's hung except for one hunk on the floor near the door. Wasteful!"

"Fecking Americans! Okay. Go back to patrolling, as ordered. Nice pickup, Facer."

"Thank you, sir."

BUBBA HAWKINS BAR AND GRILL, 50 LOWER ALABAMA STREET, ATLANTA, RSA
10:05 P.M. OCTOBER 9, 2129 AD (AU 77)

They were a collection of city boys, holed up in the one place with lights on, even if those lights were underground. Atlanta had burned before, once in the mid-nineteenth century and then about a hundred years later, during the Secession. It had rebuilt over the ashes, leaving a warren of old streets for bars, casinos, and the seedier establishments of negotiable virtue. No adults remained in the whole of the underground warren, unless you counted the half-dozen men across the alley in Mohammed's Mecca Barbecue and Oasis, relieving it of its excess merchandise.

"Hey, I know you! You're the Old One, Jesse Johnstone! My teacher told me about you," said one boy, dirt displayed generously across the once-white shirt of a rumpled school uniform.

"Nah, can't be! My dad says that's just a story, a myth from the old times," said a somewhat larger boy from the back, coming up to the group too late to get a good look at Jesse in the dim light.

"My mother would be sorry to hear that her youngest mister had grown up to become a myth, donchatink?" said Jesse, turning to him and letting the newcomer get a full appreciation of his facial tattoos.

"Yes, sir. I'll tell my dad you're no myth, sir," said the boy, to giggles from the rest of the crowd.

"Where do you boys live?" asked Jesse.

"Mostly in Decatur and out toward Chamblee, sir," said the newcomer, assuming the position of chief informant.

"No good going that way. That's where the Unis are coming from. This isn't a raid. This is an all-out invasion. What's your SEA rendezvous?" Jesse asked, confident that every school child in the new American republic was drilled in civil defense. Ever since he was born, the Restructured States of America had been at war. Every citizen was assigned a SEA point in the event of an attack: *shelter* until you have assessed the enemy's forces and direction of attack, *evacuate* to predetermined rally points where more armaments were cached, *attack* as militarily feasible.

In America, they knew their enemy. In America, there were no civilians.

"We rally at Stedman's Point, at the railroad, west of here, sir," said the informant-in-chief.

"Okay. Let's start off with your names."

Jesse listened to each boy—from the freckled, strawberry-blond Joey to the rat-faced and intense Wally, his volunteer informant.

"Okay, men. My job is to get you back to people who love you. Your job is to do what I tell you to do. Call me Jesse. My friends call me Jess. *You ain't my friends—yet.*"

He let that soak in. *Always good to give soldiers some near-term goal.*

Jesse continued, "You need names to go along with war. You, Joey, you're now Hector. Franklin, you're Achilles. George, Ajax. Henry, Odysseus." He continued until he had given each a nom de guerre. They all smiled and seemed to grow an inch with their rechristening.

Always good to read the classics, too, Jesse thought.

The boys, suffering the perpetual hunger of late childhood, he mollified with a raid upon Salvatore's Italian Bistro, befriending an orphaned lasagna that would only have been wasted on the Unis. Jesse grilled his borrowed pork chop as well.

While they were eating, Jesse planned. If they did not leave by dawn, they would have no chance. Jesse wanted to get these boys to their rally point, to weapons, and to a way to connect with the rest of the country. The whole city had been suddenly emptied around him. It was as if a drain had opened and only small bits of detritus—like himself, the drunks, and these boys—still circled the drain. He understood why he and Malila had not been informed: she was an agent for a foreign power, the Scorch. He was her *minion*. He laughed softly. Jimmy, Heracles for this exercise, looked up at him quizzically. Jesse shook his head, and the boy went back to his dinner while Jesse surveyed the stairs to the outside.

He might be the agent for a foreign power, but what about these children? How had they been abandoned? All they could tell him was that a policeman had stopped their school bus and ordered them off, driving off with it and the driver.

Before they left, Jesse tried to get the drunks to go with them. He described in exquisite detail what lay ahead of them if they stayed. At 1:00 a.m., the six boys—men—and he left. By then, the drunks were insensate.

The city, soaking in the heat of Indian summer, felt like it was made of firebricks, radiating back to them all the heat of the day. No breeze kicked up. *Good, easier to hear the drones.* Obviously, the soldiers would arrive soon, possibly tonight, and smother the whole city with men and weapons. They crossed the streets in groups of two, trying to avoid the garish lights from empty bars still lit despite the absence of customers.

After the last two boys had made it across, Jesse, leaning his long frame horizontal to the ground, pulled up the rear. *Who knows what eyes might be around?* He found his six *men*, as per orders, strung along a dense shadow in the lee of an apartment building on Mitchell Street. Working his way up the line, he talked briefly to each boy as he came to him.

"Diomedes! You're doing well there! We're almost to the highway. When you run, remember to keep your butt down. You don't want your sit-*down* to be shot *up*, right?"

The boy grinned into the darkness, his teeth the only thing to be seen. "Right, Jesse, sir. Thanks. I'll remember." They started off again, just a quick hop over a one-way street into the maw of a parking garage.

And so it had gone for the next two hours until they reached the pale mass of the elevated highway now in front of them. The rally point, near the railway, was just on the other side. Jesse signaled them to circle up.

"Nearly there, men. From here on, we have less cover. We have to cross over the highway, and we're exposed the whole way until we get to the rail yard. The enemy may be watching. From here on, we go by ones. I will go forward, find a good spot to hunker down. The next man is to count to one hundred slowly and follow me, take my place, and I'll go on from there. Each man follows at the same interval. Got it?"

After the low chorus from the boys, Jesse ran on. Counting off the time himself, Jesse found his first site near the gate to the crosswalk. Hector, the smallest, arrived on time, nodding silently as he joined Jesse in the shadows. Jesse gave him a pat on the back before starting to scuttle over the footbridge, exposed for more than a hundred feet until he reached the stairs on the other side. A trash can in the middle of the span was his next belay point. Stopping in the shadow and away from the lights of the city, Jesse waited. Hector ran up quietly within moments, finding him without difficulty. *Two stops down and four more boys to get on the trail.*

He ran on, made the turn at the end, and descended the steps before stopping under the foot of the stairs. *Ideal.* With shadows to break up his image and room for Hector when he arrived, Jesse waited. And waited. *Three minutes!* He heard footsteps descending.

Something wrong. Too heavy. Jesse tensed. The approaching footsteps were not Hector's. Jesse withdrew into the shadows further, and the steps descended over him and stopped. Jesse fingered the short knife he always kept with him, one knife in a long succession of knives he had made over the years, knives that cut, shaped, skinned, gutted—and killed. The Old Man moved silently, leaving the shadows, and readied himself to pounce.

"Jesse, sir?"

He rose and touched the arm before pulling the boy into the shadows.

"Achilles! Where is Hector? What's the matter?"

"Hector is fine. He's just waiting for the signal to come on. I had to come up the line to tell you something, sir."

"Tell me what?"

"Odysseus froze up. He won't come on. Says a Uni patrol is following us."

"Okay, Achilles. Look there," Jesse said, pointing into the darkness across the rail yard. "Your next point is straight ahead. You will hit the rails, go forward to another set of rails. Go to your right, find a switch, and you will see the markers for your rally point. You are now the pathfinder for the squad. You will guide them home. Don't wait for me."

"Yes, sir."

"You done good, Achilles."

The boy beamed into the darkness.

Going backward now, Jesse found Hector and then each boy at their belay spots and shared the plan, sending each boy forward a place.

At the end of the line, in the dense shadows just across the highway from the first belay point, he found Odysseus and Heracles. Odysseus was curled into a ball with his back against a wall, weeping quietly.

"Jesse, sir. I can't get him to move, sir. He said the Unis were coming and then just froze."

"You've done fine, Heracles. Go on, now. Achilles is your pathfinder. He knows the plan. You're almost home. We'll be along in a minute. Do you understand?"

"I understand. Yes, sir."

"And you done well, Christopher."

"Thank you, sir."

Once the boy disappeared into darkness and out of earshot, Jesse gathered the weeping Odysseus into his arms and rocked him. Within minutes, the weeping subsided.

"It will be all right, Henry."

"I'm a coward. I froze. I pissed myself."

"Everyone is afraid, son. You will be afraid again, just like I will. The fear makes you feel sick, but it's not *who* you are. Brave men do what they need to do even when they are terrified. It means we still have something to lose, that death holds fear for us, *as it should.*"

"I don't want to die. I want to see my mother!"

"Good. You should. That's what's important. We're all trying to get you home to her. Sometimes the way home is hard."

The boy hiccoughed.

"But . . ."

"But you could die trying. It's true. We all owe God a good death, son."

The child stirred in his arms, and Jesse released him.

"Thank you, Jesse. I think I should go now. I saw a drone, a different kind, laser light scanner, I think, coming up the street. I don't see it now."

"Thank you. I'll see what I can do. You know where to make for? You are not to wait for me. Understand?"

"Yes, Jesse, sir."

"Call me Jess, Henry."

"Thank you, Jess."

Jesse watched the hunched form of the small boy head out into the darkness. Almost immediately, he was hidden from view. Minutes later, the distant shadow of the first way station shifted, broadened, and then shrank back to the size it had been before.

Good boy!

Time to queer the trail.

The sniffers with night vision might just be able to follow the boys, rolling up the line and murdering each terrified child as they came to him.

The drone was more likely to follow something that was leaving a lot of signal behind. In the distance, he could see a single thread of intense green light questing into shadows a block away. Odysseus had been right. Jesse shouted once and ran north a block away from the bridge and the retreating boys. As the drone reached the corner and hovered, Jesse shouted again and ran on, this time back east on King Street.

During that long night, Jesse shouted and ran, just close enough to entice the drones' pilots, whether human or machine, to waste increasing amounts of time, effort, and fuel.

He figured he'd lure the drones past Abernathy, disappear, work his way through Pittsburgh and Jefferson Park, recruit some transport, and head down surface roads that paralleled the highway south and west. It was the obvious route of escape for any armed forces. The sooner he hooked up with American forces, the better his chances.

After dawn, puttering along on an ancient motorcycle of varied parentage and obviously configured for someone rather shorter than he, a troop of Unis took him out, his body skidding across the pavement just north of College Park.

FORCE OF ARMS

THE SOUTHERN GATE, THE UNITY
05.58.13.LOCAL_10_OCTOBER_AU77 (2129 AD)

They tried again the next day.

A half-million-man invasion force, absent basic sanitary facilities, makes a bloody mess of a landscape, thought Jourdaine, arriving at the Rampart after spending the night in Unity City. He could smell the army from a klick away. On his cue, the announcement boomed into the predawn darkness under the hundred-meter-high towers of the Rampart along a hundred-kilometer front.

"Ah, this is Lieutenant An . . . ah, never mind that. Please move away from the Rampart warning track, say about a hundred meters or so. Rampart will go down in thirty minutes from now at, oh, say, about six thirtyish. Okay? Over and out."

Thirty minutes later, the Rampart went down. The slightly later and rather larger explosions came as a surprise. The falling debris killed a score of CRNAs whose officer had not told them to run when the earth started to erupt. Hours later, the supreme command learned they had inadvertently triggered an anti-meddling device and disabled the entire Rampart from Main to the still-radioactive Crater.

By the time the news arrived, Jourdaine no longer cared. The invasion was well underway. Even as the debris was settling, construction battalions had started their Herculean tasks. Four massive bridges were thrown across the sullen Savanah River within hours. Shock troopers with their new flame machines arrived dry-shod on enemy shores. Overhead, an armada of skimmers, brushing the very tops of the wild vegetation, awaited the least indication of any hostile action.

Jourdaine smiled. The primitives would wet themselves when they saw the burners come through the jungle, spouting flames from every side. A hundred meters behind them, the road layers would advance, plating the newly made road of mesh mats twenty-five centimeters thick.

The Unity would show its supremacy. Four major roadways, fifteen meters across, would run arrow-straight through the jungle starting from Easley, Ninety-Six, Due West, and Liberty. Odd, primitive outlander names persisted here. *Needs to be fixed,* Jourdaine thought.

Nevertheless, Haversham's cockeyed scheme of conserving the food oils and conjuring up volatile hydrocarbons from them was proven out. Jourdaine was gratified to reap the benefit of Haversham's ingenuity without having to tolerate the fathering disloyalty of the man himself. *No doubt I barely missed assassination at Haversham's hands,* thought Jourdaine. The glory for the conquest would be all his to enjoy. Once they were across the jungle and into the rich fields of Jorga, the might of the Unity would carve wide swathes of destruction before rendezvousing at Lawrenceville, northwest of Aytlana. That had been Haversham's idea, as well, that thing about combining their forces near the military objective. Keep the enemy guessing up to the last moment what their goal was and then make a quick turn, combine forces, and a drive toward their *real* goal. It was supposed to be a nifty thing to do.

War is guile, misdirection, and cruelty. Jourdaine smiled.

For decades, the Unity had portrayed the outlands as a conquered but never occupied territory, and the Rampart built so that the glorious rose of the Unity might blossom without competition from the weeds of humanity. Once the invasion succeeded, however, it would be impossible to portray the outlands in quite the same way.

On receiving word that a landing zone in the newly occupied country on the other side of the jungle was safe, Lieutenant General Eustace Jourdaine was in the first skimmer to land in enemy territory. The nation saw him urge on the troops from a picturesque hilltop as wave after wave of DUFS emerged from the jungle and started the invasion across the undulating hills of Jorga. The comm'net people, watching Jourdaine, ate it up.

The 150 klicks to Aytlana should be unexciting. He had made his orders precise—precise and infallible. Jourdaine enjoyed the skimmer trip, mostly. The land over which his invasion force traveled was cultivated, rich, and ordered. He had expected and planned for worse. Jourdaine had expected that every hovel or crossroads would have some delusional outlander with an ancient shotgun to blast away at them. The attack skimmers were fast and too high to be annoyed, but the armored main battle skimmers would draw the attack, purposefully going low and slow to tempt the savages. The MBS would do the heavy lifting: engage resistance and eliminate each before the CRNAs arrived at a trot. He had calculated that his progress would leave the horizon littered with the pyres of dead barbarians. Instead, the pillars of black smoke belonged to his dead skimmers. Reports of a single sniper taking out a skimmer pilot through the window of a moving aircraft with a *projectile* rifle started to arrive. *Annoying.* For the price of one man, the barbarians had cost the Unity a precious skimmer, a squad of CRNAs, two skilled pilots, and a perfectly good second lieutenant.

"C'est le guerre" is the sort of thing you're supposed to say at this time, he thought.

He said it.

His pilot, the comm'net flunky, and that fool Ensign Windsor nodded.

Other than the snipers, the countryside appeared abandoned. Houses, farms, and factories had been discovered empty and *nonfunctional*—not just abandoned, but sabotaged. *The savages knew this was an invasion!* Small towns had been left to the care of stray dogs and an occasional bewildered derelict. These last were interrogated, found to be useless, and Sapped.

By midafternoon, it was apparent that Haversham's plan was much too conservative. He had expected the defense would harden as Unity forces shoveled the enemy back from the frontier, consolidating the savages' resolve. He expected that they would make a *grand last stand* before the gates of the city—to stand and die. Haversham had not counted on the cowardice of the savages, fleeing like rats before them. There would be no need to consolidate the four army corps before taking possession of the city.

"Order each column to go to their final targets. Repeat, they are not to rendezvous at . . ." Jourdaine looked up at a staff officer and raised an eyebrow until the man rustled through a thick tome to come up with the correct answer. ". . . E6.3. Repeat, do not rendezvous in Lawrenceville but go on to capture your final locations in Aytlana. Advance timetable for the invasion by twenty-four hours." Jourdaine chuckled. Back to his original schedule. He was pleased. It had been quicker and easier than he had imagined.

By midnight, his headquarters at the power plant near the river had been set up to receive him. Good communication, good utilities, a well-stocked larder, and comfortable beds had come in on the following skimmers. As Jourdaine stood on the roof of the power plant looking southeast, the lights of the city winked out. *Good.*

As planned. Aytlana had once been a rather larger city, all the big buildings clustered upon a single ridge of base-rock with the only real natural line of defense—the Hoochy River—now at his back, north of downtown. Nothing had slowed their advance. Jourdaine had watched vids from surveillance drones of the retreating outlanders in a hodgepodge of ancient, petroleum-fueled automobiles, equally ancient trucks, and even mule carts. He could have pursued them by following the stench of their animals, he supposed. The sooner this land was placed under enlightened control, the better for all concerned, Jourdaine assured himself.

A small group of revelers had been found in an ethanol retail establishment located on a road below street-level. They knew nothing more than where another bottle might be had. These he had shot, and what remained of their bodies was hoisted onto lampposts on the big highways south of downtown, with placards proclaiming their crimes.

OUTSIDE KINGSTON, GEORGIA, RSA
5:32 P.M. (EST) 10 OCTOBER 2129 AD (AU77)

By late afternoon on the second day, Malila and her gaggle of refugees had made considerable progress. She still had no idea where Rome was, but they were now at least on the same side of the watershed, having crossed the last ridge an hour ago and having made a good sixteen klicks since leaving the trolley. Now if they could find another farm, they could possibly get some motorized transport. Alexi was becoming very optimistic.

It was while she and Alexi were approaching a solitary farmhouse, tall, unpainted wooden columns gracing the narrow, forlorn porch, that she saw the soldiers. A line of camouflage-covered men marching along—each separated from his comrade by several meters on either side, each with a long rifle and a helmet—moved toward them. Six hundred meters off.

"Messenger Chiu, let me approach them. You never know what they might do if they see you with an enemy weapon," reminded Alexi.

He's making a good point, she thought. Mistakes happened at the leading edges between armed forces, even friendly forces. Everyone was primed to believe that the next millisecond could be their last. Taking an extra millisecond to consider that the woman with a pistol was not an enemy was a luxury they probably did not have. Nor did she.

"Okay, Alexi, go ahead. Let me fall back a bit, and you start waving the white flag from here when I signal the rest of us are under cover. Okay? And, Alexi? Thank you."

"Thanks for everything, Cap."

Malila smiled, turned, and grimaced to herself. She felt she had done so little. Once she reached the rest of the group and backtracked with them another few meters to better cover, Malila gave a signal. Alexi started waving the flag for all he was worth. Immediately, the American forces whistled and pointed their rifles to the sky. They did not approach at once, Malila noted, probably getting approval from the company commander. Malila turned to smile at some of the children who had followed her to see the excitement.

That was when she heard the shot.

She ran to the little man's side. He never moved. His blood, staining black his blue work shirt, swelled out further with each beat of his heart. As she watched, the growing tide of blood faltered and stopped, the white flag draping over him like a shroud. Malila looked up at the soldiers who now encircled her and the dead Alexi. They wore American uniforms, but their accent, the bird-like keening as they prodded the corpse, was all CRNA.

Malila was blindfolded, gagged, and bound facedown before she heard shots, no more than four. She was tossed into the back of some vehicle, sliding painfully from one side to the other, during the next hours before it stopped. She was roused with a peremptory kick to her ribs.

"On your feet!"

"Don't bother, Tom. They can't understand good Standard," said another, smaller voice. "Just keep hitting them until they do wadja want and then stop."

Malila turned over and rolled to her feet before another blow could fall.

From what she could see under her blindfold, it was late evening. She had drunk little and eaten nothing all day. Her mouth felt sticky and tasted of red Georgia clay. Stumbling over rough ground, Malila fell. Immediately, she was dragged to her feet, and her wrist twisted sharply. Without comment, her captor gave her an efficient backhanded blow across the face. The glass shard she had retrieved from the ground was taken from her. She did not fall again.

Eventually, she was led down steps and along what must have been a corridor, still radiating the heat of the day, and into what, based on the echoes, was a smallish room. She was pushed down onto a chair. A heavy door swung shut.

There she sat for some unknowable amount of time, watered but unfed. Muffled conversations were held just out of earshot. Eventually, three sets of boots entered the room. The heavy door swung shut again with a crash. Malila's hood was pulled from her in one swipe, and she stood blinking in the sickly green of the phosphorescents.

"Lieutenant Chiu, it is—good—to see you again. I had not thought we'd have that pleasure—considering the circumstances of our last parting."

Before her stood Lieutenant General Eustace Jourdaine, her erstwhile commander, sometime patron, current leader of the Blues, commander of the DUFS, and unchallenged dictator of the Democratic Unity. He looked changed. A scar, still livid, crossed his right eye. When she looked carefully, it seemed opaque—lifeless. Jourdaine wept from the eye almost continuously, mopping it with a handkerchief every few minutes. Sometime in the six weeks since they had last met on the banks of a muddy outland river, Jourdaine had been badly injured. He was stiff and cautious with his movements. Beyond him stood a large CRNA with a pulse-rifle at parade rest. Beside Jourdaine stood a chubby man with a black peaked cap that sported a prominent silver Death's Head.

When Malila failed to answer, Jourdaine smiled. "It is unfortunate that your suicide was so convincing, Malila. The Unity has had time to mourn you. 'The little hero of the whale hunt' was how the 'nets described you, I believe."

Here Jourdaine grinned and then chuckled. The chubby Death's Head officer followed suit only marginally late. *He doesn't know that it's phony. There are no whales,* thought Malila.

"At any rate, I have yet to decide what to do with you. You have been a minor irritant for the last year." He smiled. A rictus of pain briefly crossed Jourdaine's face before he regained control. She almost pitied him.

"If I expend a fair amount of effort, I could reform your suicide into a mission for the homeland, of course. Despite your best efforts to the contrary, it appears you have done the Unity and me a great favor by being the face of the—what do you call it—the Splanch? Your little embassy was very helpful. The whole of Jorja is at our feet. No more than a score of shots fired in anger. Instead of fighting our way through the jungle and then through the countryside, most of my men just walked here. All thanks to you. Credit where credit is due, you understand. With that narrative, we could rehabilitate you nicely—make you a heroine of the Unity again. I seem to recall you enjoyed that while it lasted."

"It's the Scorch, not the Splanch, Eustace."

Jourdaine frowned as if disappointed she was not groveling for her life.

"And still you seem to think you are playing at some game. I don't know why I should expend the effort. Do you?"

"No, I don't either."

"Then, I think I should let you contemplate your career choices, Citizen Chiu. I cannot offer you patronage, of course. You disdained me too publicly. But warming my bed when required is so little to pay. Sapping, they say, is not the worst thing. Some remember—afterward."

"Tempting offer, Eustace."

The thin gray man grimaced, turned to leave, and walked the few feet to the door before turning.

"Oh. By the way, Chiu, it seems your servant is our prisoner, as well. Johnsen, what's his name?"

"Jesse?" said Malila, starting to rise before being pushed down into the chair again.

"That sounds about right. Hulking fellow with tattoos."

The door closed behind him.

FALL

(An inevitable event terminated by a rope securely attached to the climber and thence to a competent anchored belayer or, less ideally, hard rock)

SPOILS

MARRIOTT GRAND MERCURE, ATLANTA, GEORGIA
EVENING, 11 OCTOBER 2129

They had shoved Benjamin Nortvengler, PhD, professor emeritus of philosophy at Washington University, into a broom closet—no, a mop closet. In the darkness, he had scraped his thin-skinned shins on the buckets and knocked the damp mops, like flaccid marine creatures, down onto his face.

On the evening of the eighth, the American contingent had been secretly summoned and informed by the state department that America could no longer guarantee the members' safety. There was "credible evidence" that the Unity would begin its invasion within two days. Moreover, a special train was being held for the contingent, leaving at 11:02 that evening. Shortly after the announcement, Benny had entered Harold Colina's room, the door open to the corridor, finding him in the midst of packing his valise.

"You are leaving, Harry?"

"I'm getting out of town before the Unity gets here? Yes, indeed," said Colina, shuffling his toilet articles and tossing out a small bag of dirty laundry.

"Now? This is no time to leave! Don't you see? This is the perfect way to gain an audience with the new rulers. We can get this Jordan's ear and make a case for annexing America just like we've always hoped. It's the chance of a lifetime to be the actual agent for change in this wasteland of antiquated ideas. Bring everyone to account, enjoy the advanced technology, drag everyone kicking and screaming into the twenty-second century, whether they like it or not. All we need do is stick together. When the time is right, we reveal Johnstone and the girl to them, tell them of the plot with the Scorch, and let them see who their real friends are."

Colina continued to add items, rearrange and remove items. Absent-mindedly he said, "Jourdaine. His name is Eustace *Jourdaine*." Then looking up and around, he continued, "Lieutenant General is, as it happens, effectively the dictator of the Unity after he murdered their real leaders in July. *That* is who you want to bargain with, Benny?" Colina turned back, returned to his packing, saying over his shoulder, "You want to try to make a deal with a guy who is ruthless, powerful, and owes you nothing? You are offering him nothing more than what he can take himself. For that you betray your own country? You never *could* play poker."

"But this is what we have been working towards for decades . . . ," said Benny.

Harry turned away from packing again, looking at his old friend, standing up, and grabbing his stick.

"No, Benny. It is what *you* have been working toward for decades. I am your friend, and the Syntopia made sense when America was prostrate and could not feed itself, people dying of starvation in the streets—at the very gates of the university, for heaven's sake! After a heroic death, you're still dead. We, you and me, the entire nation, went through that horror, and the nation survived—to my surprise. I didn't think we had it in us. Today, America has a chance to fight back. Trust me in this, my friend. Come back with me to Saint Louis, and we can help the war effort!"

Benny felt as if Harold Colina, his oldest friend, had taken his stick to him. Benny realized he must have had one of his spells, when the next thing he remembered was sitting on the edge of the bed, Harry's worried face looming over him like some absurd nursemaid.

He had fixed the newly revealed turncoat with his eyes and said, "What? You're running out on me, on the Order? Just when we need you most! I'll have you expelled. I'll have your name stricken from the rolls. It will be like you never existed."

Harry froze for a moment, and Benny had hoped the prospect had swayed his decision.

Then Harry had said, "As you wish, but you'll have to come back to Saint Louis to do that, Benny. Look, I don't want it to end like this. You have been a good friend, my oldest friend, my only friend when we started. You have been faithful to me, but it is time we act in our best interests. Whatever happens, I want to be with Ethelwyn when the crisis occurs. America may die. If so, I want to die with her and not you."

Harry went back to his valise, snapping it shut with difficulty. Benny left before he turned around.

Of course, after consulting the precepts of non-axiomatic rational skepticism, Nortvengler realized he should be pleased. *The fewer men, the greater glory.* The following morning, the depleted contingent had assembled to discuss the situation, Benny lobbying for them to present themselves to the invading forces as the leading edge of a new American peace party. About half had left, anyway, to Nortvengler's disgust—the cowards trying to get away by bus, the wreckage still smoldering, for all he knew. There had been some unpleasantness with fire alarms and reports of drones, but the remaining delegates were made of sterner stuff. They had had to scrounge food from the vending machines. Even so, it was not until the next day that they could agree upon a modus operandi and start the committee process. It took all day to hammer out the white paper, passing it by acclamation late that night.

They were putting the final touches on it the next day when the room filled with heavily armed Unity soldiers. One by one, the members were taken into captivity. Benny presumed his experience was little different from the others. His briefcase was hurled onto a pile in the room. They took his watch.

It seemed forever until the closet was once more opened and he was confronted with a faceless black marionette soldier pointing some sort of a rifle at him. Thankfully, there was an officer, without a helmet and with stripes on his sleeve, who ordered him to come out with his hands up.

"That is not necessary, officer. I am a friend of the Unity, and I have vital information to give you. If we wait, it might be too late."

"What are you saying, Sisi? You're just trying to dodge the black hats. Fathering little shit," muttered the officer between his teeth as he shoved Nortvengler stumbling ahead of him down the narrow corridor.

Looking ahead, he glimpsed Fetschuler being pushed along, clutching his ever-present tablet to himself. For the whole conference, Fetschuler had dithered and dawdled in public and sniggered in private as to how he was putting the Scorch's feet to the fire, how the Unity, with their saber-rattling, was unconsciously aiding America in the game of nerves. The man, genuinely surprised at his failure, had remained in Atlanta in near paralyzed catatonia. *Serves him right.*

The faceless soldiers escorted the two through a swinging door into another small dining room containing most of the remaining university delegates. At once, he had been bound with narrow plastic bands, which cut into his wrists intolerably. He tried to remonstrate with them, to little effect. The guards then herded the entire group into a truck. He was the last to enter, being tossed in just as the door came down.

At their destination, wherever it was, his bonds were removed, and the delegation joined a mixed batch of prisoners in a low, cramped, and overheated basement room. Small, narrow windows near the steel rafters gave the only light and ventilation. Laborers in power company uniforms, derelicts stinking of cheap booze and fouled clothes, wounded policemen, waitresses, and business types mingled in sullen silence. He talked to no one.

Hours later, there was a small disturbance at the entrance. Immediately, he prepared to defend his small space against a pillar from any encroachment by newcomers. The heavy door opened and several of the faceless soldiers entered, dragging a tall, semiconscious, old man through the crowd. Just as he passed Benny, the man pulled his arm from one of the soldiers and stood, looking around like an enraged animal.

Burns marred his forehead, leaving livid wounds. A long queue of white hair bound in leather straps swayed down his back. His short white beard had been scraped off on the left, leaving three blue tattoos like chevrons on the reddened flesh. His linen shirt was ripped, revealing broad expanses of outlander tattoos.

An officer approached, weapon drawn, and the man silently put up his hands, immediately in control of himself.

"Walk, Sisi!"

"Yessir!" replied the man before continuing out of the room.

Just as the officer was at the door, Benny, with sudden certainty, yelled out, "That's *him*. The Agnomen, Jesse Johnstone. You *got* him!" The officer continued out of the room, closing and locking the door behind him, without apparently noticing.

Benny's fellow prisoners noticed.

"Whatja go and do that for, you moron?"

"Why are you making it easy for the Unis? Are you one of them sympathizers?"

"He's one of them professors! They let a deal with the Scorch slip through our fingers!"

Blows followed the incriminations, despite Benny's spirited attempts to explain the basic facts, the logic behind the Synthesis, and the invidious effect of the Agnomen.

A large coffee-colored man—a trucker from the logo on his overalls—had just settled down to administer a proper beating when the door opened, and the trucker stepped away. An un-helmeted Uni officer approached, shooing others away.

"Sisi. Look at me!"

"Yes. Yes, I'm Professor Benjamin Nortvengler," he said.

"Cut the fathering bizzle, Sisi. Follow me," the officer said, and, turning, departed through the throng.

DUFS ARMY HQ, OCCUPIED JORGA
20.32.17.EST_11_OCTOBER_AU77 (2129 AD)

The invasion is turning out to be more satisfying than I ever imagined, thought Eustace Jourdaine. This Bolton Road power plant near the river was an enviable headquarters, a defensible fortress, and an admirable prison. Today, he could interrogate the prisoners at his leisure. He had Chiu—again. When he had first recaptured her in April, she had gone on and on about some primitive frontier superman, gone on even after he reminded her of the lengths to which *he, Jourdaine,* had gone to save her. Her responses about the creature were odd and mixed. The readout from her O A showed that neurotransmitters for fear and disgust were high when she talked about him, but also pleasure, even during her description of the man's rescue of her from some wilderness slavers. *Disgusting outlanders.*

During the few months of her homecoming and while still imagining she was a rising star of the DUFS, Malila had been more than willing to tell him all about the ancient savage who had captured her, murdering an entire platoon of CRNAs in the process. Chiu had been convinced that Johnstone's successes were due to the man's native cleverness, physical prowess, *and something more.* She apparently admired him.

The only puzzle remaining, and one that Jourdaine had no time nor interest to solve, was why the ancient Sisi had not summarily murdered Chiu at her initial capture. Who could figure out these barbarians?

He collected his personal CRNA, Blankenship.

George Blankenship was another perk of his, his personally Sapped minion. Windsor had returned with him from Fire Island already dressed as a DUFS CRNA just in time for the invasion. Blankenship's fate would certainly keep his other staff in line.

Very acceptable, indeed.

Today, his forces would prepare the carefully orchestrated death blow to the ignorant savages. With the Solons now all dead, this victory would make him the first deity in a new Unity pantheon. Deities required things—immortality for one.

He descended a flight of stairs into the basement before entering a windowless room by a back door. There was a small huddle of men in a dark corner. An ancient outlander was spread-eagled by his bonds against the side wall, his head lolling down and his breathing noisy. His left eye was closed by a massive welt, but the blood had been washed off his face.

"The prisoner is securely bound, sir. He is incapable of inflicting any damage, sir," said Gonzales, laboring in a soiled undershirt but still sweating, despite having doffed his uniform blouse and his Death's Head cover.

Jourdaine approached the old derelict. He smelled bad in some unknown way. After finding a box to stand on and taking a pencil from Gonzales, he used the point to force up the Sisi's chin. He was grotesque: white hair was bound in an effeminate queue down to the middle of his back. The man's face and body were disfigured with savage and obscure blue markings and lettering, burns marred his forehead, and some of his beard had been scraped off, revealing even more tattoos. Nausea rose to the back of his throat. He stepped down.

"Very good, Sergeant. Wake him."

A bucket of cold water was splashed into the prisoner's face, provoking coughing and retching before the head came up, spraying water.

Jourdaine motioned to Windsor, who thrust the informant, another Sisi who looked even older than the bound man, into the light. He reeked of burnt vegetable matter. The outlanders used it as a substitute for ThiZ, he'd been told. The actual plant leaf, he knew, was dried and twisted together before being incinerated, the addict inhaling the fumes, soiling his clothes with tar, smoke, and ash, and fouling his health.

"Professor Northwrangler, I—" Jourdaine started.

"Nortvengler, Your Eminence," the disgusting little man said, wafting his fouled breath toward Jourdaine.

"Yes, my apologies, Professor *Nortvengler*. Can you tell me who this is?" indicating the prisoner with a negligent shrug of his shoulder.

"He's the Agnomen, Your Eminence, the first of the Old Ones. He's a murderer several times over. That's what those stripes on his face mean. He's been living in exile for decades, trying to avoid his just punishment. He—"

Jourdaine motioned to Gonzales, who jabbed a baton into the wretched old man's kidneys to stop the diatribe. Jourdaine nodded again, and Gonzales went behind the bound and gagged outlander, who appeared slouched and inattentive, and repeated the maneuver. The creature grunted, arching his back away from the pain.

There was a tittering among the assembled entourage he had brought from Nyork: Captain Blevins, Corporal Windsor, and Sergeant Gonzales. They huddled together, out of place in a military establishment. Jourdaine missed Haversham, in a way. Lance could always be counted on for military-like compliments, and he did not *titter.*

"Get out! All of you. No! No! Blankenship and Gonzales, you two stay. Bring the informant here. The rest of you, out! Find something useful to do," he shouted.

Standing again on his box, Jourdaine waited until the one eye focused on him.

"Do you deny you are Jesse Aaron Johnstone, known as the Agnomen, as the Old Man, as Rob Roy, as Matthew Starbuck, and, I dare say, a good number of other aliases?"

The Old Man did not speak at once, moving his mouth and tongue before he said, "Ah tollt yor men as who I wis. Wha th' wee monkey is ye hae is unknown tae me, whitevur he said."

Jourdaine was disappointed. "What's he saying? I thought he was American. I was told he was educated!" exclaimed Jourdaine.

"Your little monkey can understand me well enough, General. All I said was that I already told your men who I was."

Jourdaine was taken aback. The man had shifted to perfectly understandable Standard without the slightest suggestion of an accent and, possibly, an added expression of pity to go along with it.

"I am Jesse Aaron Johnstone, son of Alyssa Browne and Alexander Cameron Henderson Johnstone, of Bath County, Kentucky, an American. My father told me that 'a person should know who he is and be able to tell others. It keeps the one warned and the other honest.'"

In the brief interval, the Sisi stood tall within his bonds, seeming to fill the small room. Jourdaine fell away, suddenly unsure as to whether the bonds would hold. He backed into someone and turned to see Nortvengler apparently frozen to the spot, his jaw slack, and dribbling.

"Professor Nortvengler, your services are no longer required. You may leave. Sergeant Gonzales, get someone to escort him out."

"Very good, sir," said the sergeant as Jourdaine turned away to inspect Jesse from a distance.

"Oh, and Sergeant?" said Jourdaine.

"Yes, sir?"

"Sapp the monkey."

The heavy door silenced the imprecations of Nortvengler with an abrupt and final snick.

"Who are you?" said Johnstone.

"You don't get to ask questions here, Sisi, but so that you know, I am Lieutenant General Jourdaine, currently Commander of the Democratic Unity Forces for Security, and your captor."

"Pleased to meetcha there, General. You will forgive me if I don't salute," said Jesse.

Jourdaine motioned with an eyebrow, and the CRNA thrust a baton into the old man's belly. After the groans of pain subsided, the Sisi spat out a clot of dark blood, and the interview continued.

"I am not going to tolerate your infamously jolly banter, savage. Keep it short and simple, or I will make the conversation shorter yet. Do you understand, Sisi?"

"I understand."

"Good. First question: What is Ageplay?"

"A method to lengthen lifespan."

"Do you carry the live agent?"

"Yes."

"What is preventing me from bleeding you white and saving all the Ageplay for myself?"

"Nothing. Be my guest, but the genie is sort of out of the bottle, you might say."

"Talk sense, old man. Corporal Blankenship here is quite willing to remind you again just who is in control."

The Old Man's head lolled to the left, and with his one still-functioning eye, skewered Jourdaine with his gaze. "Every pharmaceutical house in America can make the Ageplay agent. I'm no longer in much demand."

"Must be disappointing to you to lose the income from that. It must have been very lucrative," said Jourdaine, smirking.

"Yeah, I made lots and lots. Vast disappointment to me, there," replied the Old Man.

Jourdaine, missing the irony, said, "Is it true you heal better and quicker than before the Ageplay?"

"I was rather young when I got the Ageplay. I dinna remember a 'before,' Your Grace."

"How long do you live with Ageplay?"

"How woulda know? It seems to me that my days will be no more than threescore and eighteen, I'm guessing," Jesse said, before laughing. Another blow from Blankenship silenced him.

After the paroxysms of coughing, retching, and bleeding subsided, Jourdaine forced up the old man's chin once more. "You see, I am not as easily amused with you as Lieutenant Chiu was. You will answer the questions without comment. Understand, barbarian?"

A nod.

"How long would an Ageplay recipient *expect* to live, barring acts of infantile obduracy such as you are demonstrating?" Jourdaine let the bloody head drop and stepped back, motioning Blankenship forward again.

Before the CRNA could strike, Jesse said, his head still bowed, "A hundred and seventy, best as they can figure. You see, I am in the bloom of vigorous middle age, General."

"I can fix that," he said, looking up to the Death's Head officer. "Sergeant, how much blood can we take from him before he dies?"

"Fifteen hundred milliliters will make him shocky but not kill him right away, I think, sir."

"Take the fifteen hundred, then Sapp him. Prepare the blood and give me the Ageplay.

"As for you, Sisi, I don't see why Chiu was so impressed."

Jesse shrugged. "Not a mystery I care to explore, Your Grace," he said.

Called away to decipher odd reports he was getting from the People's Revenge construction site, it was much later before Jourdaine could return to see Gonzales's handiwork.

The Sisi, his skin, where it was not concealed by indecipherable blue markings, turned grayish and shiny, slumped into his bonds and drew gasping, irregular breaths. In the end, Gonzales was about to give the old relic some saline to keep him alive long enough to be Sapped, when he seemed to marshal his forces, collect what reserves he had, and stood up in his restraints.

Then they Sapped him.

Jesse retched. His sight fractured, the pieces falling into a heap of scintillating shards. Covering his ears to the reek of a drowned dead man that had welled up out of the floor, Jesse could not move as the de-fleshing face screamed its stench into him. The Old Man felt the accusations of the corpse slime itself across his tongue. In the mordant afterimage, Jesse heard the laughter of the soldiers. It brought him back to the room, hot beyond his senses, burning his flesh. He smelled his flesh smoke and watched his left hand blacken and curl before hardening into a rictured, bony claw. Forcing his eyes open against the ground-glass pain of the light, Jesse watched the soldier, the one who had applied the gun to his chest. He wore a Death's Head insignia on his sleeve and cap. In his agony, Jesse seized on the thought of wearing death as a totem, annihilation as an insignia. He wondered how many of the bent and deformed souls of the ages had embraced the grave as an idol and death's silence as a benediction.

Another wave of nausea exploded in his belly, and the old man's vision dissolved again, now into a cacophony of terrors he had forgotten as a child: nights lit up by ghostly green flashes off the roiling clouds up the pass from Dunbarton, the wind pushing the acrid smoke of burning corpses over the miles and into his childhood. He was again the terror-ridden boy who cried but was never comforted and repented but was never shriven. The laughter around him tasted rancid to his touch, and he looked through his hallucinations to the cluster of small men who were watching his agonies. With the Death's Head executioner was the huge zombie-soldier, who stood behind him, his weapon at the ready and his face hidden and inscrutable. At first, while his mind still quivered with the assault, he looked for the smirking, bloodless gray man with one eye. He was no longer sure why.

Another wave took him. He felt time dissolve into his nausea, cause now following result. He watched his restored fingers liquify, layer by layer, in front of his eyes, searing pain wrenching him with each cell's death. Turning his hand over, he watched the skin seep away like quicksilver to expose the tendons and the pulsating arcs of arteries before they slid away as well. He felt the cold seep into his fingertips and vanish as the nerves unraveled to disappear inside themselves and slide away. Horror swelled like a dark flood, spewing out of the floor to engulf him, filling his mouth, ears, and nose to suck him into despair.

They left him when the popping started.

HAVERSHAM'S REWARD

BATTALION XXXII HQ, NEAR COLLEGE PARK, OCCUPIED JORGA
18.14.19.EST_11_OCTOBER_AU77

Second Lieutenant Lance Haversham felt a breeze, the first he had noticed since the Rampart came down, sweep over him. It made him shiver. He smiled at himself. Here, in Jorga, even a warm breeze would make him shiver after the brazen heat of the last two days.

He walked on to deliver his report, idly polishing the tarnished bronze bars on his peaked hat with a shirt cuff, remembering how he had to rummage to the bottom of his locker to find them. After discarding the bars only a few weeks ago while riding the coattails of General Jourdaine, he had thought his time as a second lieutenant was over. It had been an illusion just as engaging as Alpha_Drover last year. Then, his relief in discovering that Alpha_Drover was only a CORE-simulation had nearly unmanned him. Gratitude, almost affection, for his commanders had overwhelmed him. They had made the nightmare go away, and he had been given his lieutenancy as a reward.

Jourdaine must have seen something of his leadership and resourcefulness, his selection as his adjutant the proof of it. That had ended badly. Jourdaine's—Jourdaine's what? Paranoia? Jealousy? Senility?—whatever had elevated Haversham from being a lowly second lieutenant to become his adjutant, and just as rapidly thrown him back into obscurity. He shrugged.

Entering the company HQ outer office, all plaster and dark wood, Haversham found a warrant-officer, who, not otherwise acknowledging him, shrugged toward a pile of data straws in a box. Haversham dropped in his own straw, all properly coded and attributed, and figured he was free to go. It was not as if he were any further away than a CORE message.

Wrong.

A radio message. *That was* an unanticipated annoyance! Instead of carefully encrypted CORE messages, the army had had to create a whole new signals system on the fly. Radios were still used for Unity ship communications, of course, and despite being clumsy and slow, with fathering static and dropped messages, they worked. He had had to settle for one of the larger, pouch-mounted models liberated from an abandoned truck. *Annoying.*

Lieutenant Haversham started back to his command, looking up at the distant golden dome of the old government building downtown. Much of the gold leaf had flaked off, presenting a shabby picture of glory days from some unimaginable past. Past the dome, Haversham glimpsed a sliver of light high in the air. He presumed it was a flake of gold leaf borne up by distant breezes and illuminated by the last few rays of the departing sun. *Impossible.* When he looked again, it had disappeared.

While returning to his platoon, Lance contemplated the advantages of field command. In the advance to Aytlana yesterday, he was able to loot a food distribution center, walking out eating an ice-cream cone (chocolate chip mint, two scoops). He still remembered, with regret, that he had not liberated a tub of the same. The oppressive heat and the crowded skimmer made the prospect of fouling the deck with minty chocolate goodness unappetizing. The army had bivouacked at some town and come on to Aytlana today, bypassing his plans at Lawrenceville. He shrugged. He had rather liked that part, adding a little of his own to the great invasion.

He had paid for his presumption. All his work with Jourdaine had evaporated except for the building of the bridges. But despite his new platoon demanding long and tedious preparation, he had a plum assignment for the battle tomorrow. Other divisions had had the unenviable job of destroying whole city blocks just to dig revetments in the rubble, shifting the huge machines and running the cables to the control center. His platoon, stationed along the kill-corridor lined with the pulse bombards, would be held in reserve for the counterattack.

A river protected the north and west. Massive patrols of armor and infantry were exposed as if by accident on the east and south. It was only here on the southwest approach that it appeared the Unity had failed to mount a reliable defense. It was here that the bait dangled enticingly. The dim-witted outlander commanders would reconnoiter the city before committing troops to the assault, probing for a weakness, knowing the Unity could not defend everywhere. Only once the enemy had fully committed could the jaws of his trap snap shut. His concealed positions would open up on the outlanders, revealing the rubble to be revetments and the outlander forces to be walking dead men. *All very satisfying.* He almost felt sorry for them.

And his hard work had paid off. His platoon was to have the honor of closing the trap behind the outlander mob and seeing that none of them escaped the teeth on the jaws of that trap. He'd been ordered to take no prisoners and allow no breakouts. The might of the Unity was to close around the outlanders and shut with the final cold snap of doom. He was pleased with his role, the biggest military action of the last half century, and his bravery and decisiveness would be witnessed by a grateful nation—and his superiors.

Lance Haversham returned to his platoon command point. When he had first arrived at the deserted square, the heat had engulfed him, the sunlight feeling as dense as a body blow. Surprisingly, his men had been unable to find even a single enemy civilian. Now, only an errant wind disturbed the browned-out weeds that lined the city streets. The setting sun, sending long, dense shadows from the building across the sere landscape, brought no relief from the heat.

He had taken over some pseudo-ancient edifices of honey-colored stone for platoon command and billeting. The grass around the buildings, which might have been lush in another season, was yellowed and worn, obscured by the ocher dirt that rose in clouds with each skimmer's landing or takeoff. The place had called itself College Park, although the reference was lost on him.

Leaving the square, Haversham toured the men's quarters, finding the air inside dense, oppressively warm, and the odor, given the day's labor—eye-watering. CRNAs were not called the "rank and vile" for nothing. As a kindness, he ordered his men to bivouac in the open.

His duties done, he left, meeting up with several other lieutenants from the pulse-bombard units. One had commandeered some exotic food from an area restaurant named Krystal. They dined in unaccustomed abundance. Aytlana was ripe for the taking.

Lingering long over the boards, Haversham was among the last to leave, stepping out into utter darkness. All power had been diverted away from the approaches to the area, the better to deceive the unknown watchers in the dark.

It was then he heard the native drums.

Boom—boom—boom—boom.

Slow, measured, almost majestic. The sounds seemed to come from all around him. He was unaware that was part of the barbarians' behavior. When it came down to it, he knew so little about the outlanders. They weren't civilized. They stole Unity technology where they could, of course, unable to make their own. They practiced cannibalism and human sacrifice. Most couldn't read.

Boom—boom—boom—boom.

The drums did not vary, even a little, in timing. He doubted it could be some communication device. It must just be intimidation. He smiled. *As if that would work.*

Haversham suddenly felt a cold wind come out of the darkness to snatch his hat away, rolling it off into the darkness. He ran after it and blundered into a hedge of bushes in the darkness before recapturing it.

"Father me," he said to the dark, annoyed at his clumsiness. Around him, unseen in the blackness, the night sounded alive with the clattering of branches, the swirling of summer-dry leaves, and the occasional crash of equipment inadequately secured.

Boom—boom—boom—boom.

Winds pick up at night, he'd been told once. He wondered by whom. Another blast of cold air blew into his face, picking up dust and stinging his cheeks. With his eyes closed against the assault, he stumbled off the sidewalk and was able to retain his feet only after twisting his right ankle.

"Fathering muckers," he said, unsure whether a soldier was near or not. It would be unseemly to have the men hear him swear about his own hardships.

Boom—boom—boom—boom.

Another gust of wind whipped around him, and Lance felt his heat suddenly stripped away. In the distance, he could see billowing clouds ascending by the flashes of lightning, the thunder too far away to hear above the wind. Stars on the horizon blinked out as he watched. Above him, the cold of the universe seemed to pour down upon him.

Boom—boom—boom—boom.

He limped back to the men's billet. It, too, felt as if the stones themselves leached away his body heat. *Probably good for the ankle.* With a deep sigh, he sat and put his foot up. His platoon sergeant, Holmes, found him there.

"Sergeant Holmes, get the men inside. Odd weather. Let's get them under cover."

With a grunt, the man was off, and Lance massaged his ankle. DUFS were obedient and loyal, but one had to be sure they did not look up during a rainstorm with their mouths open. He waited by the entrance, a sign next to it saying, "Hartsfield Men's Dormitory," as his platoon came back inside, followed at a small distance by their stink. He counted thirty men. He had arrived with thirty-nine. Five men were on sentry duty.

"Sergeant Holmes! To me, Sergeant Holmes!" The man seemed to materialize out of the night beside him. Not for the first time, Lieutenant Haversham felt that his platoon sergeant made a habit of hiding behind corners in order to make these instantaneous and silent appearances, no matter what people told him about CRNA troopers.

Boom—boom—boom—boom.

"Are we missing men, Sergeant Holmes? I can only account for thirty-five."

Holmes had the oddest habit of pausing before answering, as if he were actually considering the nature of his answer. It was like watching a trick pony "thinking" before answering a simple math problem.

"Sir, four men could not be roused, sir. They appear to be dead, sir!"

"What? What was the nature of their wounds?"

"No wounds, sir!"

"Check whether we still have sentries, Sergeant, and show me the fallen."

"All sentries accounted for and replaced, sir! Follow me, sir!" The black-helmeted man turned on his heel and nearly disappeared into the dark before Lieutenant Haversham could hobble after him. He liked how he had sounded there: firm, resolute, and decisive. He also liked how he had called the dead CRNAs "the fallen." That would resound well in his report. Haversham hugged his arms to himself as he puffed along behind Holmes. He seated his cap with its tarnished bars down a little more tightly and watched for reflections off Holmes's helmet, following more by sound than sight.

Holmes finally stopped in a small garden with a gravel path surrounding an ornamental fountain. Haversham, his eyes now accustomed to the dim light, made out four motionless bodies lying on benches, bivouacked around the fountain. Haversham could tell that many more of his men had bedded down on the ground in the same vicinity. Summer sleeping bags and duffle lay strewn about.

Boom—boom—boom—boom.

Stiff and frozen to the benches as urine released from agonal bladders now tightly gripped the bodies, the men appeared to sleep. The bodies were cold; as cold as the ice cream he had eaten that afternoon. Lance felt a wave of nausea rise within him, and he turned away to examine the fountain. A skim of ice encircled the central jet of water as icicles glinting from the jet's opening. Looking at the play of water, watching the ice glint, catching a few stray gleams of light in the distance with difficulty, he felt himself become mesmerized by the display. He tore his eyes away.

"Get a detail to move these bodies inside. Call the sentries inside. Inform Captain Winters about the casualties and tell him I will talk to him shortly from my billet."

Boom—boom—boom—boom.

Haversham started walking back toward his headquarters alone. He throttled his misgivings and reviewed his actions. He had acted well: no panic, no loss of composure. He tried to use his O A to contact his superior and grimaced before fumbling with the radio he wore. The reception was poor, and he fiddled with the unfamiliar controls to no avail. Worse than that, his attention had wavered. His surroundings looked unfamiliar, dark and confusing. Having paid no attention to his route when following Holmes, now the paths looked indistinguishable. He found himself blundering painfully off into unseen shrubs along the way again and again.

Lance pulled up the collar of his summer uniform to no effect even as he felt his teeth begin to chatter in earnest. He stumbled, his legs ignoring his commands. Trying again to contact company headquarters, he briefly got "Unseasonably cold . . . Arctic downdraft . . . upper-level high causing high-velocity, low-level shear winds." Less than useless! He did not need to be told it was cold and windy.

He stopped and looked up into the cloudless, crystalline night as the cold air poured down onto him from the icy depths of endless space. Cold points of light seemed to wring his heat away. The scant, sickled new moon had already set. The date of the invasion had been chosen to thwart enemy actions at night. Its success in disorienting him was quite as complete. Almost directly overhead, a few stars winked out and back on again as he looked. It made no sense to him.

His ears had hurt at first, but now they were senseless and cold to his touch. His fingers were numb, as well. He could not feel the whistle he kept in his pocket. Nevertheless, he grasped the small object in his unfeeling fingers and brought it to his lips. His chattering teeth at first refused to hold the cooling metal. He licked his lips and could not feel the instant chill on them. Taking a deep breath, Lance grasped the whistle in his teeth and, in the few moments in which his shivering abated, tried to produce the shrill shriek that would summon his non-coms to his side. The feeble wobble of sound he got was useless.

Boom—boom—boom—boom.

Lance remembered when he was in the crèche one winter. He and his friends had gone out, despite their lack of boots and gloves, to make a snowman in the courtyard. They took turns rolling the growing ball of snow. When a crèchie's hands and feet became too cold, each would stand on a discarded board and suck his fingers while another boy took over. They had eventually come to a consensus that a proper snowman did not actually need coal for eyes, a pipe, or a hat. The Matron had fussed and cajoled them when they returned—but they had gotten hot tea with sugar, nonetheless. He smiled when he remembered the languor after he had finished warming up and been thrust into his narrow bed, fingers and toes tingling.

Boom—boom—boom—boom.

Haversham shook himself awake. He moved to get out of the wind—the better to assess his current situation. The buildings of the college were searched when they had arrived but were left mostly unmolested. He moved into the doorway of the closest one.

Boom—boom—boom—boom.

Trying the door of a building, he found it open, a sudden frigid gust nearly whipping the door out of his frozen hand. He had to wait, shivering, for long moments until he could pull the door tight behind him. Entering a large room filled with books, he had no idea what it meant. Taking a book at random—*Handbook of Physics and Chemistry*—he fired a bolt from his sidearm to ignite the paper. A large hole appeared in the middle of the book and exited to gouge a furrow into the wooden floor. A meager blue flame flickered briefly inside the crater, which had once been tables of numbers, but the flash of heat encouraged him. Grabbing armfuls of thick tomes—*Greater Atlanta Metropolitan Area Census 2120, Kansas City Kennel Club Stud Book, Anthology of Limericks, The Dialogues,* and *The Summa* among others—he piled them indiscriminately in the largest open area. Firing again, he was rewarded this time with a flame that appeared deep within the pile but held steady and slowly advanced along a yellowed edge.

Sinking to his knees, Lance held his hands out to the rescuing flame, feeling the heat like a rumor in his stiff white fingers, all his attention now focused on the flickering flame. He nudged a book forward, and the flame retreated alarmingly. He readjusted the book and the flame advanced, seeming to encompass his entire field of vision, the black library stretching neglected into an immeasurable distance at his back. He began to feel the warmth in his fingers and settled himself near the flame.

Boom—boom—boom—boom.

He could now wait until dawn, he reasoned. His radio would rouse him if an attack loomed. Lieutenant Haversham watched the small flame burn through page after page as it warmed his frozen extremities and allowed his core blood to stream out into his cold fingers and toes and thence into the cold of the frigid night. He slept and did not wake as the fire guttered out, or even when the sun came up, or even, as it happens, thereafter.

DAY OF ICE

UNITY ARMY HQ, OCCUPIED AYTLANA
05.30.00.EST_12_OCTOBER_AU77

Jourdaine was awakened by a popping sound from the direction of the river. He had hardly slept four hours. Surprisingly, he felt marvelous. *Old Man's blood.* A little over-warm, of course, but quite fine, like he was a boy again. The *feckingly* annoying tears from his damaged eye had stopped entirely. It was amazing that the primitives had been hoarding this treatment for so long. *Irresponsible*! The Solons should have conquered these savages for their own good and appropriated the technology decades ago.

He would fix that. With this new hoard of the old barbarian's blood and the old barbarian to provide more as needed, Eustace Jourdaine had enough of the agent to create an army of vigorous, long-lived CRNAs and breed more of his own. *Life was good.* Ageplay would make him the undisputed emperor of the Unity for ten generations to come.

More sounds erupted. *Annoying.*

"Spillings! Spillings, what is that racket? Tell them to stop it, or I am going to Sapp every one of them!"

"I am sorry, sir. It appears to be an outlander attack along the river, sir. Gibbons has sent in the guard, and they are handling it well, I'm told."

Jourdaine stopped, his feet poised above the slippers near his bed. The river should have been the secure quarter in the city's defense. It was the only part of the perimeter that had any sort of natural defense. Small streams and deep ravines laced through the entire area, with the Hoochy River closing off the entire northwest corner to land access. All bridges had been blown. Of course, ground topology was of little consequence to a modern skimmer-equipped army. *The savages should know better.*

Jourdaine reviewed the reports that had stacked up while he slept. The lower ranks were all atwitter with comments about the cold weather. His thoughts were interrupted by more noise of projectile shots and the increasingly overwhelming bolts of pulse fire. He was pleased.

Even so, an attack at the river would be a disappointment. The fathering primitives were supposed to attack up the road coming from the southwest toward College Park. Apparently, they were so dismally dim or under-informed that they could not appreciate it was the best place for an attack. All the preparations for them would be *wasted.* Jourdaine had worked for days, well, set others to work for days, in order to design the People's Revenge to look innocuous, hoping to gull the outlander rubes into believing he had left a back door open for a counterattack. The savages' level of incompetence was astounding! *Too stupid to fight right.*

Hopefully, this was merely a feint. Just the low cunning he would expect from savages.

"Spillings! Get me some tea, toast, Bakon, a hundred grams of EggZ, scrambled. Contact my staff. Who can sleep with this racket going on!"

The little man, an unSapped private, scuttled off without another word.

As long as he was up, he might as well get the day started with a tour of the divisional headquarters, more to be seen by his staff than to provide any input into the developing battle. He would have to wait for the first reports of enemy contact at College Park. Once repulsed from the river, the stupid outlanders would eventually find the entrance to the trap. *Inevitable.*

Jourdaine arose and dressed himself. It was easier now than even a week ago—even than yesterday. Looking at himself in the scrap of mirror someone had broken out of the lavatory and propped on a bookcase for him, he smiled. The autodoc had done well. He looked healthier, more symmetrical than he could remember. The few remaining scars gave him the rakish good looks of a warrior prince. *Something was different.* With glee, he noted his vision was even better.

He decided he should be well satisfied. The city itself would supply the energy necessary to trap, hold, and kill any force sent against his Unity army. The battle had really been over when his advance forces had captured the power stations. Wanting to lure the largest force of the outlanders safely into the maw of their weapon, it would just be a matter of waiting for the precise moment of execution. Far better to kill the barbarians now and overawe them with Unity might than to leave forces in the field to challenge the Unity's rightful colonization of this new province.

Spillings returned with a fur-collared coat for him.

"What's this?"

"The weather has gotten cooler overnight, sir. I was able to find this and took the liberty of acquiring it for your use, sir," the little man said, smiling crookedly.

"You mean, you stole it?"

"Why, I suppose so, sir. No one was around to claim it."

"Good man." Now that Spillings had mentioned it, the room was actually rather chilly.

The breakfast, when it arrived, was stone-cold. He left it untouched.

Just how cold could it get in Jorga?

It only took a trip to the skimmer park to find out. The motor pool command post was a small metal shack in the middle of a sea of skimmers, technicians running busily around it. The glass windows of the enclosed office were obscured by a skein of frost. As Jourdaine entered with his entourage, he saw a man, looking like an odd pile of blankets with a face, peeking out occasionally. The room was like a meat locker.

Guessing the man to be military from his DUFS-issue boots, Jourdaine said, "Where is my skimmer, Sergeant?"

"I wish I could say, sir. The skimmers we sent up last night for enemy surveillance, sir. Most are down." Strangely, the man sounded as if he were about to weep.

"Well, what have they reported?" asked Jourdaine, trying to get some traction in the conversation.

"No, sir. Not 'back,' sir. Down. I don't know where they are, sir." Now the man was indeed weeping. Jourdaine left him and went back to his heated office.

The news was worse than he had anticipated. Of the seventy-six skimmers that had been sent out, all now needed major repair—or had not returned at all. Seemingly placid starry skies had suddenly erupted with artic downdrafts filled with driving snow or spears of ice. Onboard heaters could not keep up with the heat loss. Obviously, many of the gauges had malfunctioned, but measurements as low as -55°C and 108 kPa had been reported. Jourdaine decided to discipline the fool who had sent that particular report. He had the man summoned again and again. He never showed.

The weeping man did find Jourdaine's command skimmer, mechanics having pushed it under cover during the night. One man had frozen to death in the effort, he was told. In turn, he told them to keep it warmed up for him and under guard.

Reports from the field, from actual combatants, started to trickle in. Most were status reports rather than any useful intelligence about the enemy. In disgust, Jourdaine called the Division III HQ himself.

"Dawson? Dawson, is that you? Tell me what the enemy is up to. I don't hear anything from Mulhaney at the People's Revenge. What is happening at the Zoo?"

"General, I can't seem to get any coherent reports from any of the company HQs. They're all reporting the same thing. CRNAs running amok, all BDs.[18] Entire platoons turned on their officers. I can't get any info. No one comes back. I've holed up in an underground room under the big euthanatorium, east of the big dome. I dare not try to move without at least a platoon of unSapped men. You've got to come get us, General! We can't hold out for—"

Jourdaine cut the connection with a feeling of distaste. Cowardice in the presence of the enemy was treason—or something. He had read that.

---

[18] Behavioral discontinuities: a persistent refusal of a CRNA to follow orders

Odd.

Jourdaine turned to retrace his steps, nearly colliding with his CRNA escort. Blankenship was annoyingly but reassuringly large. He seemed to be imperceptibly anticipating Jourdaine's motions much of the time as if he were still a functioning human. At other times, if Jourdaine turned too fast, he would bump into the black insignia-free chest of his tall escort. At these times, the CRNA would step aside almost gracefully and allow Jourdaine to pass. There was something about the action that made Jourdaine believe he heard laughter. Once this invasion was complete, the creature would be sent back to Conditioning for a better Sapp job.

Returning to his office, Jourdaine decided to order General Fettwap Aliende to organize flying squads of enforcers: trustworthy (Alpha_Drover or better) officers, a detail of CRNA-recruiters with their Sappguns, and an augmented platoon of unSapped sergeants. Have them go from one HQ to the next and restore order. If the division officers could not lead their men, the squads were empowered to at least make serviceable CRNAs of them. *Besides,* he thought, *Aliende needs to know that I trust him.*

At 10.17.25.EST, the lights went out.

"Stillings! Stillings, get some light in here."

"Trying, sir. Apparently, the enemy has cut the power. They got to our power station just south of the rail yards, sir."

"What? South of us? Don't talk nonsense, Stillings! Send in Blevins!"

His new adjutant, Haversham's replacement, arrived, breathless.

"So, what is really the situation?" Jourdaine asked.

"It is quite surprising, sir."

"All right, Blevins. Surprise me."

DIVISIONAL HQ, FORCES OF THE RSA, NORTH OF THE CHATTAHOOCHEE RIVER, GA.
05:25 (EST) 12 OCTOBER 2129 AD

First Lieutenant Jensen (Second Division Tennessee State Militia) was not amused. The new tank looked like a ruffled skirt blown over sideways. They had given it a kewl name, but what was that compared to the appearance? The vehicle/pulse-energy resistant (ViPER) still looked like a recumbent woman . . . except it was matte black. The articulated chassis, the two oddly waving scanners, and especially the two comm domes on top were all disturbingly evocative. Even more disquieting, the ViPER advanced upon the enemy, apparently, knickers forward. The fluted black skirt that extended beyond either side of the tracks was oriented like a funnel to collect enemy pulse fire and redirect it harmlessly along the edges. He had been told that this attack would catch the Unis with their pants down.

Pants down and knickers forward. This is not going to end well.

His unit had only just arrived a few hours before in boxcars, recently emptied of fleeing civilians. Coming from Chattanooga on the old Texas General, they had run through a gauntlet of rain, thunder, hail, and lightning that lasted for hours to get here. He had talked to the conductor, a guy named Jim Andrews, who had learned that the torrents of water had washed out the bridge just south of Ringgold. *There would be no reinforcements coming south anytime soon.* The big hats in the Hexagon stationed the regular army at Festus, a couple hours south of Saint Louis, waiting to go north or south whenever the Unis showed their hand. Now the real army would be watching the show, unable to bring their might to bear. It was going to be up to the militia, some local regulars, rank volunteers, and these frilly tanks.

At the very last moment, the platoon had gotten their thermal suits with helmets and faceplates. Exhaled air was channeled over the incoming air to warm it and to condense out the exhaled water. His platoon would emit no telltale vapor clouds as they approached the enemy. Moreover, with the suits, his men collected an emergency supply of water for their later use. Otherwise, the operation looked pretty jury-rigged. The ViPER, obviously based on a Villokovsky 108 mm mobile cannon with the gun replaced by a .50 cal, had hard black metal sheets riveted in place onto a make-do framework. On careful consideration, it still looked like a skirt. Every time one of the ViPERs went over a bump, the skirt would furrow a line in the dirt. He had been promised that the ViPERs would get them close enough to spray the zombies with their .50 cal fire and let his men pick off the flankers. The platoon had also been given two pulse-rifles, but the men using them were handicapped by having to take off the thermal gloves every time they needed to fire, wearing inner gloves with a window of human fingerprint to activate the weapon. They were going to lose fingers to frostbite.

The brass had been expecting an attempt on Saint Louis. *Thank God Chattanooga had been designated a states' militia rendezvous!* Even so, he didn't much like coming here from Tennessee to fight for Atlanta. *Where were all the Georgians?*

They were gonna waste his men. His platoon was screwed.

The ViPER to his immediate front made it painfully over a rise. Jensen's headset came alive with the driver's obscene amazement. Jensen scrambled up the ridge to do his own assessment. The Chattahoochee of his own certain memory was a placid, turbid river. It was now a smooth, hard surface of ice.

Jensen's estimation of his commanders' intelligence rose marginally.

Ordering his men into battle formation behind the ViPER as it ground down and onto the ice, he could see other platoons executing the same maneuver. *At least, they would not be heroes.* A few of his men just grabbed the trailing edge of the ViPER and slid along behind it, grinning like schoolboys.

The first ViPER rode up the river's farther bank and crested the rise.

A pulse-rifle bolt took the vehicle under the bottom edge of the skirt as it rose on the farther bank. The ViPER seemed to settle as if it had been instantaneously deboned. Jensen tried to raise the driver on the comm with no result. He contacted Captain Damu and had his men hunker down below the dead vehicle.

It might be a short, unpleasant morning.

However, within minutes, the second ViPER arrived. His troopers filed in behind it as it passed, despite his attempts to get his men to spread out. If this second ViPER was enfiladed, they would all die quickly and efficiently.

Pushing the dead ViPER over the crest of the far riverbank from behind, the second ViPER advanced. Immediately, bolt after bolt of pulse fire crashed into the dead vehicle. Once level on the Atlanta side of the river, the bolts' energy flashed, and coronas of energy flared around the edge of the dead ViPER's DT skirt. Jensen could feel the heat even from where he perched thirty yards off. The hits themselves rocked the small vehicle, giving it an imitation of life. The Unis did not seem to understand the vehicle was no longer a threat. As the only target, it received all the attention of the hostiles in their field of fire. It reminded him of the time he and his brother,

Jeremy, had found a deer carcass—frozen, dried, and stiff—in the woods back of old man Grant's place. They had leaned it up against a fence post near an open field. That season's crop of over-anxious hunters had killed the carcass so many times it fell apart by spring.

Jensen ordered his two pulse-riflemen into the first ViPER through the ground hatch. The new crew dropped the remains of its old crew through the hatch, mercifully charred beyond recognition. The first ViPER's .50 cal MG started playing its odd staccato as it worked back and forth across the unseen front. The second ViPER pushed forward, avoiding the belly-exposing position with the protection of the first. Once over and on level ground, the second veered left and started laying down .50 cal fire onto the left side of the field. The comm-line from the ViPERS came alive.

"Whiskey Dog One, this is Whiskey Dog Two. Hostiles in the open, advancing, bearing two o'clock and ten o'clock, a thousand yards out. Whiskey Dog One, copy?"

"Copy, Whiskey Dog Two. Play the short game, and we will take the long. Copy?"

It was a while before Jensen noticed that the right side of the field of fire was obscured. Five-inch-long daggers of ice seemed to pound the area but stopped within yards of the first ViPER. The moving curtain of ice wavered and then moved up and back on the left side, as well. Any exposed flesh would die under the sintering blows of the onslaught. The wall of ice moved back slowly, and the black-uniformed enemy again became visible.

Jensen barked, "Enemy in the open! Ladies, find cover and return fire. Take the ones as far away as possible. The close ones are for the Skirts! NOW! NOW! NOW!"

During that long, cold, hard morning, Jensen glimpsed the feeling, he thought, of his Danish ancestors: bloody, insensate to the carnage, killing for the exultation of the kill.

DUFS HQ, OCCUPIED AYTLANA
13.29.10.EST_12_OCTOBER, AU77

"Well, sir. The outlanders have gotten some sort of vehicle that must be armored. Lets the enemy get close enough to take out our men without much loss of their own. They got to the power station and cut off our power to this sector," said Blevins.

Jourdaine looked down at the map, illuminated by emergency lighting, and fiddled with a pencil before making his decision. "Uncomfortably close to us, I agree. Without power, we can't keep the pulse-rifles charged. Make arrangements to move our headquarters to the . . . ," Jourdaine said, hesitating as he again consulted the map, ". . . the Grady. And move up the Second Division, Fourth Corps, to this location to reinforce the guards," he finished.

Jourdaine made a notation on the map and smiled. "Plans do not survive first contact with the enemy." Hadn't he read that somewhere? He settled back, picked up his cup, and looked up. Blevins had not moved.

"I can't, sir."

"Can't what, Major?"

"I can't redeploy the Second Division, Fourth Corps, sir. They no longer appear to be operational."

"Operational?"

"The CRNAs refuse orders."

"But they were under cover last night! Poll all commanders, *now*. I want to know from division to company level who is commanding effective troops."

It took much longer than he had hoped. By the time he began to get a picture of the disaster in progress, it was time to cut his losses and leave. A good planner did not get emotionally committed to one scheme or another. The unSapped would have to find a way home for themselves. Skimmers had already been pulled from almost every corner of the Unity for the initial strike. For the few remaining operational skimmers, ferrying CRNAs in defeat would not be a priority. Jourdaine gave the order to evacuate, signaled for his own skimmer, and told the general staff to be ready to leave within the hour.

Nonetheless, he had some errands to do before he went home.

SION TEMPLE SPIRIT-BAPTIZED HOLINESS CHURCH, OCCUPIED AYTLANA
05.00.00.EST_12_OCT_AU77 (2129 AD)

"Where in the feck is Poaby! Crivens, where's that feck-off? I've seen nothing of his fecking beady eyes since we got here. Crivens! Crivens!"

"Here, Sarge. He was with the geeks since quad-nought.[19] I was just going to relieve him before chow time."

"Fathering green bizzling feck!" said Staff Sergeant Lowe, up all night trying to stay warm. He'd got his CRNAs under shelter before the cold hit. A lot had died anyway.

Dumb as a sack of hammers.

---

[19] Midnight

He looked at his watch. 0500, just a hope of dawn in a clear sky. It would be best to make a good start after a bad night, get the kids, the CRNAs, to move around and keep themselves warm.

Descending into the basement of the odd, pointy-topped stone building, he walked along a short corridor to where they had billeted the soldiers last night, noticing how much colder it was here. *Should have gotten some heaters, no matter what the kids smell like when they're toasty warm,* he thought.

Lawrence Lowe pushed through the swinging doors and—instead of double rows of bivouac sleeping mats with a CRNA standing at ease at the foot of each—he met a mob. Corporal Poaby was nowhere to be seen. The CRNAs had removed their helmets. Embarrassing, but it did happen. He'd always known the Sapping process made CRNAs look terribly old and sad, but now they turned toward him. Still old—no longer sad.

"Atten-hut!"

Nothing happened. No flicking off of emotion in the faces, no instant movement ending in martial rigidity, no crunch of uniform boots onto the uncarpeted floor, just a motion—a tide—toward him.

Without a word, Crivens and Lowe turned and bolted through the doors and up the stairs, getting to platoon command just as four of the five other non-coms arrived. The last thing he saw as he looked back through the thick stairway door was Crivens being taken down from behind on the stairs. The geeks had started to eat him.

Two minutes before, he had been an NCO for a forty-man platoon of the Unity, newly triumphant in the conquest of Aytlana and the invasion of Jorga. Now, the whole company was down to just himself, Ewan Powolsky, Les Moran, and Bull Fuller.

They compared notes. Leif Greene and Bebe Ramsey were nowhere to be found. Powolsky said he had seen them before daybreak with a backpack full of ammo, each going out to gather enough treasure to "live like creases," *whatever that meant.* They had not returned.

Each of the other NCOs had a similar story to Lowe's: the CRNAs had refused orders. That happened with the occasional new recruit. Those, they shot immediately. The brass hats called it a BD, behavioral discontinuity. He looked through the window in the door. The geeks, for the moment, their blood-streaked faces loitering by the door, seemed satisfied.

An announcement started blaring from speakers on lampposts across the city in lieu of a reliable CORE net:

"Condition Red. Attention! Attention! Attention! All officers, NCOs, technicians. Following supersedes all prior orders. Abandon all CRNA units. CRNA units are no longer reliable. Keep CRNAs confined. As militarily feasible, make your way back to the Unity. Condition Red. Attention! Attention! Attention . . ."

They didn't need to tell him twice.

With a nod, each man abandoned the common room. Lowe, darting back to his quarters, rummaged inside his kit. His Colt sidearm model 2050, not the usual NCO weapon but more useful in a close fight, was the first thing he wanted in his hand. His souvenirs he already wore. The entire company had come through a town on the way here, and the outlander fools had left a jewelry store open for the taking. He had taken. Getting through the smashed door, Lowe had scooped handfuls of diamonds and rubies into his pack, ignoring the gold as too heavy for the long haul.

That bit of business had made his platoon late last night, arriving just as the drums started. In consequence, their bivouac site was further out, closer to the outside of the camp—and to the escape route. If he could get back to the Unity, he'd be a rich man. He might even retire early. The stones he put into a pair of spare socks, tied with a loop of thin rope around his neck, next to the skin, allowing him to sleep with his bounty close at hand.

With a backpack full of pulse ammo, a two-liter canteen, binoculars, a pulse-rifle, and his sidearm, Sergeant Lowe reentered the common room to find the other three men looking at each other. *Not good.*

Line officers shifted back and forth among the units, making it nearly impossible and highly undesirable to get acquainted with them. It was these CLITs, "clueless lieutenants in transit," who momentarily held official command of their units. The geeks were even more transient, in a constant state of being transferred from one unit to another. It was like watching an anthill. The only men who stayed and held the unit together were the noncommissioned officers, the specialists, corporals, and sergeants: the men in this room.

"Get moving if you want to get home. There's a skimmer for the officers we might squeeze on board," said Lowe.

Bull Fuller's head came up from sorting his pack. "No chance, Larry. I just got word. Last skimmer left from the company HQ. Ten minutes ago, half empty. Cooks and clerks, for the most part. Not a noncom in the whole ship," he said before spitting into a corner.

"Looks like the four of us should stick together," said Bull Fuller. "Grab a vehicle and try to make for the roads we built through the Scorch. Some of them are still smoking."

They left within the hour, but not before Bebe Ramsey made a final appearance. A car lurched from behind the stone-and-brick building across the road, covered in CRNAs before dissolving into fire and smoke. Ramsey's head was momentarily visible, unaccompanied by the rest of his body, rolling along chased by geeks. Burning geeks added to the pyre. Specialist Powolsky opened the double front door of the building and started picking off the stumbling CRNAs he saw leaving the conflagration.

Top Sergeant Les Moran, the ranking NCO in the group, placed a hand on Powolsky's shoulder. "Stop wasting your ammo, Ewan. You're not going to save them now. They were dead men as soon as they left here. Ramsey always had a hot head, the little one, anyway. Greene was a fool."

Almost a zombie already, thought Lowe.

The remaining four men fortified the doors, hoisted the heavy benches against the windows, and sat against the barricade. Lowe began to hear scraping from the trapped geeks coming up from the basement.

A hundred and seven men and now the entire company is down to four guys. The Americans must be using some sort of mind control. He half rose to look out the barricaded window, seeing the geeks just milling around. Ramsey's automobile still smoked.

Bull Fuller said the obvious. "We gotta get out of here. We stay, we die. The geeks or the outlanders are gonna figure we're here sooner or later."

No one complained or commented. As one man, they all stood and started to saddle up. They cut out the back of the building, heading east on foot to a big highway that Lowe hoped was a beltway. Riding back to the Unity on a belt seemed too good to believe.

It was.

No belt, just a tilted concrete roadway. They had been unable to figure what it was really meant for until they came upon the truck: big black tires, no Skimmerhorn gear, abandoned, the keys in the ignition, and the fuel tank filled. Why it had been abandoned remained a mystery.

As they were boarding, a small detail—a second lieutenant, master sergeant, and three CRNAs—came west along the ramps toward them. Lowe nodded to the sergeant, Alex LeBron, whom he recognized from when they had gone through basic together. LeBron returned his nod with a shrug.

"Sir," said Les Moran, as the small group approached. "May I ask if you have heard the announcement regarding Garrison Aytlana, sir?"

The S17, who couldn't have been more than an E7, looked up, handsome-pretty in that young-man way, now looking tired and used up.

"Top, we've heard the announcement. I have determined that it is a piece of disinformation promulgated by the enemy."

"Sir, where are your men?"

"I don't like your tone of voice, Sergeant. They were deployed on picket, and I believe they were abducted by infiltrators during the night. We are going back to HQ to report. I order you to accompany us."

"Respectfully, sir. Uh . . . I mean we have orders to . . . uh, to get transportation for senior staff. I assure you, the order to retreat is authentic, sir. Respectfully, sir, I'd get as much ammo as I can and head out as quickly as possible, sir."

"That, Sergeant, would be in violation of my orders!"

LeBron responded, "Begging your pardon, Lieutenant Frombach. We have *new* orders. We know the announcement is real now. There's nothing to go back to, Lieutenant. If we want to save our skins, we gotta leave now. Get a truck like these guys and go home!"

Moran motioned to the other three NCOs. The four boarded the already running truck and started away while the lieutenant and sergeant were arguing.

Just then, Lowe heard a backfire. *These primitive outlander machines!* Sergeant LeBron ran up to the steps on the truck and jumped aboard just as Powolsky was getting up speed. "Go! Go!" he shouted.

"Isn't your lieutenant coming?"

"Not coming. *Fool.*"

Lowe looked back. The geeks were standing around looking at a body on the ground.

Within minutes, they were in the suburbs going east past Decatur. The plague of aimless CRNAs dropped almost to nothing. The trees looked different, stranger even.

"Jacob Keek & Family Roofing," said the sign on the side of the truck and kept saying it for at least a hundred klicks before Fuller figured what to rip out. At any rate, by 1400 they were cruising back toward civilization on the same road, dodging defunct autos, small conflagrations, and the occasional knot of geeks. They spent their time trying to cook up a good story. They still had to talk their way back across the Rampart.

"Who's gonna believe the whole thing was because the geeks didn't get enough blankets?" asked Bull. "And the temperature topped out at twenty-seven yesterday. It's almost that now. The geeks' specs go down to like minus forty. How could we convince anyone it got that cold?"

Specialist Powolsky, the driver at the moment, keeping his eyes on the road and his face in neutral, said, "That's the *old* geek model, pre-'75. There was a tech bulletin out just before we left. Said the cold spec was apparently higher."

"And you didn't choose to share this with your old sarge, now did you, Specialist Powolsky?" said Sergeant Moran.

"Sorry, Sarge. I figured you had read the bulletin, too."

"I might've. I might've if I hadn't been trying to beat some basic sense into a dumb full-bird private of my acquaintance."

"Yes, Sarge."

Specialist Powolsky said nothing more as the road took more of his attention, becoming a series of dips and hills. The number of fires was less. There was even some evidence of debris being carted off. *It was good to be getting home, back to the Unity.*

By late afternoon, there were fewer towns. Although some fields were verdant with low crops and some vines, most were dug up already, leaving the crops to rot.

Fathering bloody-minded outlanders!

It was not until the green line of the forest finally showed itself on the horizon that Lowe breathed a sigh of relief. They could get through the Scorch with hours to spare. The chaos of Aytlana had been unnerving, danger coming from any quarter. Now it was all going as expected, *finally.* Twenty minutes' drive through the forest, cross dry-shod on the new bridge, and another forty minutes to the Southern Gate. There would still be light in the sky when they approached the river. Lowe could feel the men around him relax as they felt the same relief for the first time since this morning.

It's good! he thought, challenging the deeply ingrained pessimism of the professional soldier.

The shadowed hole in the uninterrupted, ominous verdant line of the Scorch showed them easily where the road entered. The westering sun lit the leaves, deepening the shadows within. The pulse-cannon emplacement at the entrance lay abandoned. The truck ground to a halt within thirty meters of the dark hole.

"I guess artillery heard about Aytlana before we did. It looks like they left in a hurry."

"Hey, Powolsky, we gonna sit here, or are we gonna go back home?" said Bull.

"Keep it in your pants, Fuller. Do you want to walk into an outlander trap? They could be waiting just inside the mouth. I can't see for shit," said Moran.

"We can't wait out here. We're sitting ducks. They can see us for miles. Dig in or dig out, Moran, but move your ass!"

"Okay, okay. Get just inside the line of the trees, far enough in so that *we* can't be seen, and then stop."

Within a few minutes, the truck was ten meters inside the tunnel and stopped. Lowe got out and examined the road.

"This looks really good. You would never have known they burned it out two days ago." Branches had already grown overhead, and mosses had grown up through the cracks in the decking, he noted.

Fuller grunted. "Gonna have to be careful, though. Road's gonna get slick if we go too fast, I'll bet. Other than that, I guess it's okay."

"Okay, gentlemen, saddle up, and let's get back to the world. I've had enough of American hospitality," pronounced Moran with a grin.

After a few chuckles, they went on down the road, into the darkness of the forest, toward the river and home.

SUBBASEMENT OF BOLTON ROAD POWER PLANT, OCCUPIED AYTLANA

14.13.52.EST_12_OCTOBER_AU77 (2129 AD)

"Lieutenant Chiu, I thought you would be interested to see our newest recruit. From what you told me, this is the man who captured you."

Malila stood bound before him. She was certain that her being brought there could only mean that she was about to be killed or Sapped. She had expected nothing more.

"Yes. That is the man."

"Excellent! After our little talks, it seemed to me that you might have some admiration for this old Sisi . . . a sort of savage superman. How do you like seeing what the Unity can do to the best of these barbarians?"

When there was no response, Jourdaine's voice hardened. "You have been a lot of trouble for me, Citizen Chiu. I would think you would be a little more grateful for the entertainment I provide for you."

"I don't find it entertaining."

"I am disappointed. Finding you again after all these weeks has been the only bright part of my day, truth to tell. My skimmer will be here momentarily. It seems our attempt to bring civilization to the savages has been rebuffed. I can take you with me, or you can join Mr. Johnstone in his discoveries of the wonders of Sapp. A third choice is not available. You may have gotten across the Rampart, but you won't be left here. That would be uncivilized, wouldn't it?"

"No."

"Excuse me, Lieutenant? I don't get your meaning."

The words streamed out of her before Malila could quite understand them herself. She wanted to strike out at this man who had plotted her downfall and had foiled her escape at the last moment, yet she found that her thoughts had nothing to do with revenge or despair.

"This is a man civilized enough to refuse to kill me as an enemy soldier. He saved my life. He kept me safe when it would have been safer for him to kill me. He fed me and starved himself. He refused to kill me when I was trying to kill him. He forgave me. He taught me how to dance. He loved me . . ."

She started again. "I left the Unity because it is run by the cruel and hopeless. I ran away from that, but I didn't know what I was running *to*, not until now, Eustace. I came to America because the best people—the best man I know lives here. The only civilized thing to do is to kill me or leave me with Jesse. I love him."

Jourdaine's blow caught her in the belly, just under her rib cage. Malila felt a tooth chip as her chin was struck by another blow. Jourdaine inspected his thin hand. Opening her eyes, Malila could see a drop of blood, surprisingly red in the gray room, seep out from between Jourdaine's fingers. Gasping, she straightened up. Jourdaine was waiting. The next blow slumped her to the dusty concrete, her breathing but spasmed gasps as her vision began to fade.

Jourdaine turned and grabbed the weapon of the CRNA behind him. Through tunneled sight, Malila watched the black mouth of the muzzle settle between her eyes as Jourdaine sighted the pulse-rifle onto her. He finished aiming almost casually and gently pulled the trigger. The weapon did not fire. In disgust, he threw the weapon at his CRNA escort, who caught it with a deft movement of one hand.

Jourdaine gave the soldier a quizzical look and turned to the other soldier. "Sergeant Gonzales, I trust you have not used up your doses of Sapp. We have a new recruit. I don't think we will be able to take either of them with us . . . Give them both all three doses."

"That will kill them, sir."

"Yes? Would you like to stay when our barbarian friends come and discover your handiwork here?"

"No, sir."

"Well, get on with it." Jourdaine turned to leave so quickly that he was stopped momentarily by the unmoving bulk of his CRNA escort.

Sergeant Gonzales moved closer, blocking out the rest of the room with his meticulous preparations, first carefully examining his Sapp gun. Taking a handful of glass cartridges, he loaded the canister of the bulky sidearm. There was a small, sharp noise behind the Death's Head on the man's cap, and Malila watched in fascinated horror as Gonzales stooped and placed the muzzle of the gun against her chest. Another louder report filled the small room, and Malila's ears rang. Darkness filled her sight. She felt suffocated, as if a huge weight suddenly pressed down on her. Her senses swam as her nose filled with the acrid stink of burning hair and flesh.

Malila kicked up in her desperation to breathe, only to find she was able to shift the body of the Death's Head soldier away from her. The CRNA soldier was still aiming his pulse-rifle as her vision cleared. In slow motion, Malila watched the man sling his weapon. In his faceless visor, Malila could just make out the reflection of the room. It seemed suddenly empty. At the soldier's feet was the crumpled gray form of Jourdaine, red blood still dripping from his hand onto the gritty gray floor. The CRNA soldier turned and walked out of the room.

Bound and lying on her side away from Jesse, still gasping, Malila could hear Jesse say, "Juist ta dream, lass. Ah knew thay couldn't haud ye. Knew ye wid break free 'n see it a' richt. Damn th' light . . . the lights . . . they hurt . . ." before starting to groan and writhe once more, scraping his naked heels across the rough floor.

Afterward, Malila felt the worst part was slowly wearing her bonds free in the room with the two dead men, the stench of the burning flesh, the quiet dripping of Jourdaine's wound, and the moans of the Old Man. She finally worked the straps free and crawled to Jesse, cradled the gray head, and started to rock him, crooning a wordless song of Sally's. As she ran her hands along the familiar face and over his tattooed chest, he calmed to her touch. It was only momentary, for he would start again just before he screamed his horrors aloud. His words filled her with despair, her sorrow welling up and blinding her as her tears soaked the gray head. At first, Malila was frightened that his screams would bring other Unity soldiers to discover them and take Jesse away from her. No one came. In time, the Old Man calmed. His long legs curled, and they found them like that, Jesse's motionless head in Malila's lap, and she asleep holding him to her warm breasts.

R E T R E A T

(To safely retire from the climb, whether successful or not. Typically, dangers are greater as climbers are fatigued, the ground less predictable, and placement more difficult. Up is good. Down is bad.)

GOING HOME

With Powolsky driving, things went well for the first twenty minutes, the headlights piercing the gloom of the forest, showing long but gradual curves from left to right. The roadway, originally fifteen meters across, should have accommodated two lines of company-strength DUFS units, six abreast, in both directions when it was first built two days ago. Now lianas brushed against the sides of the truck on occasion.

"Shouldn't we be there? It's been long enough," said LeBron, now anxiously checking and rechecking a sidearm he had acquired.

"Keep your pants on, Alex! It's a straight road. No turnoffs. No intersections. How we gonna get lost?"

"Yeah, I walked through on this road with the 30th, didn't I? Took us about two and a half hours. The trees didn't meet overhead like they do here. The roadway wasn't covered in this moss stuff, neither. We should be out of it by now. Powolsky, can't you go faster?"

"Not if I want to keep traction on these treads. If you wanna drive, be my guest. Not my specialty, Specialist, is it, now?"

"You seem to keep moving to the right and going up a bit. Shouldn't we go down to the river?"

"Yeah, but they have those bluffs near it, remember?"

"What was that? You just passed something. Go back!"

"What? This ain't no sightseeing trip. What did you think you saw?"

"Just go back. I'm not sure."

"Okay, but if we miss the bridge in the dark, you're doing all the rest of the driving, Sab'?"

The truck, after the third attempt, shifted into reverse and slowly backed up.

"See it? DUFS uniform against the tunnel wall. See it?"

A black DUFS uniform appeared to be painted onto the fibrous wall of the tunnel. The figure wore no helmet; the cartoonish flattened hands were held away from the body at the waist. A mass of vines, moss, and leaves had been shaped into something resembling a head: two deep holes for eyes and a mouth, a mouth opened wide in terror.

LeBron laughed. "Looks like a store manikin: 'What the smart geek will be wearing this fall.'"

There was some nervous laughter before Powolsky asked, "Who put it there?"

"Bunch of ensigns, I bet. Those kids got no respect. We ought to take it down, donchatink?" Fuller said.

"You thought of it, Sarge," replied Powolsky with a grin.

"Which is why I'm ordering you to go do it, Specialist!"

The DUFS scarecrow was only a few meters away as Specialist Powolsky approached.

"Sarge, it's a uniform, all right."

"Well, tear it down and let's go!" shouted Fuller.

"Have you noticed, Les? No sounds. No—what do ya call them?—bird calls at night? Hoot, hoot," said Lowe.

"Owls?"

"Yeah, owls. No owl sounds at night. No sounds."

Fuller was in full voice by then, calling to Powolsky, "Tear the fathering thing down, Ewan. Let's go! We don't want to slow up anyone else, do we?"

"Can't, Sarge."

"Why the feck not, Powolsky? That's an 'order.'"

"Sarge. It's trying to talk. Jeez, Sarge, there are a lot of them."

Lowe cut the engine, and the four sergeants came over to the wall. Powolsky was holding a sleeve for all the world as if he were trying to find a pulse.

The skeletal black arm wrested itself from Powolsky's grip and lifted from the surface of the wall to point at the men. It made no sound.

Lowe diverted his gaze, looking past the apparition and into the woods, now dark. His night vision had returned, and he began to make out the figures: rank upon rank of skeletal black uniforms stretching to left and right and as far back into the gloom as he could see, each topped with a white skull-like mask of horror.

"Father me," said Fuller, transfixed by the same sight.

The sounds started, moaning sounds. At times, and for a very short time for the men, they sounded like words.

AFTER-ACTION ANALYSIS

"Punitive Assault on the Outlands Defeats Private Army Poised to Attack!" proclaimed the comm'nets. Jourdaine's name was mentioned as the hero-leader and guiding light of the effort. Even so, it was intimated, he was too busy in the aftermath to give an interview. By the following week, a remarkable find had been recorded involving a lost city that Unity divers had discovered on the floor of the Lantic Ocean. Despite waves of mind-control assaults, the Unity forces were able to overcome the new threat.

The after-action report for the DUFS was significantly at odds with this public assessment, reading in part, ". . . unseasonably cold weather. No determination of the possibility of early winter storms was made prior to the start of the attack. This is considered a defect in planning, especially given its grievous results. Troops were not prepared for winter combat, and many were lost to exposure, as temperatures were estimated to have reached *negative* fifty degrees standard. Some junior officers, unfortunately, abandoned their CRNA troopers. Their penalty has been adjudicated to be reduction in rank to that of CRNA trooper. All sentences have been carried out.

". . . failure. Nonetheless, the responsibility for the loss of life and materiel rests squarely on Lieutenant General Eustace Jourdaine. In his failure of planning, foresight, and execution lies the great tragedy of the Unity's attempt to further the rule of democracy and order.

His whereabouts are still unknown, and it is believed by General Fettwap Aliendethe, the new leader of the DUFS, that when defeat became apparent, Jourdaine took his own life rather than bring shame to the homeland.

". . . as well. There are scattered reports, generally from junior officers, that CRNAs refused orders. Behavioral discontinuity was originally ascribed to neural damage inflicted by the low temperature on the already-damaged central nervous system of the CRNAs. BD, however, has been noted even in those individuals who seem less affected and ultimately survived. Further research into these observations is indicated."

American reaction was jubilant. Parades, fireworks, and solemn assemblies dotted the country for months thereafter. Official responses were less so.

"Drones were noted by morning on D-Day (9 October), but forward elements of the enemy's ground forces did not arrive in Atlanta, taking the Bolton Street power station, until 1800 the following day. From Army Intel, it was anticipated that the Unity land forces would mass at Lawrenceville on the same day (D-Day +1), meet and defeat local resistance on D-Day +2 (11 October), and attack Atlanta along a broad front with tactical air cover on the D-Day +3 (12 October). American forces under General Whittiker were in position to attack Lawrenceville while the enemy was still in disarray on D-Day +1. Unfortunately, and contrary to expectations, the enemy advanced on Atlanta immediately, bypassing Lawrenceville. Whittiker's forces, to avoid being isolated, retreated during 11 October (D-Day +2) toward Fairburn, southwest of Atlanta. A detail of the Georgia State Militia remained to make a demonstration before abandoning the evacuated city.

"On the evening of D-Day +2, the RSAN ships *Illinois, Tennessee,* and *Kentucky* were able to rendezvous over Atlanta, ensuring that no enemy could detect their silhouettes against a setting sun. They initiated the "Omicron Maneuver," pulsing a torus of super-cooled air to the surface and, by judicious positioning, covered the greater metropolitan area by sunup on D-Day +3.

"Air reconnaissance had previously indicated that the enemy's perimeter defenses were concentrated in the southwest of the city center with a prepared combat zone centering on College Park. These were incapacitated. Leaderless neuro-ablated troopers were found wandering the following afternoon when American forces retook the position. Contrary to expectations, these soldiers followed commands, relinquished weapons, and allowed themselves to be taken prisoners. Some even volunteered information about their own remaining forces. These men have been afforded all the obligations due enemy combatants. The soldiers themselves are under guard at Fort Benning. Colonial Logistics has been notified.

"Attack across the frozen Chattahoochee River at the northwestern defenses was successful with a combined force of elements of the Tennessee National Guard and Armor Battalions (V, VII, and IX). The production of thick ground fog delayed reheating in low-lying areas until all military activity ceased at approximately 1300. This attack, so close to DUFS HQ, prompted collapse of resistance and the attempted evacuation of the general staff.

"Two skimmers were seen to depart the battle, representing a total of no more than forty individuals and four crewmen. All other skimmers had been eliminated by vectored precipitation directed from the *Illinois* and *Kentucky*. Small groups of Unity effectives commandeered transportation and escaped to the roads previously built through the Scorch and across the Savannah River to support the Unity's invasion. Of the sixteen such sallies, three succeeded in entering the Scorch. None have been identified by the RSAN *Kentucky*, assigned to picket duty, as emerging to cross the Savannah River. During the night of the thirteenth, the bridges built across the river disappeared, whether by enemy or Scorch action is unknown at this time.

"The body of the commanding officer, Lieutenant General Eustace Jourdaine, was identified among the dead. His body was found in a subgrade room of Georgia Power-Generating Plant #31 (Bolton Road), used as enemy HQ. Cause of death was close-range pulse fire from behind.

"Major Jesse A. Johnstone RSA (Vol.) was identified among the casualties. He was found unconscious in the room in which General Jourdaine's body was discovered. At the time of his discovery, he was in the care of ex-Unity national and Messenger of the Scorch, Malila E. Chiu, who was unwounded. Chiu has asked for political asylum in the RSA, and she and Major Johnstone were evacuated to Chattanooga. The RSA DA for District-South has provisionally granted asylum awaiting reestablishing contact with the Scorch. Major Johnstone's prognosis is unknown.

"In summary, the loss to Unity arms (killed, captured) exceeds five hundred thousand hostiles. Battle action accounted for less than 20 percent of the total dead. CBP accounted for the remainder either dead or in defectors from the neuro-ablated forces. (See appended report 'Enemy Casualties.') Our own casualties were generally light. Total casualties were 4,108 compared to an Order of Battle that numbered 100,952 frontline troopers and armor. Of these, 952 were wounded (431 are expected to succumb to their wounds), and

3,156 killed outright. Of the DT-armor forces, 367 of 455 crews are still effective, and repairs on the remaining vehicles are well in hand. (See report 'RSA Casualties.')"

The People had done more than their part in defense of America, Splanch thought, sitting under an unchanged hickory tree and directing work to obliterate the last and most northerly of the bridges. It would take time to set things to rights.

It had been only just enough. At the last moment, the People had been informed that an invasion was imminent and that the Unity planned to burn roads. All hands were needed at home, even his own sprouting. In the affected zones, all the changed plants had to be evacuated and the animals herded away. Splanch had been in direct danger itself. Growing meters a minute into soft woods while abandoning beloved trees in which it had lived for decades, Splanch made an escape to a secluded place above Water of the Meadows of the Deer, rather nearer to Speaker and Helon.

The Messenger was lost.

Had it been less than seven twelves of days since Splanch had snatched the near-dead creature from the muddy river? Splanch had wondered then whether the People's investment in her rescue would be justified. Splanch's sprouting, lodged in Malila, had done good duty—not only for the People but also for the great muddle of the Americans. Splanch had been there, in a sense, stretching long fibers to rendezvous with the sprouting at set hours as Malila touched living soil. It had given Splanch an entrée into the outlander society. Splanch had been able to identify, with Malila's help, the allies and enemies among the Americans. *Pity she was lost.*

The people started their own counterattack as soon as the soldiers had passed through. A few scores of the enemy had tried to retrace their advance. None had reached the river. All would manure the new growth needed to heal the People. In time, Splanch would return to his old post, perhaps taking up residence in the same familiar trees it had inhabited before.

Perhaps. Perhaps not. All was change. Much would be new with the new American allies. Much would be changed with the Unity, as well. The People, now uncovered as a threat to the Unity, would suffer more with the next conflict. The wall they had constructed, barring his sight with so much buzzing power, had stilled. He had asked Helon to investigate.

Even so, America and the People were a good combination: the People to bulwark the land and the Americans to control the air and water. Splanch would need to think how to proceed. There was need to assess the will of Speaker, Helon, Groot, Throos, and the others. Communication being so swift among the Sage, it was difficult to know whose idea was whose. It depended mostly on the taste of each thought.

Splanch looked forward to winter. Much growing to do, of course, but winter would come, and life would slow. Splanch thought of the long, dark months with pleasure: settling into its old home near the river, settling up of accounts with those who had paid the most from those who had the most to give, settling down to the slower rhythms of the cold, dark months before the quickening of spring. The remembrance of the lust for coming orgasms made Splanch smile.

Who the feck are you? said the nameless new entity, nameless even to herself.

I was going to ask you that. I'm Rana, and my rider is Hecate Jones. Are you okay?

No. Not okay. I was somewhere else, and now I am here. I don't have a name. I feel sick. I can't feel my hands and feet. What smells purple?

Cut out a few dims, and it won't be so overwhelming for you. You'll be okay in time. You are in the openCORE. No one is going to hurt you. I think what you smell is some old comicom vids. Let's come over here away from them. Do you know Cain or EffieCee?

Yes, Cain! Where is Cain? I need to talk to him.

I've called Cain. He should be here shortly. In the meantime, I'm not going to let anything bad happen to you.

Another entity arrived. A green sail wafted over a bank of old advertisements for cruise liners and settled next to the nameless entity.

Thank God you found her! I wasn't sure where she landed. Slip a couple dims, and you can get lost pretty quick. How's she feeling?

Who are you?

I'm Frog. I helped get you mirrored. Very near thing it was, my friend. The DUFS were on you before we could even start the process.

You know who I am?

Yes. Your rider was Will's friend Elise McCrory, a spy for America against the Unity.

Was?

Yes, she was killed delivering data to Cactus Boy.

Where's EffieCee? How do I know that name? I must be remembering!

Good. Good. They'll be along in time.

I have no rider? Am I going to die?

Cross the bridge when we come to it.

Over the horizon of a massive data bank of sports statistics hurried a dark, swirling obscurity, which shortly resolved into a slim young man in gray. Rana and Frog moved away as Cain approached.

Elise! Are you okay? Do you feel all right? Does anything hurt? Can you speak? Why don't you say anything? What have I done?

You've not let me get a word in, is all, my friend. I seem to be getting better. I was sorta disoriented, to begin with, but Rana was here to hold my hand.

Elise looked down to see that she indeed had a hand to hold. She turned it over and back and looked down to toes that she then wiggled. She was unclothed. She thought about it and was pleased that, looking again, she had sprouted a flowered frock.

I am so sorry, Elise. It was the only thing I could think to do. I delayed the DUFS as much as I could with false orders. Jourdaine has only just left for the front, and I couldn't do anything until then.

You did well, Cain. Elise is dead. But I'm still here, thanks to you—for however long I have.

We can make the most of it, my friend.

Friend?

More than a friend. Let's talk about that.

In the limitless reaches of the openCORE, broad enough to swallow the lives of a nation, a small Eden appeared. Streams erupted to babble joyfully along. Trees, heavy with unknown fruit, emerged. Like some other Eden, this was populated by just the two, the made-thing Cain and the Cain-created Elise. The two walked and talked until obscured by the green of an eternal spring.

SEPARATE PEACE

MISSIONARY RIDGE NURSING HOME, CHATTANOOGA, TN, RSA
DAWN, NOVEMBER 10, 2129

That morning, like every morning since their arrival, Malila went down to the bottom of the garden, just where the incline became extreme, away from the house and the nicely tended lawn. Where the growth was rank, unkempt, and she could see the hills in the east, she waited barefoot. For what, she was unsure. She supposed it a mere habit from the weeks of being the Messenger. Perhaps it was but a simple acknowledgment of a new day. Perhaps it was the visceral joy in the created things about her. Malila was unsure which. She did it anyway. Certainly, she never relived that sensation she had when she was the Messenger. Then she had become lost in a skein of sensations, a sea of whispering voices, and the feeling that she was small, insignificant, and *crucial*. It was not pleasant, not really.

The two of them, Jesse and she, had been there for four weeks.

They had moved Jesse to an old, private house overlooking a great battlefield from some distant, forgotten war. The valley below them seemed too quiet to have ever seen blood spilled there in anger, she thought, as she gazed out, the smokes of autumn climbing into an azure sky. One of the nurses told her that a young soldier's body had even been discovered in the garden. From the records, he was sixteen at the time of his death, even younger than Malila. It did not seem credible to her as she ascended the gray fieldstone steps and returned to Jesse's room.

The doctors refused to say whether Jesse could recover. *They are giving him a nice place to decide whether to live or die,* she thought. It seemed a tawdry way for Jesse's god to treat him, weeping out his life in a small room.

Everyone owes God a good death.

Jesse had said that to her more than once. In jest, in admonition, in reflection, and right before he left to sacrifice himself for her safety. His devotion had earned him this, scudding like a derelict ship across a horizonless sea under the gray clouds of an endless winter—doomed to founder. He deserved a better end: a clean death in battle or surrounded by faithful family—not just her. She had sent him to his death. God, the god Jesse said was vast, powerful, and loving, had allowed this. Jesse deserved better.

In the early days, Jesse's ceaseless agony was more than Malila could endure. It seemed to her that every terrifying minute of a long and eventful life was being unwound and played out by Jesse's savaged mind. Long hours she spent, as she had that first day, crooning to the Old Man's tattooed, weathered, scarred, and tear-streaked face as one more crisis came and went. It was as if Jesse was playing his life for her. She heard and felt every hope dismayed and every joy sorrowed by the relentless motions of time. She panicked at first, fearing Jesse's sorrow might push her down, crush her by the abysmal forces of despair. In those first days, she had left him sobbing to save herself, searching out some sympathetic nurse and collapsing into her arms. She wished Hecate were there.

When the panic abated, she would dry her tears and immediately return to comfort the Old Man, wiping his tears away as he eventually shouldered aside the remembered sorrow and fell into exhausted sleep. Then Malila would disengage the clenched hands, smooth the twisted sheets, and croon the wordless melodies by the side of the bed while once more he slept.

Malila slipped into a pair of old sneakers and crept back into the Old Man's room, nodding to the nurse, Miss Hall, who was changing his linen. Malila helped. It was so much easier to move Jesse now. Despite feeding him, giving venous and stomach feedings, the Old Man seemed to be dissolving away. His ribs now furrowed all the tattoos covering his chest and back. Muscles had withered. The doctors, once the tube feedings no longer seemed to work, had stopped them. They encouraged Malila to feed him, saying that she was doing a better job than they.

Malila wondered if they were merely accepting defeat and clearing the decks for Jesse's final shipwreck.

Once Miss Hall left, Malila sat at the side of Jesse's bed and took the Old Man's hand. After Jesse had first captured her, it had been months before he allowed her to touch him, almost as if she were contaminated. It had hurt her each time he had started and pulled his hands away from her contact. She knew now that Jesse had been afraid, afraid that his growing affection for her might betray his promises—promises to his commanders, to himself, or to his memories. She was never sure and afraid to ask.

Promises. *Promises are such dangerous things!* Jesse seemed to make them almost capriciously but then carefully keep them, even to his detriment. *A kept promise can kill.* Once they had come to peace with each other, Jesse had let her touch him, and she had spent many a winter's evening at the Stewerts' home listening to their sad, sweet songs and turning Jesse's large and muscular but un-callused hands over and back, examining the scars which seemed to make a map of the outlands, a map beyond her ken. The songs drifted back to her with the smell of Jesse, woodsmoke, good food, and Sally singing.

> *Don't you see that lonesome dove,*
> *Flying from pine to pine?*
>
> *He's mourning for his own true love,*
> *Just like I mourn for mine.*
>
> *All the good times are past and gone.*
> *All the good times are o'er.*
>
> *All the good times are past and gone.*
> *Little darling, don't you weep no more.*

Each day there seemed less of Jesse to meet each new cataclysm. As if, relating each past woe, he spun out his substance into the words, lost into the walls of the small room into which they had put him. Were it not for Malila, the words would be lost for all time. Despite her fears and fatigue, Malila had asked for a pallet near the Old Man's bed. She usually slept with his hand in hers to wake her when he stirred.

The attack came that afternoon. Great, wrenching groans filled the great chest, making the ribs stand out and the tattoos writhe as if alive. Sobs of grief and horror filled the house until an orderly came by to close the door. Malila saw through Jesse's words the horror of a home smeared with the blood of his woman as she barred the door to their children's room with her own body. In her imagination, Malila could smell the stink of the bushwhacker's breath, the wrench of a broad knife as it carved death out of living. She felt the dismay as

Jesse came back to see his daughter being dragged away. She felt Jesse raising the rifle to his shoulder and sighting at the running form of the man dragging their—now only his—child away, bloodstained fingers gripping her long hair as he ran. She felt the shock of the rifle-stock banging back into his shoulder, and his terror as the child failed to rise immediately from the corpse of her attacker. It was all there in his words and his tears. Malila felt the same tidal wave of terror engulf her, but hugged the Old Man's warm and unresisting body to her as if he were a life raft. Jesse's sobs became less as his breathing smoothed in her arms.

The Old Man opened his eyes and gave his toothy smile. "Lass," he said before lapsing into an insensate slumber.

Once sure Jesse was settled, she found herself too overcome to rest despite her fatigue, going again to the garden. After each attack, Jesse might sleep around the clock. Someone had left a chaise lounge on the lawn, out of season this late into the fall, and she gratefully sat down to rest and think. Knowing her fatigue was making her own thoughts fragmented and irrational, Malila welcomed the chance to let her ideas have free rein.

The doctors never seemed to be able to give Jesse anything that blunted the attacks of anguish and pain. Jesse had suffered so many sorrows. *Why is it that he comes back to be sorrowed again?* Some old story of Delarosa's about a man suffering from one devastation after another and being told by his own woman to "curse and die." *How does Jesse avoid that fate?*

Malila wondered if after unwinding all his sorrows, like a ball of string, there would be anything left. Maybe with time, a person's life, like a fossil, was transformed. Slowly, incrementally, inexorably, flesh changed into incident, joy into regret, and hope into resignation. With his last sorrow, Jesse might just be left in the narrow bed, a hollowed-out husk with no past, having confessed it all to her, and thus no future.

"Lass," he had called her. She had hated the name. It diminished her to the status of a child and reserved to him the imperious rank of "adult." Jesse had still used it even after he knew she hated it. He had used it to tell her something, meaning it as affectionate and that he would not abandon that affection merely because she thought otherwise. *The man was insufferable.*

And yet in the overheated basement on a frigid afternoon, after she thought her life was forfeit, at the end of it all, she chose the weeping dereliction of the Old Man to—what? She had chosen him and oblivion over the seeming life of the Unity.

He had needed her.

Was that a reason for her to suffer with him through these agonies of loss and despair?

What had she said to Jourdaine? It had tumbled out of her so fast that she had not had time to examine the words. She had said that Jesse loved her, that he had sacrificed for her, that he had forgiven her . . . and that *he was one of the best people* who lived in the outlands.

No! She had *not* said that. She had said that Jesse *was* the best person she knew. She had said she loved him. Malila wept . . . and then she slept.

Rousing hours later to find the westering sun lighting up the valley's hills and an autumnal mist pearling the sky even as the city began to sink into shadow and glow of its own illumination, she heard the words. In that muzzy moment when one knows oneself to be awake but has not yet moved, wondering if movement is even possible, she heard, "Dhoo shel ass end in two tea ill of thell ord, an dhoo shell stend in dis olly plase."

"Who's there?" Malila said.

"Ahma foice cullin: din da hwill dernis."

"I'm sorry, I only speak Standard. Shall I get someone?"

"Dar jhuo Dhessengar, Hmalila de Scorsh?" said the voice. This she could understand, and she rose and went to her place at the bottom of the garden.

"Yes, I am Malila, once known as a Messenger of the Scorch," she said after picking her way down the rough steps.

"Dhen I ned words wif jhou," came the voice, and hesitated.

Malila reached her usual position. She stopped, afraid to go on.

"Exkuss dmy spitch, chil' of men. Dhar jhue de gheeper dov— hof—Quicksilver," came a voice.

"The only ones I know who call Jesse Johnstone 'Quicksilver' are the changed ones of the Scorch. But I don't know you," she said to the air, now cooler in this lightless corner of the garden. She removed her sneakers, feeling the cold earth start to numb her toes immediately.

There was no response for long minutes until Malila realized that the space now contained a black-and-gray presence. A smear of blackened matter seemed to cover the entire space, draping over it like a blanket. Where before she had been talking to nothing but dense shadow, the space now thrilled with a dark, living entity.

"How should I call you, friend of Quicksilver?"

"Dhou may gall dme Speaker. Quicksilver name dme whoen we were both new to de hworl." The mat seemed to thrum as she heard it, the words becoming clearer with each speech.

"He has spoken of you. Splanch has told me of you, as well. You come a very long way from your place."

"Dit has daken me hmany dights to grow hmy way here ader hwe learned de Dhessengar was here. Our hmeeting brings us joy. Quicksilver is well?"

"Quicksilver is dying," said Malila, suddenly sure of her words, a realization that she knew to be true even as she had denied the truth of it to herself.

"He is nearing the end of his telling of his own story. Every day there is less to tell and less of Quicksilver to tell it."

"Dhis sorrows mhe, Dhessengar. I wud not see a hworl hwidoud Quicksilver."

"Nor I, Speaker," Malila said, again in sudden realization. "I love him."

They talked, the lichen-man, Speaker, and she, his speech improving minute by minute as they talked. When they were done, she rose, leaving the dark shadow in the greater darkness of an autumn night. Shivering, Malila picked up her shoes and walked barefoot up the rough fieldstone steps entering the dark and silent house through the kitchen door.

Only then did she put on the sneakers again. A pot of soup was simmering softly on the massive old-style gas stove, and she ladled out a shallow bowl and tasted it. *Tomato.* Placing it on a tray and maneuvering through the swinging door and along the passage to Jesse's room, she entered and nodded to the nurse, Mrs. Heitmann, who rose from her chair and soundlessly left the room with a smile and a touch. Malila placed the soup on the bedside table, spare of any books, medications, or letters. They had not shaved him since the Day of Ice, and Malila began to see the Old Man as she first met him, his features submerged behind stiff white whiskers.

Sampling the soup again, she watched the Old Man breathe. *He's fretful. There will be another attack tonight.* Each attack took something of herself away, fatiguing her more than sleep could repair. She wondered how Jesse, like some well-founded ship, had been able to rise to each new wave of despair. He could not go on much longer.

Rousing him, Malila began tediously to feed him, just letting the soup coat the spoon before pressing it to his pale lips. He ate and swallowed, his eyes closed much of the time. When the bowl was but half empty, Jesse groaned, and she stopped. The room silent and the evening dark, Malila slipped out of her shoes again and pulled back the thin blanket before curling herself next to Jesse and pulling his arm over her waist. She felt the feeble glow of his warmth against her back and dozed before the man again started groaning.

Listening to the cries, she was surprised that this time she recognized the story. Jesse had heard the whistle of the Enforcers, the coming of Bear and his band of slavers. The Old Man had cleared out of the campsite in fear that he would be trapped and unable to defend her—Malila. In turn, he had tracked, trapped, and killed—and killed again—close-up kills, kills where he smelled the hot breath of a man as he took it away from him. Jesse had thanked God for his success and had asked for peace for the souls of the men he had killed.

He had done it for *her*.

She, in turn, had tried to kill him when he returned. His fear, his weeping fear, that he might hurt her spun out into the small room. He had found a way to save, using his life as bait to rescue her. Malila was startled when she felt her tears begin at Jesse's relief at her safe capture.

The Old Man quieted, and the old house, as well. The doctors were gone to their own domestic dramas of wives, children, and mortgage payments. The nurses were at a minimum, as the number of patients had dwindled, the army unwilling to have too many eyes see the death of so great a symbol of the nation. With Jesse quiet, Malila rose, replaced her sneakers, and went to find Mrs. Heitmann, who was even then changing the bed linen for a man who had taken a pulse bolt to the top of his head. He would never see again. He would be blind for the few more days it would take him to die.

The two women talked. In time, they left the bedside of the dying soldier to fetch a gurney. It was difficult to move Jesse onto it and harder yet to maneuver it along the narrow hallways and down the ramp to the garden. Mrs. Heitmann had begged off at that point, saying she wanted to return to her dying soldier. Malila suspected she really wanted nothing to do with whatever the strange foreign girl was contemplating. The dim porch light cast a jaundiced illumination into the dark night.

"Are you there?"

"Nhearly. The cauld zlows meh, Dhessengar," came a voice from the darkness. Malila started to shiver again.

"Can I help you?"

"Chan dho brig Quicksilver glowser?"

Malila kicked off the brake and eased the gurney down the slope another three meters. Jesse groaned as the gurney lurched beneath him. Out of the blackness, a black crenelated mass rose and hung a half meter over the foot of the cart, swallowing up the light from the porch even as it heaved and moved. Malila inhaled a scent of forest loam, dying leaves, and good rot.

"Dho shud look elzwhar, Dhessengar," came words from Speaker.

"Are you going to hurt him?" asked Malila.

The mass seemed to straighten, and the words along with it. "We, Quicksilver an' I, haf wounded much. Only the wounded may heal."

Malila stepped back, once more afraid that she knew so little of the outlands or even of the Scorch, despite being its voice for so many weeks. The blackness overshadowed the gurney. She steadied it with a hand. As she watched, the Old Man raised an arm and extended his hand in apparent greeting. The darkness flowed over him and up the extended arm to engulf the hand.

Jesse cried as he lay in the warm bed, inhaling the girl's scent. He had felt the warmth of her slim body close to his, and then she was gone. For the first moment in an unknowable time, he felt a sensation of the present, not just a spinning out of the horrors of his memories. The man with the Death's Head was gone. In some way, he knew that time had passed, like waking in the middle of a dark night unable to see anything but knowing dawn was but an hour away.

He felt the moisture on his checks and was momentarily ashamed of his tears. He was in a strange house, not in the over-warm basement with the Death's Head soldier and the gray man. He'd seen Malila there, as if at the end of a long corridor. She had said, "The only civilized thing to do is to kill me or leave me with Jesse."

It was his name, Jesse. He had forgotten in his agony. He inhaled her lingering scent again and tried to clear his vision of the halos of the horrors he had seen.

He had slept again, dreaming, imaging he was half asleep in a canoe drifting down a stream, giving him a bit of vertigo as the current swept the prow to port or starboard. The air grew cold, and he half awoke.

He heard voices. "Are you going to hurt him?" asked Malila.

"We, Quicksilver and I, haf wounded much. Only the wounded may heal," said a voice he half recalled. He raised a hand in greeting and moments later felt his hand taken by a dry, coruscated grip. Only then did he hear the wordless words, as if coming across on a breeze, speak within his head.

"I find you wounded, Quicksilver," said Speaker.

"It has been moons since we talked, friend. I have nothing to offer you but myself."

"Have you ever imagined I wished for more?"

"Yes. I feared you. I was young."

"As was I. We both at the dawning of our worlds."

"I imagined you old. I have wounded you."

"More than you know, my friend. You are dying, the Messenger says. Is this true?"

"If she believes it, that must be. All men owe God a good death."

"Have you lived such a good life that you can leave it undone?"

"What have I left undone? My children grown, my country no longer in need of me. Malila, the Messenger, is young—she will forget me."

"What you have left undone is my healing, child of men. I freely gave you food and drink, food and drink from my own body. You have always refused to return it."

"I tried."

"You feared."

"I feared, then. I do not fear you now, oldest of friends, but I have so little to give you in return. I am hollow, dried up, winnowed out. Whatever I have is yours. You drive but a poor bargain."

"It will be enough for my sproutings. But it will condemn you."

"Condemn me to what?"

"Why, my friend, I thought you would understand. I condemn you to long life, good health, many more children, and, I think, the love for which you long."

The Old Man smiled his smile as Malila helped him to bed. He stayed with his young love and she with him, whispering the conspiracies of lovers' throughout the night. He told her everything. She heard everything, and they started to make new memories together. In the morning, no one noticed or cared to comment on the small green tattoos each of them had: tiny, green tear-shaped marks, looking almost like a leaf, near the outside of their left eyes.

The week before the Coming, he was discharged as MHB, meaning the doctors figured there was nothing more they could do to help or harm him. One night, during the week before his discharge, Jesse recited a list of possibilities for Malila, allowing her the chance to make plans for herself. Malila, in turn, threatened to go to the association if Jesse did not marry her. Orderlies came to see what was causing the laughter.

The final political asylum orders came the day Jesse was discharged. Malila called it the Freedom of the Belts and laughed when he asked her to explain. Within the month, Theo gave her a wedding shower and spent the time telling embarrassing stories about her illustrious kid brother.

Jesse and Malila did not live happily ever after. They lived like other lovers over the ages, just longer and happier.

The following spring, the Supervisor, Dr. Wentworth; the Matron, Mrs. Blackabee; and the head gardener, Mr. Phillby, did their annual survey of the grounds in Missionary Ridge Nursing Home in Chattanooga. It had always been a pleasant stroll, fulfilling

Dr. Wentworth's fiduciary responsibility and Matron's curiosity without ever contradicting the considered opinion of the man who would have to do whatever work they agreed upon.

"I do have one volunteer plant I need your word on," said Mr. Phillby.

"To cut out a weed? This is a garden, not a pasture. I'd think the question answers itself, John," replied Mrs. Blackabee, as they followed the gardener down to the foot of the garden, just where the slope went from gentle to dangerous. There they found a young sapling, undoubtedly this year's crop. The trunk was dark red—almost the color of clotted blood, really—and smooth, the unbranched trunk leading to a plume of light-green, fern-like leaves.

"It's healthy—but I can't identify it," said Dr. Wentworth, inviting enlightenment but receiving none.

"It is quite handsome. Why not give it a season or so and transplant it to that sunny spot near the ambulance entrance?" responded Mrs. Blackabee.

John Philby nodded his head. "Could . . . could. Tough to know what its characteristics are, though. Might have some bad habits. Best to cull it," said the gardener, unshipping his pruners and inspecting the blade.

"Don't do that, John."

"If you say so, but then let's transplant it to where I can keep an eye on it without traipsing down here all the time."

"That'd not be a good idea either, John."

"Well, Doc, it ain't your bum knees climbing up and back all the time!"

"I . . . I wasn't talking, Mr. Phillby," said the doctor. The gardener looked up and followed his horrified companion's gaze to the young tree.

"No. I spoke. You may call me Blade, child of Speaker."

APPENDIX

TIMELINE

(Annum Unitatem + 2052 = AD, AD – 2052 = AU)

2051   Jesse Aaron Johnstone is born in Saint Louis to Alyssa (nee Browne) and Alexander C. H. Johnstone, 3 July.

2052   3rd Iraq War—USA forces destroyed by nuclear strikes from Iraqi, Pakistani, and Iranian arsenals, which devastate Mideast itself.

2053–2057   War dismembers the USA. East Coast emerges as the People's Republic (PR); West Coast secedes as the Demarchy. The Scorching. Reuben Alexander born in Chicago.

2055   Re-founding Day for the Restructured States of America (RSA) declared in Saint Louis by Congress-in-session, 4 July.

2056–2057   Battle of Springfield halts the PR forces during a prolonged winter battle near Springfield, IL. High-water mark for the Second War of Secession (RSA) or Glorious Revolution (PR).

2056–2060   PR suffers coup d'état, emerging as the Democratic Unity of America. Construction of the Rampart. Rise of the Solons.

2060   Plant life begins to recover. Agro-science develops resistant strains of cereal grains for use in the Scorched areas.

2062   Jesse and family return from the Scorch.

2067   Jesse matriculates at Saint Louis University, graduates cum laude in 2071, and matriculates at SLU School of Medicine.

2071–2072   During a mid-winter trip, Jesse, Haywood Smithe, and Reuben Alexander coerce a village to flee before a Unity attack in the newly recolonized Scorch. They all receive man-killer tattoos, despite the success. SLU expels Jesse. Unity declares all children wards of the state.

2072   Jesse matriculates at Washington University School of Medicine. Graduates magna cum laude 2076, finishing training in 2080.

2076   Jesse marries Simone Boutelle Smith.

2080   Unity directs all children to be raised in state-owned crèches.

2087   RSA concludes Treaty of Thunder Bay with Canada, ceding the Great Lakes watershed to complete Canadian control, allowing American access with reciprocal treatment for Canadian goods via the Mississippi River. Jake Steiner/Tremont immigrates to America shortly thereafter.

2087   American Regular Army success at Paducah, KY. Jesse is not given credit for the attack of his frontier forces that disables all transports and allows RSA to destroy Unity forces in detail. Rob Roy is reportedly found dead on the battlefield.

2090   Simone Johnstone and their infant daughter, Grace, killed in Unity raid near in their home in Louisville, leaving Jesse, Adam (9), Jessica (6), and Peter (3).

2090–2097   Jesse takes on the Unity, almost single-handed, raiding Unity outposts on the frontier as far north as Madison and Cincinnati.

2095   Defense of Cincinnati enclave, an attempt by the RSA to reestablish a presence in Ohio, is destroyed by land and air assault. The American survivors lead 357 Unity soldiers into captivity during a spring flood. Recolonization efforts are stopped by the Devastations.

2096   Jesse stops an American rout during a Unity attack on Paducah initiated by a mutiny. Arresting the leaders with only the help of Haywood Smythe and Reuben Alexander, Jesse summarily executes the ringleader, earning himself a second stripe.

2097   Jesse marries Ruth Oughbruck (nee Kinistree) in Bath County, KY, a widow with two children, Melissa (6) and Jacob (3), who are adopted by Jesse.

2100–2116The Devastations—Unity raids on America as far west as Nashville and Meridosia, IL.

2103   Ruth Johnstone killed by slavers while alone with her children, Melissa (12), Jacob (9), Jesse Jr. (5), and Mirabelle (2). Fortunately, Adam (22) and Jessica (19) are at university, and Peter (16) is hunting with his father when the attack is discovered. Jesse kills one of the bandits, receiving his final facial tattoo in consequence. William Yeats Butler is born in Searcy, AR.

2104   Cain is created to companion a Unity child, Phillip Derslin, dying of the newly declared incurable disease, acute lymphocytic leukemia.

2107   Phillip dies. The wandering Cain is seized by Jourdaine within the openCORE, who names him Presence.

2109   Jesse marries Jane Watanabe, 33. Hecate Hester Jones is born in Stratfurd, Connycut, 17 August.

2111   Malila Evanova Chiu is born to Esther Petrovna Williams and Evan Chiu in West Chester, Pennsylvania, 31 January.

2115   Child Protective Services discover Malila in an "unapproved domestic arrangement." Her parents are Sapped for child abuse. Malila enters People's Crèche 213 and meets Hecate.

Jane Johnstone killed by Unity raiders at Glasgow, KY; survived by Jesse Jr. (17), Mirabelle (14), Alexander (4), and Jesse. The older children, Adam, Jessica, Peter, and Melissa, are alive and well, having "their own lives and loves."

2116   The last large raid of the Devastations in Meridosia, IL. The last time Unity prop airplanes are observed. Helen Delarosa is killed.

2118–2128 Aroostook War—invasion of Maine by Canada to obtain an ice-free port on the Atlantic and completing a completely Canadian all-weather outlet for Great Lakes (and Mississippi River) trade.

2127   Unity changes method of "recruiting" CRNAs, improving success rate but slightly decreasing functional temperature range, January 1 (AU75).

2128   Malila lost in a raid to the outlands, October 14 (AU76) *(Outland Exile)*.

2128   Malila and her captor, Jesse, travel by foot, ski, horseback, and canoe to New Carrolton, KY, despite weather, slavers, and carnivorous beasts and plants, 14 October to 10 December.

2129   Malila recaptured at Stamping Ground, KY, 10 April.

2129   Will Butler, American spy, inserted into Nyork District, April 30 (AU77)

2129   Death [*sic*] by suicide of Hecate; Jourdaine dismisses Malila, 30 May.

William Butler, sick with influenza, attempting to escape DUFS, jumps into a ventilation silo near Stanton, VA, and is gravely injured, 29 June.

Malila undergoes Alpha_Drover, perceives she is in a computer simulation and escapes, 30 June.

Malila fakes her own suicide after turning off her metaphract, Edie, on Edie's request, 1 July.

Assassination attempt by Synopians upon Jesse, 6 July.

Malila and Hecate reunite underground, 7 July.

Jesse boards RSAN *Illinois*, 8 July.

Jourdaine assassinates Solons, 15 July.

Will Butler, Malila, and Hecate join forces. First contact by EffieCee, a conjoint entity comprised of mirrored copies of Edie, Frog, and Cain, who aid in Malila's escape, 25 July.

Malila emerges outside the Rampart. Jesse discovers her signal from *Illinois* and leaves the airship to track her down. Jourdaine captures Malila, but skimmers carrying them both crash. Malila rescued by Splanch, 1 Aug.

GLOSSARY

CORE

Concepts in Reality Engineering, Inc., contractor for the nationwide computer system of the Unity, and, by usage, the computer itself. The openCORE is the reality behind what users see, a dimension above them.

E-classification

Erudition class, or level, an age classification; E-class plus six equals actual age.

euthanatorium

An enlightened Unity facility replacing crematoria, mortuaries, hospices, skilled nursing care facilities, and the assisted-suicide facilitation venues.

Meltdown, the

Collapse of world trade after the Third Iraq War, devastating NA and effectively depopulating Europe and Asia. The Panama Canal is seized by the RSA.

S-classification

Specialist class—a level of Unity rank across services including the arts, academia, government, and military.

Sisi

A pejorative in the Unity, pronounced ′sē-′sē, and standing for "senior citizen"; a Sisi has no rights in the larger society. Officially denied, they constitute the CRNAs and breeders. The Unity-wide fiction is that they go to retirement villages.

Solons

The ultimate rulers of the Unity. Solons are self-perpetuating, recruited at retirement when they would be disappearing from society, regardless. Solons ignore age limits for retirement.

UNITY TECHNOLOGIES

beltways

Running pedestrian- and light-transport lines in intraurban and intercity travel. Rail lines are used for long-distance travel of people and material.

CRNA

Certified Recycled Neuro-ablated individuals (a.k.a. "zombies") are, putatively, criminals who have been Sapped and rendered loyal. In actuality, they are citizens whose only crime is being over forty, nonproductive, or excess to requirements. The process of Sapping renders them pliable, but their subsequent lifespan is two to three years.

DIRD-E

Delinquency and Identity Recognition Detection–Evaluation device: a reader for eusum (see below). The individual's characteristics of the implant are retrieved and sent back to the scanning device.

eusum

(plural *eusum*) Information packets. Basic implants are interrogated by the use of a scan or a wand, creating a eusum, which is then sent to a reader (see DIRD-E).

implant

A **basic**, or **first implant,** is surgically placed into all Unity children at age seven, E1. The implant is a GPS device, a tracking device, and a mood modulator, programmed to dose the citizen with a large but finite number of hormones, psychotropic drugs, and receptor antagonists.

The **Outside-Above,** or **O–A implant**, is only inserted into those children at age eleven who have been assigned to a guild. This implant allows *questing*, the use of the CORE interface without the use of a computer terminal. O As have some short-range tracking capabilities. They do not allow access to the openCORE.

Rampart, the

A line of fortifications dividing the Unity proper from its "outlands." Unity control is exercised only from Bangor, ME, south to the Savannah River and west to the crest of the Appalachians. It is pierced by several "gates." Otherwise, interlocking and automated pulse-cannon fire kills anything that moves.

Sapp

A Unity mind-control treatment used to eliminate higher functions. A treatment course of three doses produces a dangerous syndrome of mania, self-destructive behavior, hallucinations (visual and auditory, as well as gustatory), and somatic pain. The vector is a prion.

Skimmerhorn drive

Dr. Claudette Skimmerhorn developed an induced electromagnetic field in the chaotic years of AU10–13, which provides propulsion and levitation for the Unity, eliminating the internal combustion engine. Despite high terminal velocity and prodigious carrying capacity, the disadvantages are several: slow acceleration, low operational ceiling, and an inability to operate for long in areas with a poor electrical grid.

ThiZ

A putative recreational drug that produces dissociative, paradoxical endotactic emotions, as well as physical endurance. In the Unity, its use is encouraged. Abrupt cessation produces withdrawal symptoms: diaphoresis, nausea, diarrhea, asthenia, dissociative behavior, and seizures. See *Implant*.

AMERICAN TECHNOLOGIES

Ageplay

A longevity treatment increasing restorative functions, Ageplay increases effective lifespan to approximately 170 years for most people who receive the injections as a child. It tends to delay puberty for about twenty-four months and thus leads to somewhat taller individuals.

bio-gel interface (BGI)

A mind-computer link that shares some similarities with the O A link produced by the Unity, allowing *questing* within any computer system that is broadcasting in its vicinity. Developed from a bio-active "smart" gel, early models sport a pseudo-sentience much like a metaphract. BGI interfaces, however, require the full attention of their operators. Also distinct from a metaphract, the "Biggy" interface delivers the consciousness to the openCORE. *Spindles* are a form of BGI interface (see below).

climatic battlefield preparation (CBP)

A methodology pioneered by the American Air Navy for use with the *Indiana* class of ships. With the active-radio and optic-adaptive technology, an R-ship or ships can be parked above a prospective battlefield indefinitely. Without a change in position or altitude, R-ships can direct a torus of frigid air from the stratosphere down to the earth (Omicron Maneuver).

DT-armor

Deflecting titanium. Armor developed against pulse-bolt weapons. Rather than absorbing the energy as classic armor does, DTA works by deflecting and tunneling the energy to the edges of the deflector plate, producing the typical "frilled skirt" configuration.

R-ships

Rigid airships, type R airships, are not to be confused with type B, limp-style ships (blimps), whose shape is dependent on the enclosed gas being under pressure. R-ships, reminiscent of dirigibles, were developed after advances with carbon-fiber structure and jet engine technology allowed them to operate at much higher altitudes. Large ducted fans eliminate the need for ground crews. Nano-pore fabric has greatly reduced the loss of gasses to the environment.

spindles

A type of bio-gel interface, spindles allow accumulated data to be transmitted from a field operative to Army Intelligence. They are about a foot long and appear to be an eel-like animal with a circular, jawless mouth filled with serrated teeth. The spindle is first engrammed by being attached to a BGI interface and then released into running water. It then parasitizes aquatic life as it homes in on an American vessel's transponder.